PRAISE FOR GUARDIANS UNLEASHED

"Jerusha Agen once again delivers top-level suspense and thrilling action. *Covert Danger* kept me looking over my shoulder and flipping pages. Fast-paced suspense at its best."

DIANN MILLS, BESTSELLING AUTHOR OF *CONCRETE EVIDENCE*

"Hang on! This action-packed story doesn't let up until the good guys win!"

NATALIE WALTERS, AWARD-WINNING AUTHOR OF *LIGHTS OUT* AND THE *HARBORED SECRETS SERIES* ON *COVERT DANGER*

Hidden Danger kept me reading and on the edge of my seat from page one through the end. Jerusha Agen writes a gripping suspense filled with danger, romance, and K-9s complete with a strong faith thread.

SHAREE STOVER, BESTSELLING AUTHOR OF *FRAMING THE MARSHALL*

"Fast-paced, explosive thriller. I couldn't turn the pages fast enough."

CARRIE STUART PARKS, AWARD-WINNING, BESTSELLING AUTHOR OF *RELATIVE SILENCE* ON *RISING DANGER*

"*Rising Danger* grabbed me from the first chapter and never let go. Don't miss this edge-of-your-seat story of suspense and romance."

PATRICIA BRADLEY, AWARD-WINNING AUTHOR OF THE *LOGAN POINT* AND *MEMPHIS COLD CASE SERIES*

UNSEEN DANGER

BOOKS BY JERUSHA AGEN

GUARDIANS UNLEASHED SERIES

Rising Danger (Prequel)

Hidden Danger

Covert Danger

Unseen Danger

Lethal Danger (2024)

Untitled Book Five (2024)

SISTERS REDEEMED SERIES

If You Dance with Me

If You Light My Way

If You Rescue Me

UNSEEN DANGER

GUARDIANS UNLEASHED  BOOK THREE

JERUSHA AGEN

Published by SDG Words, LLC
www.JerushaAgen.com

Library of Congress Control Number: 2023907591

ISBN 978-1-956683-24-0

ACKNOWLEDGMENTS

It takes a village to create a good book. Or, more precisely, the perfect individuals God brings along at just the right time. Such was the case in the effort of bringing *Unseen Danger* to fruition.

Thank you to my old friend, the real Andrew Allen, for giving me the information I needed to accurately write about the world of hip-hop. (Any errors are mine.) I didn't make you a bad guy after all. A good guy seemed more fitting.

Thanks to Robin W. Pearson for providing authentic insider details I wouldn't have thought of on my own.

Carilyn Bergner, instructor at Gracie Jiu-Jitsu, what a blessing that God connected us at the perfect time. I'm delighted to find in you not only an expert resource for all things jiujitsu but also an avid reader and sister in Christ. Thank you for your warm welcome to Gracie Jiu-Jitsu and for sharing your expertise.

A huge thanks goes to Natalya Lakhno, Angelique Daley, and Anne S. for giving me feedback and catching errors on the earliest drafts of *Unseen Danger*. Your positive response and enthusiasm to read my stories is such an encouragement.

Thank you to the readers of the *Guardians Unleashed Series* who kept asking me when the next book would be released. Your eagerness for more stories kept me going through the rough patches in getting *Unseen Danger* to print as soon as possible.

To Mom—brainstormer, editor, proofreader, encourager, cheerleader, friend. Thank you. I couldn't do this without you.

To the correctional officers who serve with courage and kindness. Your job is usually thankless, but so necessary. You keep us all safe. You are unsung heroes. Thank you for your service.

Soli Deo Gloria

You came near when I called on you;
you said, "Do not fear!"

Lamentations 3:57

ONE

The building quaked, helpless against the pounding onslaught. D-Chop was famous for his ear-blasting hip-hop concerts, but Nevaeh Williams was glad she wasn't backstage at the moment. She could do her job of security specialist a lot easier with some hearing left.

Alvarez followed by her side as she turned the corner into the hallway that housed the dressing rooms. The K-9's heavy panting was a welcome, softer sound as they continued their patrol through the limited-access sections of the Power-Source Center.

One of D-Chop's bodyguards stood outside the rapper's dressing room just ahead. The guy was about six feet and buff but a mere mortal compared to the two dudes who had flanked the star when he'd arrived at the venue.

D-Chop hadn't spotted her when he'd made his entrance amid a mob of raving fans, kept at bay behind barriers. Would he have recognized her if he had? Probably not now that he was a world-famous hip-hop headliner. And the last time he'd seen her, she'd been a kid.

Didn't matter. She was just glad to be helping him out in some small way after all these years.

The bodyguard by the empty dressing room gave her a

curt nod as she passed, leaving plenty of space between them.

"This is PT3, east wing clear."

Nevaeh smiled at the sound of Jazz Lamont's full voice coming through her earpiece. Didn't think she'd ever tire of hearing her best girlfriend back at work with the Phoenix K-9 team, healthy and strong. Though the worry something could happen to Jazz might never go away since she'd nearly died in the explosion during their big job three months ago.

A kid probably no more than nineteen with a stage crew ID around his neck smiled broadly as he approached, going the opposite way up the hallway as she and Alvarez.

She straightened her lips and met his appraisal with a *cool it* stare.

Down, boy. I ain't smilin' at you.

His gaze dropped as he neared. Message received. And then some, judging from the way he paled as he darted a glance at the thick rottweiler mix at her side.

Checking over her shoulder to be sure the teen kept walking, she paused at the door that led to the stage. "Here goes, buddy." She glanced down at Alvarez, earning a look from his big brown eyes. "Sorry about the noise."

The music would be even harder on the dog's sensitive ears. But Phoenix Gray and Marion Moore had trained Alvarez to be cool around gunshots, so he should be able to handle the measly noise of a hip-hop concert.

Nevaeh pushed through the door into the dark, black-walled world of the immediate backstage area.

The steady beats from the DJ's turntables on stage, backed up by the guitars and whatever else D-Chop had brought with him, slammed into Nevaeh's ears.

Her wince shifted into a wry grin. She must be getting old. Used to be she couldn't get enough of hip-hop and especially D-Chop's beats.

Several people in black clothing rushed around, weaving in and out of the thick curtains that created a maze behind the stage. She kept her eyes on them just long enough to verify they all wore crew IDs.

Nevaeh and Alvarez veered between the gigantic curtain closest to the stage and the set pieces that formed an elaborate backdrop for D-Chop's show. The music was nearly deafening from so close, but this would also be the most likely place for a would-be attacker or trespasser to lurk.

As she came out the other end, movement caught her gaze.

A huge man stood at the entrance onto the stage, watching the performers.

She froze.

Buzz-cut black hair and coffee-colored skin. D-Chop's bodyguard.

She let out a breath.

He turned his head her direction, like he knew he was being watched. Good instincts.

She pushed her feet forward and looked away, clasping Al's leash a little harder to hide the tremor that tumbled through her fingers. Lucky he wasn't a hostile. Wouldn't want to have to tangle with that dude.

Or the other one she'd seen escort D-Chop into the building. He'd stood out even more than this guy, maybe because he was unexpectedly blond and light skinned. Or could've been because he had another couple inches in height over the Brutus guy she'd just passed and a similar measure of extra muscles. She'd better not bump into him suddenly backstage.

Her pulse sped up as an alarming image flashed in her mind. The big guy, jumping out of the shadows and—

She shook her head as she stalked toward the stage exit opposite the one she'd entered through. "Just give me a good smack, will you, boy?" She muttered the suggestion to Alvarez, half hoping he'd figure out how to follow through with it.

She'd told Phoenix she could handle this assignment, even though there might be triggers around. She was in good shape. Or at least she had been, before the assassin nearly blew up her best friend in front of her eyes.

Seemed like that incident shouldn't be connected to the reason for her PTSD. But somehow it was. Or maybe something else was bothering her now. Something she didn't dare think about.

She leaned into the bar across the door. Her nerves were—

Pops halted her movement.

Not gunshots, more like—pyrotechnics?

She breathed again as the sputtering and popping continued.

Boom.

The explosion shook the floor under her feet. No way was that normal concert pyrotechnics.

She spun back as screams filled the air like the death cry of the music that suddenly choked to a halt.

"With me!" She shouted the command to Al as she sprinted toward the opening that led onstage.

The big bodyguard she'd just seen ran at her.

Her heart leaped into her throat. She lurched to the side.

"D1 this is D2, explosion onstage." The guy barked into coms, his voice hitting her ear as he jogged past her.

D-Chop hunkered close to the bodyguard, nearly tucked into his side.

Her heart dropped back into place. Of course, the bodyguard hadn't been charging at her. He was protecting D-Chop.

"Package clear, moving to safe zone."

She glanced after them as the bodyguard and D-Chop disappeared offstage, probably headed to the dressing room.

"D2, negative." A deeper voice came across coms. "Go for evac."

"Roger, D1."

She could barely hear the radio chatter over the screams and shouts from the arena that were nearly as deafening as the music had been seconds before.

There was another noise, too. A hissing sound she couldn't identify.

She stepped out onstage, her hand going toward the Sig Sauer pistol in her hip holster.

Chaos rippled through the audience below as people rushed for the exits, a mob probably taking down others in their panic.

A scream much closer yanked her attention to the right. At the other side of the massive stage, orange flames lit a man on fire.

Nevaeh sprinted across the stage, dropping Al's leash as she ripped off her windbreaker.

She ran at the screaming man, the fire consuming his back as he stumbled.

"Drop! Drop and roll!" She yelled the directions, and he leaned forward like he was going to lower to his knees.

Not fast enough.

She launched herself the remaining four feet, jacket outstretched, and tackled him to the ground.

TWO

Branson Aaberg dashed through another hallway, the fastest route from the security center to the main stage.

The image he'd seen on the camera feed burned in his mind—flames engulfing Kicker. Branson prayed someone would reach the man and help him before it was too late.

Chatter from the PowerSource security team sounded in his earpiece. He listened for a second longer to verify they'd called for paramedics and police backup. Their leader also gave instructions for evacuating the massive audience.

He switched his coms to channel six as he braked at a fire extinguisher housed in a case attached to the wall. His security team should've switched to that channel as soon as the fire started. "D2, this is D1. Give me status."

Branson whipped his Glock 19 from its holster and smashed the grip into the glass. Knocking away the jagged edges that remained, he snatched the fire extinguisher and took off.

"D1, package en route to exit." Darren Tremblay didn't have D-Chop out of the building yet. He wasn't secure.

Branson sprinted past the door that would've led him to the stage. Every instinct screamed at him to go put out the fire, to save Kicker. But his priority always had to be the principal. Always.

He grit his teeth as he headed for the rear exit. "D3, status."

"D1, this is D3. With package." Louis Kursko was with D-Chop, too. Maybe Branson could turn back.

Two PowerSource security guards in black uniforms jogged past him, going the opposite direction as their radios sputtered with chatter.

"D1, this is D2." Darren's disgruntled tone sounded in Branson's ear.

"Go."

"The package wants you to stay behind and see the band members are safe."

The image of Kicker on fire seared Branson's memory. He'd like nothing better than to help the guy. But he had to prioritize...

"D2, what's your status?"

"D1, we're in the pocket. Ready to leave."

The tension in Branson's chest eased at the code name for D-Chop's private limo. "D2, go ahead. I'll check on the others."

"Roger, D1."

Branson spun around and ran hard in the opposite direction. Would he be too late to help Kicker? He hoped someone else already had or the guy wouldn't have a prayer.

The lighting and décor grew darker as he wove through the final hallways just before the stage access. He dashed past the dressing rooms and veered into the metal stage door, slamming it open to dart around the black, sound-absorbing walls and curtains that had been put up for this concert.

He had to dodge scrambling crew members that were beating a quick exit instead of going onstage to help fight the disaster.

Ty Leeman, the keyboardist too new to have come up with a unique monicker yet, jogged past. Going the wrong way, but at least he was one D-Chop band member accounted for.

Branson hit the stage, rapidly taking in the scene. No sign of Kicker or anyone on fire.

Thank you, Lord.

A loud *whoosh* jerked his gaze to two men in PowerSource security uniforms who stood by a backdrop that was lit with flames. One of them sprayed a fire extinguisher at the blaze.

The orange menace climbed higher than the short guy seemed able to reach. It spread horizontally across the backdrop above the extinguisher's spray.

Branson rushed over to attack the fire on the far left. He sprayed the extinguisher he'd brought with him in a sweeping motion at the base of the flames that climbed vertically and then slanted right at about six feet and kept crawling.

He blasted the highest licks of fire with the extinguisher, his tension easing as they weakened, flickered, and petered out.

"Call it in?" He glanced at the security guard closest to him. The man nodded and started his report over coms as Branson turned to check on the band members.

JipJag looked okay, standing about twenty feet away from the backdrop examining the electric guitar Branson theorized the man slept with.

Pinky bent over his drums, his wild red hair somehow as unsinged as the rest of his intentionally ripped attire.

"Branson!"

He swung his head to the source of the urgent call.

B-Puff hurried toward him, the man's bling—two long and clunky silver necklaces—catching the light from the arena's overhead fixtures that were powered on for the evacuation.

"Kicker's hurt." The widened whites of B-Puff's eyes showed his panic. "He got burned up."

Branson put his hand on the DJ's shoulder. "It'll be okay, man. There's an ambulance on the way. Where is he?"

"With the chick." B-Puff nearly stumbled as he turned away. "Over there."

Branson spotted a person kneeling in the area B-Puff pointed to, far out on the connecting stage. Even from behind, there was no missing the womanly curves, but his gaze locked on her red T-shirt with *Phoenix K-9* printed on the back. She must belong to the K-9 unit the PowerSource Center's head of security had added for D-Chop's concert.

He started in her direction.

"She saved his life." B-Puff's gruff voice made him pause and look at the shorter man. "He was burning up, and she came out of nowhere and was just there. He was running, and she tackled him and put out the flames. It was..." He slid a hand over his bald, brown head and shook it slowly back and forth as he blew out a breath.

"Okay. You'd better sit down, B-Puff." Branson gently thumped the man's bicep. "Why don't you sit on Pinky's stool until I see how Kicker's doing. Then we'll get out of here, so long as the police don't need to talk to you guys, all right?"

B-Puff wandered toward Pinky with a wobbly gait.

Branson swung back toward the woman who was apparently some kind of heroine, if the DJ's drug-fogged account could be trusted.

As he continued her way, Branson assessed the scene.

Kicker lay still on the stage floor in front of her.

Movement on the far side of the woman caught his eye.

Was that a dog? A square, black and brown head came into view. The stocky dog Branson guessed was a rottweiler watched him with a pink tongue hanging from its mouth.

The woman's voice, husky and rich, floated to Branson as he came up behind her. "I know it hurts, Eddie."

Eddie? Kicker had let this woman call him by his real name?

Maybe he'd been charmed by her mesmerizing voice.

Or maybe it was the hair. Branson's gaze locked on the black bounty as he paused a few feet away. He'd never seen such an abundance of curls as those surrounding her head. A crazy urge to touch the black spirals to see if they were as soft as they looked twitched his fingers.

A pained groan yanked him out of his temporary insanity. Kicker must be hurt badly, but at least he was alive.

"I need you to breathe for me, okay, Eddie?" The woman's tone stayed even and calm. "The ambulance will be here soon, and we'll get you help with the pain."

Branson stepped to her side, where he could see she held Kicker's wrist in her slim fingers, apparently checking his pulse. Was she a medic instead of security?

Her bounty of natural curls blocked her face from view.

He crouched beside her. "How's he doing?"

She started and leaped away faster than the pond frogs back home.

His heart jumped as he stood and reached for her in case she toppled as she landed five feet from him.

But she jerked back before he could touch her. Her eyes were wide, and her nostrils flared as she stared up at him as if he'd tried to attack her.

A hot zing blazed through his chest as he took in her deep brown eyes, flawless skin, and full lips. Ironic to say the least. D-Chop had given Branson an unsavory nickname because of his disinterest in the female groupies among the hip-hop star's entourage. Now here he was, attracted to a girl for the first time since high school.

And he'd clearly just scared her to death.

Low-pitched rumbling pulled his gaze down to the rottweiler that stepped in front of the woman and stared at Branson, its lips curled in a menacing growl.

A spike of apprehension flared behind his ribs. The dog wouldn't attack him, would it?

"Sorry." He held up both hands in front of him, palms out. "I didn't mean to sneak up on you." He slowly reached into his pants pocket and pulled out his ID, flitting his gaze between the dog and the woman. "I'm the head of D-Chop's personal security detail." He raised the ID toward her. "I just wanted to check on Kicker. I saw him catch fire on the security cameras."

Her chest still rose and fell rapidly, and her eyes were full of fear.

His stomach twisted. His goal was to protect people, not scare them. He tried a smile. "My name is Branson Aaberg. Are you part of the K-9 unit hired to supplement the venue security?" If she was, it seemed peculiar she was so easily frightened. But maybe she'd been traumatized by the explosion and seeing a man on fire.

It was a terrifying sight. And she'd apparently had the courage to put out the fire that could've killed Kicker.

D-Chop's hype man said something in a pain-tightened whisper that drew the woman's attention.

She put a hand on her rottweiler as she knelt by Kicker again. Her touch seemed to have a calming effect, making the dog relax its lips and break the stare it had held on Branson.

"I wish I could do something more for you, but I don't have any medical equipment with me. Just hang on. You're going to be okay." She threw Branson a glance over her shoulder, her eyes widening again as if she'd forgotten what he looked like.

He'd had a lot of encounters with women in the celebrity protection racket, and, if they chose to notice him at all, he seemed to have an effect on them. Usually a positive one. Sometimes too positive, and that created another kind of problem. But terrifying a woman with a simple introduction was a first.

Activity at the stage entrance drew his gaze from the peculiar woman. A team of two paramedics—or maybe EMTs—rushed across the stage toward them.

The woman in red moved quickly to her feet and backed away with her K-9, giving the professionals room to treat Kicker.

She shot Branson another apprehensive glance. Was she afraid he'd sneak up on her again? Maybe he made her nervous because of his size. At six feet five inches and with a muscular physique he worked hard to maintain, he was used to intimidating some people. It was an asset in the protection business.

But this slim woman was in perfect physical shape, as far as he could see, and just the right height. A man wouldn't have to bend in half to—

"Nevaeh." Another woman—a tall redhead in a green windbreaker—came from the other side of the stage with a harnessed dog on a leash.

Branson recognized the Belgian Malinois breed from his time serving in the Navy. The dog and its handler stopped by the woman whose name must be Nevaeh. That's what Kicker had whispered to her, but Branson hadn't recognized the word. A beautiful name that fit the stunning woman well.

"Excuse me. Did you see what happened?"

Branson turned toward the voice at his side.

A female paramedic looked up at him, questions in her eyes. He did his best to answer what had happened to Kicker, but after explaining for a couple minutes, his gaze drifted as if of its own accord to peer over his shoulder at Nevaeh.

She was gone. Along with the dogs and the redhead.

"Do you know if he has next of kin we should call?" The paramedic's question demanded his attention and an answer.

He gave both on autopilot. His mind was completely preoccupied with the huge brown eyes, smooth-as-a-still-lake chestnut skin, and distracting pink lips of the vibrant woman who'd somehow left a gaping empty space in an arena that seated thousands.

THREE

He was coming.

Footsteps echoed in her ears.

Nevaeh darted a glance over her shoulder.

The white wall of the women's bathroom directly behind her back was still there. Just like when she'd checked three seconds ago.

No man lurking behind her shoulder. Ready to grab her and—

Stop it. Breathe. Focus on now.

She reached for Alvarez's blocky head. Felt his short fur.

If only she'd brought Cannenta. Nevaeh loved Alvarez dearly. But he wasn't a natural comforter or a trained PTSD service dog.

He stood facing away from her, his back end touching her knee as he panted heavily. He held his small, dropped ears pinched close to his head, a sign she was stressing him out. Or that sitting here without action was getting to him.

It was getting to her, too. But not for the same reasons.

Footsteps sounded again.

Her imagination or something real?

They grew louder.

She looked behind her.

Nothing.

But the footsteps wouldn't stop.

She shrank back into the corner that should be hidden behind the door if it opened.

His shadow crossed before her eyes, the only warning she'd had before—

"Nev?" Jazz's red wavy hair, followed by her emerald-green eyes, stuck through the opening as the door swung in. She blinked at Nevaeh and quickly stepped inside, her mouth turned down.

Nevaeh straightened from the near-fetal position she'd somehow adopted without meaning to. Her breaths came shallow and hard-earned, but she tried to hide the panic symptom behind a shaky smile.

Lucky it was Jazz who found her. Sofia was awesome, but there was nothing soft about her. She'd report this to Phoenix for sure.

But Jazz understood. She got it.

"You can beat this, girl." She stepped closer and put her hands on each of Nevaeh's shoulders as if to prove her thoughts true. "You've done it before. You're strong."

Nevaeh met Jazz's fierce gaze and nodded as she hauled in a deep breath.

"You could've choked out that guy in a second if you'd wanted to." Jazz showed her brilliant white smile. "Even if he was bigger than Hercules. And awfully cute." She winked.

Nevaeh couldn't help the laugh that bubbled up and the grin that found her face. She gave Jazz a playful shove. "Get outta here. We got work to do."

"Yeah, no joke." Jazz bent to grab Flash's leash from the floor. Nevaeh hadn't even noticed the Belgian Malinois slip in with Jazz. "Thomas gave us a new assignment to guard the stage and backstage until all the band members and every last audience member is gone. Basically until the building is closed. They put Sofia on the same area, too."

Nevaeh groaned. Since they'd been hired by the venue, the PowerSource head of security could technically change their assignment whenever he wanted. But she didn't exactly feel like staying here late into the night now. Especially with the possibility of the gargantuan strongman appearing out of nowhere again.

"You good?" Jazz looked back as she held the door open.

"Yeah. Sure." Nevaeh grabbed Al's leash and followed Jazz and Flash into the hallway that led past the dressing rooms.

"Oh, and we're supposed to talk to that guy, D-Chop's head of security, to find out if there was foul play involved in the fire."

The tension that had only started to release clenched Nevaeh's muscles again. "Why?"

Jazz glanced at Nevaeh as they fell into step with each other, dogs at their sides. "Sofia told Phoenix what happened, and Phoenix wants us to find out."

"I guess Sofia can ask, then."

"I thought you'd want to since you two already had such a nice chat." The humor in Jazz's voice dampened the instinctive flicker of fear in Nevaeh's chest.

She shot her so-called best friend a narrowed-eye glare.

Jazz laughed. "Fine." She let out a dramatic sigh. "I'll just have to talk to him. And you can eat your heart out from the sidelines."

They veered across the hall to the backstage door as Nevaeh snorted. "No clue what you're talking about. He wasn't even hot."

Jazz arched an eyebrow as she reached for the door handle. "Somebody wasn't looking."

That was an understatement. All she'd seen was a hulk appear behind her, all muscles, massive shoulders, and broad chest. The power to—

"There's Sofia." Jazz's voice stopped Nevaeh's dangerous mental spiral. "Why don't you find where she wants us posted, and I'll go talk to the guy who apparently blinded you with his good looks."

More like his potential to be as dangerous as the man in her nightmares. But Nevaeh rewarded Jazz's attempt to distract her with a smile. "Maybe you can get his number."

"I'll do that." The redhead's musical laugh trailed behind her as she and Flash disappeared around the partition that blocked the stage entrance from view.

"Get burned?" Sofia's voice, suddenly behind Nevaeh, would've startled her. But four and a half years at the Phoenix K-9 Agency had gotten her used to the boss, who could appear from nowhere even more quietly than Sofia.

Nevaeh turned toward the petite woman, her waves of black hair disappearing in shadows on her shoulders.

Raksa, her German shepherd protection K-9, swished his tail at Alvarez.

"A little." Now that the adrenaline and fear were fading from Nevaeh's system, the pain in her left hand finally registered. She lifted it to look at the palm. "Some of the flames tried to sneak out when I was smothering them." The extent of the damage was hard to assess in the dim lighting.

"You should treat that."

"Looks like first-degree. I'll be fine."

"You're the expert. You're also an instant legend from the stories I'm hearing." Sof's white teeth sparkled in the darkness as she smiled. A new smile Nevaeh was still getting used to.

It was still big, but not as frequent and quick as the smile Sofia used to flash when she went by Amalia Pérez. Truthfully, it seemed like she meant it more now. Like there was more...warmth to it. Which was a strange word to use for Sofia. She'd never been anything close to warm. Awesome and fun, but not warm.

Going through an identity change, getting married, and adopting a kid all in the span of a few months was bound to have some kind of effect. Nevaeh had only just started to adjust to Amalia's new name, Sofia Gomez, when the woman married Michael and changed her last name to Barrett.

"A legend, huh?"

"Yeah. Superwoman. You apparently leaped on the burning man in a single bound and put out the flames with your red cape."

Nevaeh laughed. “Some superheroes don’t like capes, but I always knew mine would come in handy.”

“Obviously.”

“Don’t worry. I won’t do anything heroic enough to threaten your superspy status.”

The former CIA agent’s dark eyes twinkled. “I’m too busy being a mom these days to engage in any such behavior.”

“It is so weird to hear those words come out of your mouth. ‘Mom?’”

“I know, isn’t it?” Sof shook her head with a grin. “Okay. Back to work. You take the stage. I’ll cover back here. Tell Jazz to patrol the backstage hallways.”

The stage was where the Hulk still was. “Care if I swap with Jazz?”

“Any special reason?” The look Sof gave her was too suspicious. Did she know?

“Never mind. Stage is fine.” Nevaeh swung away. “Come on, Al.” She and Alvarez headed in the direction of the stage with a confident stride she hoped Sof would buy.

And she should be confident. Jazz was right. With everything Phoenix had taught her, Nevaeh was a whole new woman. She knew how to handle herself. She could take out any guy she needed to.

She rounded the barrier and walked out on stage.

Her gaze found Jazz. Standing behind the man with the bodybuilder physique that undid any benefit from her pep talk in two seconds flat.

Even his baggy, hip-hop style cargo pants and drapey black sweater couldn’t hide the fact that every inch of him was pure muscle. His chest and arms practically rippled through the sweater that was supposed to be loose-fitting. This dude would make mincemeat out of her.

Not that he’d try anything. He was probably a law-abiding citizen. Maybe even a good guy. Just because he was big and strong didn’t automatically mean he was dangerous.

Her brain knew the facts. And she even believed them. She was being ridiculous, and she felt every bit a coward for knowing she'd panic again if the bodyguard or anyone like him got close.

But PTSD didn't listen to reason.

Good thing all she needed to do was avoid the burly dude for a few more hours. Then she'd never have to see him again.

"You should head on home." Branson squeezed Pinky's scrawny shoulder. "I'll give you an update on Kicker as soon as I hear anything. B-Puff's with him, and he'll keep us posted."

Pinky's cloud of loose red curls bobbed with his nod. "Cool." He sauntered away toward backstage, his body sagging with each step.

They'd all been through the wringer tonight.

"Mr. Aaberg, is it?" A female voice behind him made Branson turn.

Disappointment sapped the hope that had flickered before he even realized what he was thinking. The redhead, though lovely enough to draw the interest of most men, wasn't the woman he'd hoped to see. Though why he was getting so hung up on a perfect stranger, he didn't know.

"Yes. Call me Branson." He extended his hand to her. "And you are?"

She put her hand in his for a firm, confident shake. "Jazz Lamont." She glanced down at the Belgian Malinois that stood at her side, panting. "This is Flash. We're with the Phoenix K-9 Security and Detection Agency."

Branson smiled. "Right. I met one member of your team earlier."

"Yeah, I heard." Jazz's mouth turned up into a grin broader than he'd have expected. As if there was some added meaning behind it.

Had Nevaeh said something to her about meeting him?

His pulse might've missed a beat or two at the thought. His gaze couldn't help but drift toward the backstage entrance.

A profusion of black curls were framed in the opening. She was there.

Something squeezed in his chest. He couldn't make out her face in the shadows. Was she watching him?

Then she shifted. Slipped away.

His foot started to move. To follow as if by some strange instinct.

"My boss wanted me to find out the cause of the fire." Jazz's question stopped him. Brought him back to reality. To his job.

What was off with him tonight? He'd never been distracted by a woman in his life.

"Do you know if it was intentional?"

He looked at the tall redhead. Curious thing for her boss to want to know since the K-9 agency had only been hired by PowerSource as supplemental security for one night. At least that's what he'd been told. Maybe her boss was concerned about liability. "I was just waiting to find out."

He twisted toward the fireman who was overseeing the takedown of what remained of the set piece. He caught the fireman's eye, and the man walked their way. "Any conclusions?"

The fireman tipped his helmet back on his forehead as he stopped by them. "Can't say officially until the fire investigator does his thing." He wiped his fingers along his bristly jaw as he met Branson's gaze, his eyes inviting more questions.

"Okay. But unofficially?"

"Unofficially, there's a lot I can tell you." A brief smile created more creases in his weather-beaten face. "Looks like the pyrotechnics equipment was tampered with so it would malfunction and spray sparks in a different trajectory than planned. There's also evidence of accelerant on the objects that caught fire."

Arson. The truth Branson had suspected sank into his

gut. Was it related to the other incidents? D-Chop's favorite mic disappearing, B-Puff's turntable getting broken, the power outage at the previous concert venue. Seemed like small, harmless stuff. Accidents. Maybe carelessness.

Had they been something more? Intentional sabotage?

If they were all connected, it could signal a pattern. Escalation.

Someone could be targeting Branson's principal, the man he was supposed to protect. But why? And more importantly, how far was the culprit prepared to go?

If worsening attacks were planned, or if harming D-Chop was the end game, whoever it was would have to go through Branson first.

FOUR

The cool fall breeze slipped under the collar of the jacket Jazz had loaned Nevaeh as she and Alvarez walked away from the PowerSource Center.

"Whew. What a night, huh?" Jazz tossed the question into the air as she rounded her navy blue SUV with Flash.

A shiver trickled through Nevaeh. But not from the chill.

She stopped at the parked SUV and peered into the night.

Tall lamps lit the parking lot at the back of the Power-Source Center. Several vehicles peppered the huge lot, all of them somewhat close to the building. Made sense, since D-Chop's security dude was still there along with rescue personnel, the fire investigator, and the PowerSource security crew.

But cars didn't explain the tingling of her nerves.

"Nev?"

She brought her gaze to Jazz, who walked along the hood from the opposite side to see Nevaeh.

"I just felt...weird. Like..."

Jazz's eyebrows lifted to fill the silence. "You're being watched?"

Nevaeh gave a nod. Her throat tightened as she scanned the shadowy lot again, then cast a look over her shoulder at the still-lit building.

"We'll check it out." Jazz stalked back around the SUV and tossed Nevaeh the keys. "You get in and lock the doors. Flash and I are going for a walk."

"I can—"

"Hey," Jazz's tone meant she didn't want any arguments, "you've been through enough tonight. Give yourself a break." Her features softened, and she winked. "Flash and I missed out on the fire, so this'll keep us from getting bored."

Nevaeh's throat closed up further as she nodded again and opened the back door of the SUV for Alvarez to jump in. She cast a glance at Jazz.

The tall redhead moved in and out of the shadowy places with Flash as they navigated between parked vehicles.

Nevaeh grabbed the passenger door handle with a shaking hand and cowardly slipped inside. She pressed the button to automatically lock the doors.

She needed to get a grip. If this kept up, she'd have to give up hiding her relapse from Phoenix and admit it before she crumbled completely on the job. When it really mattered.

She'd been doing so well, feeling more confident.

And she would again.

She sucked in a breath. It was just a rough night. How was she supposed to know a huge muscleman would appear out of nowhere. Just like—

She shook her head. She needed to get home. To Cannenta. The sweet dog would help Nevaeh calm down and get out of this triggered cycle of memories and—

A knock on the driver's window launched her heart into her throat.

Jazz's familiar face appeared in the glass as she pointed her finger at the lock.

Nevaeh's pulse raced, trying to catch up from the lost beats as she unlocked the doors.

"Sorry." Jazz lowered into the driver's seat. "Didn't mean to startle you."

So she'd noticed. Of course, she had. Jazz knew her maybe better than Nevaeh knew herself.

Nevaeh handed over the keys, not bothering to deny she was that jumpy right now. Jazz would see through it anyway.

"We didn't find anything out there. Empty vehicles. Flash didn't alert at all. Did Alvarez?"

Nevaeh shook her head.

Jazz locked the doors and started the engine. "Do you think someone was there?" She tossed Nevaeh a glance as she drove across the open lot, crisscrossing the painted stall lines and ignoring the arrows.

"Probably my imagination."

"Or your instincts. They're good."

Nevaeh's mouth tugged into a partial smile. Jazz was always her champion. No matter what. "You saw me tonight. I don't think my instincts are doing anything right now. It's all panic and cow—"

"Don't say that." Jazz's eyes flashed. "You are *not* a coward."

"Sure. Because every normal person has to hide in a bathroom after some guy gets within six feet."

Silence hung between them.

But it wouldn't last long. Not with Jazz.

"You went through something no 'normal,'" Jazz made bunny ears with the fingers of one hand in the air, "person has experienced. Something that would've turned most normal people into vegetables who'd never step foot outside again. You're the bravest person I know, Nev."

Jazz turned her head away from the road and looked at Nevaeh long enough for the sincerity in her gaze to spark hot tears in Nevaeh's eyes.

A lump stuck in her throat, and she swallowed, blinking back the tears so she wouldn't have to add *crybaby* to her list of failings for the day.

"You saved a man's life tonight. Don't forget that."

A perfectly timed reminder. Typical from Jazz.

"I mean, come on, girl." She reached across the console and gave Nevaeh's shoulder a shove.

A smile found Nevaeh's face, lifting her heart. "Yeah. I guess there's that."

"Yeah." The emphasis Jazz gave the word that might as well have been *duh* bubbled a laugh up Nevaeh's throat.

They laughed together as the tension she'd been holding for hours started to ease.

"Seriously," Jazz smiled as their amusement wound down. "That was amazing what you did for that guy."

Nevaeh lifted her shoulders. "I guess once an EMT, always an EMT." Even if she couldn't cut it on the job when she'd tried. Though not for lack of knowledge or skill.

Jazz's eyebrow arched. "Not sure that's standard EMT training, but I'll let you retain some humility. Don't want my BFF getting a big head."

"Me?" She pretended to fluff the natural coils around her head with her hands. "Never."

Jazz laughed.

Nevaeh grinned as she looked out the window. But her own reflection in the darkened glass caught her attention instead.

Her smile faded. Like it was a mask she couldn't keep wearing for long. Without the mask, nothing but fear stared back at her.

"I know it wasn't the fire that scared you." Jazz's voice reached for her, but Nevaeh didn't turn. "The hulking bodyguard was a trigger, I know. But you haven't been...yourself for a while now."

Nevaeh stared at the lights outside the window. The gas station they passed. Street lamps.

"August twenty-ninth."

Jazz's words plunged into Nevaeh's stomach. She'd kept track? Of course she had. If things had been the other way around, Nevaeh would know the date, too.

"That's when he got out, right?"

Nevaeh slowly turned her head and met her friend's gaze.

The green orbs were filled with hurt. For Nevaeh.

"Yeah." Nevaeh whispered the word, fighting desperately

not to let her memory conjure his face. His horrible, angry, brutal face.

"Do you think we should tell Phoenix?"

Nevaeh looked down at her hands in her lap, clenched into a ball. How long had they been like that? She took in a breath. "She's gotta know already. The boss always knows."

"You don't think he'll—"

"No." Nevaeh's rational mind suddenly kicked in, probably a survival mechanism to save her imagination from exploring the most terrifying possibility. "The judge gave him a lifetime restraining order. She made it clear he'd go back to prison if he came within fifty yards of me."

"Right. That's good." Jazz nodded as she stared out the windshield. "He'd have to be stupid to come near you."

"Yeah." Nevaeh's heart rate sped up despite their words.

She was all too relieved a few minutes later when Jazz said she'd spend the night at Nevaeh's house.

Because their arguments for why he wouldn't come close were only giving lip service to what they both hoped would be true.

The man of her nightmares would do whatever he wanted. And maybe, like before, no one could stop him.

As Branson pushed open one of the double doors, the squeaks, buzzers, and commentators of a basketball game blared from the twenty-foot screen of D-Chop's home theater. Not the kind with tiered seating, but simply a giant screen that stretched along one end of a big room populated with sofas and recliners.

Branson navigated his way past the pool table, bar, and arcade games that filled the space behind the seating area.

Darren stood to the right of the inset wall that held the big screen, his back to the basketball game as he watched the room.

Branson gave the personal protection specialist a nod as

he approached behind the sofa where D-Chop sat. He rounded the end so the rapper could see him.

Slumped into sofa cushions, beer can in one hand and wearing a sports team's hooded sweatshirt instead of the bling and flashy vest he'd worn onstage, D-Chop looked like any ordinary Joe relaxing at home after a hard day's work. Redness rimmed his eyes—whether from fatigue, worry, or too much of some substance, Branson wouldn't guess.

He'd learned a long time ago that it wasn't his place to be the moral compass or conscience for his clients. His job was to keep them safe from outside forces. He couldn't keep them safe from themselves.

But the fact D-Chop's frequent grin was nowhere in sight was a sign he'd taken the night's events to heart more than he did most things. How much had he heard?

"How's Kicker?"

"I haven't received any recent updates." Branson met D-Chop's gaze. "B-Puff said he'd call."

The door opened at the far end of the room, drawing Branson's attention.

Peter Volrath entered, his glasses reflecting the recessed lighting as he headed their direction, carrying the smart tablet he almost always had in his hand.

"Maybe he texted me." D-Chop reached in the pocket of his low-slung jeans. "I don't know where I left my—Hey, Petey, my man."

Peter leaned past Branson to hand D-Chop his smartphone.

"You my main man, Petey." D-Chop threw out his traditional praises absently as he thumb-scrolled on his phone's screen. "Here it is. They gave him something for the pain. He's feelin' better. Gonna need a skin graft, though."

D-Chop tossed his phone on the cushion beside him and let out a long, beer-scented breath. He covered his eyes with his hands, then drew them down across the thin side sections of beard that bordered his jawline and attached to his goatee. His gaze locked on Branson. "What happened, man?"

"The fire investigator said it was deliberate. Someone sabotaged the pyrotechnics and painted accelerant onto the set pieces so they'd be sure to catch fire."

"Why?"

Branson studied D-Chop's face. The man had a lot of secrets in his past that he didn't like to talk about. But his face tended to reveal everything. Everything he was thinking at any given moment, at least. And right now, genuine bewilderment appeared to be all that was on his mind.

"I don't know. Can you think of anyone who'd want to make life hard for you? Maybe scare you?"

D-Chop grunted. "Nobody'd try to scare me if they know me. I don't scare."

An expected answer. Maintaining his reputation as a tough rapper with plenty of street cred was the reason he hadn't wanted to report the other incidents, the thefts and vandalism.

But from what Branson had seen, it wasn't all bravado. Even now, fear wasn't the emotion that reflected in the hip-hop star's eyes. It was worry. For himself or for Kicker?

"Rock here told me some chick saved Kicker's life."

Branson glanced at Darren, who kept his features schooled. He'd given Darren the news about what had happened to Kicker to pass on to D-Chop. Maybe should've omitted the part involving a woman. Especially since it was Nevaeh.

"Someone with the Phoenix K-9 Security and Detection Agency." Branson kept his expression bland in the hope D-Chop would let it go. "I didn't see it happen, but B-Puff says she put out the fire on Kicker's back."

D-Chop swore with a grin. "My kind of woman. Gutsy. I heard she's hot, too."

Branson gave Darren another look, this one out the corner of narrowed eyes. The man talked too much. "I wouldn't know."

"You never do, man." D-Chop laughed. "Let's bring her here."

"What?" Branson's chest pinched. Nevaeh here? With D-Chop? Like the other women he had over to—

"Yeah, hire her." D-Chop swung his gaze back to the basketball game. "And another one, too, if they've got more than one hot chick there."

Frustration tangled in Branson's ribs as he bit back the response he wanted to give. They weren't playthings. They were security professionals, just like he was. And they were women who deserved to be treated with respect.

But he couldn't say that to his boss. His job could be on shaky ground as it was after the incident tonight.

He could try reason, try assuming D-Chop's mind wasn't in the gutter where it lived so often. "I think we have enough security at your estate right now."

D-Chop looked away from the big screen, his dark eyes landing on Branson. "You doing a'ight, B. But I'd feel safer with more protection. And guard dogs, man. Them is dope. They have 'em, right?"

"Yes." Branson fought to keep his face blank as his abs tightened. They both knew D-Chop didn't feel unsafe. He wanted to get the women here so he could—

Branson clenched his jaw to stop the train of his thoughts. He still had a job to do, no matter how unpleasant it could be at times. "Given what happened tonight, I think we should go to the police and tell them about the other incidents that have happened lately, too."

"What incidents?"

"The smashed turntable. The theft of your mic. The—"

D-Chop blew a whoosh of air past his lips and waved off Branson with a dismissive hand. "Accidents. And I still think Petey took my mic just to try it out. Eh, Petey?" D-Chop grinned at his assistant.

"I'm sorry, what was that?" Peter glanced up from his tablet with his characteristically bored expression.

"Be sure to bring the girls in here when they come, a'ight?" D-Chop grinned at Branson, not bothering to wait for Peter to answer his joke. "It'll be nice to have somebody hotter to look at than you and the Rock over there."

Branson glanced at Darren. The man maintained his professional stoic silence now, though he apparently got chatty when Branson wasn't around.

"What's the problem?" D-Chop cut him a look. "Don't worry, man. I ain't gonna replace you with a bunch of hot chicks." An angled grin accompanied the assurance.

But Branson's gut twisted. The fact D-Chop even went there suggested the man had considered replacing him. Or was questioning if Branson was able to do his job to keep D-Chop fully protected.

Branson forced a closed-lip smile. "No problem. I'm just thinking through where we'll put them. Nighttime patrol on the grounds would be the best use of the K-9s. They'd have an advantage in the dark."

"Sure." D-Chop returned his attention to the big screen. "Just make sure they come in here sometimes."

"Will do." Branson forced the pleasant words through clenched teeth. He spun away and stalked to the door midway along the room.

"Hey, B." D-Chop's voice stopped Branson with his hand on the sliding door.

"Don't wake the chick in my room."

Branson hid a cringe. Of course, he'd have brought home some groupie, as usual. Hopefully, she was at least legal age.

"She couldn't handle—"

Branson held up a hand, palm out, to stop any graphic descriptions he didn't want to hear. "I got it. I'll be quiet."

He went through to the hallway where D-Chop's bedroom suite was. Branson headed for his own room next to D-Chop's. As the rapper's head personal protection specialist, the proximity was a precaution in case of overnight threats.

But he couldn't be happier that the security system in place at the estate and D-Chop's preference for independence and privacy meant Branson didn't need to be on active duty right now. He couldn't wait to shed the baggy hip-hop clothes D-Chop liked his security personnel to wear for public appearances.

More than that, he wanted to shed the dirty, slimy feeling that crept along his skin every time he had to live in such close proximity to the lifestyles of the celebrities he protected.

Not exactly the wholesome, Christian family environment he was raised in. And had wanted for himself someday.

He locked his door, a precaution he took whenever women visited the house, and pulled the loose-fitting sweater off, leaving on the black T-shirt he wore underneath. Fatigue from more than the evening's events weighed him down, heavier than the sweater.

Why was he so tired lately? It wasn't exactly a physical fatigue. He still had energy for his intense workouts, felt strong and healthy. But weariness seemed to rest on his shoulders like a weighted barbell he could never set down.

He checked his watch. *12:15.* No wonder he felt tired tonight. He usually tried to be in bed by nine thirty. Ten at the latest. Staying up beyond that made it more challenging to arise at four thirty a.m. Maybe he'd let himself sleep in till four forty-five.

But sleep wasn't going to make this situation look any better. The fact that Darren was still watching D-Chop right now meant the rapper must have told him to stay. The PM routine at the estate was for Darren and Branson to retire while Louis monitored the cameras and security system from the security room overnight. Despite his bravado, D-Chop must have been a little shaken by the fire.

Branson hated to think it, but what if D-Chop wanted the Phoenix K-9 women to provide security for another reason beyond his desire for eye candy? What if he really was questioning Branson's abilities as the head of his security and his personal protector?

Branson could not lose this job. Not now, with so much at stake.

He'd have to call Phoenix K-9 in the morning to hire Nevaeh and another woman. Probably the redhead he'd seen last night, since she also fit D-Chop's superficial criteria of beauty.

It meant he'd see Nevaeh again. He wouldn't mind that a bit under different circumstances. But though D-Chop was a nice guy, he was also a habitual womanizer. His behavior toward women was disrespectful, though most females Branson had seen with the rapper didn't seem to mind. Would Nevaeh be like that?

Not that it mattered. He should be more concerned about the possibility that if the strange incidents around D-Chop continued to escalate, the Phoenix K-9 Agency could take over his security position permanently.

The consequences of that would be too great. He couldn't let his family down. Not in that way.

No matter how lovely and competent the Phoenix K-9 women were, he'd have to make sure they didn't charm their way into stealing his job.

FIVE

Nevaeh sucked in a deep breath as she followed Jazz into the breakroom at PK-9 headquarters. The smell of coffee filled her nostrils and traveled down to her belly—the precursor enjoyment of the energizing brew. Her droopy eyelids opened farther already.

"Bless you, Cora." Jazz smiled at the blonde as she took the offered mug.

Flash swished his tail at her side like he was also anticipating the coffee.

Cora's sweet smile beamed, mirrored by Jana, her golden retriever who wagged her tail as she greeted the newcomers. "It's the least I can do after your hard night."

"Hard night?" Sofia cast them a glance from the sofa where she sat with Gaston, her chocolate Newfoundland. The water rescue dog rested his head on her lap and hogged the other cushions with his sprawled body. "If that was hard, this team is getting soft. Maybe we need to do some more drills."

"Shh." Nevaeh aimed an exaggerated look at the doorway where Phoenix would enter when the meeting was going to start. "The boss might hear you."

Sof snorted. "She might hear you call her 'the boss,' too."

Nevaeh wrinkled her nose at Sof.

A whiff of coffee jerked her gaze to Cora.

The lovely blonde held out Nevaeh's favorite mug, molded and painted in the shape of a rottweiler's head. Steam curled off the surface of the liquid inside, but it was the fabulous smell that made her mouth water. They didn't usually have flavored coffee in the breakroom. "Caramel?"

Cora's smile grew. "I wanted to give you something extra special since you saved a man's life yesterday." The expression in her soft blue eyes turned more serious. "We're so proud of you and thankful God gave you the courage to do what you did."

The courage. How much did Cora know? The PK-9 team members all knew something was off with Nevaeh. They had to. They'd been in enough situations together to have noticed Nevaeh had...issues sometimes. That she could get shaky. And, of course, they all saw her bring Cannenta to meetings and other places when she wasn't on duty with Alvarez.

She looked down at the thirty-pound corgi mix who sat quietly on the floor by her foot. The PTSD service dog was a dead giveaway to everyone that Nevaeh wasn't the same as they were. That she had a weakness.

But they probably didn't know why, thanks to Phoenix's rule that the private details of their pasts remained secret to all but her unless they voluntarily shared the stories themselves. Though as the office manager and technologies specialist, Cora probably had access to all their files.

And Cora had been there from the beginning, the only one already working for Phoenix at the agency when Nevaeh came on board. Nevaeh had been such a mess back then, Cora probably couldn't have missed the obvious signs of PTSD.

"Nevaeh? Did I remember wrong?" Poor Cora still held the mug, her smile faltering.

"Nah, it's great." Nevaeh snatched the mug so fast the coffee nearly sloshed over the edge. She held the brew to her nose where she could get the full body of caramel coffee aroma. A naturally induced grin lifted her spirits. "Food and drink have always been the way to my affections." She winked at Cora. "Thanks, girl."

"Of course. I'm thankful you're okay, and that the man you saved is, too."

"Have you heard any updates?" Jazz asked the question from the love seat where she sat.

"Updates on what? The caterers?" Bristol Jones rushed into the room with enough force to create a breeze, probably because she was just under the wire for the meeting's start time of eight a.m. "Hey, everyone." She flashed a smile at Nevaeh and Cora, then swung her gaze to include all the women in the room.

A black blur darted past her. Nevaeh's eyes followed long enough to ID the phantom as Toby, the energetic black Labrador that took playing with Raksa as seriously as he took his explosive detection work. He and Sofia's German shepherd protection K-9 wagged their tails vigorously as they smelled each other near the air-conditioning vent that they hadn't figured out wasn't providing cool air anymore. Flash, though Jazz had let him off leash, hung back and watched the two buddies.

"Welcome." Cora smiled at Bristol. "No, I'm still looking for a different caterer, I'm afraid. My father decided they weren't suitable for our wedding and canceled the booking."

"Because they catered his competitor's company banquet?"

Cora raised one skinny shoulder slightly at Bristol's question. "At least he's agreed to let me select the caterer now. The trouble is most of the reputable options are booked or unable to handle a wedding of this size."

"Should've gone small like Michael and I did." Sof grinned at Cora. "In and out without a fuss. No caterers or headaches." She held up a finger like she wanted to mark the most important thing. "And *no* fittings."

Nevaeh snorted. "Yeah, like Cora's the type to elope."

"We did not elope." Humor twinkled in Sof's eyes. "You were all there, along with my parents and the pastor."

"And Grace." Cora tilted her head as her features melted to mush. "She was so darling in that little pantsuit."

Sof chuckled. "Couldn't get the girl to wear a dress any more than me."

"Which reminds me..." Cora glanced at Nevaeh, then swung her gaze to include Bristol and Jazz. "All the adjustments have been made to your dresses, so you can pick them up whenever you like."

At least that meant the fittings were done. Never enjoyed all that playing dress-up, which was probably exactly why Sof refused to be a bridesmaid. But it was sweet of Cora to ask Nevaeh and especially Jazz since she hadn't been with the team a year yet.

It probably would've been easier to stick with having only Bristol as maid of honor given that Kent's brother, his best man, was his only living relative. But because Cora wanted more of the PK-9 team in her wedding party, Kent had recruited Remington and Michael to be groomsmen. She'd heard from Cora that the PK-9 husbands were becoming friends anyway.

"But enough about the wedding." Cora pressed her hands together in front of her smile like she'd secretly love to keep chatting about her big event. "To answer Jazz's original question, I did receive an update about the man whose life Nevaeh saved last night. I called the hospital and was told he is expected to recover, though he'll need to have skin grafts."

The hospital wouldn't normally give that kind of information about a patient to a non-family member. But Nevaeh didn't ask. Probably another one of Phoenix's sources. Or maybe Cora's. The angelic-looking blonde had more tricks up her sleeve than most people expected. It was a mistake to underestimate anybody on the PK-9 team.

"Praise the Lord he'll survive." Bristol voiced the churchish saying as if she meant it. And she did. Both she and Cora did. It was obvious in the way they lived out their faith all the time.

"Amen." Sof added the addition. So weird coming from

her. The woman had been Nevaeh's partner in joking about Cora and Bristol and their church talk, their mini sermons, and frequent mentions of God. Sofia's jokes had seemed to carry more of an edge to them than Nevaeh's. Like she had more serious issues with God or religion.

But just like that, Sof had joined them. The cold CIA agent fighting machine had gotten religion. And a husband and daughter.

If any more drastic changes struck her PK-9 family, Nevaeh was going to get whiplash.

At least she was sure Jazz wouldn't join the religious trend. She had too many reasons not to.

And there was no way Phoenix ever would. The idea of religion and Phoenix Gray was like trying to pair…

The boss entered the room and strode past Nevaeh before she could finish coming up with an appropriate comparison.

Dagian, her sandy-colored multi-purpose K-9 kept in step at her side, as usual, though he was off-leash.

"Let's get started." Phoenix reached the farthest armchair she always sat in and turned to face the group.

Nevaeh glanced at her watch as she took her coffee and Cannenta to the love seat. Eight o'clock on the dot.

She'd never get how Phoenix could always be exactly on time and always in the nick of time for any unscheduled danger.

Nevaeh plopped onto the cushion next to Jazz, and Cannenta jumped up to sit between them, placing her paw on Nevaeh's leg.

Jazz gave Nevaeh a smile over the corgi mix's head. Having only been back for nine months, Jazz was still getting used to Cannenta's cute behaviors.

But they were so much more than cute. Cannenta putting her paw on Nevaeh was intentional. She'd probably sensed the small spike in Nevaeh's blood pressure because the meeting was about to start. Not that she dreaded these meetings. Hanging with her PK-9 family was one of the best things life had to offer, right next to hanging with her blood relatives.

But she figured what would be on the agenda today. Debriefing from last night.

How much would they cover? She didn't want to think about the...triggers Cannenta and Jazz were still helping her recover from. And would Sof have noticed anything about Nevaeh's behavior—her fear—that she'd feel she had to share with Phoenix? Or question Nevaeh about?

"First, commendations are in order for Nevaeh's actions last night." Phoenix's dark blue eyes locked on Nevaeh across the distance. "You went above and beyond to save a life. Well done."

"Yeah!" Sof started clapping as she grinned at Nevaeh. The other PK-9 girls joined in the applause, and Jazz added a whistle that drew the shocked gaze of every dog in the room.

Even Gaston lifted his furry head off Sofia's lap to stare at Jazz.

Heat rushed to Nevaeh's face as her pulse accelerated. What if they talked about the other things that had happened last night? Jazz would never snitch, but Phoenix always seemed to have ways of finding things out. Sof could've noticed Nevaeh's absence when she lost it and went—

A small body moved onto Nevaeh's lap. Cannenta. Her solid presence, the contact and warmth between her and Nevaeh's chilled legs, interrupted the early start of a spiral.

Nevaeh donned a grin. "Stop it, gang. Y'all will make me blush." The smile felt more real by the moment as her family smiled back at her. She'd missed the look in their eyes. No judgment. Just pride and joy.

The same way she'd felt when Bristol had bested the terrorist bomber, when Cora had survived the drug cartel's attacks, and when Sof had, well, done everything awesome she always did as easily as normal people drank water.

"Intel on the fire indicates arson," Phoenix continued in her emotionless delivery. "No progress in finding the perpetrator as of yet."

Arson. Someone had intentionally sabotaged D-Chop's concert? Jazz had probably learned that last night, but Nevaeh had been such a wreck at the time, she could see why Jazz hadn't told her.

"The perp apparently didn't use any explosives." Bristol gently scooted Gaston's back end off the cushion at the far end of the sofa so she could sit there. The dog pulled his hind legs under him and sat up between Sof and Bris, his massive body taller than they were.

Nevaeh chuckled at the sight as Bris finished what she was saying.

"Toby and I checked the equipment on stage in our search before the concert."

"Correct." Phoenix turned her head slightly toward Bris, the angle causing a shadow to fall over her eyes under the bill of her gray baseball cap. "The pyrotechnics had been tampered with."

"Should we investigate who caused the fire?" Cora, seated in the other armchair, stroked Jana's ear as she looked at the boss.

"We'll give the police more time." Phoenix and Dag, sitting at her side, looked like immovable statues as she responded. "We were not in charge of overall security at the venue, so the responsibility isn't ours, unless we let someone slip by while we were patrolling. Given that we weren't scheduled to arrive until the doors opened, I'm quite certain we weren't at fault. A job like this one was likely executed hours in advance."

"But why?" Nevaeh couldn't keep the question from slipping out. All eyes turned to her. "I mean, why would someone want to sabotage D-Chop's concert? Do you think they meant to hurt him instead of his hype man?" The thought thumped her pulse harder for a different reason.

Phoenix stared at her for a second. "The motivation and perpetrator aren't our concern. I'll only look into it if there's evidence we were lax in our duties."

"Sorry, but I...have history with D-Chop."

Silence filled the room as they all stared at her. Except for Jazz, who already knew the story.

The others wouldn't ask. They knew the PK-9 privacy policy. But it wasn't like a big secret she needed to hide. And she couldn't stand the weird silence for another second.

"He and my big brother were..." As much as she loved these girls, her mouth wouldn't form the words to say Jordan had tried to muscle in on another gang's territory. "They were caught in a bad scene. Jordan got shot. All the other jerks ran, but D-Chop stayed with him. All the way to the hospital. And he sat there with him until he died."

She glanced up at the girls, their sad, serious faces all trained on her. Man, this was awkward. She grabbed for a smile. "Sorry, gang. Didn't mean to go all gloom and doom on you." She shrugged. "I just feel like I owe him."

Bris nodded. "Completely understandable."

Phoenix didn't say a word, but she gave Cora a look. One of those silent signals the two used to communicate like they had a secret language between them. Kind of like Nevaeh and Jazz, in a way.

Cora aimed her blue eyes, full of compassion, at Nevaeh. "You'll probably be pleased to hear this, then. We received a phone call this morning from Branson Aaberg who is the head of D-Chop's personal security detail."

Nevaeh's stomach clenched at the bodyguard's name. But Cora seemed to think there was some good news involved, so she tried to focus on that possibility.

Cora's eyes widened as she smiled. "D-Chop was so impressed with your actions last night that he wants to hire you for overnight security beginning this evening at ten thirty p.m. to six thirty a.m."

Awesome. She could help protect D-Chop from whatever danger he was in. What better way to pay him back for her family's debt? For her brother?

But alarm pumped through Nevaeh's system as if she'd overlooked a threat only her instincts could see. The bodyguard called to hire her. Was it really D-Chop who wanted her or the oversized bodyguard? How could she be around the guy and not lose it again? And what if he was purposefully trying to get her there alone, isolated?

Nevaeh's gaze landed on Cora. And the worry that tensed her mouth.

Nevaeh must be showing too much of the panic pulsing through her. She scrambled to control her features, channel Phoenix's expressionless vibe.

Jazz cleared her throat and cut Nevaeh a side-eyed glance that rapidly darted to the others like she was afraid they'd think her bestie had gone nuts.

Apparently the effort to hide emotion was just making Nevaeh look like a contorting lunatic. The thought was enough to push a laugh up her throat.

"Are you okay?" Bris half smiled as she peered at Nevaeh.

"Yeah." Nevaeh grinned and laughed again. "I'm just wondering if this makes me a paid groupie. I used to dream of following D-Chop around on tour."

Cora smiled gently, but her eyebrows pressed together as if she was concerned by the thought. "I think they want you because of your security expertise and the K-9s. Mr. Aaberg mentioned he thought the dogs would be an asset to have on the estate at night."

"Chauvinist, huh?" Jazz quirked her mouth into a smirk. "Women can be security assets, too."

"You'll get your chance, Jazz." Cora glanced at Phoenix and then back to Jazz. "He asked to hire you, as well."

"Me, specifically?" Was that a blush that colored Jazz's peaches and cream cheeks?

Nevaeh snickered. "Looks like you want somebody to think you're an asset."

"What is this?" Bris jumped on the hint, always eager to make anybody pay for the ribbing they'd given her when she was falling for Remington, the guy who was now her husband.

Of course, Jazz wasn't on the team at that time, so

Nevaeh should probably defend her. But teasing was way more fun.

"Do tell all, Nevaeh." Sof's dark eyes gleamed as she leaned forward with a grin.

Nevaeh opened her mouth to tell the others about the muscle-bound bodyguard Jazz had a crush on, but then she pictured him. What she remembered of him anyway. Too large, strong, overpowering...terrifying. With a deep voice that shook the ground and the confidence she'd worked so hard to build.

"We met Branson Aaberg. Super cute." Jazz's amused tone seeped through Nevaeh's rapid, panicked thoughts and wrapped around her like a warm blanket. "Muscles for days." She tossed Nevaeh a grin, but her eyes reflected understanding, their shared secret she would keep.

"I guess Nevaeh was right." Bris grinned at Jazz. "You do sound pretty dreamy already."

"I admit I like a tall man. They're hard to find."

"It's so hard to be height-challenged." The very petite Sofia chuckled.

"Very." At five feet nine inches, Jazz wasn't kidding.

"Good thing you'll be working so closely with your dream man, then." Bris laughed, and Sof and Jazz joined in.

Nevaeh may never have loved Jazz more than at that moment. Nevaeh could normally take a good ribbing as well as she could dish it out but having to focus so much on the bodyguard right now...she'd probably have ended up running off to have a meltdown in the bathroom again. And then she'd lose this job.

Couldn't risk that, especially with the mess it sounded like D-Chop was in. Whether someone only wanted to make life hard for him or wanted to do worse—like harm the rapper himself—Nevaeh couldn't sit back and leave him on his own. Not when there was a chance she could help him. Jordy would want her to do that, and so would Pops and Grams, if she were still alive.

D-Chop had been there for Jordy—for her family—when

nobody else had. She'd do what she could for D-Chop now. Try to keep him from a fate like Jordy's.

Even if it meant she had to risk being around the burly bodyguard who reminded her of the past she needed to forget. D-Chop had risked a lot, including jail time, to stay with Jordy that night. She could risk getting triggered to repay him.

"You're to visit the estate at one o'clock for a tour in daylight." Phoenix's deep voice interrupted Nevaeh's inner pep talk.

So they'd have to go sooner than she thought. And the Aaberg dude would probably be their tour guide.

Nevaeh swallowed. She could do that. She'd have Alvarez with her. And Jazz and Flash. She'd be fine.

"Just remember," Phoenix seemed to watch Nevaeh instead of Jazz, though it was hard to tell for sure under her cap, "D-Chop is hiring additional security for a reason. Be alert at all times."

The warning snaked a shiver down Nevaeh's spine. Alert —more like downright yellow—was the only thing she seemed unable to *stop* being at the moment.

Phoenix always told her to use her fear. That it was a warning she should listen to, the signal to get ready for danger. If only Phoenix, just this once, could be wrong.

SIX

Branson should not be excited to see the two women and K-9s walking from a navy blue SUV to D-Chop's house. And he probably shouldn't be spying on them from the camera feed in the security room.

Then again, he was the head of security here. And he was also nervous, a foreign experience for him. He hadn't felt a tickle in his belly like this since the first day of basic training.

He dashed out of the security room and hurried through the hallway, sliding his hand over his short hair that he'd added more gel to than normal to make sure it'd stay in place.

Cutting through the expansive rooms designed and decorated to impress, he barely glanced at the surroundings. Would they impress Nevaeh? Or did she care about more important things when—

The thought halted the instant he realized what he was thinking. *When looking for a man?* Good grief.

He'd spent his entire adult life without so much as a girlfriend, and now he was suddenly hoping for a serious relationship? With a woman he'd only talked to for about twenty seconds.

And she'd barely said two words in return. If she'd even said that many.

He hadn't really noticed. All he'd been able to notice were her eyes, her abundant curls, her perfect features. And the way she gave him a breathless feeling when he was standing stock-still.

"This way." The voice of Marsha Phillips, the housekeeper, echoed from the entryway as Branson reached it. "Oh." The tall woman with high cheekbones and soft-styled wavy hair, the brown color belying her sixty-some years, gave him a smile when she saw him. "I was about to bring these ladies to you. They're from the Phoenix K-9 Agency."

He turned in the direction she looked, his gaze skimming across the redhead and locking on the target it had sought from the beginning.

Nevaeh. She was every bit as breathtaking as he'd remembered. No, even more so in the daylight.

Sunrays streamed through the windows behind her and cast a warm glow on her richly colored black hair. Her features were more defined in this light—her full lips, perfectly shaped nose, and gorgeous eyes that...were staring right at him.

Gone was the fear he'd seen in them last night, but they also didn't hold the friendliness he'd hoped for when he'd imagined talking to her again. They were cool, almost hostile, as was the shape of her lovely mouth.

He squelched the urge to clear his throat and looked at the housekeeper. "Thanks, Marsha. Have you already introduced yourself?"

"I have."

"Great. I'll take it from here."

She nodded and moved off in her elegant way.

He took a breath and faced the two security agents. Given the coolness in Nevaeh's demeanor, he'd do well to think of them only in their professional capacity. And to remember they could be a threat to his job. The job he couldn't afford to lose.

The thought lent a note of formality to his tone when he spoke. "I believe you both already know my name, Branson

Aaberg." He looked at the taller woman. "And you're Jazz Lamont."

"Correct." She smiled. At least one of them was friendly. Though he noticed she was packing a knife in a sheath on her hip in addition to her firearm. Probably not for whittling.

He slowly brought his gaze to Nevaeh. Wouldn't do to let on he'd been eavesdropping and cared enough to remember the name he'd heard Jazz use.

"Nevaeh Williams." She didn't extend her hand, so he didn't offer his. Her eyes broadcasted a stay-away message even he, no genius at reading women, couldn't miss.

The words he'd prepared to say—*what a beautiful name, it's a great pleasure to meet you,* and other such nonsense—died before reaching his throat. It was for the best anyway. No sense in schmoozing the competition.

"Okay, let's get down to business." He crossed his arms over his light blue T-shirt. "You've been brought on to enhance our overnight security. Darren Tremblay and I are D-Chop's primary security personnel during the day at the estate. D-Chop likes his freedom and privacy, so we survey the premises and are usually only with him when he has visitors. At night, I'll give you any updates and directions needed when you first arrive, but then Darren and I go to on call status overnight."

"You live here?" Nevaeh's voice made his pulse do an odd skip.

He met her cool gaze. "Yes. Darren stays overnight, as well. A third personal protection specialist, Louis Kursko, comes in for the overnight shift. If D-Chop wants to be alone or is sleeping, Louis spends his shift monitoring the security cameras. We have some indoors in select hallways and non-private areas. And we have them outside at all the entry points. I'm sure you noticed the guard at the front gate when you came in?"

Jazz nodded.

"He's a daytime security guard we contract through a local company. He doesn't have the training and experience of a PPS, but he is armed. He won't be here at night when you are, though, unless D-Chop holds a party, which happens pretty frequently."

"Will we patrol the house at all?" Jazz watched him with big green eyes.

"You'll mostly be on the grounds. The dogs' extra senses should be an advantage in the dark out there and act as a deterrent. But I'll have you make occasional passes through the house, as well. The security system is armed at night and during the day except when we allow visitors through the gate. We take it off only to let people in and out. It's an advanced system, so we can feel comfortable relying on it with less security staff overnight."

"Sounds good." Jazz glanced at Nevaeh and then back to Branson.

"Was the fire at the PowerSource Center the first suspicious thing to happen to D-Chop?" Nevaeh caught him by surprise again, this time not only from speaking but from the pointed nature of her question. Her full lips pressed into a firm, plush line, but something in her gaze belied her attempt to look disinterested.

D-Chop didn't want anyone to know about the recent incidents for fear news of them would reach the press, and he'd look vulnerable or weak. Sometimes this job meant protecting information as well as people. "You're going to be asked to sign a non-disclosure agreement. Let's introduce you to D-Chop, then get the NDA done."

Nevaeh's eyes cooled again and narrowed slightly.

Branson turned away, disappointment settling in his belly. This wasn't how he'd envisioned their second meeting.

He led them in silence through the parlor that was far too large, cold, and stylized to be called a living room and then cut across a hallway to reach the music room.

Since D-Chop had only moved into the house two weeks ago, he hadn't yet enacted his plan to turn the room into a recording studio. But it seemed to suffice as a rehearsal space.

Heavy beats shook the floor outside the room as Branson opened the door.

He glanced inside, noting Darren stood near D-Chop as the rapper spewed out rhythmic lyrics into a microphone.

Branson stepped back and held out an arm toward the door. "After you."

Jazz's eyes widened, and a smile played on her face as she passed him with her Belgian Malinois and went through the doorway.

Nevaeh—Ms. Williams—didn't move. Her big eyes looked larger than before as she glanced at him, then away. "Go ahead." She suddenly shoved her hand in the pocket of her red windbreaker. "I have to take this." She pulled out a cellphone and turned away.

Weird. He hadn't heard it ring. Must have vibrated in her pocket. Though that wouldn't account for the strange expression on her face. As if she were afraid of something.

Maybe she hadn't met a celebrity as famous as D-Chop before. Some fans froze up before meeting him, while others went crazy with excitement. Everyone was different.

He entered the room ahead of her but stepped to the side just beyond the door. He didn't want to think she could be up to something bad, but it was his job to be suspicious, cautious, and ready.

She followed within seconds. Quick—and very silent—phone call.

His suspicions increased. What was she up to? He'd have to watch her closely.

Not that he'd mind. He squashed the smile that tilted his lips at the thought. Cold or not, she was still the most beautiful woman he'd ever met.

And she was about to meet one of the biggest players he'd known. The thought pulled his mouth into a frown as he followed Nevaeh toward D-Chop.

The rapper lowered his mic and signaled B-Puff to stop his turntables. The other band members followed suit, Pinky lowering his drumsticks and Leeman taking his hands off the keyboard. JipJap kept his guitar strapped onto his shoulder.

Jonesy Baker, the hopeful trying out for the job as D-Chop's new hype man, grinned at the women.

His glee didn't match D-Chop's. The gleam in the rapper's dark eyes was like the look of a tiger eyeing his prey. "Life just got a whole lot better, boys."

Branson's jaw clenched. All he could do was try to lend an air of professionalism that D-Chop would no doubt shoot down as soon as he opened his mouth. "Ms. Lamont and Ms. Williams, may I introduce D-Chop."

D-Chop laughed as he crawled over cords to reach Nevaeh. "Would you listen to him? Like we're meeting at a ball or something. Though I wouldn't mind meetin' you anywhere, baby." His gaze raked Nevaeh in a way that he apparently meant to be flattering.

But it churned like raw meat in Branson's gut.

Nevaeh's eyes brightened and her lips angled upward.

No way. Don't tell him she was going to fall for D-Chop's disrespectful treatment. Branson clenched one hand into a fist at his side.

She tilted her head, her mass of curls following the movement. "That line work for you these days?"

Branson's fist relaxed with the surprise that loosened his jaw. Hadn't expected that. Though it could be her way of flirting.

D-Chop apparently thought so, too. His grin widened, and he took a step closer. "You mean I don't need it?"

A growl rumbled through the room. The stocky rottweiler by Nevaeh stared at D-Chop.

The rapper glanced down, his grin dropping as he stepped back. "Hey," his tone was a little shaky, "your dog's supposed to protect me."

"I always come first for him. It's a relationship thing." Nevaeh smiled, revealing white teeth that lit up her face, nearly blinding Branson with her beauty. "But if you drop the player routine, I might tell him not to rip your throat out."

A snicker tried to escape Branson's mouth, but he swallowed it down. Couldn't keep the grin from reaching his lips, though. The woman had spunk. And apparently no celebrity worship.

D-Chop's gaze shifted to the redhead, and his eyes brightened with that gleam again.

"What Nevaeh said goes for me and my K-9, too." Jazz delivered the warning with a smile and friendly tone.

These women were something else. Knew how to put a predatory man in his place without sacrificing their professionalism or showing an ounce of fear.

"Nevaeh?" D-Chop swung his attention back to her. "Nevaeh Williams?" He peered at her, but the flirtatious gleam was gone. "You aren't..."

"Nice to see you again, Darius." Why would she use his name from before his rapping career?

"No way." D-Chop grinned—a real, happy show of teeth. "Jordy's kid sister?"

"Yeah." Nevaeh's smile softened.

"Wow." D-Chop looked her over, this time devoid of the usual ogling that set Branson's teeth on edge. He looked at her like a big brother or uncle might, as if she was a long-lost relative. "Last time I seen you, you were this high." He indicated his chest-level with his hand. "You gone and grown up, girl."

She shrugged. "You've changed, too."

He wiped a hand over his goatee, ending at his chin. His gaze shifted away from her, almost shy. Or ashamed? "Well... I got out." His focus returned to her, as if the thought renewed his self-confidence, which never seemed lacking.

"Yeah. You did." She held his gaze as something passed between them. What kind of shared past did they have?

At least it didn't seem to be romantic. Sounded like she'd have been too young for that. That didn't guarantee something couldn't develop now, though.

"It's crazy you're here. You knew who I was when you took the job?"

"Sure." Nevaeh met D-Chop's quizzical stare. "I owe you."

Another voiceless moment passed between them. Then D-Chop nodded. "We should hang out sometime. Relive the old days."

Branson's muscles tensed. Was that an invitation to something more? She might've been too young for D-Chop before, but she was full grown now.

"Maybe when I'm off the clock."

"A woman with purpose." D-Chop chuckled. "That's a'ight. I can tell B's gettin' uptight anyway." D-Chop threw Branson a grin.

Had he been that transparent? Hopefully not. He needed to stay on D-Chop's good side.

The rapper returned his attention to Nevaeh. "Good to have you and your dog protecting the place. I'm cool, you know, but my family comes here." D-Chop's usual bravado buoyed his tone. "I need it safe for them."

Did that mean he was starting to think it wasn't safe enough? Branson's unease returned. Maybe D-Chop was questioning the job Branson was doing with security. And maybe he really would get the Phoenix K-9 Agency to replace him. If they even did long-term security jobs.

But he hadn't been replaced yet. Branson stood a little straighter. "Then we'd better get going with the tour."

The women turned to look at him, though Nevaeh darted her gaze elsewhere as soon as possible.

He stifled the urge to shake his head. Never did understand women very well.

"I'll show you the parts of the grounds I want you to patrol." He stepped to the side to let them pass through the doorway first, as his mama had taught him.

Nevaeh hurried to move in front of Jazz as if she wanted to be first out the door. Odd.

But Branson had bigger things to worry about than the woman's strange behavior. His job security, for one. And protecting his client.

The women paused in the hallway and waited for him.

"This way." He focused on business as he led them through one of the back doors and outside into the afternoon sunlight that warmed the crisp air. Made the temperature comfortable enough that it wasn't a problem he hadn't thought to grab his jacket on the way out. Sunglasses would've helped, though.

He shaded his eyes with his hand as he looked out across the pool and patio to the landscaped garden beyond. "On the other side of that fence," he pointed to the wooden privacy fence that isolated the pool and garden, "is about an acre of open land behind the house. It's secured by a chain-link fence. If you'll follow me, we can go around to the front, and I'll show you the perimeter there and the entry."

"Lead the way." Jazz gave him a smile.

He nodded to her, keeping his eyes away from Nevaeh as he stalked past the pool and out the gate of the privacy fence. He led them around the large house, pointing out spots that tended to be shadowed and the location of the security lights that would be on at night.

"The side door is lit and wired to the security system, but I'd like you to check it when you make your rounds past there."

"Got it." Jazz responded as the women followed a few feet behind him.

Nevaeh was back to complete silence again. Maybe she was shy. Though that didn't match the vibrance she seemed to give off, even when silent. And there was nothing shy about the way she'd handled D-Chop.

They followed the curve of the driveway and walked past the decorative stone in the middle that encircled a couple trees and other plants.

Once cleared of the plants that had blocked the view of the road, Branson's gaze moved ahead to the security gate and guardhouse. Which looked empty. Where was—

One of the dogs growled just as Branson saw his answer.

A body lay sprawled on the pavement.

SEVEN

Nevaeh broke into a run behind Aaberg, scanning the surroundings for danger, for an explanation as to why a man was down.

She reached the fallen man at the same time as Jazz.

Aaberg already crouched by him, reaching for the man's neck.

Jazz gave her a look, along with a tap on her hip holster, that said she'd cover Nevaeh.

That was all she needed to know. Nevaeh quickly went to the side opposite Aaberg and kneeled on the driveway beside the young guy dressed in a tan uniform with a badge clipped to his chest pocket. The gate security guard.

The door to the small guardhouse hung open behind Aaberg.

"I think I feel a pulse." Aaberg lifted his head. Hope and uncertainty filled the blue eyes that found her face.

She hadn't noticed their color before. A very nice, unexpectedly gentle shade like the blue that would decorate a baby boy's room.

She yanked her gaze away and pressed her fingers to the guard's neck. "Yes. Pretty strong pulse. Call 911. He'll need an ambulance."

Aaberg nodded and pulled a phone from his pocket as he stood and walked a few feet away.

Nevaeh shifted her hands to the back of the guard's neck and felt her way up his skull.

Her fingers reached something sticky. Blood. A gash and swelling.

The guard groaned and shifted his head.

"It's okay." She checked his badge for a name. "James, it's okay. I'm Nevaeh. And your boss is here. Branson." Or did he know him as Aaberg? It seemed the guy liked to be pretty formal, given how he'd introduced her and Jazz as Ms. Williams and Ms. Lamont.

The guard's eyes slowly opened. He started to lift his head, but a moan pushed through his lips.

Nevaeh braced her hands behind his head as he lowered it back down the quarter inch he'd managed to heft it. "Try not to move much, okay? We've called for an ambulance."

Denim-clad legs moved into view. She slid her gaze up, way up, to take in the giant of a man that was Branson Aaberg. She'd noticed when they'd arrived that he wasn't dressed at all like he had been last night.

The dark and baggy hip-hop outfit had been replaced by cowboy cut jeans, wide belt, and a tucked-in blue T-shirt that didn't do much to hide his massive muscles. She'd guess D-Chop wanted his bodyguards to fit in with the rapper's style in public appearances. But she had to admit Aaberg's chosen look made the most of his physique.

She could almost understand why Jazz had been mooning over him. He did have a certain appeal if a girl was into huge strongmen. Which Nevaeh definitely was not.

"They're on the way." Aaberg's deep rumble seemed to fall from the heavens, sunlight backlighting his face so she couldn't see his features, even with her head tilted far back.

She hid a shiver by pressing her fingers to the guard's pulse again.

His breathing was slightly labored.

"Head hurt?"

The young guy, probably no more than twenty-one, grimaced. "Yeah."

"Help will be here soon."

"Hang in there, buddy." Aaberg lowered his large form on the other side of James. "Can you tell us what happened?"

This close to the bodyguard, his deep tones seemed to vibrate right through her. Nevaeh stood, the increase in distance and height instantly allowing her to breathe easier.

"I think..." James squinted, maybe trying to remember or just avoid the sunlight. "I remember a man pulled up in a car. Wanted to see D-Chop."

"Did you know him?"

"I don't think so. I can't say for sure."

Nevaeh shot Aaberg a glance, her nerves tensing. Was he the type of boss to get irritated with an employee who messed up?

His features stayed smooth, except for the dark blond eyebrows that were already dipped. "It's okay. Just relax. The memory will come back."

Surprise soothed some of Nevaeh's frayed nerves. Wouldn't have guessed Aaberg would be that patient and...nice.

As soon as the thought popped into her head, a spasm of guilt followed. He hadn't done anything to make her think he wouldn't be nice. He just happened to be unusually big, strong, and intimidating. To her, at least.

She knelt next to her patient and cut Aaberg a glance she hoped didn't look too apologetic. But his attention was on James, his hand on the guard's shoulder.

If she could focus only on Aaberg's face, she might not be so nervous around him. Straight, long nose, and a soft mouth with a crease in the skin on one side of his lips that suggested he smiled a lot. Light brown stubble emphasized his strong jawline while the top of his head was shaped with closely shaved blond hair on the sides and inch-length strands on the top, styled in a short wave. His sun-bronzed skin sold his swoony, city-cowboy vibe all the way.

Jazz was right. Nevaeh might state it even stronger than *cute*. But Jazz would rib her for days if she admitted she'd been wrong about the man's looks.

"I remember..." James's strained voice drew Nevaeh's attention. "The guy in the car had on a cap and sunglasses. Couldn't see his face."

She wasn't sure whether that was suspicious or ordinary for D-Chop's visitors. But judging from Branson's frown, she'd go with suspicious.

"D-Chop wasn't expecting any visitors today."

"Right." The guard squinted into the sun. "I asked for his name for the list."

Nevaeh leaned forward and held her hand above James until it cast a shadow over his eyes.

"He said he couldn't hear me, so I left the booth and went over to his car. Then..." The guard's features scrunched. "Somebody slammed something into my head." He directed his gaze toward Branson, though Nevaeh's hand might've blocked his view. "That's all I remember."

"Okay. Hang in there, buddy." Branson gently thumped the man's arm with his fist, then pushed to his feet.

His enormous size took her breath away. And not in a good way.

She popped up and took a few steps back. Far enough for air to return to her lungs and her pulse to slow its teetering sprint.

He tapped the earpiece she'd noticed he wore when they'd arrived. "Team leader to D1. Threat at front gate." Aaberg's voice deepened more, if that was possible, commanding and in control. "Secure D-Chop until we clear the property."

He suddenly looked right at her.

Her pulse jolted. But she forced herself not to look away. Not to show the cowardly feelings inside that made her want to curl into a fetal position.

"I told the dispatcher they should send the police, too." His tone softened slightly when he spoke this time.

She nodded. Her throat seemed to have shrunk smaller than her pinky at the moment, so she wasn't about to get any words out.

"D-Chop won't like it, but I can't keep this one quiet if there's a chance the police can catch the person who did this to James."

"Why wouldn't D-Chop want the police called?" Jazz stepped closer to Nevaeh, facing Aaberg.

He lifted one sculpted shoulder. "He doesn't want to risk the press finding out and making a big deal out of him being preyed on. He doesn't want to look weak or vulnerable."

That, Nevaeh could understand. Being, not just appearing, weak and vulnerable was even worse.

"You said 'this one.'" Jazz's sharp gaze fixed on Aaberg. "Have there been other incidents?"

He peered at Jazz, then Nevaeh. Like he was trying to read how honest they were.

"Wait till the NDAs are signed?" Nevaeh laced the question with a sardonic tone.

His mouth slanted, the curved line by his lips deepening like he wanted to smile. "I guess you've already been baptized by fire."

She tilted her chin up to see him better. Weird expression for a rapper's bodyguard to use.

"Yeah. There were a few suspicious incidents before the sabotage at PowerSource. D-Chop's favorite mic went missing, the power went out for no apparent reason during his concert at the Regent Arena two weeks ago. Someone slashed the tires on his limo. And a turntable got smashed when it was unattended at a venue."

"And none of those were reported to the police?" Jazz never was one to hide her emotions. Incredulity widened her eyes and lifted her eyebrows.

"Like I said, D-Chop wouldn't let me. My hands were tied." Branson looked down at James, then lifted his gaze again. "Truthfully, I think he's also worried about the custody battle he's engaged in right now with his soon-to-be ex-wife."

"You mean because the court might not want the kids with him if his lifestyle seems dangerous." Nevaeh tried to focus on his soft blue eyes rather than the bulk of his size as she spoke.

"Exactly. But the police will hear about this one. James should be able to press charges against whoever did this to him."

Sirens sounded in the distance.

Nevaeh glanced at Jazz. "We'd better search the property. The attacker's probably long gone, but we might find something."

Jazz nodded, and they started to turn away.

"I don't know if that's a good idea." Aaberg's deep voice made them pause.

Nevaeh cautiously angled back toward him.

He hadn't moved.

She breathed easier as she waited for him to explain himself.

"It might be dangerous."

If anyone but a giant of a man who left her on the brink of a PTSD episode had said those words, she'd have snorted with laughter. Or at least given him the smirk Jazz delivered now instead.

He lifted his large hands with a small smile that almost looked embarrassed. "Sorry. You're professionals. Go to it."

Jazz gave him a forgiving smile. "We'll let you know if we find anything." She spun away with a bounce in her step.

"Come on, Al." Nevaeh shook her head as she followed with Alvarez, lengthening her stride to catch up with her long-legged friend.

Jazz shot her a grin as soon as Nevaeh fell in step with her.

"Don't tell me you really do have a crush on the giant bodyguard." Nevaeh's stomach swirled as she waited for a response. Probably because it wouldn't work at all if her BFF had a boyfriend who terrified her.

"You mean the very muscled, strong, and attractive bodyguard?"

"Oh, man." Nevaeh rolled her eyes before scanning the chain-link fence they were headed toward. "You are falling for him."

Jazz's musical laugh usually made Nevaeh smile. But it grated over her tense nerves this time. "You're hilarious, you know that?"

"Uh-huh. I'm famous for it." Nevaeh didn't look at her annoying sidekick as she moved her gaze along the fence line ahead, some of it blocked from view by trees with leaves of vibrant orange and red. "Do you think we should split up?"

"I mean, you're jealous."

Nevaeh jerked to a stop. "What?" She stared at Jazz with an expression she hoped showed the redhead how crazy Nevaeh thought she was.

Very much the same look Alvarez was giving her right now, actually. He'd even stopped his usually constant panting to tilt his head at her.

Jazz laughed again. "You like him, and that's why you're acting so funny about me just being friendly with the guy."

Nevaeh blew out a breath and started forward again.

"And, yes, I think we should split up. There's a lot of ground to cover."

"Fine. I'll follow the fence starting there," Nevaeh pointed the fifty feet ahead to the metal fence, "and you can cut across to cover the east fence line."

"Sounds good. But Nevaeh..."

A touch on her shoulder made her stop and meet Jazz's gaze.

"He is super cute, but he only has eyes for you."

Nevaeh's pulse pounded as her throat started to close again. "I hope not. You know he freaks me out."

"I know." The humor left Jazz's green eyes as she pressed her lips together. "But I don't think there's a reason to be afraid. He seems very nice. Maybe you can give him a chance."

Just the suggestion was enough to send her heart rate soaring and make her next breath hard to find.

Jazz backed away, Flash turning to follow her. "Maybe at least speak more than five words to him next time? I've never seen you so quiet and shy in my life."

Nevaeh snorted as Jazz spun around and cut across the lawn with Flash. If only shyness were the real problem.

"Come on, Al. Let's check this fence. We're looking for entry points. Any sign of somebody going over or through." The rottweiler mix walked close to the fence while Nevaeh kept pace on his other side, her thoughts returning to what Jazz had said.

No reason to be afraid. As if PTSD cared about reasons.

But Jazz was right about one thing. She'd have to get control and stop being so skittish around Aaberg if she wanted to keep this job. She needed to keep it. Her family would want her to do this for D-Chop, to repay him for what he did for Jordy.

"We're so proud of you." Cora's smile filtered through her memory along with her words from that morning's meeting.

So maybe there was another reason Nevaeh didn't want to lose this job. Or have Phoenix take her off duty completely. Which she would if she knew how much Nevaeh was slipping, how her PTSD was slowly taking over again.

Alvarez let out a low growl and pulled against his leash.

"What've you got, Al?" Nevaeh's pulse accelerated as she sped up to let Alvarez follow whatever scent or instinct called him forward.

As she trotted behind him, she scanned the ten-foot-high fence with an angled top. It'd be a challenge to climb.

She spotted the odd-looking links of the fence just as Alvarez slowed to a stop. She stepped closer.

The perp hadn't climbed at all. He'd slashed the fence and curled the two cut sides back, creating a hole large enough for a grown man to crawl through.

Had he had the guts to cut the fence in broad daylight?

Nevaeh crouched, looking for anything the perp might've dropped.

Nothing. Except footprints in the thin grass that had given way to dirt under the pressure of someone crawling and scrambling to stand. A heavy, male someone, judging from the prints.

The footprints went in and went out.

At least that meant the attacker was gone. But when would he come back?

Branson leaned forward in the steno chair and peered at the screen as he reviewed the security footage.

Everything was exactly as James had described to Branson and the police when they'd arrived right after the paramedics.

The car, a dark blue sedan, pulled up to the gate at ten minutes after one. The driver was impossible to identify under his cap and sunglasses, especially in the shadowed interior of the car. All Branson could make out was the guy was heavyset, dark-skinned, and wore what looked like a black canvas jacket.

The two cameras, angled to capture only the drivers and vehicles trying to enter through the gate, caught James's hands from the wider angle, but not his attacker. Not even a shadow or reflection.

The driver gunned the engine, screeching his tires as he backed out and headed north. Probably after or during the attack.

Was the driver in on the attack? The decoy? Seemed likely, given the car didn't have a front license plate. Not that it mattered either way.

Branson didn't have a plate number and couldn't ID the guy or the off-screen attacker. He grunted and pushed hard against the edge of the desk, sending the chair rolling backward.

A gasp sounded behind him.

He flew out of the chair and spun to—

Rich brown eyes and a cloud of black curls grabbed his gaze.

Nevaeh.

His breath caught. Man, she was beautiful.

Even though her eyes were unusually widened again. It seemed they did that a lot when she looked at him. Though probably for a good reason this time. Judging from the position of the chair and where she and her dog stood, he might've nearly hit her.

He gave her a smile that probably wobbled as much as his suddenly nervous insides. "Sorry if I..." *Almost hit you?* That didn't sound good. He scrambled for a better alternative. "Sorry if I startled you. I was just looking at the security footage."

Her tongue slid over her full lip. "Oh." Her gaze flitted to the screens to his left. "Anything?" Her voice sounded smaller than before. Not as rich and confident.

He shook his head. "Nothing. Can't ID the guy just like James said. The attacker knew enough to stay off-camera. He apparently didn't come through the gate at all. The wide-view camera would've caught him."

"No, he didn't."

Branson quirked an eyebrow.

She shifted her hold on her dog's leash. "We don't have coms yet, so I came to tell you I found a hole cut through the fence on the west side."

"You're kidding." He reached a hand up to smooth over his hair.

She jerked back slightly, the movement so small he almost missed it. Like an instinctive reaction.

He reviewed what he'd just said. His voice had sharpened. Maybe he'd sounded angry. Which he was, but not at her.

She was a security specialist who likely faced dangerous

situations, or at least the possibility of them, for her job. Surely, she wouldn't be afraid of a little irritation in his tone. He must've imagined her response.

"The fence line is a challenge. There's a lot of it." He tried a smile. "We can't exactly run voltage through it given we're in a residential neighborhood."

Her features seemed to relax as he continued in a friendlier tone.

"But the house was secure the whole time. The security system stayed on and didn't trigger any alarms. All the house cameras show no activity at the entrances. D-Chop was safe." Was he trying to convince her of that or himself?

Her, obviously, in case she'd talk to D-Chop about what had happened. They were apparently buddies. A fact that for some reason churned his stomach.

Though if it meant D-Chop kept looking at her with the brotherly affection he'd switched to when he'd learned who she was, then Branson was grateful for their shared past. If D-Chop suddenly realized Nevaeh was all grown up and tried to capitalize on the friendship, that'd be a different scenario.

"Why would someone attack D-Chop's gate guard?" Nevaeh's lovely voice, growing stronger again, interrupted Branson's effort to figure out the best way to tell his boss a woman was off-limits. "Was he trying to get to D-Chop?"

"I'm not sure." He turned away to grab the folded piece of paper next to the control board for the cameras. He swiveled to Nevaeh and took a step toward her, extending the paper.

She moved back.

He tried to keep his eyes from narrowing. He hadn't imagined it. Was she afraid of him? He cleared his throat. "I found this in the guardhouse after you and Ms. Lamont went to search the grounds. Well, this is actually a copy I printed out from the photo I took of it with my phone. I sent the real note with the police for analysis."

She stared at the paper in his hand as if afraid it might bite her if she touched it.

Now what? Should he break the awkward silence and

read the note? It would help if he knew why, or if, she was afraid of him.

He withdrew the paper and opened it. “It’s a typed note. It says, ‘I can get to you anytime anywhere. Don't forget, you owe me.’”

Nevaeh met his gaze, something that looked like grim determination sliding into her eyes as her timidity disappeared. “The attack was personal.”

She was right. The threat to D-Chop had just become a more dangerous reality.

But he needed this job more than ever. And he wasn’t about to let a client get harmed on his watch.

Whoever had tried to breach the estate today made his first mistake—he’d made this personal for Branson, too.

EIGHT

She could do this. Nevaeh gripped the steering wheel as she drove home on the freeway and continued the effort to psych herself up for the return to D-Chop's estate in about seven hours.

She'd survived being in the same room with Branson Aaberg. Alone. The funny looks he'd given her suggested she probably hadn't hidden her nervousness very well. But at least she'd gotten through it without having a PTSD episode.

Though she might have one now on the way home. She took a deep breath and blew it out slowly. Then again. The slow breathing was supposed to help. Seeing Cannenta at home would help more.

She reached into the back seat of her pickup truck's extended cab and managed to touch Alvarez's ear.

The big dog moved away to stick his snout out the window she had open a few inches.

So much for trying to make the protection K-9 into a service dog.

A wry smile curled her lips as she retracted her arm and rested both hands on the wheel. Something about having any dog around was still a comfort, even if only for the humor.

The beats of one of D-Chop's hits sounded from Nevaeh's phone in the cupholder.

She grabbed it and checked the screen.

Sherinda. Work conflict, date, or money problems?

Nevaeh tapped the button for speakerphone. "Hey, sis."

"I'm in a jam."

Nevaeh pressed her lips together. No surprise there. Sherinda didn't call for any other reason. Though that still meant she called about every other day.

"I have to take a double shift tonight. Can you drop the kids off at school tomorrow?"

"Um..." Nevaeh did the math in her head. She'd get off at D-Chop's at six thirty in the morning. Should leave enough time to drive to Pops' and pick up the kids to get them to school by eight. "Yeah, I can make that."

"Thanks, Nev. They'll like going with their favorite aunt anyway."

Nevaeh smirked. "You sure it's for a double shift this time?"

"I said it was." The gratitude in Sherinda's voice vanished as it took on a defensive edge. "I only did...something else once."

Or more than three times. And one of those times when she'd lied about what she was doing had resulted in her sixth baby. The one-year-old boy was crazy adorable, but Nevaeh's kid sister needed to focus on getting things together this time. Pops had spent enough of his life raising kids that weren't his own. Nevaeh and her siblings were lucky their grandparents had taken them in. But Pops shouldn't need to keep doing the same thing for more generations.

"Eyes on the prize, Sher. You're almost set for the apartment, right?"

"Yes." Her tone grew more insulted. "That's why I'm taking the double shift, so I can afford it."

"Cool. And I'll help you move in like I promised." If Sher made it this time instead of spending the saved rent money on a guy or a good time.

Nevaeh tapped the brakes as she pulled up behind a slow semi.

"You can plan on it."

Nevaeh grinned. At least keeping after Sher was a way to give her the kick in the pants she needed to actually follow through.

"I'll do that." Nevaeh flicked on the blinker and checked her rearview mirror.

That black Dodge Ram sure was sticking around. It'd been two cars behind her for the past ten minutes. Of course, that wasn't all that strange on the freeway.

"I'll tell Pops to expect you in the morning." Sher's proud tone made Nevaeh smile again.

She slipped into the left lane to pass the semi. "Look at you, being all organized."

Sher blew an exasperated puff of air over the line. "You're so annoying." There it was. The little sister Nevaeh knew and loved anyway. "Love ya, too, Sher."

"Yeah, yeah. Love you, I guess." The smile in Sher's voice came across the line just before she ended the call.

Nevaeh chuckled as she pulled back into the right lane ahead of the semi. Nothing like some family time to right her world. Her siblings might be messed up, but they always grounded her.

She glanced in the mirror again.

The black pickup switched lanes to fill the space behind her in front of the semi.

Her nerves tingled as she looked forward, then checked the truck's reflection.

The license plate was caked with dirt, making only one number and one letter clear. Couldn't run a search with only that much of the plate. Dried dirt splattered most of the truck itself, like it'd been taken off-road or maybe to a construction site.

A sign for the next exit ramp grew large as she passed it. Her usual exit wasn't for six more miles, but she signaled to take this one.

How long had the pickup been behind her? She wasn't watching as closely as she did on the way to a protection job.

Then she followed Phoenix's protocol to constantly check for tails and automatically throw in extra turns and take roundabout routes to the destination.

But she didn't bother when she was headed home. And her concentration wasn't at its best given she'd been battling PTSD when she started off from the estate.

She checked the mirrors as she took the ramp, slowing for the stoplight at the bottom.

The black truck zoomed past the ramp at freeway speed.

Nevaeh let out a slow breath and relaxed her grip on the wheel. "Pretty pathetic, huh, Al?"

The rottie mix faced forward and stuck his head past her shoulder to look out the windshield.

"Now I'm imagining somebody's following me. Don't tell anyone, okay, bud?"

He swung his head past hers as he turned away, giving her a heavy dose of doggy breath from his panting mouth.

He didn't seem to care enough to tell anyone. But if she didn't get a grip on her PTSD nerves soon, Phoenix or someone else from PK-9 would notice.

Or, worse, it could keep her from doing her job. And someone could get hurt.

"Two Phoenix K-9 agents on their way to you." Louis's voice sounded in Branson's ear through coms as he finished pouring two mugs of coffee. The brew smelled tempting, but he'd resist since he would be going to bed soon.

His stomach might not like it anyway. Enough anticipation fluttered there to remind him of his one high school crush.

A laugh floated from the hallway outside the kitchen just before they entered. It was musical and joyful. Was it Nevaeh's laugh? He hadn't heard her laugh yet. He'd settle for seeing a real smile if he could get that far.

Jazz appeared in the doorway first, her wavy red hair

pulled back in a ponytail. But his gaze didn't stay on her or her dog, instead hopping to the woman who'd had him checking his watch, counting down the hours all afternoon until she'd return.

Nevaeh's hair was styled in a mass of tight coils around her head as before. Her skin was just as smooth as he'd remembered, her full lips just as distracting, and her eyes—just as cool.

"Welcome." He gave her one of his biggest smiles.

She didn't look away, but her distant expression didn't change either.

Probably his fault. He'd been so focused on the threat they posed to his job earlier today, he'd been more brusque and less friendly than his norm. But they'd helped, not hindered his work.

And D-Chop had taken the news of the gate attack in stride. He'd recognized he had been safe in the house, and Branson's security hadn't failed to protect him. His only concern had been the press getting wind of it since Branson informed the police. But Branson had assured him the police said they'd be discreet and leave D-Chop's name out of it.

Whether or not these women were a threat to his job security, he knew better than to treat them with less friendliness than he would anyone else. He was supposed to show Christ's love to everyone, no matter the circumstances.

He would do a better job of that with both ladies tonight, even if Nevaeh didn't respond in kind.

So he hung on to his smile as he grabbed the mugs and held them out to the women. "I made you coffee. In case you'd like an energy boost before your patrol."

Jazz glanced at Nevaeh, then returned Branson's smile. She stepped closer and took one of the mugs.

Nevaeh didn't move, staring at his hand the way she had when he'd held out the note that afternoon.

Jazz moved between him and Nevaeh and took the other mug.

The first mug sat on the island counter where she must've left it, and she handed the second one to Nevaeh.

Nevaeh's eyes narrowed slightly at the corners as she looked at her friend, but she accepted the mug.

Had Jazz known Nevaeh wanted coffee, or was she forcing it on her for his sake?

Being friendly was more complicated than it should be sometimes. But given the apparent subtext between the women in the look they'd shared, he'd be smart and move on.

"I see you have some added protection." Both women sported black armored vests under their open jackets and even the dogs were geared up in K-9 versions.

Jazz ran her hand down the black material. "Given the attack today, our boss thought it best to be cautious."

"Good call. Your coms are there." He nodded to the wireless earpieces he'd set on the island for them. "We use channel one."

"You said you're off during our shift?" Jazz's green eyes found his face.

"On call. I'll be sleeping but available in emergency situations." He hooked his thumbs in the pockets of his jeans. "Since this is your first night on patrol, feel free to call me on my cell with any concerns or questions. I keep it on overnight. I've written my number on the notepad there."

The notepad that sat next to the earpiece Nevaeh lifted off the counter. Her eyes lowered to the paper as she tucked the earpiece under her hair.

Heat crawled to his face. Hopefully, she wouldn't think he was trying to exchange numbers with her. Though he wouldn't mind doing that. But under different, outside-work circumstances, of course.

She took out her phone and moved her thumb over the screen. Entering his phone number, he assumed.

Why that filled his chest with a strange warmth, he didn't want to ponder at the moment. He was trying to stay professional and friendly here.

Nevaeh slid the paper to Jazz and reached for her coffee mug. She lifted it, then paused midway to her mouth. Her big eyes raised and landed on his face. "Caramel."

He hid a cringe. "Yeah. Sorry. Maybe you prefer unflavored coffee?"

She rolled her lips in and slid them against each other. Her gaze dropped to the brew in her hand. "It's fine."

"It's her favorite." Jazz gave him a smile.

Nevaeh shot her a glare, but that didn't stop the thrill that spiked through Branson as if he'd guessed the numbers of a winning lottery ticket.

Friendly and professional, boy. Friendly and professional. She was probably used to getting hit on by men all the time. Especially players like D-Chop, whom she handled like a pro —a pro who did not appreciate such treatment.

He'd never hit on a woman in his life, so that wasn't a risk. But he didn't want to appear as if he were disrespecting her or devaluing her in any way. And he didn't really know anything about her either. He wasn't the kind of guy to chase after beauty without first knowing her character and whether or not she shared his faith.

The reminders worked like a splash of cold water. He needed to get the ladies started on their shift and get to bed. Without making a fool of himself before then.

He shifted his gaze to Jazz so he could concentrate better. "I'll show you the security room and introduce you to Louis, the protection specialist on duty during your shift. But before we head there, I wanted to ask if you'd be willing to work D-Chop's benefit concert tomorrow night."

"Instead of patrol here?" Nevaeh's question drew his gaze back to her. An easy and comfortable destination.

"Yes. If D-Chop is the target of whoever attacked James today, I don't think the estate will need to be patrolled when he's away. Though you'd have to start at five p.m., so I hope to ask your boss for subs for the late overnight hours here after the concert."

"We have a couple other security specialists who could probably cover that." Jazz lowered her mug as she spoke.

"Great. D-Chop asked that you be at the concert."

"Is he getting worried?" Nevaeh's full voice surprised Branson and made his pulse skip a beat. She was talking more now. Maybe a good sign.

He smiled at her. "I don't think so. He's pretty chill about these things. But I think he likes having you around."

A laugh sprang from Jazz. The sound he'd heard earlier in the hall. What would Nevaeh's laugh be like?

"I'm not sure whether to be insulted or take that as a compliment." Jazz grinned at Nevaeh, whose lips shaped into a smirk.

"It's kind of both with D-Chop." Nevaeh let her gaze move from her friend to Branson, and her eyes kept their glint of humor. "But he's pretty harmless. He means well."

Only if the woman didn't fall for his charms. Branson knew what she meant, though.

D-Chop was a magnanimous guy. Generous to a fault with all his buddies and anybody he'd ever known, it seemed. He was always getting jobs for his homies from back in the hood, as he referred to them. Sometimes even giving them money to get them through a rough patch.

Nevaeh glanced away again, and the break in connection brought Branson back to his mental agenda. Get them set up, then go to bed and get some sleep. Considering the effect a woman he barely knew was having on him, he apparently needed the rest.

"If you'll head back up the hallway you came from, that will take us to the security room."

Nevaeh, closest to the doorway, grabbed her mug and turned. "Oh—" She stopped abruptly, her body jerking like she'd stumbled into something as coffee sloshed over the edge of the mug.

"Are you okay?" Branson stepped close to the island to see over it, looking for what she'd tripped on.

"Yeah." She shot him a quick glance, then looked down at

the dog standing in front of her. "Sorry, Al. I should've told you we were moving."

The rottweiler looked up at her as if he understood. And his wagging tail said he forgave her.

Jazz chuckled. "Poor guy was settling in for a nap. Did coffee get on him?"

"No." Nevaeh maneuvered around the big dog. "Just got all over the floor." She reached for the paper towel roll on the counter along the wall and tore off some sections.

Branson mentally kicked himself. He should've thought to hand her some right away. Cleaning up kitchen spills wasn't his specialty.

She squatted to sop up the brown liquid as he rounded the island and ripped off more paper towels.

He wouldn't be able to go around without bumping into her, so he waited behind her, ready with reinforcements.

The towels she had were already soaked through, brown and sopping as she wadded them up on the floor.

He crouched and extended the clump of fresh paper towels past her small shoulder. "Here you go."

Her head twisted toward him with a rapid jerk.

He caught a split-second glimpse of her widened eyes before she sprang up and nearly crashed into her dog again as she scrambled away from him.

Her nostrils flared as she looked at him for a second, her dark eyes filled with…terror.

"Did your leg cramp again?" Jazz went to Nevaeh and took her dog's leash. She gave a convincing wince as she glanced at Branson. "Hate it when that happens. Nothing like muscle spasms to make you have to move." She smiled. "Mind if we head to the security room while you finish cleaning this up? It'd be good to walk off the cramp. Right, Nevaeh?"

Branson's gaze went to the woman who scurried toward the doorway like she couldn't get away fast enough. She maybe gave a short nod before disappearing with her dog.

Jazz lingered, her smile seemingly real and untroubled.

Was she unaware or simply unbothered by her friend's strange reaction? Or was she that good at covering for a friend?

"Sure, no problem." Branson tried for a smile but wasn't nearly as successful as Jazz. "Follow this hallway, then cut through the foyer and take the east hall. It'll be the first door on your right. Louis will let you in, and I'll catch up with you there before you go on patrol."

Branson stood still until Jazz's Belgian Malinois, the last to leave, entered the hallway and moved out of sight.

What had just happened? The look in Nevaeh's eyes when she'd stared at him—he'd seen it before. In the eyes of good men he'd fought beside in battle. And the ones who were still fighting battles of the mind stateside.

First time he'd seen such fear caused by him, though. Assuming he was reading the situation correctly. It could make a man think something was wrong with him. Maybe Nevaeh found him so repulsive that he frightened her. Like the way his sisters felt about centipedes and spiders.

He didn't like that explanation. Not one bit, given how attracted he was to her.

And his gut didn't buy it either. Her fright was too extreme, her response too primal.

As he soaked up the remainder of coffee from the white-tiled floor, unease stirred in his belly.

Was Nevaeh in some kind of trouble? Or perhaps she had been in trouble before, and now she was battling the ghosts of memory.

He clenched his jaw as he stood and tossed the wet paper towels in the trash where they landed with a *thunk*.

Either way, he wouldn't let her fight alone.

NINE

His arms snaked around her neck and shoulders, immovable beams of steel.

He was behind her? How?

He dragged her off the chair. Laughing.

A whine broke through the flash of memory. The nightmare that bled into reality.

Nevaeh pushed her mind to focus on the feel of the leather leash in her hand. She gripped it tighter as she looked at Alvarez.

His wide pink tongue was the easiest feature to see in the dark night as they patrolled D-Chop's estate.

Supposed to be patrolling anyway. Alvarez was. But Nevaeh only managed to walk beside him, her pulse sprinting as the flashbacks assaulted her in barrages that left her wobbly.

Al whined again—a sign he was stressed. By her again.

"Sorry, bud." She stroked his head as they trudged over the lawn along the fenced perimeter of the property. "It's okay."

But it wasn't. Branson sneaking up behind her and startling her like that had left her so shaken Jazz had asked if she needed to go home.

Nevaeh thought she'd managed to say she was good to

go. Must have somehow been convincing since Jazz hadn't stopped her from going out on patrol and had left to do her own patrol pattern with Flash.

Why couldn't Aaberg have stayed on his side of the island in the kitchen? She'd been doing great until he'd suddenly appeared almost on top of her. Just like—

No. She shook her head, pushed her thoughts back onto the track that was slightly safer. Aaberg.

To be fair, he probably hadn't meant to sneak up on her. He was only handing her paper towels. A perfectly normal thing to do.

Only *she* wasn't normal. Neither was her nervous system.

And he was massive. A beast of a man ready to assert his strength on others, to strip them of control, to make them feel powerless.

His face loomed in front of her, his ebony skin darker in the dim light.

His eyes pierced her with fury, violence. But he laughed.

Swung his club-like fists.

Her foot caught, jerked her to the night, the blackness surrounding her. She took a quick step to save herself from falling as Alvarez scooted out of the way.

She peered at the ground. Just a lump of uneven ground in the lawn.

Her hot, quick breaths billowed in front of her in the chilled air.

When had she gone from thinking about Branson to…

A shiver trembled through her. She shifted the looped handle of Alvarez's leash to her wrist and zipped up her black PK-9 windbreaker over the bulky armored vest.

The quiet of the night wasn't helping her concentration. But she couldn't keep letting flashbacks assault her or she'd end up in a full-blown panic attack, scrunched into a corner somewhere.

"You could say something, Al. Talk to me, you know?" She forced her attention to her partner's heavy breathing. The sound of her footfalls in the grass, stalled in its growth by the cold snap. The feel of the uneven surface beneath her feet. The cold of her fingers.

She should've brought gloves, even if Jazz would've teased her about how she was always cold.

So cold.

Was she dead?

Numbness crept through every fiber of her body.

He swung his fist again.

Kicked his leg toward her.

She saw movement through the gap between her hands, the last-ditch try to protect her face, her head. But she couldn't feel the blows anymore.

This must be it. Death.

It was so cold.

A growl. Something bumped into her knee.

Alvarez.

Nevaeh blinked into the darkness.

The rottie mix stood tall, stiff, staring through the fence with his head and ears alert. Had he heard or smelled something?

"What is it, Al?" She stepped closer to him and peered into the shadows. They were on the street side of the fence now where a few streetlamps lit the sidewalk and empty road.

Blood rushed in her ears, but not because of the darkness. Or Al's growl.

The memories lurked over her shoulder. Just like he had. Only she could see them coming. The flashbacks, the PTSD overwhelming her. The fear paralyzing her.

Your fear is a tool. Harness it. Control it. Use it. Phoenix's instructions filtered through the panic.

Yes. Nevaeh could use her fear. It had taken months of intense training for Phoenix to get her there.

She let out a long breath and focused on what her body was telling her. It was primed for danger.

Like Alvarez, who let out another low warning as he took a step toward the fence so his snout nearly touched the links.

She let her gaze dart around as it wanted to, searching the dark shadows for danger.

She listened. A dog barked in the distance.

Was that what Alvarez was concerned about? He'd been trained not to automatically bark at other dogs, especially on patrol. But he wasn't perfect at that particular trick. His desire to talk back to other dogs and be the toughest on the block sometimes won out.

But no, her rapid pulse told her something was wrong.

Unless that was only the PTSD?

Frustration crowded her throat, wanting to escape in a grunt. Telling the difference between legit fear, the kind that warned her, and the irrational kind was the problem she never seemed to solve.

But at least her nerves kept her ready, on alert either way.

A squeak reached her ears.

Alvarez barked, his attention locked on the darkness somewhere down the sidewalk. Or in the bushes there?

She pulled her Sig from her hip holster.

"PT2, this is PT1. K-9 warning at north fence line."

"PT1, Roger." Jazz's voice answered her instantly through the earpiece. "Want backup?"

"Negative until ID."

"Roger that."

Al barked again. Twice.

Nevaeh kept her eyes on the darkness beyond the farther lamp, her muscles wound tight. Ready.

A shadow shifted. Movement.

She let Al keep barking. He might scare off the threat.

The movement came closer, a shadow inching along a row of bushes that bordered the sidewalk about sixty feet away.

A silhouette appeared. Moving slowly.

A head, body. Looked like a man from the bulk and structure, dressed in dark clothing.

Something smaller moved along the ground beside him.

Was that...a puppy?

She relaxed her grip on her gun, still held low at her side.

Alvarez yipped. So much for the protection K-9's ferocity. He always was a sucker for puppies.

The man continued walking toward them on the sidewalk. He passed under a streetlamp, the light hitting his gray hair and illuminating the puppy's small, wriggling body. Looked like a black Labrador puppy, probably seven or eight weeks old. It was almost eleven p.m. now, but no doubt the old guy had to take the pup out late to avoid accidents.

Nevaeh holstered her weapon as Alvarez barked again. A playful bark this time.

"That's enough, Al." She put a hand on the dog's head, his muscles taut under her hand.

He whined, his tail wagging as he shifted his weight between his feet, staring at the puppy.

Looked like the only challenge would be keeping Al from jumping the fence to get to the pup.

She'd better report to Jazz that they were clear. "PT2, negative on the threat."

Except the one still in her mind. The one she might never escape.

TEN

"You do good work, Branson. Clients will always respect that." Andrew Allen's firm voice came through Branson's Bluetooth earpiece.

Branson could think of a couple who didn't respect his good work. Modella Hughes came to mind, the only client who'd fired him. Although she'd been under the influence of alcohol and maybe other things at the time. But he knew what his mentor was getting at. "So you mean I shouldn't worry about it."

"You know what I always say."

A grin stretched Branson's mouth as he went to the side of the leg press machine and lowered the peg to add more weight. "Don't worry about it. Do something about it."

"Good to know you listen sometimes." Humor eased Andrew's tone. "Focus on doing good work, protecting your client, and you'll be fine."

A clang sounded, probably Andrew setting down a set of weights at his home gym. Thanks to D-Chop's desire to stay buff, Branson got to take advantage of the massive gym at the estate. And at five a.m., D-Chop was sound asleep, so Branson had the expensive equipment completely to himself.

"You're right, as usual." Branson sat on the bench and

positioned his feet on the large plate in front of him. "I just can't afford to lose this job right now, you know?"

"Because of your dad."

"Yeah." He straightened his legs, pushing against the resistance.

"How's your dad doing?"

Branson bent his legs, releasing the pressure. "I don't know for sure, really."

"Haven't you talked to him recently?"

"Sure." Branson pressed with his feet again as he thought back to how long ago he'd called his parents. Maybe three weeks. Probably too long. "I get the feeling they don't like to tell me the hard stuff. I think the treatments are going okay, though."

"You should give him a call. Find out." Andrew's last word cut off in a heavy breath, as if he was in the middle of a bench press or something.

"I will. Hopefully before I have to tell them I can't send money anymore."

"From what you've told me, I don't think your client should have reason to doubt your abilities."

Branson completed another press and sat up. "But there's been a series of these things. And now escalation with the guard getting attacked. The fence was breached on the estate."

"No one got near the house, right?"

Branson reached for the bottled water he'd set on the floor. "True."

"No actual threat to the client? He was secure all the time?"

"Yes."

"You did your job, Branson. You kept the client safe and secure. You can't foresee every threat that might come, but you can be ready to respond to keep everyone safe. You did that."

The affirmation calmed the unease in Branson's belly. "Thanks."

"I don't give compliments, pal."

Branson smiled at his mentor's familiar reminder.

"What are you doing about the fence going forward?"

"Cameras will be installed tomorrow, two on each fence line." Branson walked over to the rack of free weights. "And we have K-9 teams patrolling at night now. I'm pretty sure the perp must have cut through the fence in the dark the night before. Too likely he'd have been seen otherwise."

"Great idea about the K-9 teams. Dogs are excellent at night, even for the deterrent effect."

"Well, I can't take credit. It was actually D-Chop's idea."

"Your client thought of it?"

Branson chuckled and briefly explained D-Chop's motivation for bringing women on for security and the fire rescue that inspired the idea. He maybe lingered more than briefly on his description of Nevaeh and her heroics in saving Kicker.

"Sounds like an impressive lady. And she's on one of the K-9 teams patrolling the estate?"

Branson recognized Andrew's change in tone. He was smiling.

Heat surged up Branson's neck. He had probably said a little too much about Nevaeh. Or maybe it was the way he'd said it. He intentionally firmed his tone as he responded. "Yes. One of two women and K-9 teams. I don't plan to see them much, since I'm off when they come on. And I'll run myself ragged if I keep staying up late to see them when they start at ten thirty. I'll probably let Louis brief them, if necessary, when they get here from now on."

Though then he'd miss seeing Nevaeh, a thought that didn't sit well at all.

"Good thinking." The amusement still lingered in Andrew's voice.

Branson crouched to grab a set of fifty-pound dumbbells off the rack. "I hope they'll be a deterrent, like you said, and scare off whoever is hounding D-Chop. It won't look good to any potential investor either if I lose this position."

"Have you found anyone interested yet?" Andrew's breathing grew heavier for a few seconds.

"My friend Cooper White is talking to his investor about me."

"He's the security specialist who started his own security company in Florida?"

Branson began alternating bicep curls. "Yeah. He started with corporate like I want to do, though he has a lot of private clients now, too. He got going with this investor's backing."

"Well, I know you're eager to leave the celebrity protection racket, so I hope it works out soon."

"Me, too." Though a new concern loomed in Branson's mind. Starting out on a business venture, even with an investor, could be risky. And he wouldn't make as much income initially. Would it be enough to still cover his dad's treatments?

He might be stuck with celebrity protection longer than he'd hoped. Which meant more days of slogging along under the growing sense of pointlessness in his daily work. The growing impatience with the shallow world D-Chop and Branson's previous clients lived in. The deepening disgust with the immorality of their lifestyles and the spiritual darkness that defined their world.

But at the moment, D-Chop's life, or at least his well-being, could be at risk. And thanks to the heroism of the man on the other end of this phone call, protecting any person in danger had been the goal of Branson's life since he was twelve years old.

That was the only purpose he needed to fulfill today. Well, that and maybe figuring out how to avoid frightening a certain woman who was somewhere outside right now but much closer in his thoughts.

Nevaeh should not be there.

Nothing wrong with being on the grounds. She was hired to patrol them.

But she wasn't being paid to stare at a guy in the gym.

It wasn't her fault. She'd been minding her own business, making rounds with Alvarez. They were supposed to check out the entry points on the house.

She wasn't the one who'd designed the house with floor-to-ceiling windows as the outer wall of the gym. With the lights on inside and the pre-dawn darkness outside, she couldn't help but see in.

And see the man working out.

Branson Aaberg appeared to be alone, though his mouth moved like he was talking. She'd figured out after a minute or two that he had a Bluetooth earpiece and was on the phone with someone.

She probably would've noticed it sooner if she hadn't been so mesmerized by the display of muscles and strength more impressive than anything she'd seen before.

"Wow." Jazz's familiar voice came from Nevaeh's right.

Nevaeh looked to see her approach in the darkness with Flash.

Nevaeh really needed to train Al to warn her of friends approaching, too, so she wouldn't be caught in such compromising situations.

"Some view, huh?" Jazz stopped next to Nevaeh and faced the windows.

"I was just making sure it was only Aaberg in there. Checking for threats."

Jazz snorted a laugh. "Right. And that's why you're still here."

"I just got here."

She shoved Nevaeh's arm and grinned at her. "I saw you from way over there." She waved a hand at the darkness behind them. "You've been here for like five minutes."

"Whatever. Maybe two, tops."

"Come on, girl." Jazz draped her arm across Nevaeh's

shoulders. "Admit the guy's a hunk. I mean, look at those muscles."

Nevaeh was looking. And had been for the past however many minutes. She'd thought his T-shirt earlier in the day had shown off his muscles, but that was nothing compared to the loose-fitting tank that left his arms bare.

When she'd first spotted him, he'd been doing curls with weights on a barbell that looked heavier than her whole body, his biceps bulging. Now he was flipping huge tires as if they weighed nothing, his massive muscles rippling in his arms and in his calves beneath his shorts.

The sight should've terrified her. But there was something so magnificent about him, like Hercules come to life. She couldn't seem to look away.

Even weirder was the tingling that stirred in her belly. Not like the usual nerves of fear. But something else. Something closer to that time Gary Benson had asked her to senior prom.

A low growl woke her up.

She glanced down at Alvarez

The K-9 stared at Aaberg through the windows as he growled.

"Easy, bud. He's one of the good guys."

As she gave Aaberg one last glance through the windows, he flipped another tire, his head angling toward the windows. His features bunched together, aggression contorting his face.

A shiver tracked down her spine, and she swung away, marching back into the darkness.

One of the good guys? She may have just lied to her dog. And to herself.

ELEVEN

"Somebody smells nice." Louis swiveled away from the security room monitors with a grin as Branson stepped up beside him for a look at the screens.

"That would be me. Time to head home and hit the showers, brother." Branson hid a cringe behind the teasing. Maybe he'd overdone the cologne.

He'd probably also spent a little too long making sure his hair laid right and touching up the stubble along his jawline.

But his eyes scanned the monitors to spot the reason for all the unusual attention to his morning preparations.

Nevaeh's black jacket and curvy figure appeared on monitor C as she, the dogs, and Jazz headed for the house's rear entrance.

His heart thumped against his ribs, nearly startling him. He stifled the urge to shake his head at himself and the strange feeling. There was something about Nevaeh Williams.

"Have a good day, man." He clapped a hand on Louis's shoulder before he hotfooted it out of the security room and headed toward the back of the house.

He should not be this excited to see Nevaeh. Especially since he'd somehow frightened her. Again.

He couldn't figure it out. She wasn't a timid or fragile

person. That much was clear from her heroic effort to save Kicker from being burned to death. And from the bold way she handled D-Chop and the fact she was in the protection business.

Yet he'd seen fear in her eyes when he'd gotten too close in the kitchen last night. And before, at the scene of the fire. He'd been close behind her then, too, apparently without her being aware he'd approached.

Maybe she just had an unusually heightened sense of personal space?

He did tend to get physically close to people, thanks to his upbringing in a hugging, touchy-feely type of family. Not everyone was used to that.

He'd be careful to keep his distance this time. Which would be a challenge given how she seemed to have the opposite effect on him, her mere presence making him want to move closer.

Feminine voices reached his ears, sending a surge of warmth through his chest. Sounded like they were in the parlor just ahead.

The wall ended to his right, opening into the wide room.

Two women with dogs walked his direction across the gray and white marble floor as they laughed about something.

A smile curved Branson's mouth at the sound of Nevaeh's laugh. Rich and vivacious. Like the woman herself seemed to be.

Except when she looked at him. As she did at that moment, all trace of amusement instantly gone from her face.

"Oh, hi." Jazz gave him a smile and moved closer with Flash.

Nevaeh slowed to a stop with her dog a few feet behind and to the side, positioning Jazz between her and Branson. Was that intentional?

He tried to shrug it off. They were here for a job, not a singles mixer. It didn't matter if she liked him or not as long as she did her job and didn't interfere with his.

The squeezing sensation in his chest called him a liar. But he donned a smile. "Anything to report?"

"No. Nothing alarming." Jazz turned her head to look at Nevaeh. "You want to tell him about the puppy walker?"

Nevaeh took a couple steps closer on the other side of Jazz, enabling Branson to see her better.

Fatigue that hadn't been there earlier lingered like a shadow under her eyes and in the set of her mouth. Eight hours was a long shift for patrol, but the scheduler at Phoenix K-9 had told him that was standard for the agency. That didn't necessarily mean it couldn't take a toll.

"A man in his early sixties came by the property on the north side at five to eleven. He was walking a black Labrador puppy."

"Oh, Tim Wilson." He grinned. "Great guy. I've met him and Gilligan—that's his puppy—on my runs."

Nevaeh's already big eyes widened slightly, but she didn't give any other response.

"She determined he wasn't a threat, as well." Jazz drew her gaze away from Nevaeh to land her green eyes on Branson. Did she always do Nevaeh's talking for her?

A disappointed sigh bunched at the base of his throat, but he swallowed it down. So much for his hopes he could engage with Nevaeh and have a better interaction this time.

The coolness had returned to her eyes and her stance. Worse than that, she had an edginess about her now. And was keeping her distance, as if afraid he was dangerous.

"Well, thanks for your good work tonight. I'll—"

A strange sound, like a cross between a growl and a strangled whine, cut Branson short.

"Flash, leave it."

The Belgian Malinois strained at the end of his leash, ignoring Jazz's stern command.

Branson turned to try to see what the dog was pulling toward.

Movement by the far end of the nearest sofa caught his

gaze. A fluffy white tail lingered past the lime green upholstery.

"Princess?" Branson walked toward the suspicious bit of fur and gently lifted the escapee. He gathered up the pure white, seven-pound cat and held her against his chest as he walked back to the ladies.

And the dog that let out a yippy bark.

"Flash, leave it. Look at me." Jazz watched Flash as he finally looked her way, his stare locking on her face. "Yes." She reached into her pocket and pulled out what he assumed was a treat. The dog gulped it up too fast for Branson to actually see it.

"Sorry about that." The redhead gave him a chagrined smile. "Cats are his weakness, I'm afraid."

"No problem. Princess is used to having admirers, aren't you girl?" He scratched the cat under her tiny chin, and she rewarded him by crawling higher in his arms to rub the soft top of her head under *his* chin.

"She is beautiful. And so darling." Jazz sent Nevaeh a look he couldn't quite read, but he didn't try once his eyes landed on Nevaeh.

Her gaze shifted from Princess to his face as she closed her mouth that must've been slightly open. The coldness in her expression was gone, replaced by...curiosity? Or maybe just perplexity. Maybe she thought he was weird. Most people didn't expect a guy in his line of work to have a cat.

But at least she seemed to be letting her guard down. So he tried another smile. "Could you both do me a favor and keep it to yourself that you saw Princess out here? She's technically not supposed to leave my room. I must not have closed the door tightly when I left." In a rush to make sure he didn't miss seeing Nevaeh, but he'd keep that part of the explanation to himself. "D-Chop's not a fan of cats."

"Why is that?" Nevaeh actually asked the question. Without hesitation, her gaze not leaving his face.

"He says cats don't go with his tough-guy image."

"I can see that." Her gaze traveled to Princess and back up to him.

Then it happened. Her lips shaped into a gentle curve—a hint of a smile that was like the lovely prelude to the most beautiful of sunsets.

Something in his chest twisted almost painfully. If that was the prelude, he didn't know if he'd be able to handle Nevaeh's full smile. But he'd sure like to find out.

"I wanted to ride shotgun." Six-year-old Carrie stuck out her lower lip in a dramatic pout that only made her look cuter than usual.

Nevaeh hid a smile as her niece climbed into the back seat in the extended cab of her pickup, piling in beside two older siblings and Alvarez, who soaked up the attention from the narrow floor. "As soon as you're big enough, you can get a turn."

"Yeah, you're just a *baby*." Dawton leaned past his sister Lillibet to tease his youngest school-aged sibling.

"You know what you are compared to me, Dawton?" Nevaeh twisted her head to see in the back seat and cut him a look.

The nine-year-old's smirk faded into a charming smile as he met her gaze, then stared down at the smartphone she wished her sister hadn't bought him. The kid needed another vice about as badly as her sister needed another expense.

"All ready, Pops?"

Her grandpa took the concrete walk from the old house to her pickup parked at the curb, gripping Felice's hand in his. "Spit shined and ready for the world."

He released the eight-year-old so she could dash ahead of him to the passenger door.

Nevaeh's gaze lingered on her grandpa's movement. His walk was getting slower these days, the limp he'd had her whole life more noticeable lately.

Her heart squeezed. What would she do without him if something happened? What would her sister do? Losing Grams had been nearly unbearable. Like having the foundation of their world, of their lives, ripped out from under them.

"Don't get lost again."

She blinked. Pops had apparently made it to the truck while she was thinking, and he swung the door shut behind Felice. The girl slid onto the passenger seat looking no happier than earlier when she'd misplaced her homework.

Pops braced his hands on the windowsill, the window all the way down. His hands were marked with age spots and wrinkles now but were still strong and lean like she remembered. His dark brown eyes captured her in that all-seeing stare that had been her comfort and her nemesis throughout childhood. "You gettin' lost in that darkness, child. Focus on the blessings."

The words and the love in the voice that said them wrapped around her like a warm blanket that chased away the chill from the crisp morning air. "Thanks, Pops. I'll try."

He peered at her a little longer, both of them ignoring the kids' squabbling in the back seat.

"I'm okay." She gave him a small smile.

"That ain't my girl's *okay* smile. I know you been worse lately." His fingers flexed on the windowsill. "Know why, too."

Of course he did. He'd always had a mind like a steel trap. He'd have remembered when Walter had gone to prison and the length of the sentence. Knew when he'd get out. And knew how it would affect her. Though if she were more like Pops, it wouldn't affect her this way at all. The man was a tower of strength.

"That fear gonna own you if you let it." His words to her six years ago sounded in her memory.

He'd been right, of course. He was always right. But that hadn't stopped the fear from taking over her life for nearly two years. Until Phoenix.

"Keep fighting, honey. God will help you. You just got to ask."

"Sure, Pops."

"Don't 'sure' me, child." His thin lips shifted into a line halfway between stern and smiling. "What I say is true. God's bigger than this."

Nevaeh squashed the urge to roll her eyes and checked the clock on the dash instead. "Gotta roll."

His warm smile appeared, filled with knowing and gentleness. "We gonna talk about this later."

"Uh-huh." She flashed him a grin. "You sure you're okay with Handon and Crieg until Sher gets off?"

"Don't let this bum leg fool you, honey. I can keep up with all six of these rascals." He cast his gaze over the fidgeting, arguing kids, starting with Felice and ending with the three in the back seat. "You the one I worry about."

Nevaeh laughed. "Me, too, Pops."

"That's better." He pointed at her smile as he gave her one of his own. He pushed off the truck and backed up a few steps.

"Say goodbye to your grandpoppy, gang." Nevaeh's direction was followed with enough enthusiasm to damage her ear drums as she pulled onto the street.

Pops stood at the curb, his hand raised in a still wave until she could no longer see him in the mirror.

"Auntie Nev, do you have a boyfriend?" Felice aimed her big brown eyes at Nevaeh.

The image of Branson holding his tiny cat against his broad chest sprang instantly to her mind. For some crazy reason.

"Not right now." Though a smile found Nevaeh's lips. Branson Aaberg cuddling the miniature cat had to be one of the most adorable things she'd ever seen. And he hadn't shown even a trace of embarrassment or awareness that babying a white fluffy cat named Princess might threaten some men's sense of their masculinity. Didn't damage his a bit. It did make him seem much more—

"What would you do if Riley St. James asked you to be his girlfriend?" Felice's voice cut through the thoughts that were doing odd things to Nevaeh's pulse.

She caught the groan in her throat before it released. It was going to be a long ride.

But thanks to Felice's constant questions and the kids' fighting in the back, the time flew by, and Nevaeh soon pulled up in front of the school to let the critters loose. With two minutes to spare.

"Okay, go, go, go!" She hopped out on the driver's side and rounded the front of the pickup to help the kids out onto the wide sidewalk.

"Bye, Auntie Nev!"

"Bye, Auntie Nev!"

Dawton's and Felice's farewells overlapped as they took off.

"Be good!" Nevaeh's reply was echoed by a bark from Alvarez, who'd stayed in the cab like he was supposed to. Didn't stop him from watching the action with his ears perked.

Carrie teetered as she tried to insert her arms into the straps of her pink backpack. Nevaeh stepped closer to help, but Lillibet beat her to it. The seven-year-old struggled with the weight of her pack almost as much as Carrie, but the mothering effort was too cute for Nevaeh to interrupt. They could be Nevaeh and Sherinda all over again.

"Okay." Lillibet patted Carrie's shoulder. "Be good."

Nevaeh tried to hide her smile as Carrie scurried off with a "Bye, Auntie Nev!" and Lillibet turned toward her.

Her large, soft eyes blinked up at Nevaeh. "Boys are silly. You should've told Felice."

Ah, so Lillibet had been listening to the boyfriend discussion from the back. Not surprising. Unlike her siblings, Lillibet did a lot more listening than talking.

"They aren't bothering you, are they?" The idea of any boy trying to tease or be a so-called boyfriend to her seven-year-old niece raised Nevaeh's hackles.

Lillibet shrugged her skinny shoulders beneath the straps of her backpack. "I can handle 'em."

Nevaeh smiled. "I know you can. You're tougher than they are."

"Yep." Her gaze drifted beyond Nevaeh as if she wasn't fully paying attention.

"You better dash inside or you'll be late." Unusual for Lillibet to linger. She was the only one of her siblings responsible enough to care about things like being late for school.

"Auntie Nev?"

"Yeah?"

"Why is that man staring at us?"

Nevaeh's stomach clenched. "What man?" She spun toward the direction of Lillibet's gaze, her pulse speeding up.

A few people, hurrying moms and kids, peppered the grassy patch across the driveway and the parking lot beyond. No men.

Her heartbeat kept an uneven rhythm as she looked at Lillibet. "I don't see anyone."

She shrugged again. "He was just there."

"What'd he look like?"

"Big."

Nevaeh's throat started to close. Big…like Walter.

"Like daddy."

Nevaeh's panic stalled at Lillibet's addition. The girl had only seen her dad two times. And he was no more than an inch taller than Nevaeh. Not a big guy at all.

The school bell sounded, probably not for the first time if Nevaeh had been paying attention. "Okay, you gotta run."

Lillibet took off toward the building, raising her hand in a backward wave. "Bye, Auntie Nev!"

"Be good!" Nevaeh watched until her niece disappeared into the school, then turned to scan the driveway and lot again.

She walked around the front of the pickup and got in behind the wheel, her gaze lingering on the suddenly still and lifeless span of pavement and parked cars. Everyone was either gone or inside now.

Alvarez rumbled a low growl.

She jerked to look at him. His head was behind her seat, posture alert as he stared out the back window at the parking lot.

Where Lillibet had seen a man. Watching.

Nevaeh's fingers trembled as she started the engine and drove away from the school, trying to keep from pressing the pedal to the floor to get away faster.

Fathers dropped off kids, too. Sometimes.

Lillibet was smart and responsible, but she was only a kid. She'd probably seen a dad watching to be sure his child made it inside and thought he was staring at them instead.

Nevaeh's instincts were shot right now. They'd react to any suggestion of men. The fear clenching her muscles didn't mean anything.

But Alvarez didn't growl at nothing.

That thought kept her stomach in knots and her eyes on the rearview mirror all the way home.

TWELVE

"It's so good to hear your voice."

"You, too, Mom." It was true. His mom's voice filtering into Branson's ear from his Bluetooth was like a wave of everything warm, familiar, and grounding. "How's Dad?"

"You can ask him yourself. I've put you on speaker."

"Hello, son." Dad's voice wasn't as familiar, thanks to a weak, fatigued quality that hadn't been there before.

"Hey, Dad. How are you feeling?" Branson cringed as soon as the question slipped from his mouth. "Sorry. I know you get asked that all the time." At least that's what his dad had told him on a previous call. And then he'd asked the same question like an idiot.

"It's okay. I'm thankful people care enough to ask. The treatments are going well."

Branson stroked Princess as he set her down next to her food and water dishes in the bathroom that attached to his bedroom. He didn't miss that his dad avoided answering how he was feeling. Probably meant not well. "That's great." He crouched to scoop kibble from the bag on the floor and sprinkled it into Princess's dish.

"Thanks to you."

Branson's chest tightened as he straightened. "I wish I could do more." Like find a cure for his dad's cancer. He was praying for that. But sitting around and waiting for someone else to take action drove him crazy. Especially when he let himself think about the six-month prognosis. Six months to live unless this treatment worked. That would mean only four months left now.

"Oh, sweetie." His mom's soothing tone washed over him. "Your willingness to pay for this experimental treatment has given us so much hope. You have no idea."

He tried to swallow around the lump that ballooned in his throat. "I'm glad." The words sounded tight with emotion, even to him.

"How is your work?" His dad's question shot apprehension through his system instead, a perfect antidote to sadness but almost equally uncomfortable. Did his dad suspect there might be a problem funding the treatment?

He shook off the thought as soon as it crossed his mind. His dad always asked about work. And he asked about his dad's. One of the few things they talked about.

"It's good. We brought on some additional security personnel." *We* was a stretch, since D-Chop had insisted on it over Branson's objections. But he didn't mind nearly as much as he'd thought he would.

Nevaeh's beautiful face appeared in his mind as vividly as if she were standing in front of him. With that sweet almost-smile that had shaped her lips that morning. Heat flared in his rib cage.

"Oh. That sounds interesting." Dad's effort to find something to say pulled Branson back to the present.

"Yeah. They're K-9 units."

"Oh, they have dogs? What are they used for?" His mom did a better job of conveying genuine interest.

Not that Branson blamed his dad for the lack of it. Pastoral ministry was his life and passion. Their jobs had so little in common, it was hard to find anything they both enjoyed discussing or that would help them relate to each other.

He watched Princess eat and drink as he explained the

patrol and security function of the K-9 teams, ending with praise for their work. "Both women seem skilled, and their dogs are well-trained. I'm impressed so far."

"Women?" His mom's voice lifted with the question. "I expected men."

His gut tightened. He knew that tone. "They're from a security agency that's made up completely of women agents and K-9s, actually."

"What are their names?" The curiosity and hope in his mom's voice multiplied.

He rubbed the back of his neck with his hand as he absently followed Princess out of the bathroom. "The women at the agency?"

"No, the two you're working with."

"Oh." He hesitated. His mom's matchmaking instincts were legendary. She already boasted two successes—the relationships that had led to marriages for his younger brother and sister closest in age to him. "Jazz Lamont." He worked hard to keep his tone even as he came to the next name. "And Nevaeh Williams."

"Tell me about this Nevaeh."

He lifted a fist in the air as he silently grimaced. The pause must've given him away. "She's great." Shoot. Why had he let that come out? He hurried to cover the slip. "She's very professional. She works with a rottweiler named Alvarez." He floundered for something safe to say. "She actually got the job by..." He caught himself this time. His mom never liked to hear about the dangers of his work. She'd end up worrying more about him if she knew of the fire and that his client had been threatened. "Doing very well on security detail at a venue where my client performed."

"Oh. Well, she sounds lovely."

Branson didn't know where his mom got that idea from the little he'd said, but her ability to read between the lines when it came to her children was always a mystery to him and his siblings.

A hard cough came sharp in his ear. His heart squeezed as

if a fist clenched around it. Was a cough part of the cancer? "You okay, Dad?"

"Just a bit of a cold, I think. It's the season for it."

But wouldn't a cold be dangerous for him with his low immunity? Branson's gut twisted.

"Don't worry about me, son. You're taking care of us by paying for my treatments so I can get well."

"It's my privilege." And exactly what he wanted to be able to do—to take care of his parents and the rest of his family, if needed. With his siblings ranging from middle school age to college or buried in college debt, he was the only one in a position to help financially.

And given that his dad's cancer was a rare form, the only option was an expensive, experimental treatment that insurance wouldn't cover. Since Branson was the eldest, had been in the workforce longer, and got paid well, he'd been able to put away sizable savings. He'd started saving even more when he began to realize celebrity protection wasn't for him and aimed to start his own corporate security firm instead.

That money was dedicated for his parents' use now. And he didn't regret that for a moment. His first duty and desire was to protect his family.

But it meant he needed an investor to allow him to leave the celebrity protection business that seemed to be slowly draining his soul. Or at least his sense of purpose in life.

And most of all, it meant he could not lose this job with D-Chop. His dad's very life might depend on it. Then again, with the increasing danger surrounding the rapper, D-Chop's life might depend on Branson, too.

His massive hands gripped her neck. Squeezed.

The security alarm blared. Someone had activated it.

Why hadn't they come to rescue her?

Pounding at the door. Were they there?

Barking pierced Nevaeh's consciousness.

She opened her eyes, groaned at the daylight that poured into her room through the sheer curtain covering her bedroom window.

Just a dream. Wasn't real. At least not anymore.

The reminders she had to run through when she woke up the last few weeks had become a routine she could do practically in her sleep.

Fatigue pulled her body down into the mattress, her head against the pillow, pleading for more sleep despite the nightmares that might meet her there.

But the noise wouldn't allow it.

An alarm blared near her head. Her alarm clock. She fumbled for the off button, the blurry numbers *4:47* barely registering as other sounds penetrated her numb senses.

Alvarez was barking. But at home that could mean anything. Even a loud truck going by on the road.

A loud ding rang through the house, prompting more barks.

The doorbell?

Nevaeh moaned as she shoved her eyelids open all the way and pushed to sit up.

Cannenta blinked at her with an equally sleepy expression from her spot on the extra pillow of the double bed.

Nevaeh's feet protested as she stood, apparently a little sore from last night's patrol. She picked up a sweatshirt off the chair on her way out of the room as a knock reached her ears.

And made Alvarez sprint for the front door, barking all the way.

"Okay, Al." She pulled the sweatshirt over her satin cap as she plodded on bare feet through the kitchen and into the hallway that led to the front door.

Alvarez pranced back and forth on his feet as his bark gave way to a whine. Did he know the visitor was friendly or was he just hoping?

She looked through the peephole.

A weirdly magnified view of a familiar gray baseball cap greeted her eye.

Phoenix. What would she be doing here? She'd only been to Nevaeh's house three times. Once when she'd helped her move in, once to help with at-home training for Alvarez, and the other time was when Nevaeh hosted a PK-9 gathering.

Unannounced visits weren't Phoenix's style. Unless something had happened.

Nevaeh flipped the bolt and yanked the door open. "Is Jazz okay?"

If Phoenix was surprised by Nevaeh's greeting, she didn't show it. But she never showed anything, so that didn't mean much. "Fine, to my knowledge." She stroked Alvarez's head as the rottie mix pressed through the doorway to greet her.

He left Dagian alone, and the sandy dog stayed quietly by Phoenix's side.

"Okay." Nevaeh tried to calm her breathing. Wouldn't help her situation to let Phoenix see how rattled she was by the sudden visit. "So you're not here with bad news?"

Phoenix's dark blue eyes moved to Nevaeh's face. "No."

"Great." Nevaeh curled her toes on the cold vinyl floor. "Want to come in?"

Phoenix moved forward, and Nevaeh pulled Al out of the way to let her boss and Dag through.

"I was about to put on some coffee." Might as well act like she'd already been up. Though Phoenix would see right through that one. Especially since Nevaeh was wearing the blue cap on her head to protect her natural hair while she slept.

And anyway, Phoenix wanted her security specialists to get enough sleep between shifts. They had to be alert to be effective, she'd said. Which is why Nevaeh was sleeping at almost five p.m. "Do you want some coffee?"

"No." Phoenix angled off the hallway into the living room and turned back to face Nevaeh. "This won't take long."

Her ominous statement brought Nevaeh's heartbeat to a

screeching halt. Had she found out about the PTSD flaring up? Jazz wouldn't have outed her.

Phoenix didn't say anything. Just watched Nevaeh as if waiting for her to confess.

Survival instinct must've started Nevaeh's pulse again because it thudded in her ears as dread gripped her insides. "Please don't take me off this job." The words tumbled out as she took two steps closer to Phoenix.

"You know your PTSD can't interfere with your work or others will get hurt."

Nevaeh pressed her hands together. "I owe it to D-Chop to protect him. Like he did for my brother."

"I understand."

Despite the unemotional, almost cold lack of light in Phoenix's eyes, Nevaeh believed she did understand. She'd seen too much of the good Phoenix did for others and the way she treated the PK-9 team to believe otherwise.

"But I can't allow you to jeopardize the safety of any client or member of this agency."

"I know. I—" Nevaeh swallowed, fighting for the calm demeanor Phoenix always had. Showing fear about this wouldn't help her case. "But it's like you said back when you recruited me. Remember?"

Nevaeh did. Remembered like it was yesterday. It was the day she'd gotten Cannenta and been invited to the work and community that would give her a new life.

Phoenix had shown up unexpectedly that day, too, at Nevaeh's apartment door. The mysterious, intimidating woman had arrived with a corgi mix and a quiet, sandy-colored dog. The little corgi mix, Cannenta, was for Nevaeh. A gift, Phoenix had said. A rescue trained by a prison inmate to be a PTSD service dog.

Nevaeh had heard such a training program had started at the prison after she'd left. But she wasn't about to take one of the dogs herself. Not when it would constantly remind her of inmates and the prison—everything she needed to forget.

But Cannenta had settled on Nevaeh's lap as soon as

she'd sat on the sofa, her warm body like a blanket of warmth and comfort.

And Phoenix had spoken the words that changed Nevaeh's life. "I'll teach you how to find your courage again. And you'll learn to use your fear so it's an advantage, not a hindrance."

She'd promised a job at Phoenix K-9. A job she had said Nevaeh could do because she would have a protection dog.

Emboldened by the memory, Nevaeh met Phoenix's cool gaze. "Remember how you said Alvarez would supply any courage, strength, and ferocity I needed whenever mine was lacking?"

She'd never forget the empowerment and hope she'd felt as Phoenix had said those words. "And that's what Al is doing. He can practically do this job without me." She gave Phoenix a smile that was probably a little wobbly. "Though I hope you'll let me keep being his partner."

Phoenix stared at Nevaeh for another moment. A long, silent moment.

Nevaeh's throat dried. Should she say something more? Try another pitch?

"We'll need to do training sessions again."

Nevaeh nodded as hope sped her pulse. "Absolutely. I'd like that." The martial arts training Phoenix had given Nevaeh before she'd declared her ready for protection work had been the key to battling her PTSD and restoring her courage. At least as much as seemed possible. Especially when Nevaeh had finished the training, she'd felt so much more in control, knowing she had the skills to handle dangerous situations, even aggressive men.

At least, that's what she'd believed then.

"I don't mean your monthly reassessment. I mean intensive sessions with me, three days a week."

"Got it." Nevaeh smiled, a more genuine expression this time. "Honest, Boss, I'd love it. I think if I can show myself I'm in top form, I'll feel better, you know?"

"We start tomorrow." Phoenix abruptly moved around her

and headed back to the hallway.

Nevaeh hurried to follow with Alvarez.

Cannenta's nails clipped on the vinyl as she appeared from the direction of the bedroom, trotting to catch Phoenix before she left.

The boss turned and squatted to greet Cannenta. She murmured something to the dog that Nevaeh couldn't hear, then straightened.

She gave Nevaeh another long look. "Do you remember what else I told you? About fear?"

Nevaeh moistened her lips. Phoenix had told her a lot of stuff about fear during their training. But she could guess what Phoenix meant now. "If I don't control my fear, it will control me."

"Your fear is there for a reason. Use it as a tool, and it will serve you well. Let it run wild, and it will destroy you."

Nevaeh gulped. Was it too late? Had she already let the fear run unchecked too long in the last couple months? She opened her mouth to ask.

"You're due at Wilton High School for the concert in thirty-five minutes." Phoenix's reminder shut Nevaeh's mouth with a surge of panic—of a different kind this time. Punctuality was one of the boss's top rules for her team, especially on jobs.

"On my way."

For once relieved that Phoenix never wasted time or words, Nevaeh locked the door after the boss and rushed past her two dogs to get ready. She'd have to skip the shower she'd planned on taking, but that's what deodorant was for. Since she didn't wear makeup on protection jobs anyway, all she needed to do was change, touch up her curls, feed the dogs, and grab her and Al's gear.

And get a grip on the anxiety that lurked as a subtle churn in her belly, waiting to take control of her at the slightest sign of weakness.

Though if her fear was legit, the fear itself could be the least of her worries.

THIRTEEN

Security was going to be a challenge. It was admirable and typical for D-Chop that he wanted to support the high school he'd attended, but Wilton High wasn't set up to host a celebrity of D-Chop's fame, or one who was being threatened.

Even so, things were starting to look brighter. Branson smiled as he spotted Nevaeh's familiar abundant curls and red jacket through the glass front entrance. Jazz and a woman he didn't recognize walked alongside her with their dogs, but his eyes didn't stray from Nevaeh more than a second.

His heart beat faster as he opened the small gate to bypass the metal detectors and made his way to the double doors. He gave a little wave through the glass as he unbolted one door and swung it open.

"Welcome." He smiled as he held the door wide. "I feel better already now that you're here." He moved his gaze to include all of them, but they exchanged peculiar smiles with each other as they passed through the opening.

Nevaeh scooted through last and moved away quickly—not before he caught her raised eyebrows.

A flush crawled up his neck. Did they think he meant he felt better because Nevaeh was there? It was true, but he hadn't meant to announce it like that. He rushed to explain.

"The security here isn't great. You and your K-9s will really help." The clarification sounded weak to his own ears. Moving on. "You must be the bomb detection team." He switched his gaze to the newcomers, a brunette with a black Labrador on a leash.

The woman gave him a friendly smile and extended her hand. "Bristol Jones. Nevaeh's conscience."

Branson paused mid-handshake and sent Nevaeh a curious look.

She rolled her eyes, a good-humored smile shaping her closed lips. "Bris is also one of our resident Bible thumpers. Never leave home without it, do you?"

"Not when I know you're going to be there." Bristol grinned. "You need all the help you can get."

Nevaeh's dark eyes glimmered with amusement as she chuckled. "Meanwhile, Jazz and I have to put up with impromptu sermons and random Bible quotes at every team meeting."

"And you wouldn't have it any other way."

Nevaeh wrinkled her nose at Bristol. "All families have their weird children. But we love you anyway."

"Back at you."

Branson couldn't help but smile at the friendly banter, especially since it exposed a lighter side to Nevaeh than he'd seen before. It didn't come as a surprise. Somehow he'd sensed she had a fun sense of humor, maybe from the glimpses of her laughing and chatting with Jazz before she'd get close to him and go quiet.

But two other realizations tampered his enjoyment in seeing Nevaeh's real personality. Bristol sounded like she was probably a Christian. What a wonder that would be since he'd never encountered fellow Christians in his line of work.

The second reality made it hard to retain his smile. Nevaeh, though clearly teasing, didn't seem in favor of the Bible or Christian behavior.

That should've been the first thing he'd wondered about once he knew he was interested in her. The state of her soul should've been his primary concern. Maybe he'd gotten farther away from a Christian mindset than he'd realized. Being immersed in the highly secular celebrity culture for years had taken a toll, in more ways than one, apparently.

"And this guy," Bristol brought him out of his disturbing thoughts as she glanced down at the black Lab who wagged his tail as he watched Branson, "is my partner, Toby, explosives detection K-9."

"Glad to meet you both." He was tempted to pet her friendly dog, but the K-9 handlers he'd known didn't like that while the dog was working. "Are you the team that cleared the PowerSource Arena before D-Chop's concert?"

She nodded, her smile shifting to a wry angle. "Don't hold that against us."

He chuckled. "I doubt your dog's trained to detect tampering with equipment."

"Not yet." She laughed.

"Glad to have you on board. I'd like you to concentrate most of your attention on the stage and seating areas, of course, but go ahead and check the rest of the facility, too."

"Right." She adjusted her dog's leash in her hand. "We'll cover the whole place, starting with the performance areas. I'll let you know when we're done."

"Great. Go ahead and take the gate past the metal detectors."

She nodded, then gave Nevaeh and Jazz a salute as she and her K-9 moved toward the detectors.

"Where do you want us?" Jazz scanned the entry.

"I'll have you make rounds. Nevaeh," his gaze went where it had been wanting to go, to Nevaeh's lovely face, "you'll be posted here at the entrance with Greg Smith and Terence Robbins, the high school's security guards."

"Got it." The amused sparkle was gone from her big brown orbs, but at least he didn't see any fear this time.

A definite improvement. Now if he could avoid ruining that…

Staring at her probably wouldn't help. He forced himself

to look away, casually and naturally. He hoped. “How about we do a quick tour?” He went to the gate by the metal detectors and held it open.

As Jazz passed through with Flash, she cast Nevaeh a smile over her shoulder, as if there was a shared secret between them.

“What?” The question popped out before he thought, delivered on the wings of his curiosity about all things Nevaeh.

He expected Jazz to answer, since she seemed to be the bigger talker of the two. But she kept silent as Nevaeh paused before going through the gate.

“I went to high school here.” The words came out in the reserved, almost cautious tone Nevaeh usually used with him —a far cry from the easy, lively tones she’d used with Bristol moments before. The light in her eyes shifted, a hint of discomfort and maybe fear creeping in.

He took the hint this time, tabled the gentlemanly behavior he’d been brought up to exemplify since he was a kid, and went through the gate ahead of her himself. *Sorry, Mom.*

Disappointment settled in his belly from much more than not being able to hold the gate for her. If she couldn’t even stand to be close to him without getting nervous, a relationship would never work. Not to mention there was the fact she didn’t seem to be a Christian.

He should give up his silly notions now. So what if she was the first woman he’d ever been attracted to. That didn’t mean he was supposed to marry her. It wasn’t like him to get obsessed about a woman anyway or to have romantic feelings.

He’d think of her only professionally from now on. A security specialist he would work with temporarily. He could do that.

“Hey, Nev. Is this where you and—”

“Uh-uh.” Nevaeh rushed up to Jazz with a sharp warning sound that she smoothed into something lighter when

Branson looked their way. She gripped Jazz's arm with one hand and gave Branson a half-smile so cute it shot a jolt of warmth through his chest.

Maybe it wouldn't be so easy to think of her only as security personnel.

"I suppose you have a lot of memories here." Branson ventured a smile. "D-Chop was sharing stories yesterday. Did you attend here after he graduated?"

"Yeah."

Branson had hoped for more of a response than that, but he'd take it. "If you have any personal belongings you want to stash somewhere, we can use the principal's office, since that has some impressive locks."

Nevaeh let out a little snort-like laugh.

He shot her a look. "Is there a story behind that?"

"They might've beefed up the security thanks to one of my cousins. He didn't like it when the principal told him he couldn't graduate with his GPA." She cut Branson a sideways glance as they continued up the hallway. "It was totally his fault, but..." She shrugged.

Branson tried to keep from staring. What a different world she'd grown up in than he had. "Did they have the metal detectors when you went here?"

"Oh, yeah. Though most kids figured ways around them whenever they wanted to get something through."

They turned the corner to another wide hallway, and her mouth tilted at an amused angle. "I'm guessing you didn't have anything like that at your school?"

He chuckled. "Well, considering I grew up in a town of about nine hundred people and went to a Christian school with one hundred students, nope. No metal detectors."

"Where was that?"

Was she asking him where he grew up? His heart thumped against his ribs at the sign of interest. *Whoa, boy. Professional relationship only, remember?*

"Sunnybrook, Idaho."

She nodded, that amused smile still in place. "Makes sense."

"I noticed that here the security seems aimed more internally than externally."

"If you mean protecting against the students instead of intruders trying to get in, you get a gold star." Nevaeh glanced at Jazz, who nodded as if she already knew of the school's problems. Had Jazz attended this school, too? The two did seem to be close, though that could come from being coworkers.

Branson pointed farther up the hallway to a door on the right. "So you probably know the stage entrance is there. We'll use the room across from that for a dressing room." He pointed to the closed door on the left. "But D-Chop is going to arrive only fifteen minutes before the concert."

"Let me guess." Nevaeh smirked. "Accommodations not plush enough for him?"

Branson grinned. "You know him well."

"It's nice of him to do this benefit concert, though." Jazz inserted the comment as Branson had them stop by the dressing room door. "It's for music scholarships?"

"Yeah. D-Chop set up the program to help students interested in music like he was." Branson turned the knob and swung the door open, looking at Jazz. "I'd like you to check the dressing room every time you make your ro—"

The eyes of both women widened as they stared past him through the doorway.

He jerked his head to look.

Next to the mirror on the wall of the dressing room hung a D-Chop poster.

With a knife blade stabbed into the rapper's face.

FOURTEEN

This one was vicious.

The image of the knife cutting into the D-Chop poster wouldn't leave Nevaeh's mind as she and Alvarez stood guard at the front entrance.

Greg and Terence, the high school's security guards, directed concert attendees to pass through the two metal detectors one at a time, then patted them down on the other side as an additional precaution.

The process took time and created a line of people out the glass doors. Some people who'd cleared security clustered on the other side of the detectors to wait for their friends or family before heading to the theater.

The unusually cheap ticket price for this D-Chop benefit concert meant the low-income students who attended Wilton High could afford to see the rapper in person. No wonder the turnout was big. Hopefully, the high school-sized auditorium would have room for them all.

She'd heard D-Chop himself had insisted on making the concert affordable. His goal was to give back to the school, to help kids like him pursue a better future. That would take community effort and ownership, as well as generous donations like D-Chop's to the scholarship program.

It was the kind of thing D-Chop did. Taking care of his own, giving back. But had it gotten him in trouble this time?

Not everyone liked change or appreciated a hero coming into their lives and telling them to aim higher, even if that hero gave them the means to achieve their dreams.

The knife in D-Chop's face on the poster felt different than the previous incidents Branson had told them about. And different than the fire or the gate guard.

This was a direct attack on D-Chop. Or at least a photo of him.

It felt…angry. Like someone driven by a personal vendetta.

Or it could have been a teenager playing a prank, like Jazz had hypothesized after they'd found the knife. She'd pointed out this was a school day, so students had been there. Any one of them could've visited the dressing room, knowing about the concert that night, and decided it'd be funny to fake a threatening message.

Could've been the result of a debate between teens about who was the best rapper. She'd seen much worse result from equally lame disagreements, especially among teens posturing, one-upping, and scrambling to survive.

But even though it seemed more intense than the other threats on D-Chop, the knife message could've been from the same perp who attacked the gate guard and started the fire. If it was, he could be escalating. Moving in on D-Chop, trying to get closer and more intimidating.

Either way, Branson had been right. D-Chop should've canceled the concert. Nevaeh had heard Branson's end of the conversation when he'd called D-Chop after discovering the knife. And she'd seen the concern bunching Branson's eyebrows as he finished the call. D-Chop refused to cancel and wouldn't let Branson tell the cops about the knife. Thought it'd make him look lame, reporting a harmless prank.

D-Chop had a point. The media could spin it that way. But he'd only look bad if it was a prank, if whoever left the knife hadn't intended the menacing threat her gut said was behind it.

She'd thought about calling Phoenix to send Sofia and Raksa for more security presence. But then she'd remembered Sof was playing bodyguard for Michael tonight. Some meeting with a source for an investigative series her journalist husband was writing. Given Michael's track record of getting into trouble, even if it was always for a good cause, Sof shouldn't leave him unprotected.

Nevaeh's gaze paused on a male, probably sixteen or seventeen, standing in line to go through the detector. He wore the typical baggy clothing of a hip-hop fan and the unwritten uniform of most boys at Wilton. His sullen expression, tinted with defiance, matched the majority of guys she'd known in high school.

But it was the red color of the bandana he wore, peeking out from under his crooked baseball cap, that caught her attention.

That and the way he angled off to the side of the line every time it moved forward and stared at someone farther up.

She followed the direction of his gaze.

Another guy, taller and lankier, maybe a year older, stood in line sporting a black bandana tied like a headband.

Adrenaline rushed through her veins as she spoke into coms in a low voice. "W2, be alert. We have opposing gang members in line at front entrance, eyeing each other."

Greg stayed calm and casually glanced down the line as he sent a teen girl through the metal detector. "PT1, Roger."

She could've told him in person, but that would've involved walking over to him. Could've drawn too much attention and added pressure to the situation.

If these kids were anything like the ones she'd gone to school with, they wouldn't be deterred by someone knowing what they were up to. They'd only be encouraged by the expectation.

"PT1, this is PT2." Jazz's voice sounded in Nevaeh's earpiece. "Do you need reinforcements?"

"Negative, PT2. I've got it." This, she could handle.

"Roger, PT1."

Nevaeh glanced down at Alvarez, gauging if he was ready on short notice. He sat shifted on his hip, looking bored as he watched the people he knew he wasn't supposed to greet. But he'd come alive the instant anyone became a problem.

"Don't let him in." The shorter guy farther back stepped out of line and marched toward the front where the taller dude was next up for the metal detectors.

Here we go.

Alvarez growled as Nevaeh started forward with him.

Tall Dude lunged out of line like he'd expected the confrontation, shouting threats that were supposed to be intimidating.

The two juveniles stood chest-to-chest, spitting expletives into each other's faces. The precursor to the physical fight.

She scanned them as she moved closer.

They hadn't gone through the metal detector yet. Was there a reason Short Guy had started the fight now? He could be packing heat.

Out the corner of her eye, Nevaeh spotted Terence stepping away from the metal detectors. "W3, hold your position." She used coms to be heard over the shouting. "Could be a diversion." She doubted it was planned, but anyone could take advantage of the security guard not paying attention and slip through with a weapon.

She stepped closer to the two jokers. "Break it up, boys."

They kept shouting, aggression twisting their features as they became more heated.

"Al, all in."

Alvarez immediately planted his feet and unleashed powerful, snarling barks.

The teens sprang apart, their bodies angling toward the K-9 as their eyes bugged out.

"Al, enough. On guard."

Alvarez stopped vocalizing but held his ground, keeping the gang members in his stare.

Nevaeh swept her gaze over the two teens. "Either of you packing?"

They both glanced at her, then quickly looked away.

"I figured. Unload your weapons here. Set them on the floor slowly and back away." She jerked a nod at Short Guy. "You first."

He glared at Tall Guy, then reached under his jacket behind his waistband. Probably a gun.

Nevaeh rested her fingers on her holstered Sig as she watched his hand come around his body, gripping a Glock. "Put it down. Slowly." She kept her voice firm and steady as she watched his every move.

He placed the weapon on the floor.

"Step back."

The kid hesitated, then finally brought his defiant glare to her face.

Alvarez growled without her needing to ask him to.

Short Guy's focus shifted to the K-9, and he backed up a few steps.

"Your turn." She glanced at Tall Guy, needing to wait for him to back up before she risked approaching the gun on the floor. "I want to see all your weapons on the ground."

His demeanor was more relaxed than Short Guy's. Too relaxed.

Nevaeh's nerves twitched as he swung his right hand around to the back of his waistband like he was going to retrieve a gun.

But his left hand went to his hip at the same time.

Nevaeh lunged at him.

The knife appeared at the same moment he spun toward Short Guy.

She grabbed his left arm, brought it into her torso, and twisted his wrist as Alvarez charged.

"Al, on guard!" She shouted the command just before the

K-9 would've bit down on Tall Dude's arm or leg to defend her.

She didn't have to twist harder for the guy to drop his knife.

She glanced at Short Guy in time to see his gaze dart to his discarded gun. "Don't even think it. My K-9 would love to sink his teeth into something right now."

He looked at Alvarez, who gave him a low growl. Short Guy held up his hands and took another step back.

Nevaeh released her hold on Tall Dude and swiftly pushed away, snatching up the knife and gun from the floor while Al held the teens in place with his intense stare.

She glanced around at the people watching. Searched the small crowd that had gathered on the cleared side of the metal detector.

One woman with salt and pepper hair stared, her features pinched with dismay like she knew one of the boys.

"Is that your grandma?" Nevaeh let anger infuse the question as she looked at the teens.

Short Guy dropped his gaze to the floor.

"Are you kidding me?" She glanced at the woman before locking her gaze on the boy. "Haven't you shamed her enough yet?" Nevaeh would bet anything the grandmother didn't want to see her grandbaby in a gang let alone witness one of his brawls. She'd probably raised the boy.

"Both of you get outta here."

"Hey, I got a ticket." Tall Dude dared to challenge her. Doubly ironic since he probably hadn't even gotten his ticket honestly.

"You also got an attempted assault charge and some K-9 teeth marks if you don't beat it in the next ten seconds." Nevaeh met his stare with a glare of her own.

His gaze darted from her to Alvarez and back again. "Whatever." He spun away and stalked out one of the doors marked *Exit Only*.

"You." Nevaeh pointed at Short Guy. "Escort your grandma home and see she gets there safely." Nevaeh pivoted to find the grandma in the cluster of people. "Ma'am." She waved, and the woman headed their direction.

Nevaeh glanced at Greg as he let the woman back through. He gave Nevaeh a thumbs up.

She nodded but didn't relax until Short Guy left the building with his grandma and she reported on coms the situation was contained.

If that was the most exciting incident to happen tonight, they'd be doing all right.

This wasn't over yet.

Branson watched closely as Louis patted down each person who showed him a ticket to enter the exclusive meet and greet with D-Chop in a backstage room. Technically, it was a teacher's lounge, but it was the best option at the high school.

Branson glanced at D-Chop. The rapper stood near a short sofa and posed for no-touch selfies with fans one by one under Darren's careful watch.

They'd made it through the concert without incident, thank the Lord. Other than the scuffle at the entrance that Nevaeh had handled with impressive ease. But a meet and greet was always a moment of possible danger for celebrities.

People were allowed closer than usual, and the expectation was that they were friendly, there to fawn over their favorite idol. After all, they usually had to pay for the privilege.

In this case, some of the fans had paid an additional price, but most were chosen because they were students who attended Wilton High and were excelling musically or academically. Their parents were allowed to accompany them, so many of the twenty-five fans were adults, too.

Security should be well in hand. Louis stood outside the door, checking invitations and searching for weapons, Darren was posted by D-Chop, and Branson worked the room. But the knife incident still set Branson's instincts on edge.

Nevaeh had pointed out that it seemed malicious. She was right.

Malicious and angry. Violent.

What would a person who had left that kind of message do next?

A direct attack on D-Chop seemed like the probable next move.

Branson needed to make sure that didn't succeed.

He scanned each of the ticket holders' faces as they entered the room. An informal line formed leading to D-Chop, though the fans were free to go anywhere in the room and enjoy snacks and drinks laid out on the counter that lined one wall.

The people who had already met D-Chop and gotten their selfies wandered toward the refreshments, some chatting excitedly with each other as they threw glances at the rapper.

Another teenager with an adult woman and man Branson assumed were the girl's parents entered through the doorway.

The two females paused at the end of the line, while the man drifted farther into the room.

Curious.

Maybe the guy wasn't a D-Chop fan and had only come for his daughter's sake.

Branson kept an eye on the middle-aged man as he meandered toward the food and drinks.

He didn't look at D-Chop at all. Not once.

Branson's on-edge instincts raised warning flags in his mind. Even if the guy wasn't a rap fan, wouldn't he at least look at a famous celebrity out of curiosity? Or to see what his daughter was so excited about?

But he didn't look at his family either. If the woman and the girl were his family.

Each student had received the invitation to attend with a

notation they were encouraged to bring their parents. So there was only one invitation postcard per family unit.

The man picked up a chocolate-dipped strawberry and struck a lounging pose with his elbow propped on the countertop. He still didn't look at D-Chop, but he wasn't staring at nothing either.

He darted quick glances, without moving his head, at the door first. Checking for Louis?

Then his gaze went near D-Chop, but appeared to pause too far to the left. Watching Darren?

His eyes flicked to Branson. A fast dart.

Branson didn't look away from the man, letting him see he was noticed. Maybe that would deter him from taking whatever action he might have planned.

The guy turned fully toward the counter again, stuffing the strawberry into his mouth. He walked around a teen boy at the counter and went to stare at some other food options. But Branson didn't buy it.

The move had allowed the guy to increase the distance between himself and Branson.

His fingers twitched as he watched the man.

D-Chop was sensitive about how his biggest fans were treated. He wouldn't want Branson to scare anyone who didn't deserve it.

The man could simply be a disinterested dad who was there for free food and nothing else. Maybe seeing all the security made him uncomfortable.

But Branson's instincts were rarely wrong. And right now, they were telling him the guy wasn't there for a social call or to make his daughter happy.

Branson glanced toward Darren.

His dark eyes met Branson's.

Branson shifted his gaze to the man at the counter, then back to Darren.

The protection specialist gave a tiny nod.

Good. Darren would be ready if Branson's senses weren't lying to him and something went down.

He sauntered closer to the refreshments where the guy pretended to peruse the vegetable tray.

But the man's fingers gripped the edge of the counter. Hard.

He turned around, attempting to lean back against the counter in a relaxed pose.

His eyes gave him away. They aimed at D-Chop this time. And they were full of fury.

The man pushed off the counter and sprinted for D-Chop with a blood-curdling shriek.

FIFTEEN

Branson lunged, flinging his arms around the man's waist.

He was half Branson's size and weight, but desperation or hatred fueled him, rolling off him in waves as he twisted and strained. His arms reached toward D-Chop, fingers stretching and curling as if he wanted to choke the rapper.

"You killed him!" His scream shook the silenced room. "You murdered my boy!"

Branson held the man in place, trying not to injure him if he didn't have to.

"I'll kill you! Let me go." He turned on Branson, his fingers reaching to scratch his face, gouge his eyes.

Branson turned his head away and grabbed one wrist, then the other in a solid one-handed grip. "Sir, you have to calm down."

"Let me kill him! He killed my boy." He tried to kick at Branson with his legs.

"Sir. Enough." Branson pulled the man's arms at an awkward angle, as if to twist them around the guy's body. "I don't want to hurt you, but if you don't calm down, I may have to for the safety of everyone here. Do you understand?"

The beginning of discomfort pinched the corners of the man's eyes. The fight drained out of him, and he sagged, all but collapsing against Branson.

A sob quaked his body.

Holding the guy up, Branson half-carried him over to the sofa, bystanders parting to let him through.

He lowered the attacker to the sofa but angled him so his back faced out. Branson grabbed a zip tie from his pocket and cinched it around the man's wrists before turning him to lean his back against the sofa.

Branson straightened and took in a breath as he scanned the room, his gaze landing on D-Chop.

Darren stood in front of the rapper who now inched around his protector to see the attacker.

Darren should've gotten D-Chop out of the room entirely, but the rapper had probably refused to go. Didn't help when the principal thought he was too tough to let them do their jobs.

D-Chop walked toward them, his eyebrows drawn together in a pensive expression Branson had rarely seen on the rapper's face.

Branson stepped a few feet away from the perp to hold out a hand in front of D-Chop. "That's close enough."

"DT3, clear the room." Branson didn't bother identifying himself over coms since Louis was watching from the doorway.

"Roger." His response came through Branson's earpiece as he moved into the room and spoke to the fans. "Meet and greet is over. Clear the room, please."

Murmurs and some groans came from the people as they drifted toward Louis and the doorway. But they looked peaceful enough.

"What did you mean?" D-Chop's voice was raspy and quieter than normal as he stared at the attacker as if he'd never seen a man before.

The guy's eyes were mostly covered by his lids, his gaze fixed downward. "My boy was happy. Smart. A good student. He was going to make something of himself. Until he started listening to your trash." The man went silent. As if that were enough explanation for why he wanted to physically attack someone.

"I don't make anybody listen to my music." D-Chop's tone took on a defensive edge, though his consternated expression didn't change. "They listen 'cause they love it."

The attacker's gaze finally lifted and aimed at D-Chop with eyes so full of hate that a warning jolt shot down Branson's spine. But tears pooled there, too. "Do they love being told to ruin their lives? To take drugs until they die?"

D-Chop's eyes narrowed, but he pressed his lips together, then let them go—his tell-tale sign he was uncomfortable or nervous.

"You hooked my boy on drugs. He killed himself with the stuff, listening to your trash."

Branson braced his jaw at the depth of raw pain in the man's voice. *Dear Lord, please help this man.* Such a loss, especially that way, would be devastating. It was destroying the father just as his son had been destroyed.

Compassion wrenched Branson's heart. He opened his mouth, wanting to share words of comfort with the grieving father. The only words of comfort that could make a difference. The comfort of Christ and His redemption, His defeat of evil, the hope He offered.

"Police are here." Darren nodded toward the door where two uniformed police officers entered.

D-Chop jerked his head toward Darren. "You called the police?"

Darren stayed silent. Louis had probably called it in when the attack started. Good move. Though D-Chop wouldn't like it.

Branson looked at the rapper. "We can't let this one go." The attacker was too dangerous.

As if he could read Branson's thoughts, the grieving father glared at D-Chop through watery eyes. "You better lock me up. Or I'll still kill you."

One of the officers moved in and raised the man to standing as the other one started asking questions.

Branson took the lead on detailing the incident and charges. By the time he finished, and the officers escorted the angry dad from the room, he found D-Chop nursing a glass of wine as he sat on the same sofa his attacker had vacated.

Branson exchanged a look with Darren, who stood by the arm of the sofa. He lifted his eyebrows and flattened his lips in a uniform line that said D-Chop wasn't cooperating with whatever he had suggested. Probably that they take him home.

"Ready to get out of here?" Branson scanned D-Chop's face, noting the bags under his eyes, the thoughtful frown, the furrows between his eyebrows.

"Do you think he's right?"

Branson paused. He'd learned the hard way that clients rarely wanted an honest opinion, even when they seemed to ask for it. He could pretend he didn't know who or what D-Chop was referring to, but dishonesty and subterfuge was never a good idea. "Are you asking if I think it's your fault his son OD'd?"

D-Chop leaned forward, bracing his elbows on his knees as he held the glass between the fingers of both hands. He didn't look up at Branson. "Yeah."

Branson waited. Another technique he'd learn to navigate these tricky situations was to keep silent. More often than not, people wanted to talk and be heard more than they wanted answers.

Sure enough, D-Chop opened his mouth again before Branson had to respond. "I just wanted to make good music, you know? Just wanted to get out of here." He leaned back, casting his glance around the room that perhaps, to him, represented the school and world he'd come from. "To make it. That ain't wrong, is it?" He looked at Branson this time, his brown eyes sharpened with angst and a glint of fear. Maybe the fear that he was guilty.

Answers D-Chop needed to hear swirled through Branson's mind. That he was guilty because all people were. Everyone did wrong and needed God's forgiveness.

That D-Chop's raps celebrated violence, drug abuse, and sexual promiscuity as well as other immoral and sometimes illegal behaviors. That his music wasn't the harmless escapism he liked to pretend it was. That he was lying to himself about that and a lot of things so he didn't have to face the truth about himself and his need for a Savior.

But Branson couldn't say any of that. One word about God or sin—the most unpopular topics in the celebrity world—could get him fired. Even by an easygoing guy like D-Chop.

He was paid to protect D-Chop and occasionally build him up, make him feel better about himself when he invited conversation. If Branson dared to speak the truth about guilt and the Gospel, he'd be out on his ear. And his dad could lose his life to cancer because of it.

He pushed a safe response through his lips. "You'll have to answer that one yourself." An unfamiliar, creeping sensation of cowardice inched through Branson's torso, settling uncomfortably in his tense gut. But what other choice did he have? "Let's get you home."

Home. The word sprang the image of his dad instantly to mind. In his office behind his desk, poring over the Bible and commentaries as he prepared for his sermon every week.

He would be ashamed.

But at least he'd be alive.

Branson clung to that most important factor in a failed effort to soothe the sting of shame he apparently didn't need his dad to inflict.

She was missing something.

He stopped to talk to her. They laughed.

It was familiar. Like all the times before.

But something was different.

His face was hidden in shadow. She couldn't make it out.

He walked away with a laugh.

He was gone.

Until he grabbed her from behind.

Somehow, she saw his face.

Blue eyes, features contorted with anger, violence. It was Branson.

He swung his massive fist.

Bone-crushing pain surged—

Nevaeh jerked awake. She pushed up in bed, breathing hard. Sweat dampened her body, her cotton T-shirt clinging to her torso.

Something brushed against her chest.

She jumped.

A warm nose touched her chin. Cannenta.

Air filled Nevaeh's lungs as she sagged against the small dog in desperate relief, wrapping her arms around Cannenta's furry body.

She held Cannenta, or maybe Cannenta held her, for as long as it took for the trembling to stop.

For the flashes of the nightmare that had once been a reality to fade.

Why had Walter changed to Branson this time?

A shiver shook her body. She tightened her arms on Cannenta.

The little dog rested her head on Nevaeh's shoulder. Calm, real, peaceful. Safe.

Before Cannenta, there had been no way to stop the nightmare even when Nevaeh opened her eyes.

Phoenix said this fear was a tool. But how could something so terrible be useful?

Walter's face flashed before her eyes.

The searing pain pierced her skull, her ribs.

Cannenta shifted, her small tongue gently licking Nevaeh's face.

Nevaeh blinked the memory away. It wasn't happening now. Not again. It was over.

She sucked in a deep breath. Slower, longer. She took in air again, this time focusing on counting out seconds. *One, two, three, four…* In, out. Slowly.

Another shiver twisted through her. She kept breathing.

In, out.

Cannenta's body was warm, her short fur soft beneath Nevaeh's skin. She was here now. This was real.

So was Alvarez, his panting louder than Nevaeh's controlled breathing.

His blocky head appeared at the end of the bed, and he rested his chin on the blanket, his dark eyes aimed at her as he briefly closed his mouth.

Then he opened it again without lifting his chin off the bed or breaking eye contact as his tongue lolled onto the blanket.

A chuckle bubbled up her throat and slipped out her lips. "Are you trying to tell me something?" She leaned back from Cannenta, looking down at her sweet comforter. "I guess Al wants a walk."

Fresh air would be good for her right about now, too. Maybe Alvarez knew that. Or at least knew he wanted to get out of the room with the crazy person. For all she knew, she might've screamed or something in her dream before she woke up.

Poor guy had to live with a nut. No picnic for anyone.

Nevaeh glanced at the clock on her nightstand. *1:18*.

Jazz and Sof would be at D-Chop's estate still on patrol right now. Probably a good thing Sof had taken Nevaeh's shift since she'd been on duty at the concert. Of course, Jazz had, too.

But Jazz had volunteered to be the one to pull the all-nighter. She knew it didn't do Nevaeh any good to get short on sleep—that her PTSD would get worse. So Jazz had pretended she wanted to stay up so she had an excuse to sleep all the next day.

No surprise. Nevaeh and Jazz had been covering for each other since they were seven years old.

Nevaeh slowly pulled away from Cannenta and shifted toward the edge of the bed. She swung her feet to the floor, her bare skin greeted by plush carpeting. "You want to come, too?" She looked back at the corgi mix.

Cannenta's amber eyes gazed back at her.

"I know. You'll go if I need you, right?" Nevaeh smiled and leaned over to kiss Cannenta's head. "It'll be chilly, and you don't like that." She smoothed her hand over the dog's ears before she stood. "You stay cozy in here, and we'll be back in a few minutes."

As if she understood perfectly, which she maybe did, Cannenta returned to the spot where the blanket and pillow met, turned around two times, and nestled into the softness, her body curled so she could rest her face on her feet.

A healing laugh flowed from Nevaeh as she watched her little friend. Made going back to sleep look more tempting. But Nevaeh wouldn't be able to sleep again. Not yet.

Fresh air and escaping the confines of her room usually helped.

She soon had a leash clipped to Al's collar, not bothering with the harness for this quick trip, and grabbed her PK-9 windbreaker.

They stepped out the back door where the security light illuminated her small yard and the back of the neighbor's fence.

Crisp air slapped her face, and she sucked in an involuntary breath. She zipped up her red jacket.

Colder than she'd thought. Fall might not last long this year again at this rate. Winter always came fast in Minnesota. Way too fast. Summer could've stayed much longer.

She shivered. "If you want to do anything, you better get to it, Al. I think Cannenta had the right idea."

Alvarez seemed to take the cue, and he tugged her toward the side of the house.

She focused on breathing in the chilled air. On the sounds of the night.

A brave cricket hanging on despite the coming cold.

The sound of the breeze passing through the leaves of her bushes as she and Al walked along her house.

Al's steady panting. Wasn't cold enough for him yet.

They rounded the corner of the house to reach the front, and she scanned the neighbors' houses across the street.

All was quiet tonight. Except in her mind.

She forced her thoughts away before they conjured more memories, more waking nightmares.

She pushed her gaze to take in her surroundings, the moonlit street.

A pickup truck.

Her heart stalled at the same time as her feet.

Alvarez growled.

The truck stood parked in front of her northern neighbor's house.

A dark color. Black? Like the one she'd seen on the road? The one that could've been following her? The nearest streetlamp was too far from the pickup for her to be sure.

Alvarez rumbled again and tugged the leash as he walked in the direction of the truck.

He was right. They should check it out.

She hadn't brought her Sig. But she shouldn't need it.

Use the fear. Her nerves already on edge, she'd be ready for anything. Her senses were heightened, alert and prepared.

She could handle a lurker. She'd moved here to get away from the crime of the neighborhood she'd grown up in. But it was up to the residents to keep this neighborhood safe.

"Let's check it out, Al." She marched toward the truck, Alvarez trying to outpace her in his eagerness. He sure pulled harder without the harness. But she kept her eyes trained on the pickup.

A silhouette of a head became clear as she got closer.

Someone was in there.

Thirty feet away now.

The engine revved. He was leaving.

She broke into a run, charging the truck as Al started barking.

It peeled away from the curb, tires squealing.

She strained to catch the plate number.

No good. It was covered in mud.

SIXTEEN

What was he doing?

Branson paused in the middle of his shave, switching off the electric razor as he stared at his reflection in the mirror above the bathroom sink.

"You'll have to answer that one yourself."

What had he been thinking? That had to be the dumbest answer any Christian had ever given when someone was practically begging them to share the answers.

Answers he had. Hope he had.

Be prepared to make a defense to anyone who asks you for a reason for the hope that is in you.

He'd known exactly what he should've said. Exactly what would help D-Chop with his guilt and the dark hopelessness of his life.

But Branson had practically run the other way. His views —the truth, the Gospel—weren't welcome in the world where he worked and lived. He knew that. Others before him had tried to speak and been cancelled or fired.

He couldn't afford that. Not right now.

He turned the razor back on and finished shaving the skin above the light stubble that lined his jaw.

Setting the razor on the sink, he turned away from the mirror.

A squeak made his feet freeze. Just in time.

His gaze dropped to see Princess scoot out of the way.

"Sorry, little girl. Are you okay?" He bent to pet the cat that his hand nearly covered from head to tail. He fought the urge to scoop her up. She never liked that when she was trying to eat.

She arched her back in a gentle stretch under his hand as a purr reached his ears. Appeased, she went back to the kibble in her dish.

The smile that curved his lips as he watched her quickly dropped away.

The shame that had gripped him last night still pinched his chest. And rightfully so. What had happened to the boldness that had been enflamed into a fire within his twelve-year-old's heart the moment he saw the shooter aim the gun at his dad, the second he saw Andrew take him down?

Of course, if there'd been a physical threat, Branson would've acted instantly. He wouldn't have held back.

But this was different. Revealing his Christian faith at the wrong time to the wrong person, to any celebrity or person in this culture he worked in, would be the end.

He couldn't risk that. Not now, when his dad's life depended on his income.

Surely the Lord knew that. He'd provided Branson with this job in the first place, with the funds at just the right time when his dad needed them.

And Branson was so grateful for that. As long as he kept working hard and didn't let anything or anyone endanger his client, Branson's job would be secure, and his dad would have a future.

Branson grabbed the T-shirt he'd left on his bed and pulled it over his head.

Was the irate father from last night behind everything that had happened lately? The knife in the poster, the attack on James at the gate? And the fire?

Branson had considered the possibility at length last

night. Even talked to the police about the gate guard being attacked in case they wanted to investigate a connection.

It was possible the grieving dad was the culprit. But would he have attacked another young man to get at the rapper he blamed for his son's death?

Maybe. Grief and anger made people do things that didn't make sense.

But Branson wasn't sure. It would be great, in a way, if the father had been behind everything. Then the threat to his client would be over, now that the man had been arrested.

D-Chop likely wouldn't press charges, though. Giving handouts and forgetting wrongs—not prosecuting people—was more his style. Half his friends had criminal records, as far as Branson had been able to ascertain.

And with how guilty D-Chop had obviously felt last night, there was no way he'd stick it to the grieving dad.

Branson paused at the door as the memory of D-Chop's crestfallen, lost expression seemed to block his way.

Why hadn't he helped him? The answers Branson should've given him bombarded his mind. And he'd thought of them in that moment, too. He didn't have an excuse of being tongue-tied or going blank. He'd known what to say. He just hadn't said it.

He banged his fist against the doorframe and spun away.

"I'm sorry, Lord." His whisper filled the silence of the room. "Please forgive me."

This is what six years in this shallow world of celebrities—parties, greed, sexual obsession, drugs, immorality of all kinds—had reduced him to. He needed to get out.

It'd been exciting at first, like the stepping stone to the future success he'd wanted. He could protect people every day, like he'd dreamed of since he was a kid. He'd trained for this, worked hard, and stayed focused. He'd enlisted in the Navy SEALs at eighteen like Andrew had, gaining the experience and training he would need to be a protector for civilians back home. It had all gone according to plan.

He'd gained a positive reputation among celebrities,

except for the dismissal by Modella Hughes. But even her friends knew she was unstable. He'd landed this coveted job with D-Chop that was more than being a bodyguard. It was the final step up he'd needed—managing a security team.

Now he could finally escape this celebrity culture before it reduced him to a shallow, purposeless creature as lost as the clients he protected.

Corporate security would enable him to find fulfillment and meaning in life again. He'd be working with better people in an environment where he could choose his clients and be free to set his own rules. Including the freedom to allow himself and any employees to share their faith openly without repercussions.

But he had to hang on a little longer. See if he could land an investor now that his money had to go to his dad's treatments.

He ran a hand over his hair. But how could he make sure he didn't lose his faith in the meantime? That he didn't fall away from Christ and lose hold of the truth during this time when he had to hide his beliefs from others?

The memory he'd thought of yesterday, his dad reading his Bible, returned to the front of his mind.

Branson had fallen away from the personal Bible study that used to be a staple in his morning routine. He checked his watch.

6:00 a.m.

He still had a half hour before he needed to meet Jazz and Sofia Barrett for a debrief when they went off patrol. No Nevaeh to see today.

He shook off the disappointment that settled in his stomach at the thought. The point he should focus on was that he had time to get in the Word. To remind himself of what was real and most important.

He went to his nightstand and opened the drawer. He frowned. Hadn't he put his Bible in there?

After a few minutes of searching, he found the thick study Bible. Still in his suitcase.

He sat on the edge of his bed, and Princess jumped up to nestle beside him as he realized he'd better begin with prayer. For forgiveness and help to find his purpose again.

And for wisdom to know if what his gut was telling him was true—that the threat to D-Chop wasn't over.

The assailant grabbed Nevaeh from behind, her arm latching around Nevaeh's neck and dragging her backward.

Nevaeh quickly slid her fingers inside the arm that held her and hung her weight to stop the backward drag. She stepped her foot behind the attacker's leg, then pivoted and snapped her leg to topple her boss.

"Good." Phoenix jerked a nod as she looked up at Nevaeh from the mat. "Don't forget to brace your knee into me here." She tapped the lower right side of her stomach where Nevaeh should've had her knee planted to hold her boss down while keeping her extended arm captured.

"Right. I forgot."

"That's why we practice." Phoenix got to her feet in one swift motion. "Go again."

They drilled the same defensive technique for the fourth time during their morning training session.

Nevaeh's confidence had been returning with every technique they practiced—every defense, chokehold, or escape she executed effectively. She could do this. Maybe she had just forgotten that she could.

She'd needed the dust knocked off her skills and her brain, but now her muscle memory was firing again. Though this was only with Phoenix.

While the boss was intimidating, she wasn't a huge, strong guy—the trigger that changed everything. And given the way Nevaeh's panic and PTSD flared so easily around Branson, a nice guy who still fit the bill, she knew the results of an encounter with an aggressive man wouldn't end well. If Walter came back, she—

"Don't let your thoughts spiral." Phoenix's voice halted her pulse's sprint.

How had she known what Nevaeh was thinking? Nevaeh met the boss's gaze.

Phoenix's eyes gave nothing away, not even a glint of her special knowledge. "Control. Discipline. At all times."

"Or my fear will control me?"

"Let's take a break." She led the way to the bottled waters they'd left on the mat by the wall of the jiujitsu school Phoenix had reserved to use for an hour. The boss picked up her water and unscrewed the lid. "What were you thinking about?" She casually took a drink, as if that wasn't the strangest question she'd ever asked Nevaeh. Or anyone, probably.

Nevaeh fiddled with the lid on her water bottle as she looked at Dag, the dog quietly holding a down stay by the bench along one wall.

Phoenix never showed curiosity about others or pried into anything remotely private. And she certainly wasn't into small talk or getting to know people in the normal way. But there was no point in trying to hide anything from her. She always seemed to know.

"About Branson Aaberg." Nevaeh lifted the bottle to her lips, pausing just before taking a swig. "How I get nervous around him because he's...you know." She took a drink that nearly got stuck in her throat.

"It's natural to instinctively guard yourself against the type of person who hurt you before."

"But I don't think he's like that." Nevaeh surprised herself with her hurry to defend him. "I mean, he doesn't seem like that kind of guy. Not..." Violent, aggressive. She couldn't say the words out loud for some reason. Probably because they summoned a memory she had to mentally fight to keep at bay. *Control your thoughts, girl.*

"I agree. I checked his background. He's a former Navy SEAL who served two tours and earned a Bronze Star. He has an impeccable service record and a solid reputation as a personal protection specialist."

A smile stretched Nevaeh's lips. Why, she wasn't sure. Maybe because she had confirmation her instincts were better than they used to be. She'd thought Branson was a good guy. If only her PTSD would believe her.

"But he still matches the category and type that your survival system has determined is your greatest threat. That isn't wrong."

"It isn't?" Nevaeh's confusion probably showed on her face.

Phoenix pushed her long, blond braid over her shoulder. "Your survival instincts are there to protect you. You feel the fear to warn you that danger is possible, perhaps even likely in some cases. Your fear was right to prompt caution with Aaberg before you knew him."

"But even after I figured he was okay, I still..." Nevaeh shrugged and dropped her gaze to the green mat beneath her feet.

"Rightly so."

Nevaeh lifted her gaze to Phoenix.

"If your fear still tells you danger can be present, it's probably right. Don't ignore that. You can never be sure about anyone. Better to be prepared and aware at all times."

"Does that mean I have to stay scared all the time?"

Phoenix finished another swallow of water before responding. "No. The fear is your warning danger may be near. You acknowledge the warning, then assess, make sure you're prepared, and dismiss the fear with the knowledge that you are ready."

"So that's what you mean by using the fear?"

Phoenix bent to set her water bottle on the floor, taking her time to answer as she often did. She straightened. "Fear can enable you to consider all possibilities and motivate you to prepare for everything."

"Isn't that exhausting?"

Phoenix pinned her with a steady look from her blue eyes. "How badly do you want to survive?"

Nevaeh let silence hang between them. They both knew the answer to that question. She glanced out at the middle of the room where they'd been training. She could do the right things, be ready to survive against Phoenix in a studio or even against two brawling teenagers at a hip-hop concert.

But if it was him...or someone like him. Nausea twisted her belly, and she closed her eyes.

"You see him in your nightmares. In your flashbacks."

That was more the boss's style. Statements instead of questions. Probably more efficient for someone who knew everything.

Nevaeh nodded, opening her eyes before those images could flash in front of them again.

Phoenix stepped closer, an odd move for her, though there was still a good three feet between them. Intensity darkened her eyes as she stared at Nevaeh.

The hairs on Nevaeh's arms stood on end. She'd never seen any kind of emotion in Phoenix's gaze before. And there was something frightening about this one.

"The next time you see him, turn the tables."

Nevaeh blinked. "What?"

"When he appears in your mind, in your dreams—you're not the victim. You are the aggressor. You are the one in control. You are his worst nightmare. Make him fear *you*."

Nevaeh stared at her boss, shock and wariness freezing her in place.

Phoenix stepped away. "Let's go again."

Nevaeh watched her walk to the middle of the mat as her words sunk in. Could Nevaeh do that? Would it work?

"You're not the victim. You are the aggressor."

A shiver shot up Nevaeh's spine. How empowering that would be. If she could do it. If she could believe it.

"We have ten minutes left." Phoenix's reminder pushed Nevaeh's feet forward, and she met her boss on the mat.

But instead of launching a surprise attack without warning, Phoenix looked into Nevaeh's eyes. "Is there something you want to tell me?"

Nerves tickled her stomach with the question, as unexpected as most things were with Phoenix.

The pickup truck. Nevaeh had planned to bring it up this morning. But she'd thought better of it. Phoenix already knew her PTSD was flaring up and had barely agreed to let her stay on D-Chop's security detail. What would she do if she knew Nevaeh might be imagining dangers that weren't there and leaping to conclusions?

There were plenty of dirty pickups driving around Minnesota. And most of them were probably black. The one outside her house last night didn't have to be the same one she'd seen on the road.

And despite Phoenix's warning to take her fear seriously, Nevaeh was pretty sure that didn't include irrational, paranoid fears that would mean she couldn't be trusted and couldn't do her job.

She couldn't risk Phoenix knowing she was that far gone. And besides, with this extra training, she was already regaining confidence and skills. Soon she wouldn't be imagining pickup trucks or freaking out around muscular men. She shook her head. "No, not really."

Phoenix swung a punch at Nevaeh without giving her a moment to think. But that was the point.

And this time, Nevaeh was ready.

SEVENTEEN

Something was different about her. Branson noticed the change as soon as he opened the front door, and Nevaeh and Jazz entered the large foyer with their dogs.

To begin with, Nevaeh almost smiled at him. Well, maybe it was more the hint of a smile, of friendliness in her eyes. But he'd take it. Much better than the cool expression or fear that had been the pattern before.

"How are you doing tonight?" He tried to throw in a glance at Jazz when he asked the question, but his gaze returned to Nevaeh like a magnet.

"Great. Ready for hours of keeping this place safe." A note of humor colored her voice, then her full lips angled in a closed-lip smile. At him.

His pulse skittered. A responding grin stretched his mouth as he fought not to stare. "Glad to hear it." He forced himself to take a turn looking at Jazz. "We haven't had any more incidents since the concert last night."

"No escaping cats?" Nevaeh's unexpected question shot his gaze back to her face. One dark eyebrow quirked.

Was she teasing him? His heart thumped hard against his ribs. "Not that I know of." He made a show of glancing at the floor behind him.

Nevaeh chuckled, a hearty sound that warmed him from

the inside out. "What kind of cat is Princess? I've never seen one so small."

A personal question. Branson tried to keep his breathing even as his heart continued to pummel his ribcage. "She's a Himalayan Persian."

Nevaeh watched him for a moment, probably the longest she'd ever looked at him, at least without frightened, widened eyes. "Did you pick her name?"

A grin tugged at his mouth. She wasn't the first to ask that. "My sister did."

"Your sister?" Both eyebrows went up.

Man, her expressions were cute. "Yeah. She's twelve and very opinionated. I told her she could choose the name, and she insisted on Princess. Said my kitty was too beautiful to be called anything else. Couldn't argue with that logic, could I?"

Jazz laughed, but Nevaeh kept his attention riveted. Because her lips parted in a full, glorious smile.

A jolt shot from his chest all the way down to his toes. Whoa.

"Team Leader this is D2." Louis's voice crackled through the coms earpiece Branson wore.

"Excuse me a second. Louis is talking to me." He gave Nevaeh a smile as he activated his coms. "Team Leader, D2, go."

"The garage entry gate is open."

Louis must be in the security room watching the monitors. He'd probably let himself in the side door as he usually did.

"Roger, it's not working right. I'll take a look at it."

"Roger, Team Leader."

Branson gave the women a smile. "Sorry about that. The gate by the garage is sagging so much it's scraping the blacktop. I have to see if I can get it closed before I turn in."

"I guess we'd better get going, too." Jazz glanced at Nevaeh.

The black-haired beauty gave him another cute smirk as she turned to leave.

"Have a good night." His words trailed as he watched them leave, disappointment sagging his shoulders.

Though as he headed for the east side door out of the house, the closest to the standalone garage, the memory of Nevaeh's smile buoyed his steps.

Why was she so different tonight? Was it having seen his cat? Maybe Princess made him seem less threatening. Or maybe it was just from having been around him more at Wilton High for the concert.

They both shared concern for D-Chop's safety, as was obvious in her reaction to the knife in the poster. Her anger and concern had been written all over her expressive face. And she would've known Branson cared since he'd tried to talk D-Chop into cancelling the concert.

Branson pushed through the door and headed across the stone footpath that led to the garage.

He scanned his surroundings as he walked—a precautionary habit but also a search for the woman who was occupying his mind.

The security lights at the front of the house illuminated the curved driveway to his left. The blacktop split off from the main driveway to connect with the building he was headed for where D-Chop's car collection was housed.

Branson left the stone path and cut across the grass to reach the narrower driveway that led to the garage.

The security lamps above the four garage doors cast enough light for him to see the wide, chain-link gate they always closed overnight for added security. No one should be able to get on the grounds without being spotted by Louis on the cameras or the Phoenix K-9 teams. But if someone did manage to sneak in with a mind to steal a car, they'd have a hard time driving it through the locked gate without being heard.

Darren was supposed to close the gate before he turned in for the night, but he'd reported it was sagging too much to latch with the post on the other side of the driveway and lock in place.

Branson slowed his quick walking pace as he reached the gate. It stood in the open position, drooping so that the bottom corner rested on the blacktop. He blew out a breath. So much for this being a quick fix. And so much for getting enough sleep tonight.

Though it was more than worth cutting his sleep short every night if it meant he could see Nevaeh.

He scanned the darkness behind the garage. He didn't know where she and Jazz started their patrol patterns. They were supposed to vary them every night so no observers could predict where they'd be at any given time.

Movement caught his attention along the east fence.

Even in the moonlit night, there was no mistaking the silhouette of Nevaeh's mass of curls and curvy figure. Or the way his heart pounded harder at the sight of her.

But it wouldn't do to be caught staring. Especially when she was just starting to warm up to him.

He forced himself to focus on the gate repair. Better push it into the closed position first to see how much he needed to raise it for connection with the latch.

He grabbed the gate and swung it across the driveway, grimacing at the loud scraping sound of trembling chain links and metal along the blacktop.

Loud barks made him stop.

His gaze instantly shot to where Nevaeh had just been.

Alvarez stood in the shadows, barking.

Where—

Nevaeh's body was crumpled on the ground.

EIGHTEEN

She cowered behind the desk, covering her head with her arms and hands.

The blows didn't stop.

He'd been so friendly. So normal.

What had she missed? Why had she turned her back?

"I ain't good enough for you, huh?" Another punch to her head.

"Won't even give me your keys." A smashing kick to her ribs.

Searing pain. Trying to crawl away.

Grabbed. Pinned for more blows.

Helpless, powerless.

"You don't say no to Buzz."

Hands on her shoulders. Shaking her.

"Nevaeh?"

She tightened her arms around her head. Couldn't survive another blow.

"Nevaeh, honey, it's okay. It's me, Branson."

The voice was deep. Deeper than Walter's. Someone else?

"You're safe." Strong arms went around her.

But it didn't hurt.

She blinked, her senses and vision clearing.

Moonlit darkness, crisp air, cold grass beneath her.

And a man, cradling her.

Branson. He was on the ground beside her, holding her

against his muscled chest. His arms cocooned her in his warmth. "It's okay. You're safe."

Something in the words, maybe the aching gentleness in his voice, the sweetness of his protection, made her break.

A sob lurched from her throat, and the tears came. She dug her fingers into his sweater as she trembled against him, crying like she'd never be able to stop.

He stroked her hair, rocking her, holding her. His strength seemed to slowly transfer to her, giving her the courage she needed to get ahold of her tears.

She sniffed and swallowed. Relaxed her strangle hold on his poor sweater.

But it was harder to pull away. The scent of him, masculine and spicey, played with her senses. His warmth, his strength formed a shelter of comfort she didn't want to leave.

Alvarez whined close by. Poor boy. She'd probably freaked him out.

She managed a shaky breath and leaned back, moving away from Branson.

Her gaze found Alvarez, panting a couple feet away.

And then the embarrassment came. She'd been on patrol. A professional security specialist representing Phoenix K-9. What would Branson think of her? Of the agency?

She reached for Al as she stood, scratching behind his ears and fiddling with his harness. Anything to avoid looking at the man who now knew her darkest secret. Who'd seen her cowering and weak. All because of some noise that reminded her of a prison gate and triggered the flashbacks. The panic.

"How long have you had PTSD?" His deep voice was softer than she'd ever heard it.

She closed her eyes. Oh, yes. He knew. All of it.

Her only hope was to own it. To act professional about it now, at least, and try to erase his impression of the last however many minutes. She wiped the moisture off her cheeks before facing him.

He was standing now. A tower of strength and power, looking down at her.

Somehow, her instincts didn't tell her to fear him this time.

Maybe it was his eyes. The light from the moon seemed to make them glow with gentleness and concern. Vertical lines formed between his eyes as he watched her, his mouth in a pained line.

She cleared her throat. "Six years."

He dipped his chin in a small nod. No judgment. Just sweetness in those soft blue eyes.

He probably had questions. Probably wanted to know why she had PTSD. But she couldn't tell the story. Not now. He'd already seen her more vulnerable than any man since…

A shiver trembled through her body.

"You can take the night off. Go home and get some rest."

Her belly clenched. Was he going to fire her? She shook her head and forced herself to meet his gaze with boldness she didn't feel. "No. I'm fine."

"Are you sure?" Concern seemed to lace his tone rather than skepticism.

Relief threatened to weaken her knees, but she firmed her jaw to keep from showing anything but strength. "Totally sure. It was just a fluke. I'm great once it passes. It won't happen again." Most of the words weren't exactly true, but she kept her eyes on his to sell the story all the way. She would be able to do her job the rest of the night. She'd make sure of it.

Though she didn't really get why she'd had an attack now. She'd felt so good after the training with Phoenix. So strong and in control. Enough to be friendly with Branson.

Jazz had even teased her about flirting with him. Maybe she had, a little.

Then all it took was a noise, a harmless sound, to send her reeling.

"Okay. If you're sure." Branson's response brought her

attention back to him, to the size of him and the heat of him that she could feel across the feet that separated them.

And to the darkened blotches on the front of his pale green sweater.

A hot flush surged up her neck. She'd just had to sob all over his nice sweater. Probably his favorite. Though that blue one yesterday had brought out the color of his eyes. *Get a grip, girl.*

She moistened her lips. "Yes. I am." She lifted the leash in her hand. "We'd better get back to work."

"Right." He stepped aside as if he'd been blocking them. "Call me if you need anything."

"Uh-huh." More heat warmed her cheeks. At least he wouldn't be able to see it. "Alvarez, with me."

The K-9 took off at a fast clip, hitting the end of the leash as if desperate to run away from the scene of the meltdown.

Her muscles clenched with the urge to do the same. To run, to flee, to forget.

She forced herself to stay at no more than a fast walk. Embarrassment and guilt swelled uncomfortably in her chest. Probably should've said *thank you*.

But there was no way she'd risk looking back.

Then she did anyway. A quick glance over her shoulder.

He stood in the same spot, watching her, hands stuffed in the pockets of his jeans, creating a large, impressive silhouette.

At her look, he turned away.

So did she. But something in her said that was wrong. That she should go back and stay close to him for the rest of the night.

Sounds of joy danced in the air. D-Chop's three kids giggled and laughed uproariously as they tumbled and jumped in the piles of leaves the groundskeeper had left for them to play in during their visit.

Branson scanned the property as he watched them.

Afternoon sunlight bathed the leaves of the trees, firing their reds, oranges, and golds in an awesome display of God's beauty through His creation. The warmth of the sun seemed to do battle with the cold air, crisp enough for Branson to wear a light jacket over his sweater as he provided security for the children.

Darren usually handled the kids' security alone when they visited their dad, but given the recent incidents, Branson joined him as an extra precaution.

Darren stood closer to the children, switching between observing them and scanning the area as Branson was doing.

At least the schedule today was for D-Chop and the kids to hang out at home. With the security system at the house protecting D-Chop, Branson and Darren should have no problem ensuring the children were safe.

Tomorrow, the kids had some outings scheduled, which could pose more of a security risk. Usually, Darren and their nanny were enough. But Branson might call in Louis to accompany them this time while Branson stayed with D-Chop for his meetings at the estate.

Branson checked on the kids again before letting his gaze wander past the garage to the place where Nevaeh had collapsed. Where he'd held her in his arms.

He hadn't been able to enjoy the moment the way he would've liked, not when she was in emotional anguish. But she'd still felt so...*perfect* in his arms. So right. Like she'd been made to fit them.

But a vise had squeezed his chest at the way she'd trembled. And when the tears came, every sob had wrenched his heart like someone was twisting and crushing it.

Several of his buddies from service had PTSD, and he'd witnessed more than one of their episodes. Terrifying to watch. He couldn't imagine what it must be like to be the one experiencing it.

More giggles brought Branson's gaze back to the kids.

D-Chop's two sons, Samson and Bear, rolled in the leaves

while his daughter, Destiny, between the two in age, shrieked with laughter at their antics.

At least the kids could enjoy an interlude of happiness in the midst of their parents' hostile divorce. The press, agog about the divorce, had attempted to follow the children onto the estate when they'd first arrived this morning, but the new gate guard had kept them at bay.

Still, the grounds were large. Press members were one of the threats Branson watched for as he guarded the kids.

Was the other threat, the person behind the fire and the attack on James, neutralized now? The bitter father who'd tried to attack D-Chop two nights ago was in jail. He could've been responsible for all the strange occurrences.

He certainly could have put the knife in the poster at Wilton High. He didn't seem like the type to have set up the gate attack and knocked out James, though. He'd probably be physically capable of it, especially if fueled by the rage Branson witnessed after the concert. But his rage was so personal. If all he wanted was to make D-Chop pay for the death of his son, wouldn't he go after D-Chop more directly, as he had at the high school?

And how could he have accomplished things like the disappearance of D-Chop's mic or the smashed turntable? He couldn't have. Though maybe those incidents weren't connected to the others.

The fire probably was. Would the father of a high schooler, owner of a local laundromat, have had the knowledge and access to sabotage the pyrotechnics and prep the set pieces to burn?

Branson rubbed the back of his neck as the questions he couldn't answer swirled in his brain. Maybe he should—

Pops rent the air.

"Get down!"

NINETEEN

Branson charged for the kids, rapidly assessing as he whipped out his Glock.

The pops came from the garage.

Darren grabbed Destiny and laid her flat as Branson reached them.

He swung the two boys in his arm, bringing them to the ground as gently as he could, lying them in the leaves. "Stay down."

More pops. Not gunshots. More like...fireworks?

Something smashed. Shards of glass flew as the window burst at the side of the garage.

Sparks spewed from the opening.

Branson caught Darren's gaze, signaled with his hand he was going to check it out.

Darren jerked a nod and stepped between the kids, crouched as he took Branson's forward position.

Branson stayed low as he moved out. He darted at an angle away from the garage first, then headed back, zigzagging in case the culprit was in there with bullets to add to this party.

He used tree trunks as cover when he could.

Still no activity. No signs of movement.

But bushes lined the garage. And there were a few objects around the house someone could hide behind.

He'd kept a close watch, so it wasn't likely anyone had gotten into position without his knowing.

But he didn't know how someone could've started fireworks in the garage either.

The pops stopped for the last several seconds it took him to reach the structure.

He inched along the bushes at the side of the building. His height meant he could see through the opening that had been the window.

A sound like a rain shower caught his ears just before he saw the reason for it.

The sprinkler system was dousing the entire garage, giving the lineup of cars a wash.

If there was someone in there, they were probably huddled somewhere trying not to get wet.

He turned back and headed for the door at the front of the garage. Typing in the code on the keypad, he waited for the lock to release, then reached for the knob.

He turned it. Took in a breath.

Pushing the door open with one hand, he raised his weapon and scanned the left side of the garage.

Empty.

He inched just inside, then darted to the left and swung his weapon in a sweep to the right.

The sprinkler water soaked him like a heavy rain as his gaze searched the cars, the tidy gardening tools and weedkiller the groundskeeper used.

Someone could be hiding in one of the vehicles.

He made a pass by each of them, looking through the windows to make sure they were unoccupied.

As he rounded D-Chop's Porsche, something dark on the garage floor caught his eye.

Three small stands held the casings of what he assumed were fireworks. Wires ran from them to what looked to be a receiver of some kind. Perfect setup for remote-controlled fireworks.

He gritted his teeth. He'd have to check it over more thoroughly after he made sure the kids were safe.

"DT1, we're clear." He spoke into coms as he made his way out of the garage. "Wait to move the packages until I get there." He didn't want to make the mistake of not taking enough precautions. Especially not with the children. There was always a slim possibility someone could still be lurking somewhere on the grounds.

"Good job, guys." Branson forced cheerfulness into his voice as he neared the kids, their little heads poking up above the leaves. "Think you can beat Darren and me to the house?"

Grins lit their faces, and the game was on. A game for the boys, anyway.

With Darren carrying Destiny in his arms, they ran to the house. Branson and Darren kept pace beside the boys, staying between them and the garage until they were safely inside.

Marsha hurried toward them across the vast foyer. "I heard loud noises."

"Just fireworks." Branson kept his voice light as he gave her a look he hoped communicated the need to stay calm for the kids.

She didn't miss a beat, pressing on a smile as she turned to the children. "Your snacks are prepared in the kitchen. You go on ahead, and I'll be right there."

Branson gave Darren a nod, signaling he should follow the children as they dashed to the kitchen where they'd no doubt annoy the chef who was prepping dinner.

"What's this about fireworks?"

Branson gave Marsha a brief explanation of the little he knew.

"Should we call the police?" She whispered the question though the kids had already disappeared.

"I don't think D-Chop would like that. And if it's only

fireworks, that's not exactly a serious criminal offense. I'll need to check it out first. Would you find Peter and tell him I want to talk to him?"

"Of course." Concern filled Marsha's blue eyes.

He hadn't missed that she'd been getting attached to D-Chop's children. Branson touched her arm. "It'll be okay. The kids are safe. And they'll stay that way."

She managed a small smile with her nod. "I'd better go before the children make Chef Cox threaten to quit again."

He returned her smile, but it faded as soon as she walked away.

He spun and headed out to the garage with the grim premonition he wasn't going to like what he'd find.

Fifteen minutes later, his jaw was more clenched than before as he returned to the house. The gate guard hadn't seen anything unusual all day, aside from the initial press visitors that morning. But someone had managed to set up remote-activated fireworks to explode in the garage, damaging two of D-Chop's expensive cars.

The damage was superficial, mostly scarring the paint. But that was vandalism, which probably made it a misdemeanor. Could even be a felony depending on state laws in Minnesota and the extent of damage. That meant it was something they should report to the police.

And he still needed to report the whole incident to D-Chop, unless Darren had already. Either way, Branson needed to see his client and discuss the incident.

Darren had reported via coms that the kids were fine, now playing in the game room.

As Branson went to the hallway that housed D-Chop's suite, he silently gave thanks that the children were unharmed, physically and emotionally.

Then he inhaled a deep breath and knocked on the door of D-Chop's bedroom suite.

"You know what to do." D-Chop's answer came through the door in a lazy tone. Good. He didn't sound more intense or serious than usual.

Branson opened the door and went in, scanning the lounge area.

D-Chop sat on one of the two white sofas in the center of the room, leaning back against the cushions. He wore a thick bathrobe and watched Branson with a darker expression than he'd hoped to see on his client's face.

The rest of the room appeared unoccupied, other than discarded wine glasses, beer bottles, and women's clothing strewn on one of the sofas—leftovers from D-Chop's visitor last night.

"Darren filled you in?" Branson headed directly for D-Chop and stopped at the end of the coffee table in front of him.

The rapper leaned forward, his movement slow and painstaking as if the effort cost him something. "My kids are here, B. Nobody threatens my kids." D-Chop lifted his gaze to Branson, intensity shining from deep within his dark eyes.

Branson didn't look away. "I know." He thought a moment, then added, "We kept them safe. We'll always keep them safe."

D-Chop entwined his fingers together, folding his hands in a prayer-like position between his knees as he moved his gaze to stare as if unseeing at the wall. "Yeah. But if they tell their old lady, I'll lose the chance for custody. I'll never see 'em again." His eyes angled up toward Branson. "I can't let that happen. You feel me?"

Also D-Chop's way of saying he didn't want the incident reported. Since the rapper was the only victim, Branson would have to abide by that. "I understand."

D-Chop shifted his jaw and leaned back into the plush sofa cushions. "You sure you got this under control, B?" The question was delivered in his usual laidback tone.

But it stiffened Branson's muscles anyway.

"We can hire more security if you want help." Meaning D-Chop thought he needed help?

Branson's chest clenched. He could not lose this job. He drew in a slow, calming breath through his nose before he responded. "I've got it, D-Chop." He kept his tone even but firm. He had to convey the confidence his client needed to see right now.

"Okay, man." D-Chop pushed off the sofa and stood. "Get Nevaeh and her dog to watch the kids tomorrow. They going to that Fun Land place."

D-Chop didn't trust Branson to protect them. Not fully. The realization settled like a hard rock somewhere behind his abs. "She's scheduled for overnight patrol. She wouldn't be able to do both."

"Then get that other girl to cover for her at night, the Latina chick Darren told me about." D-Chop shoved his hands into the thick pockets of his robe, a deceptively relaxed gesture. "Just get her here." His gaze angled up to Branson's greater height. "I want my kids protected."

Branson nodded. "They will be."

D-Chop didn't break his stare.

"I'll get Nevaeh and her K-9 for tomorrow."

"A'ight." D-Chop dipped his head in a nod, then turned and headed for the door that led to his bedroom.

Branson watched him go with a clenched jaw. If these incidents didn't stop, he was going to lose his job. And his dad would lose the chance at treatment. At life.

If D-Chop wouldn't let the police investigate, whoever was doing these things would keep going unchecked. And probably escalate for whatever purpose the culprit had in mind.

That was not going to happen on Branson's watch. He'd have to do some investigating himself and determine who was behind the attacks. Soon.

Because each attack hit closer to home. And the next one could be deadly.

"Time to get this party started!" Nevaeh grinned at her PK-9 family as she marched into Cora's house with a bowl of cheese puffs in her hands.

"Nevaeh's here!" Cora's beaming smile stood out among the crew as they all greeted her with warm laughs and *hellos* from the open living room.

Looked like everyone was there, including most of the dogs, some lounging near their humans on the sofas and chairs, and others wandering around sniffing each other.

Alvarez and Cannenta, off leash, were already enjoying a friendly greeting from Toby and Raksa.

"Here, let me take that for you." Cora smiled at the orange contents of the bowl. "I knew I could count on you to bring cheese puffs."

Nevaeh winked. "You know it." Her hands freed, she grabbed the wrapped package from under her arm. "And a shower gift."

"Shh." Cora's sparkling blue eyes belied the warning. "We're not calling it a shower, remember? Sofia and Phoenix will leave."

Nevaeh laughed. "I forgot." The idea of Phoenix or Sof telling someone they went to a bridal shower was enough to make Nevaeh snicker. They were no doubt both armed and would be watching all the entry points during the whole party.

"Bris and Jazz did an awesome job with the decorations for your *party*." Nevaeh scanned the light blue streamers that decorated the ceiling of the living room, the balloons in the corners, and the *Here Comes the Bride* banner that hung at the far end of the room.

"Didn't they? I'm so grateful."

"Good thing Jazz volunteered to help Bris instead of me. Or you know it would've all ended up in red."

Cora's gentle laugh trickled from her lips. "That wouldn't be the worst thing. But this does match my wedding colors better."

"Uh-huh. And you."

Cora acknowledged the statement with another smile, her pale blue sweater intensifying the color of her eyes. "They know me well."

"Did I hear a compliment of our decorating job?" Jazz's voice drew Nevaeh's gaze to the redhead who approached with a grin. And Flash, who nuzzled his head into Nevaeh's hand when she reached to pet him.

"You never did miss a compliment." Nevaeh chuckled.

"A girl's gotta boost her self-esteem somehow."

"You boosted enough, girl." Nevaeh gave Jazz's tall figure an exaggerated scan from toe to head. "You're always towering over us little people as it is."

"Can I help it if you're vertically challenged?" Jazz flipped a wave of hair off her shoulder in a perfect imitation of the head cheerleader they'd both had to put up with as students at Wilton High.

"I'll give you a vertical challenge." Nevaeh reached for Jazz, who dashed playfully out of the way.

Nevaeh grabbed again, and Jazz wrapped her in a loose hug as they laughed.

"You two." Cora shook her head, holding the bowl away from them with an amused smile.

"I know. We never grew up."

"You mean *you* never grew up." Jazz shoved her away with a teasing grin.

"Hey," Bris waved at them from the floral-patterned love seat, "when you two are done messing around, we have serious matters to discuss over here."

Cora chuckled. "Make yourselves comfortable. I was just about to get plates for the snacks."

"You shouldn't do the work at your own party." Jazz's tone was friendly as her eyebrows dipped. "Remember, Bris told you that? I'll get the plates, and you sit down and enjoy."

"Well, all right." Cora smiled at Jazz. "Thank you."

Nevaeh and Cora stepped into the living room where Cora set the bowl of cheese puffs on the coffee table crowded with other snacks. She then crossed through the encircled sofa, love seat, and armchairs to reach a floral-upholstered chair that sat directly beneath the banner, clearly intended for the woman of the hour.

Nevaeh's path to the light blue sofa where Sof sat on the close end was blocked by several dogs. First Jana, then Toby and Gaston stalled her progress as they crowded in for petting.

"Somebody's popular today." Sof smiled at the happy crowd.

"Hey, I'm this popular all the time." Nevaeh sent her a grin as she gave each dog a turn of ear rubs and chin scratches.

"Yeah, that's what we heard." Sof's teasing tone set off warning bells in Nevaeh's mind as she joined her on the sofa.

She narrowed her eyes at Sof's grin.

"Seems a certain hot bodyguard wants to see you so badly that he switched you to days."

Heat seeped into Nevaeh's cheeks, but she covered with a snort. "More like he needed a babysitter for one day."

The women laughed—all except Phoenix, who sat in a blue armchair and kept an eye on their shenanigans with Dag lying next to her.

"I don't buy that." Sof's dark gaze swung to include everyone. "You should've seen how disappointed he looked when I showed up at the estate instead of Nevaeh the night of the concert. That's when I knew it isn't Jazz he's into."

"I think I was the one he was sad to see." Jazz bounced into the room with a stack of plates she set on the table. "He probably hoped I'd take the night off instead of Nev."

Great. What happened to Jazz covering for Nevaeh by pretending to like Branson?

"Now that she's flirting with him, the poor man's a goner for sure." Jazz plopped onto the middle cushion between Sof and Nevaeh. She angled an annoying grin at Nevaeh. Knew exactly what she was doing, egging them on.

"I did not flirt with him." Not exactly. Had she? "I only asked him about his cat."

"He has a cat?" Cora's eyes were the only ones that looked innocent in this bunch of jokers.

"Yeah."

"A tiny little...what kind did he say it was?" Jazz nearly burst with her eagerness to share, and Nevaeh knew why.

"A Himalayan Persian."

"That's right." Jazz nodded. "Her name is Princess."

"Aww," Bris's voice carried over Sof's snorting laugh, "that's adorable."

"Well, from what I've seen," Sof talked through her grin, "he's one of the rare guys who doesn't need to worry about having a kitty named Princess. Right, Nevaeh?" She winked.

Something welled up in Nevaeh at Sof's observation. Almost felt like pride. But she didn't have any business taking pride in Branson and his indestructible masculinity. She reached for a plate and stood to fill it with cheese puffs.

"I think it's very sweet." Cora smiled at Nevaeh. "It shows he has a gentle side."

The image of Branson snuggling with little Princess flared in Nevaeh's mind. She dropped back onto the sofa and popped a cheese puff into her mouth before she said something that would give away her fluttering pulse.

"Exactly." Jazz put her hand on Nevaeh's shoulder. "He's perfect for our girl."

Nevaeh rolled her eyes, landing them on Bris. "Didn't you say you had something serious to talk to us about?" She crunched another cheese puff.

"Oh. Yes." Bris lowered her eyebrows and straightened her mouth. Only for about a second. "Your date for the wedding." A grin broke her serious expression. "We all think you should bring Branson."

Surprise tangled with the cheese puff in Nevaeh's throat. She coughed, raising a fist to her mouth.

"You okay?" Jazz patted her back, totally failing to hide her laughter.

Nevaeh managed to swallow. "You all should wear a

warning label: 'Lame jokes. Choking hazard.'" A residual small cough escaped her throat.

"Here you go." A glass of water appeared in front of her in Cora's extended hand.

"Thanks." She met the blonde's sympathetic gaze.

"Hey, we've been waiting a long time for payback." Sof's gleeful grin didn't hold a hint of apology.

And it shouldn't. Nevaeh had been the instigator of teasing Bris, Cora, and Sof when they'd met the men who were now their husbands. Or about to be, in Cora's case. Nevaeh sniffed dramatically. "Well, at least I knew what I was talking about. I knew you'd found your soulmates."

"Oh, yes." Sof laughed as she stood to grab some snacks. "That was all because of you."

"That's why we want to return the favor." Bristol's tease drew Nevaeh's gaze. "Branson could be your soulmate, and we wouldn't want you to miss out."

"Besides, he'd look awfully good in a tux at the wedding." Jazz nudged Nevaeh's arm.

As if Nevaeh could even consider inviting Branson to the wedding, sitting close to him at the reception. But Jazz's words conjured a tempting image in her mind. Branson in a tuxedo, watching her stand in front as a bridesmaid. His smile soft and warm.

Yeah, *awfully good* was an understatement.

"I think we've lost her to daydreams of a bodyguard." Sof's mirth-filled tone cut through the too-pleasant picture.

Bris laughed. "Boy, you've got it worse than I thought."

"All right, you've had your fun." Nevaeh grinned at her PK-9 family. "Not as much fun as I had at your expense, of course, but it's a decent try." She glanced at their silent boss, her eyes steady and observant beneath the bill of her charcoal baseball cap. "If we don't knock off the boy talk, Phoenix is gonna wish she hadn't come."

It was probably cowardly to use Phoenix as a diversion, but she figured the boss wouldn't care. And Nevaeh was getting desperate. Mostly to stop the images from coming to mind that the girls were putting there. Images that made her think way too much about the strong, handsome man who'd held her in his arms last night. So gently, as if she were someone to be cherished instead of crushed.

And then, after he'd seen her at her weakest, he'd let her go to stand on her own two feet. Given her a chance to show she could be strong.

He hadn't taken advantage of her. Hadn't hurt her when he could have. He'd kept her safe.

And the truth was, she didn't know what to do about a man like that. It was scary in a different way. Especially because, according to her skipping pulse and emotional reaction to every mention of him today, her heart was already getting ideas about Branson Aaberg. And those could set her up for a whole different kind of hurt.

TWENTY

"There. That's it." Branson pushed off the hand he'd braced himself with as he leaned over the monitor in the security room.

Louis pressed in closer from the chair as he paused the recording on the shot of Jill Jacquet, D-Chop's wife, driving her white Ferrari out of the garage. He blew out a breath and ran his fingers through his short brown hair, leaving a tuft of it sticking up at the back of his head. "So Jill, Peter, Brian. They all had access and opportunity."

Branson folded his arms over his chest. "Yeah. Peter didn't tell me Jill took her car when she was here until I asked him if anyone had been in the garage today. Apparently, she made a big thing about it with D-Chop when she dropped off the kids, and he let her have it since he'd bought it for her as a wedding present. He said he thought it'd give her one less thing to fight him about in the settlement."

"Brian goes in there pretty much every day, so I don't know that we should suspect him."

Branson nodded. The groundskeeper always had complete access to the garage since the landscaping supplies were housed there. And Branson couldn't think of a motive the man would have to harm or threaten D-Chop. But maybe he should run that down in case he was missing something.

"Peter went in when he took the Bugatti for the tune-up?" Louis looked at the monitor and rewound the video again, stopping on the time-stamped section where Peter entered the garage. "At ten fifteen a.m. He's not carrying anything."

Branson moved closer to watch over Louis's shoulder as Peter disappeared into the building. "True."

Louis sped up the video to a minute later when Peter backed out in the expensive sports car. "He drives those cars all the time to one thing or another for D-Chop. And he always has complete access to everything around here. Nothing unusual."

Branson couldn't see him wanting to harass D-Chop either. The man had a cushy job with generous pay and plenty of perks. Branson had never heard him complain.

D-Chop had shown off his car collection to friends just last night. They'd walked through the entire garage with Branson accompanying them. Whoever had planted those fireworks would've had to do so after that tour.

According to the security footage, no one had gone in or out overnight. And only three people had entered and left during the daytime hours.

Only Jill had obvious motive as well as opportunity.

"But do you think Jill would endanger her own kids?" Louis must be thinking along the same lines.

"I don't think she did endanger them."

Louis swiveled in the chair and faced Branson head-on, his eyebrows lifted.

"She knew Darren and I were with them and that they don't have access to the garage. With the remote setup, she could've even watched with binoculars through the fence somewhere to be sure the kids were a safe distance before she set off the fireworks."

"But how would Jill know how to set up something like that? She's not exactly a mechanical genius."

Definitely an understatement. She'd once demanded that Branson show her how to operate the toaster when their live-in chef in Los Angeles had the day off. "She is smart, though.

Maybe she had someone show her how to do it. Or there are probably video tutorials online." Seemed to be a video for everything these days.

But could Jill have done the other things? Her motivation fit—someone who felt D-Chop owed her something. She wanted money in the settlement, custody of the kids, and wanted to win. She also talked about the waste she thought her years with D-Chop had been, as if he owed her for that time. And for the philandering, even though she was guilty of the same sin herself.

Did she have the access and ability to carry out the fire and the attack on the gate guard? Probably not. But she could've hired someone. Though no one unusual had accessed the garage or come on the premises except for D-Chop's guests, and they'd been monitored during their visit.

Unless...

"The window." Branson stepped to the desk next to Louis.

"What?" Louis swiveled to the screens.

Branson leaned over and pointed at the current view of the garage from the camera attached to the house. "We can't see the window. If a person approached the garage from the back, he or she could scoot around the side and enter through the window while staying out of view."

"Did you check to see if the window was jimmied?"

"Can't." Branson straightened. "The fireworks destroyed it." But if his guess was right, Jill wasn't the only suspect. Any member of the staff or even one of D-Chop's guests could've accessed the garage last night or this morning.

"Looks like the ladies are here." Louis's statement brought Branson's gaze to movement on the monitor that showed the front entrance.

His heart lurched in his chest, then sank as he saw Nevaeh wasn't one of them. Pretty pathetic. He'd known she wasn't coming tonight since she would work tomorrow during the day instead. But apparently the hopeful part of him hadn't gotten the memo.

He'd think about why that was later when he had the energy for it. "Keep an eye out, man." Branson thumped Louis on the shoulder and left the room, heading toward the foyer.

The two women, Jazz and Sofia, smiled as he let them in.

"Heard you had some excitement today." The black-haired beauty aimed intense dark eyes at him.

He nodded and filled them in on the fireworks incident and what he'd found. "So stay on the alert out there tonight. Though it seems whoever the culprit is might be brazen enough to do the dirty work in daylight."

"Or clever enough to know we have the nighttime locked up." Jazz looked at Branson.

"True."

"All right." Sofia glanced at Jazz. "Let's get on it. Start at the front tonight to change things up."

Jazz nodded, and they turned to go out the front door.

"Jazz, could you stay a second?" Branson blurted the words before he gave them enough thought.

The women exchanged a look, then Jazz glanced at Branson with her eyebrows raised. "Sure." Hesitation lengthened the word.

Sofia gave Jazz another short stare he couldn't read, then went outside with her German shepherd.

"Sorry, I didn't mean to be awkward." He rubbed the back of his neck with his hand. "I just wanted to ask you about Nevaeh, but I didn't know how much Sofia knows about..."

Jazz's green eyes locked on him. "Her PTSD."

"Yeah."

"She does keep it private, so I appreciate your discretion."

He nodded, but his mind was on the woman with black curls and big brown eyes. "How is she?"

"You mean in general or..."

"No, after last night. Is she okay now?"

"She's doing better." Jazz closed her mouth, seemed to hesitate, then opened it again. "Thank you for what you did. For helping her."

A lump slid into his throat at the memory of the way his heart had seized when he saw her on the ground. And the way she'd felt in his arms, her body trembling as he cradled her. Her grip on his sweater, as if she needed him and didn't want him to let her go.

He nodded, not trusting his voice to sound normal at the moment.

"So we can count on you to keep this to yourself?" Jazz's voice brought his attention slowly to her face.

He had to admit he'd wondered if Nevaeh's boss knew about her PTSD. Jazz's question suggested she did not. Couldn't that be a problem in this line of work? He thought a second before venturing a question he hoped was tactful. "Is she okay to do security work with her PTSD? I wouldn't want her or anyone else to be in danger because of something she can't help."

Jazz's mouth set a bit firmer. "Nevaeh is tough. Only certain things trigger her PTSD. She's fearless with everything else." She glanced down at the Belgian Malinois panting at her side, then brought her gaze back to Branson's face. "There's no one I'd rather have watching my back." A flash sparked in her green eyes. "And I watch her back, too."

Branson inwardly squirmed. Maybe he'd gone too far, but he had to know Nevaeh and everyone she'd impact in this work were safe. He kept eye contact with Jazz.

"She's starting to trust you."

A jolt shot through his ribs at the statement. Nevaeh trusted him?

"She doesn't do that easily." The redhead took a step closer to him, her tall height meaning she didn't have to tilt her head up as far to see him as most women. "If you hurt her in any way, I may have to use you for target practice."

Movement at her hip drew his gaze to where she tapped the hilt of her sheathed knife.

The threat was clearly meant to protect her friend. And as such, he didn't doubt Jazz would act on it if needed. "Good to know she has someone to protect her. I respect that. But I'm not a threat."

"I don't know about that." She scanned his face. "You like her, don't you?"

He squelched a surprised grunt. Hadn't expected that one. He slid his hand down the back of his neck as a goofy smile slipped onto his face before he could stop it.

"Thought so." Jazz moved her fingers away from her weapon, and the expression in her eyes lightened. "I approve of you so far." She gave him a nod. "Anyone who looks like you but can make Nevaeh feel safe has my vote."

Not sure what that meant, but it sounded good. "Thanks?" Should he add he couldn't pursue a relationship with Nevaeh until he knew where she stood with God? Maybe he should ask Jazz about that.

No, that was a conversation to have with Nevaeh. But he didn't think they were there yet. Given what he'd seen last night, he'd have to go slow with her. Would she be more comfortable around him now?

From what Jazz just said, he gathered there must be something about his appearance that was a trigger for her PTSD. Which explained her nervous behavior around him before. She'd been getting better. But after the episode last night, would she feel more afraid or awkward around him?

He hoped it would have the opposite effect. That she would trust him more now, like Jazz said. That she would know he'd never hurt her. That he'd keep her safe.

Protective instincts stronger than they had a right to be fired his chest as he remembered her tears, the vulnerability of the strong woman. What had happened to her to cause such fear?

Part of him didn't want to know. But another part did, so he could find the person and make him pay. He reigned in the kneejerk instinct. As a Christian, he would leave any vengeance to God. But he would do everything in his power to shield Nevaeh from having anything bad happen to her again.

The sense that protecting her was his duty—what God intended for him—stayed with him after Jazz left for patrol, and Branson went to bed. As he lay down, Princess snuggling into his chest, the thought that grew more intense in his mind with every moment coiled his muscles.

Nevaeh needed protection. Like the instinct that warned him the bitter father had been going to attack D-Chop, somehow, he knew—Nevaeh was in danger.

Nevaeh was in trouble. If she didn't get to sleep soon, she wouldn't function well tomorrow. She'd be more likely to have issues with…everything. Couldn't exactly risk a mental crisis in front of D-Chop's kids when she was supposed to protect them.

She blew out a breath and punched the pillow under her head.

Cannenta shifted, the pressure of her body against Nevaeh's back a grounding comfort.

The switch from the overnight shift to daytime was always a challenge for Nevaeh's inner clock. Though that wasn't the only problem tonight.

She was supposed to meet Phoenix for training first thing in the morning. Should she tell the boss about her PTSD episode last night?

Nevaeh caught her lower lip between her teeth as she stared at the dark wall beyond her bed. Phoenix was patient and understanding, but that only went so far. If she knew Nevaeh had lost it on the job…

But it was the first time that had happened while working for PK-9. She'd had flashbacks and less intense episodes, like at the PowerSource Center. But this all-out episode, where she'd completely lost all awareness of reality, had never happened when she was on the clock for PK-9. She should be allowed one mistake, shouldn't she?

It wouldn't happen again. She was getting better, thanks

to working with Phoenix again. Her confidence was coming back, her courage growing.

She stiffened her jaw. She wouldn't let it happen on the job again.

The memory of ending up on the ground, a weak blob of mush at the estate she was supposed to be guarding stuck in her craw. And Branson had found her like that.

Embarrassment should've flooded her at the thought.

But instead, her silly pulse skipped. And warmth seeped from her chest out to the fingertips resting on her pillow.

It was almost hard to believe she'd been afraid of him before. Would her system still go on alert if he got close to her again?

The anticipation that coursed through her at the thought told her she'd likely have a very different response now.

Her mouth curved into a smile. Was he disappointed not to see her tonight since Sof and Jazz were taking the patrol shift?

'Cause she sure wished she could see him.

His handsome face, strong features and jawline, and his soft blue eyes filled her vision as her lids drifted shut.

Vicious snarls yanked her from sleep.

She sat up, her gaze locking on Alvarez at the foot of the bed as she tried to clear the fog clouding her brain. She must have fallen asleep. How long ago?

Alvarez growled and barked, his lips curled as he stared at her bedroom window covered by a thin curtain.

Nevaeh's belly clenched. This didn't look or sound like a casual, car-drove-by-on-the-road kind of barking.

She leaned over to her nightstand and pulled out the drawer. Gripping the Sig inside, she silently flipped off her blanket and lowered her feet to the floor.

Cannenta stared at Alvarez as the protection dog barked furiously.

He edged closer to the window while Nevaeh crept to the wall beside it.

Al backed her up with snarls and growls as she reached for the curtain.

She slowly pulled the edge away from the window frame.

A face covered with a black ski mask stared in her window.

TWENTY-ONE

Nevaeh jerked back from the window, letting the curtain fall over the masked face.

The next second, she stepped forward again. She raised her Sig and yanked the curtain aside.

He was gone.

"Come on, Al." Anger and adrenaline pumped through her veins as she dashed to the front of the house. She quickly clipped a leash on Al's collar and opened the front door, Sig in hand.

A silhouette hurried toward a black pickup parked on the street.

"Hey!" Nevaeh sprinted toward the truck, gun leveled as Al kept pace, barking all the way.

The engine started.

She rushed up to the passenger window, Sig aimed. "Stop! Show me your hands!"

The man twisted his masked head toward her as he peeled away from the curb, engine rumbling.

Her gaze dropped to the license plate. Covered in dirt.

Same truck as before. She was sure of it.

Her chest heaved as she lowered her Sig, and Alvarez launched barks at the escaping creep who thought he could scare her that easily.

"Okay, bud." She put her hand on Al's broad shoulders. "We probably already woke the whole neighborhood."

She reached for a phone in her pocket but felt the flat side of her pajama pants instead. No pocket. No phone.

She headed back inside, making sure to lock the door and arm the security system behind her.

Cannenta greeted her outside the bedroom, concern in her hesitant tail wag and cautious stare. "It's okay, girl. Some jerk thought he could scare me by being a creep, I guess." She bent to give Cannenta a quick pet as she passed through the doorway.

Nevaeh grabbed her phone off the nightstand and navigated to the saved numbers. She tapped Phoenix's name.

No way had she imagined the guy this time. Her paranoia hadn't created this or the previous night she'd seen the truck. Or the time he'd followed her on the freeway. Maybe the sense she was being watched hadn't been off either.

The comfort in that realization only lasted a second. Because it also meant the threat was very real.

Maybe he should call her. The thought that had nearly made Branson reach for his phone last night to call Nevaeh made him lower the weights in his hands now.

He looked at his smartphone he'd set on the stand near the door that held a water dispenser and towels.

The feeling something was wrong or about to go wrong hadn't left him even after a night of sleep. A very shortened night.

His standard morning workout was harder than normal today, thanks to trimming his hours by staying up late to greet the Phoenix K-9 team every evening and the worry about Nevaeh that had kept him awake for a while last night.

He'd ultimately decided that praying for her would be safer than calling. She may not even want to talk to him after he'd witnessed her PTSD episode. She may be more uncomfortable than ever with him now.

The thought thickened his throat. Not conducive to getting enough air for the incline dumbbell fly he was doing.

A ring in his ear signaled the call he'd been waiting for. He sat up fully and glanced at his phone to verify the caller ID.

"Hey, Andrew."

"Branson. Couldn't believe it when you said five thirty instead. I'm already halfway through my workout."

Branson chuckled as he set one dumbbell on the floor. "Yeah. Too many late nights."

"Burning the candle at both ends?"

"Something like that."

"Is it the situation with your client?"

"That's part of it." Branson briefed his mentor on the fireworks scare yesterday as he lay back on the bench and began reps of the single-arm fly. "The fact that his kids were there seemed to shake D-Chop's confidence in me. It's the first time he's openly questioned my work or wondered if I can handle it."

"But he didn't say your job was on the line, did he?"

"No. He did bring on more protection for his kids today, though. Nevaeh Williams." His pulse thrummed as he said her name. "One of the Phoenix K-9 patrol teams. I don't have a problem with her at all." Quite the opposite. He sat up and tried to keep his thoughts in check so they wouldn't affect his voice and make Andrew suspicious he had feelings for her. "She's very capable, and I can see why D-Chop would want her and her K-9 with the children."

"But?"

Branson sighed. "It's not a good sign he feels he needs to add to my security team and recommendations." He slid his hand over his hair. "Dad needs the money I make so badly right now, and I need to look good to investors. This whole thing with D-Chop and his wife—he has women coming in and out of here like a...well, a lot. His wife has some weird reality show that my security staff tell me about. I can't even believe some of the stuff she says and does on there, according to them. And that's after six years in this business. Which is feeling like five years too many." He lay back on the bench and switched the dumbbell to his left hand.

Andrew didn't say anything, letting a silence fall across the line.

Branson cringed at how much he'd dumped on him. But given that Andrew had mentored him since he was twelve, the man had heard far longer tirades before.

"You're putting a lot of pressure on yourself." Andrew's tone was thoughtful, and Branson could picture the way his graying, thick eyebrows probably dipped as lines crossed his brow. "I've been thinking about what you said last time and about your corporate security plan. If you're able to get the investors you need, are you sure corporate security, having your own firm, is what you're really looking for?"

The question nearly knocked the wind from Branson's lungs. He quickly lowered the dumbbell to the floor before he dropped it on himself. He sat up and took a deep breath before trying to answer. "I'm not sure what you mean."

"What if the celebrity aspect isn't the problem? Or not the only problem."

Uneasiness gurgled in Branson's gut. Why, he wasn't sure. He didn't even understand what Andrew was getting at. "What else could it be?"

Another pause.

Branson would pick up his weights again, but he didn't want to risk surprise from another left-field question.

"Have you talked to your dad about it?"

Good thing he hadn't been in the middle of a heavy press for that one. "No. You know how he is. He doesn't understand me wanting to do this kind of work at all."

"I get that. Do you remember that when you were younger, you wanted to be a pastor like your dad?"

"Of course." His parents had reminded him of that incessantly when he changed his mind. Even though they knew why.

The day the shooter came to their church had changed everything, for more people than Branson.

A twelve-year-old didn't expect to see a gun pointed at his dad. Didn't expect to see his dad try to persuade the shooter not to hurt anyone. Didn't expect to see the shooter start to pull the trigger but be gunned down instead.

The moment had happened within seconds, but his memory recalled it in slow motion, right through to the shooter falling to the floor and to the moment Branson saw Andrew Allen standing beyond, his gun aimed—smoking, victorious.

Andrew had saved over one hundred lives that day. Including Branson's family and Branson himself.

After that day, how could he choose anything other than to try to be the hero Andrew Allen was? Branson's path became so clear. He wanted to be a man who saved lives and protected people from violence.

And Andrew had been kind enough to take Branson under his wing, guiding him in the training and education he'd need to excel in the Navy SEALs, as Andrew had. Branson had decided to specialize in private security after the SEALs rather than following Andrew's path into law enforcement, wanting to avoid the politics and paperwork involved in the latter.

But every decision Branson had made led him to this point, to being a highly trained security specialist with the skills to protect others and save lives. He'd been able to do just that several times in the military and when protecting celebrities.

But it gave him the most satisfaction to know he'd be able to protect his family if needed or anyone else even if an unexpected scenario occurred. He was always ready. Just like Andrew.

"You still there?"

"Yeah." Branson cleared his throat. "Sorry. Just got me thinking."

"Good. Because I have one more question for you."

Branson's abs tightened as he stood. "Shoot."

"Have you asked God what *He* wants you to do?"

The question punched into his gut as if his mentor had delivered it with a fist. It shouldn't have. It should be easy to answer.

But the only answer Branson found as he searched his mind, his memories, was one even he couldn't believe. It was *no*.

TWENTY-TWO

Weird feeling to enter a PK-9 meeting at headquarters with the boss herself.

Nevaeh and Alvarez followed Phoenix and Dag through the hallway at the PK-9 Agency, headed for the breakroom.

Phoenix and her K-9 didn't look any worse for wear after spending the rest of the night patrolling outside Nevaeh's house while she tried to sleep. The boss still stood straight and tall, her walk alert and strong, mimicked by the dog at her side.

Voices drifted out of the breakroom as they approached, but they stopped as soon as Phoenix turned through the open doorway.

So this is what it felt like to be Phoenix. Kind of.

They all adored their boss, but she did have a certain presence that tended to quiet whatever jokes they were in the middle of when she arrived. Once she was there, though, they all relaxed into their banter again, kind of like kids around their mother.

"Hey, Phoenix."

"Morning, Nevaeh."

The welcomes and smiles from Bris, Sof, and the others were dampened more than usual this morning. Probably because they'd heard what had happened.

As Phoenix crossed the room to her armchair on the far side, Nevaeh went to the love seat where Jazz sat, Flash lying on the floor with his head on her feet.

"Hey." Jazz's green eyes held concern as Nevaeh sank into the cushion beside her. She rubbed Nevaeh's shoulder with a comforting hand. Jazz had already shared her worry and frustration when she'd called as soon as she got off patrol at D-Chop's a half hour ago. Frustration because she hadn't been able to leave and go to Nevaeh right away. Phoenix had told her to stay on duty when she'd notified the team via text that something had happened.

"Some coffee?" Cora's soft voice drew Nevaeh's gaze to the blonde who bent close and held a steaming mug out to her.

Jana had apparently followed Cora over, and the golden greeted Alvarez with the usual tail wags and sniffing.

Nevaeh caught a whiff of caramel. "Flavored again?"

Cora smiled. "We may have to make it a permanent treat if you keep earning it."

Nevaeh laughed. "One way or another, I guess." She took the mug. "Thanks."

Cora straightened. "We're all so sorry for what happened, Nevaeh. But so thankful God protected you."

"I think Alvarez and Phoenix took care of that." As soon as the words left her mouth, Nevaeh wanted to pull them back. She didn't usually flat-out contradict any of the team members' Christian stuff. They were free to believe whatever they wanted. But something about Cora's words this time, or maybe the situation, sparked irritation in her chest. God wasn't in the business of protecting Nevaeh. That much had been proven.

Still, she wanted to kick herself for causing the awkward silence that filled the room.

Cora's sweet expression didn't waver, making the guilt even worse.

Nevaeh scrambled for something to say. "I don't think he wanted to hurt me anyway. Just scare me."

Cora walked back to the sofa she'd been sharing with Sof when Nevaeh and Phoenix had arrived.

But Jana decided to stay with Nevaeh for some reason. The golden sat down in the place by Nevaeh's leg that Al vacated, the rottie mix apparently headed for the open carpet where he could rest without a crowd.

"But who would want to do that?" Bris leaned forward in the other armchair, the movement drawing Toby to her for some petting. She obliged, her mouth curving into a smile as the black Lab pushed his head into her palm.

"It would be strange for this to happen out of the blue." Sof aimed her dark eyes at Nevaeh. Raksa slept on the short carpeting a couple feet from her, probably exhausted from the overnight patrol. "Did you notice anything else unusual lately? Anyone watching you?"

Nevaeh glanced at Jazz before answering.

Jazz didn't nod, but her eyes said she thought she should tell them. Nevaeh had planned to tell Phoenix last night anyway, but the boss hadn't asked questions. Just told Nevaeh to get some rest while she guarded the house.

"I thought I was maybe being followed a couple of times."

"You mean when you were driving?" Bris's eyebrows lifted above her gray-blue eyes.

"Yes. And when I was outside the school my nieces and nephews go to."

Sof, Bris, and Cora looked toward Phoenix. Nevaeh did the same, her stomach clenching at what she might see.

Would Phoenix be mad? Not that she'd show it on her face if she were. Did she even get mad like regular people? The random thoughts bought Nevaeh time to see that the boss's expression was as unreadable as always. Who knew what she was thinking or feeling? If she felt at all. The woman clearly thought circles around pretty much everyone.

"Tell us everything that happened leading up to last night." Phoenix's deep voice was steady and firm.

Nevaeh opened her mouth to say she wasn't sure about any of it.

"Everything." Phoenix read her mind. "Even what you aren't certain of."

Nevaeh moistened her lips. "Okay." She told them all she could remember, working backward from last night to two nights before when the truck had been parked on her street. She told them about seeing it following her on the freeway and the morning Lillibet said she saw a man watching them. Then she finished with the first night outside the Power-Source Center when she'd felt like she was being watched.

Jazz sucked in a breath. "Oh, Nev." All the women stared at Jazz, but she watched Nevaeh. "That night at Power-Source, when Flash and I went to clear the parking lot, I saw a black Ram. It was parked by..." her gaze went to the ceiling as she thought, "a gray sedan and a black SUV."

"Did it have mud spattered on it?"

Jazz shook her head. "I don't think so. But I didn't get the tags. I'm sorry. It was empty and dark like all the other vehicles in the lot when I checked. And Flash didn't notice anything." Vertical lines bunched between her eyebrows.

"Don't worry about it." Nevaeh gave her a smile. "You're a smart girl, but I don't expect you to go around memorizing fifteen tags every time I get spooked."

"So why didn't you guys mention any of this earlier?" Bris asked the question everyone probably wanted to. The woman had softened a lot since she'd gotten religion, but she was still painfully blunt sometimes.

Jazz looked at Nevaeh, letting her decide how much she wanted to say.

"I've been..." Nevaeh glanced toward Bris. "I haven't been myself lately." She inwardly scoffed at that. Maybe she was herself, but not the one she wanted to be. "I thought I might be imagining things because of being...stressed. I didn't want to make a big deal out of something that wasn't real. I couldn't be sure about any of it. Until last night."

"That makes sense." Cora nodded.

Warmth filled Nevaeh at the understanding in her gaze and the lack of judgment in the others' eyes.

"Back to Bristol's first question." Sof glanced at the brunette before bringing her attention to Nevaeh. "Who would want to scare or hurt you?"

The face of the most obvious choice flew in front of her eyes, filling the screen of her mind.

Panic rose in her chest, her heart rate elevating.

A touch on her arm paused the fear racing through her veins. Jazz. But she didn't look at Nevaeh as she spoke to the team. "I wondered if it could be the person who's bothering D-Chop."

Bless Jazz's loyal heart. She always had Nevaeh's back. But the PK-9 team was family now, too. And these girls always had Nevaeh's back, like she had theirs. Maybe she should tell them about Walter.

"It's a possibility." Sof apparently thought Jazz's suggestion was a good one anyway. Maybe they wouldn't have to talk about him.

"Do you mean because she's helping to protect D-Chop?" Cora reached for her notebook computer on the coffee table and moved it to her lap.

"But if that's the reason, why would they go after Nevaeh?" Bris's gaze switched between Cora and Sof. "Why not Jazz, too, or you?" She landed her focus on Sof.

"Your senses told you someone was watching you the night of the PowerSource concert." Sof looked at Nevaeh as if wanting confirmation.

She lifted a shoulder, still uncertain if she'd really sensed it or just imagined it. "I guess."

"And Jazz saw the pickup that night."

"Correct." Jazz tucked her wavy red hair behind her ear.

"The three of us were all there, but we had different assignments. Jazz and I were on the front entry points and crowd control."

"But Nevaeh was backstage." Jazz angled her head toward Nevaeh, her eyes widening as if she'd realized what Sof was getting at.

"So?" Nevaeh looked at the women.

"You could've seen something we didn't." Sof's dark eyes trained on her.

"Something the perp didn't want seen?" Bris turned her attention to Nevaeh as if to puzzle out what she didn't know she knew. "Maybe you saw the perp himself. Or herself. Whoever messed with the pyrotechnics and started the fire."

"He could be afraid you can ID him." Worry colored Jazz's eyes again. "Or she, I guess."

"Phoenix?" Cora looked at the boss, and they all waited to hear the one-word question answered. Nevaeh wasn't even sure what Cora was asking, but good things usually came of the pair's secret way of communicating.

"We'll investigate the D-Chop case."

The PK-9 team members exchanged surprised glances. All except Cora, who immediately opened her computer as if she'd expected Phoenix's decision and was already getting to work.

"The theory that the same person behind the attacks may be the one stalking Nevaeh is viable." Phoenix turned her gaze toward Nevaeh.

Stalking. The word sent a shiver down Nevaeh's spine. As if she didn't have enough to be afraid of.

"We don't tolerate threats on this agency. Since the police have not been invited to be involved in this case, we'll need to solve it ourselves to ensure Nevaeh's safety."

"I was hoping you'd say that." Sof grinned.

"Me, too." Bris added a big smile.

Nevaeh's heart swelled behind her ribs. These girls were the best. Especially Phoenix. She gave the boss a look she hoped expressed her relief, but Phoenix was already focusing on Cora.

"Suspects."

Cora looked up from her screen. "Right. The list I have so far is short since I only know about D-Chop's basic staff and his publicly known associates."

Nevaeh blinked. That's more than she'd have expected

Cora to have since they weren't investigating the case until ten seconds ago.

"Marsha Phillips, live-in housekeeper." Cora read off the screen. "Peter Volrath, personal assistant, Jaycee Hyman, the maid who comes in daily, and band members JipJag, Pinky, B-Puff, Kicker, and Leeman."

Bris and Sof snickered, drawing Cora's gaze.

She smiled over her computer. "I'll have to do more research to find their legal names."

"Kicker's name is Eddie Bosworth."

Cora's gaze jumped to Nevaeh.

"He told me when I was waiting with him for the EMTs."

Cora smiled. "Excellent. That will save me some time." She looked back down at her computer. "Then there's D-Chop's wife, soon-to-be divorced, Jill Jacquet." Her gaze lifted. "We know the security team is Branson Aaberg, Darren Tremblay, and Louis Kursko. They all have impeccable records, but I thought we should include them."

Sof nodded. "Records don't tell the whole story."

That was for sure. Walter had a great record while in jail. He'd even earned privileges for good behavior, working his way up to the inmate maintenance crew.

She pushed her mind away from him and back to Cora's voice as quickly as she could.

"I think we'll need more information about D-Chop. I'm sure he has more associates than I'm aware of, from his past and now."

"We can ask Branson when we go on patrol." Jazz looked at Cora.

"Good idea." Cora nodded. "I can do more extensive research, as well, given more time."

"We should probably investigate other theories, too." All eyes went to Bris. "I agree this could be about D-Chop. But we don't want to overlook other possibilities, right?"

Sof brought her gaze to Nevaeh again. "She has a good point. Are there other people in your past who might have reason to stalk you or bother you now?"

The truth she'd been hoping to avoid stuck like a lump in her throat. Silence hung thick in the room as they waited for her to say something. Could she talk about it without…

She moved her gaze over these women's faces. Her sisters.

Only Sof and Bris didn't know now. At least she guessed Cora knew part of it from having access to their employee files.

None of them would ever use the information against her. She knew that. They would only support her one hundred percent like always. Maybe two hundred percent if they knew what had happened.

She struggled to pull in a thin breath. "Yes." She pushed out the word. Once that one was out, others followed more easily. "I worked as a correctional officer at Whitlow Heights Prison. While I was there…" She dropped her gaze to her lap. Her hands trembled. She should've brought Cannenta with her.

Jazz put her hand on Nevaeh's leg. "Do you want me to…"

"No." The touch gave Nevaeh the courage she needed to lift her head again. To meet the gazes of her sisters as they watched her. No pressure. Just compassion and love. She took in another breath. "An inmate attacked me."

Frowns marked the girls' faces, their concern almost palpable as they listened.

"It was my fault in a way. I was friendly with him like I tried to be with everyone who responded to that. I let him out of the pod to go on his maintenance shift, and we chatted like usual. I let him go around the desk, get behind me, and I didn't turn to watch him." The worst mistake she'd ever made in her life. Trusting someone like Walter Johnson. Thinking someone like him could be a friend and would respond to her kindness like people should.

She stopped. If she went any closer to it, she'd risk flashbacks, a PTSD episode. She loved these girls, but they didn't need to see that first thing in the morning.

The humor in the thought gave her the strength to quirk her mouth and find distance from the memory. "You know how it is. Somebody does something to you, but they blame you for it. He'd only had one year left to serve at the time. So I was the reason he had to do more time. I heard he was pretty mad about that."

"That's insane." Anger undergirded Bris's statement.

"Yeah." A laugh somehow found its way to the surface and escaped Nevaeh's mouth. "That's a good word for him." She fought not to picture his face, the craziness in his eyes as he'd—

Sof suddenly got to her feet, startling Raksa into standing. She stalked around the coffee table and stopped by Nevaeh, then sat on the edge of the table in front of her.

Raksa followed the odd path, stopping to smell Jana when he arrived by the love seat.

"Was there a motive for the attack?" Sof's dark gaze held something Nevaeh hadn't seen there before—a blend of fury and compassion that seemed to throw sparks from her eyes.

Nevaeh cleared her throat, unable to look away. But to answer she'd have to remember what he said, have to hear his voice in her head. She couldn't risk that.

Jazz gently squeezed Nevaeh's leg.

Nevaeh knew what she meant without looking. She nodded.

"He wanted Nevaeh to give him her car keys so he could escape." Jazz's voice was thick with emotion as she explained. "It was a stupid plan. None of the COs were allowed to keep any personal keys with them in the prison. And there was no way he could've gotten all the way out without other officers stopping him anyway."

She paused and gave Nevaeh another squeeze. "He got angry when she wouldn't help him escape. And he claimed she'd been stringing him along, flirting with him. Which, of course, she never did. She was only trying to treat all the inmates like human beings."

"I get the picture." Sof's eyes sparked enough for lightning to be housed in them. She put her small hands on Nevaeh's. Possibly a more startling thing than the man staring in her window last night. Sof was never a toucher. Never.

"Where is he now?" Her voice held a sharp, barely restrained anger, like she was ready to finish him right now if she found out his location. Was that for Nevaeh's sake?

Her cold hands warmed beneath Sof's touch and protective passion. "He would be out now. His sentence was done seven weeks ago."

Sof looked deeply into Nevaeh's eyes. "You've got this. And you know we've got your back."

Nevaeh swallowed, the assurance infusing her limbs with strength, slowing the trembling in her hands and arms. She didn't care Sof had probably noticed. Her support, no matter what, was obvious. And having a fighter like Sof in her corner sure gave a girl a boost of confidence.

"Always." Bris nodded in agreement. "Thank you for telling us. You're incredibly brave, Nevaeh."

Brave. That was one thing Nevaeh never was when it came to Walter and the memory of the attack. But it was awesome of Bris, former bomb tech with nerves of steel, to say it. "Thanks."

"Do we have a name and location for this thug?" Sof stood as she aimed the question at Cora.

"Walter Johnson. Phoenix had me locate him as soon as he was released and again three days ago."

Nevaeh glanced at Phoenix. She shouldn't be surprised. Of course, Phoenix knew when Walter's sentence was up. And Nevaeh should've known the boss would be monitoring him and the situation. She always thought of everything.

The shadow cast by the bill of Phoenix's gray baseball cap hid her eyes. But she seemed to be watching Nevaeh.

"He's in the Los Angeles area of California working on a stock car racing pit crew." Cora looked at the other women above her computer screen. "I haven't been able to verify yet that he is actually there and showing up for work every day.

His employers won't give out that kind of information. But I believe Phoenix has a lead we might be able to use for that." Cora angled her head toward the boss.

No surprise there either. Phoenix had connections better than a U. S. President's.

"How likely is it Johnson would want to track you down?" Bris asked the question Nevaeh would give her right arm to know the answer to.

Her fear screamed one answer—that he must be close, in the Twin Cities, right now. But her fear had said that even when he was behind bars. "He was mad at me when they..." Her throat started to close.

Jana leaned closer and rested her head on Nevaeh's lap, as if, like Cannenta, she knew Nevaeh needed comfort and grounding.

Nevaeh focused madly on the golden, stroking her soft fur as she forced her mind away from the memories. "When they caught him, he was furious at me. At least, that's what they told me later." She'd finally passed out, maybe become unconscious, when the officers came in to stop him. "They told him he wouldn't get out for a lot longer because of what he'd done."

"How long did he get?" Sof paused her pacing behind the sofa across the room.

"Five years for third degree assault."

"You're kidding." Bris's features twisted with incredulity.

"That's nowhere near long enough." The anger that flashed in Sof's eyes was obvious even from this distance.

"That's what the judge said, right, Nev?"

Nevaeh gave Jazz a nod, the okay to tell the rest.

"She said she was 'dismayed,' wasn't that her word?" Jazz didn't stop for Nevaeh to answer. "Dismayed that five more years was the max she could legally give him, since she knew he was a threat to others and society as a whole. And then she slapped him with the lifetime restraining order."

Everyone turned their focus to Nevaeh again. She moistened her lips with her tongue. "Yeah. He'll go back to prison if he comes within fifty yards of me."

"Well, that's something." Bris leaned back against the sofa cushions. "He'd have to be a world champion idiot to bother you then. Unless he loves living in prison."

Bris was right. Logically, Walter probably wouldn't come near Nevaeh again. For his own sake, he shouldn't want to.

But her fears didn't listen to logic.

"Until we can eliminate him with a solid alibi or other evidence, Johnson is a suspect." Phoenix's voice cut through the worry clouding Nevaeh's mind. "But not the only possibility." She turned her head slightly, seeming to aim her gaze at Cora from the shadow under the bill of her cap. "Also track down all inmates who served time at Whitlow Heights Prison while Nevaeh was there."

"That will be a lot. I was there for two years."

"No problem." Cora gave Nevaeh a small smile. "If you can provide the date range, I can match that with the incarceration records." Her mouth shifted into an apologetic press of her lips. "And if you can let me know if you had any problems with other inmates, that would be helpful."

That was a new idea. Nevaeh hadn't thought once about any of the other inmates since she'd left. For obvious reasons, since any memory of the prison could trigger her PTSD. Surviving this conversation was nothing short of a miracle of will power and support from the girls.

"Good idea." Bris reached for her coffee mug on the table. "We don't want to overlook anyone by focusing only on the most obvious suspects."

There were too many suspects now. All of the inmates she'd ever had contact with plus all of D-Chop's acquaintances, which Nevaeh was pretty sure could end up well over one hundred if they went into his past, too. How would they ever narrow down a list that huge?

"In the meantime," Phoenix halted the overwhelm rising in Nevaeh's chest, "you'll stay with Sofia until we can isolate the perpetrator."

"What?" The word popped out before Nevaeh thought. She glanced at Sof, who gave her a teasing grin.

"That's the reaction every hostess wants to hear. Afraid to see the condition of my house?"

Nevaeh chuckled. "No. But you have a kid now and a husband. You're newlyweds."

Sof wrinkled her nose. "Yeah, who have known each other our whole lives. Don't worry, I promise we won't gross you out with any PDA."

Public displays of affection weren't Nevaeh's concern, but the idea of Sof and Michael grossing out her and Grace with their romantic affections made her laugh with her teammates. "My point is you have a full house and a full life already."

Sof shook her head. "Never too full for family."

Nevaeh shook her head with a smile. True, they were family, but she couldn't intrude on Sof's new household, and she needed space of her own. As much as she trusted Sof's support, she was not about to have a PTSD episode in front of her young daughter and husband. And if someone really was after her, there was no way she was bringing that kind of danger to the doorstep of ten-year-old Grace. "I really appreciate it, Sof. But I'll be better off at my own place." She slid her gaze to Phoenix. "I need that."

The boss watched her in silence. Was that agreement or her thinking? "Jazz can stay with you instead."

Perfect. Jazz had already seen the PTSD. They both knew the worst and best about each other. Hadn't fazed them yet.

"We'll patrol your house as we can on an unpredictable schedule."

Nevaeh probably should save her pride by saying she didn't need the extra protection. But the truth was she didn't mind a bit. Knowing Phoenix or Sof were out there could help keep her fears at bay.

And could ward off whoever had paid her a visit last night.

Most of the possible suspects, she could handle like nothing. She'd like to see the spoiled, social media sensation Jill Jacquet try to come after her. And even a lot of men she could face and take down on her own.

"We'll find the person behind this threat." The angle of Phoenix's head shifted slightly, just enough that the shadow cleared her eyes, and Nevaeh could see they were trained on her. "And we will stop it."

Phoenix's confidence should've been enough to clear away Nevaeh's last bits of doubt and anxiety.

But Bris's remark about Walter needing to be an idiot to come after her lurked in the back of her mind.

No one would ever accuse Walter Johnson of being smart.

TWENTY-THREE

Branson checked his watch for probably the tenth time in the last half hour. He returned his gaze to Jill, D-Chop, and their lawyers where the group sat on opposing sides of the dining room table. But he didn't really see them.

A flawless face with big brown eyes filled his vision instead. Nevaeh and Darren were escorting D-Chop's children from school to Fun Land now. Darren reported Nevaeh had met him at the school as planned thirty-six minutes ago.

Branson had almost asked to talk to Nevaeh when Darren called. Ever since Jazz told him before she went off shift that morning that something had happened to Nevaeh, he'd been going crazy with worry. It was as if his mind and emotions had hopped on a roller-coaster ride he couldn't stop.

Jazz hadn't told him exactly what happened. She'd spit out the information that something had happened to Nevaeh as if she hadn't meant to say it. She'd clearly been worried about her friend. Which only worried Branson more.

Jazz had said Nevaeh wasn't hurt. But the deep concern on her face and the way she'd practically run out the door to go to her friend did nothing to back that up.

Nevaeh must be okay, though, since she'd come on duty for the kids' protection detail as planned. The Phoenix K-9

Agency was professional enough that they would've called or sent someone else if she wasn't able to perform her duties.

The reassurance only slightly loosened the knot that twisted his gut. He needed to see her. Needed to verify for himself that she was all right.

And being okay physically was not the same as being unharmed emotionally. What if whatever happened had worsened her PTSD?

An itching sensation twitched his fingers. If only he could've swapped assignments with Darren today. But he couldn't leave the estate when Jill and her lawyer were scheduled for this meeting with D-Chop.

His number one priority had to be D-Chop's safety. And if Jill was behind the threatening incidents that had been happening, he couldn't risk leaving the rapper with anyone but himself. He'd even brought in Louis for the meeting to make sure they were covered if Jill or her lawyer tried anything. And to be able to follow either of them if they wandered off to enact more sabotage.

But the knowledge he was fulfilling his duty and doing his job well was little consolation for the tension compressing his chest. D-Chop was not the person he wanted to protect right now.

He should be protecting Nevaeh.

His heart thudded into his ribs.

When had he started to think that way about her? The night he'd held her in his arms, trying to shield her from the demons in her mind?

No. It was before that. The first time she'd sprung away from him. At the PowerSource Center when he'd startled her, and she'd looked at him with fear in her gorgeous eyes.

He wanted to be the one to protect her from that fear. From any dangers she faced.

In a way, that was normal for him. He wanted to protect anyone in danger. But this was different. It was...personal.

Why did—

"That's the least you can give me." Jill's raised voice

grabbed Branson's attention. "You owe me everything." She stood and leaned across the table.

"I don't owe you nothin'." D-Chop jumped to his feet on the other side and pointed a finger in her face. "You owe *me* everything!"

"You cheating..."

Branson shut out the expletives Jill screamed as he and Louis stepped forward to break up the celebrity couple before they came to blows.

Protecting Nevaeh and puzzling out his feelings for her would have to wait. She was a capable and strong woman who probably didn't need his help. He only hoped she might want him around anyway.

It paid to be a celebrity's kid. D-Chop had rented out the entire Fun Land facility, a building that had probably been a warehouse before it was converted to a family recreational center that featured ball pits, trampolines, arcade games, and every other entertainment a child could want.

Nannies, on the other hand, weren't paid enough. From what she could gather from D-Chop's chatty children, they'd scared off their most recent nanny—something they apparently did a lot—and were very happy without one until the replacement was hired.

Today was Shawnee Blackwell's first day, and Nevaeh guessed she wouldn't last many more.

The girl stood off to one side, fingering her beach wave extensions as she stared at her smartphone. She'd apparently given up on trying to be the kids' new buddy. Buying them a bunch of snacks and junk food only went so far, and D-Chop's hooligans saw right through the befriending con.

She was obviously too young and inexperienced. Judging from the curves she'd barely squeezed into a tight, supershort skirt and a top with a plunging neckline that left nothing to the imagination, it was obvious D-Chop hadn't hired her for her childcare qualifications.

"Hey, Nev! Watch this!" Eight-year-old Destiny waved as she bounced high on the trampoline and flipped in the air.

"Cool." Nevaeh gave a thumbs up.

"I can do that." Bear, the adorable six-year-old who didn't seem old enough to be away from his mother so much, brushed against Nevaeh as he ran onto the in-floor trampoline with his sister. He jumped and tried to flip before he got high enough. He tumbled in a somersault instead.

Samson snickered and pointed at his little brother.

"You can do better, Sam?" Nevaeh pushed back on the boy who reminded her of Dawton even though Samson was a year older. He needed to be challenged by someone.

"If I wanted to." He crossed his arms over his skinny chest, apparently smart enough not to try what he knew he couldn't do.

"Uh-huh."

Destiny and stocky little Bear hopped off the trampoline and ran into Nevaeh like she was there just to stop their progress. "Can Al come on the trampoline with us?" Destiny fiddled with Al's ears as she looked up at Nevaeh.

"I don't think he'd like that."

Though he was loving the attention from the kids. Little Bear hung his arms over Al's back while Destiny's small hands massaged his face.

The dog's eyes sagged at the corners, his panting grin a sign of sheer bliss.

Nevaeh laughed. "But he definitely loves you."

"I love him, too." Destiny planted a kiss on Al's broad head.

"Time to go." Darren's deep voice came through the earpiece Nevaeh wore. She glanced at him, standing guard at the metal back door they'd entered through.

"Roger that." She glanced at the nanny. "Miss Blackwell."

The girl, who probably wasn't more than nineteen, looked up from her phone.

"Time to take the kids home."

"Right." She tucked the phone into her slim purse. "Let's go, kids." She headed for the door instead of the children. Like they'd all just follow her.

Nevaeh rolled her eyes.

"Aw, do we have to go?" Samson led the whining Nevaeh had expected.

Destiny and Bear added their own complaints in simpering voices.

"Don't you want to go with your mom? She's waiting at the house to pick you up."

"Not really."

Rats. That was the motivation Nevaeh had planned to use, but Samson's answer shot it down. "You want to stay with your dad instead?"

The boy nodded, looking away, his slim jaw set.

Compassion for the kid's situation made Nevaeh take a second. Her nieces and nephews had the same problem. Wanting to be with their dad, needing two parents who loved them and cared enough to spend time with them.

But she'd turned out all right without a mom and dad. Thanks to grandparents who filled the gap. Who did these kids have to fill the gap?

She swallowed the lump that stuck in her throat. "I didn't see my dad or my mom much growing up." She gave Sam's shoulder a quick squeeze. "But I made it. And I helped my kid brothers and sister make it. You can do that, too."

A little hand slipped into hers.

Bear. He didn't look at her as he did it, just took her hand as naturally as if he'd known her for years instead of one afternoon. Poor desperate kid.

"You guys want to know how to make Al walk when you want him to?"

Three pairs of dark eyes looked up at her. Samson and Destiny nodded.

"You say his name and then 'with me.' Sam, you want to try?"

"Sure." He glanced up at Nevaeh before looking at Alvarez.

"Wait a second. Stand next to him first, and then walk with him when he walks."

Samson stepped to Al's opposite side. "Al, with me."

Nevaeh started forward to prompt Alvarez to listen to the boy.

Samson shot her a grin as the K-9 walked alongside him.

She returned the smile. The trick worked to happily move the kids all the way to Darren at the back door.

"Stay between Nevaeh and me, got it?" Darren repeated the direction he'd given them when they'd arrived at Fun Land. "And if anything happens?"

"Do exactly what you say," Destiny and Samson repeated together.

"You got it." Darren looked at Nevaeh from a safe distance away. The guy seemed professional enough, but he was almost as big as Branson. His size and muscular build didn't help her frayed nerves.

The ride here in the limo had been touch and go. Lucky it was a very big limo or having to sit in there with the massive man would've prompted a full-blown PTSD episode for the kids to see. The idea of getting in the limo with him again was making her sweat.

"I cleared the lot a minute ago." He spoke to Nevaeh over the kids' heads. "No press."

"Great." What a weird life these kids had, having to enter and leave places the back way to avoid reporters and cameras.

"I want to go first with Al." Destiny pushed between Samson and Alvarez, earning a shove from her brother.

"Hey, that's enough of that. Al and I will go first, and if you both behave, you can follow us and sit by Al in the limo. All right?"

Darren stepped away from the door to move behind the nanny who hung back, staring at her phone again.

Nevaeh gave Darren a glance, and he nodded. She pulled

open the door and started to step through with Alvarez, but Samson and Destiny squeezed past and darted ahead.

She walked into the chilly air. “Hey, stay with—”

Alvarez snarled.

Shots exploded beside her.

TWENTY-FOUR

Nevaeh whirled to see the nanny dart into the building as Darren crashed to the blacktop. Shot.

Two men in ski masks rushed out from behind garbage bins, carrying guns. Kidnappers?

Alvarez barked and snarled.

"On it!" She dropped his leash, pulled Bear behind her legs, and gripped the boy's arm with her left hand as she drew her Sig. She didn't want to shoot someone in front of Bear, but she'd do it to save his life.

Alvarez launched himself at the closest man, gripping his wrist in powerful jaws and thrashing.

The man screamed, and his gun dropped.

The other one tried to aim at Alvarez, but he'd probably hit his pal with how much Al was moving.

"Don't try it." She leveled her Sig at him. "Drop the weapon."

Brakes screeching jerked her head to the right.

A black van pulled to a halt six feet from Sam and Destiny.

"Kids! Run to me!" She holstered her Sig, scooped Bear into her arms, and sprinted for the other kids as they ran her way.

They met midway, the kids grabbing hold of her jacket and leg.

Alvarez had taken his target to the ground, the guy trying to grab his mangled arm from the dog.

"Al, to me!"

He instantly dropped his hold and dashed to her, too fast to catch the other guy's bullet, she hoped.

But he didn't try to shoot, just stalked toward them. Maybe because the kids he wanted to kidnap stood too close to her now.

A sliding sound signaled the van door opening. She spun to check.

Two more men in black clothing and masks dropped out.

She set Bear on his feet. "Hold on to him, Sam." She shot the older boy a look she hoped would scare him into action. "Protect your family."

She looked toward the building. The survivor continued her way, gun in hand. He wouldn't use it if he wanted the kids alive. And she couldn't risk drawing his fire by shooting with them so close.

"Al, stay. On guard." He launched a warning growl as she whirled to face the kidnappers from the van.

She jumped out in front of the kids, distancing from them to push the kidnappers back.

The smaller guy lunged at her.

She dodged, but her head suddenly yanked sideways.

He had her hair in his grip.

She reached above her head and grabbed his wrists. She locked her grip as she turned in and down, slamming his arm beneath her as she took him to the ground.

He didn't let go, so she braced her leg against the blacktop and forced his forearm into an awkward angle. He still held on.

She yanked.

He shrieked as the elbow broke. And so did his grip.

Nevaeh pushed up, landing in base, a ready stance.

But something heavy and strong engulfed her from behind.

Walter.

She smelled him, heard his breath. His sickening laugh.

The blows would come next.

The crushing, bone-splitting—

"Nev!" Destiny's shriek cut through the panic that flooded Nevaeh's system.

She focused on the little girl, the fear on her face. Bear's wide eyes. Sam's brave hold on them both.

Alvarez moved away from the kids, snarling and spewing barks as he neared Nevaeh and the attacker who gripped her.

"Al, no! Stay on guard." The dog whirled around and darted to the other side of the kids just in time to stop the gunman from reaching them.

She had to fight. It wasn't Walter. She could do this.

Step back. Wrap the leg. Take him down.

She started to execute the moves she'd practiced with Phoenix.

But another man appeared. Walked in front of her like he was going for the kids.

"Hey! Freeze!" The deep shout had to be Darren. And the shot that rang out, probably taking down the gunman.

A siren sounded nearby. Police.

A new burst of adrenaline surged through her, and she tried to pivot around the big guy. But the new attacker lunged at her and grabbed her shoulder, stopping her movement.

"Let's get out of here. Just take her."

Her legs swung off the ground as the big thug picked her up.

She kicked and thrashed.

A cloth pressed hard over her mouth. The stench of chloroform seeped into her nostrils.

She should fight. Use a jiujitsu move to slip out of the hold. Deadly to get in the vehicle.

But if she kept them there another moment, the kids could get hurt. It could be them or her.

She went limp, faked the chloroform was working as he carried her into the seatless back of the dark van.

But her bluff was too late.

Her vision blurred.

She'd be unconscious in a second. Panic rushed in her ears.

The kids were safe. If she died, at least she could know it was worth it.

Branson's heart stopped. He couldn't have heard Darren right. "What do you mean they took her?"

"They shoved her in the van when I threatened to shoot and police sirens sounded." Darren coughed. "They already had ahold of her. I think they panicked. Wanted to cut their losses and scram."

Nevaeh. Kidnapped. The victim of the attackers' panic move when she thwarted their plan.

"Excuse me." A female voice came across the line.

"Who is this?"

"A paramedic with Saint Paul Emergency Medical Services. Your friend is badly injured and cannot talk on the phone. You'll have to come to Districts Hospital and see if you can speak to him there."

Darren had mentioned the kidnappers shot him. But he was apparently well enough to talk. "Ma'am, this is a life and death situation. I need to speak with him."

"Sir, this is life and death for your friend. He's unconscious and needs immediate medical attention. I'm sorry."

The line went dead.

Branson's gut clenched. The damage was worse than he thought. *Lord, please keep Darren alive and give the doctors wisdom.*

He shot out of the chair behind the monitors in the estate's security room. Jill and her lawyer had just driven away. He'd watched to make sure they did so without any stops or tricks.

"DT2, this is Team Leader. Meet me en route to principal." Branson whipped open the security room door and took the hallway with long, fast strides.

His stomach churned, pushing an unpleasant taste up his throat. Where was Nevaeh now? What were the kidnappers doing to her?

Logic kicked in. They hadn't intended to take her. They'd wanted the kids. Probably for ransom. They would want to attempt the same end goal with her, so they'd keep her alive. Probably wouldn't hurt her. At least not initially until they decided what to do, maybe contacted someone for ransom.

Would they try for D-Chop, hoping he'd want to pay to get one of his employees back?

Either way, it wasn't going to go down like they wanted. Branson tightened his jaw as he stalked through the parlor. He'd get her back.

"Branson." Louis's voice brought him to a halt. The man walked toward him across the tiles.

Branson glanced around the room to verify they were alone. "There's been an incident." He quickly filled Louis in on the little he knew. "I want you to go get the kids and bring them back here. Be sure to bring your guardian verification so the police will release them to you."

Louis nodded. "Got it." He didn't move.

Branson looked at him.

"What about Nevaeh? What's—"

"I'll get her back."

Their gazes met, Louis searching for something, probably some reassurance in Branson's eyes. Then he nodded again, apparently satisfied enough to get moving.

Branson covered the rest of the ground to the music room in record time, launching into a jog at the end. "D-Chop."

The rapper lowered his mic as Branson burst into the room. He was alone, probably trying to de-stress after his wife's visit.

"I need you to sit down."

D-Chop stared at Branson for a second, but then he

returned the mic to its stand and went to the plush armchair against the wall. He looked up at Branson. "Shoot, man."

"Your children are fine. They're unharmed. But several assailants tried to kidnap them as they were leaving Fun Land."

D-Chop's eyes sparked. "Who did it?" His voice pitched low with an edge Branson had rarely heard from him.

"I don't know. Darren was shot and is being taken to the hospital. According to what he told me over the phone, Nevaeh held them off, and they took her instead when the police were closing in."

"They took her?"

Branson's response exactly. He nodded.

"Get 'em, man." D-Chop pushed up from the chair. "Go get her back. She don't take the fall for this, you hear me?"

Thank the Lord. Branson was going to go after her either way, but having D-Chop's blessing would help and speed up the process. "I'm going after her right now. Louis is bringing the kids back here. I'll arm the security system on my way out."

D-Chop waved a dismissive hand. "Just get her, man."

Branson headed for the door.

"Hey, B."

Branson looked over his shoulder.

"Do whatever you have to. I'll back you."

Branson met D-Chop's gaze, the rapper's eyes filled with a ferocity he'd never seen there before. Branson jerked a nod and left, breaking into a run to reach his pickup as quickly as possible.

Thoughts, images of Nevaeh battered his mind as he ran. He'd find her. But with her PTSD, what would this do to her? Would there be long-term effects, even if they didn't hurt her physically?

The image of her crumpled body by the fence of the estate loomed in his mind. Paralyzed with fear. Helpless. Vulnerable.

A beautiful woman someone could prey on. Someone like

the violent kidnappers who held her hostage now.

No. He'd find her before that happened. And he'd rescue her. He had to.

TWENTY-FIVE

Not Walter. Not Walter. The self-reminders pulsed through Nevaeh's mind as quickly as the rapid beats of her heart thudded in her ears.

But the burly man who'd dragged her into this room with his buddy was strong enough to overpower any attempt she might've made to escape his hold. If she'd been more than barely conscious at the time.

As her consciousness slowly returned, so did the fear. It coursed through her limbs, numbing them more than the drug.

She closed her eyes, struggling to breathe through her nose above the duct tape that covered her mouth.

I am not powerless. Not helpless.

The zip tie on her wrists and the gag called her a liar.

But she could deal with those. She forced the reminder to stay in her mind, hoping it would stop the spiraling panic. She knew how to escape zip ties, and then she could remove the tape from her mouth. She could breathe and be free anytime she wanted to.

Until that man or any of the others came back.

They could do anything to her then. Maybe they'd be mad to see she'd freed herself. Would they—

The image of the biggest thug, slamming his fist into her face flashed before her eyes.

She jerked, wincing as if the blow had been real.

No. She opened her eyes and shook her head, her hair rubbing against the wall the thug had propped her against. She had to stay calm. Couldn't give in to the flashbacks.

This was different. They didn't have it in for her. She wasn't the intended victim. She was convenient, a panicked decision.

They'd be scrambling now, trying to figure out what to do to salvage something from their botched kidnapping attempt. They'd have potentially gotten a way bigger ransom from holding D-Chop's kids. But if they were like most kidnappers, they'd try to leverage what they ended up with—her.

Would they contact her family? She snorted, instantly regretting it as the action clogged her only means of getting air at the moment. Her family wouldn't be able to pay a thing, even though they'd want to.

The idea of Pops being contacted by these jerks, told they had his granddaughter, shot hot fury through her torso. They were not going to put him through that. He'd been through enough in his lifetime, and she'd always aimed never to add to his burdens. She wasn't about to mess that up now.

She'd have to get out of here before they made it that far. At this point, they probably wouldn't even know who she was. Unless…

She lowered her bound hands to her hip pocket. Her driver's license and ID were gone.

Right. So they did know who she was. She didn't keep any next of kin or contact info on her. That should help.

But she had to get out of here before they located her family and asked for a ransom her kin didn't have.

She took in her surroundings as her vision sharpened.

Desk, filing cabinets. Some kind of office.

Gritty floor beneath her. The air that seeped into her nostrils smelled of wood and metal. A factory or warehouse?

Windows topped one wall halfway up. If she got closer,

she could probably see out by kneeling. Hopefully without being seen herself.

She'd have to give it a shot.

She eyed the corner of a metal set of shelves. Should she break the zip tie now?

No, she'd better scope out the situation first, in case she needed to pretend she was helpless for longer.

Pretend. Laughter at the bluff she tried to sell herself bubbled in her throat. She swallowed it back. Probably would choke her with the tape over her mouth. That'd be an ironic way to go: *Kidnapped woman dies of lying to herself.*

Whatever. If she needed to bluff herself to get out of here, that's what she'd do.

She leaned forward and pulled her feet under her. She managed to shift to her knees, teetering slightly as her vision tilted.

The rest of the drug should wear off in a few more minutes. By then, she needed to be ready for action.

She moved toward the windows on her knees, sliding one leg forward at a time. Every muscle in her body protested. Probably thanks to her fight with these thugs and the manhandling while she'd been out.

Voices reached her ears as she neared the windows. Male voices.

She ducked a little lower as she crawled forward, trying to make sure her hair wasn't high enough to be spotted.

The voices grew louder. Were they coming to the office?

She reached the nearest window and stopped, ducking low.

"...wasn't my mistake."

"...told me to take her."

The wall between her and the men muffled their gruff voices, keeping her from hearing every word. But there was no missing the frustration in their tight tones.

"...hot."

"Didn't...a looker."

Wait. Were they talking about her? She leaned closer to the window just above her head.

"...we could have some fun while we wait."

Her insides clenched. No doubt what kind of fun the jerk meant.

Panic surged up her throat. She'd choke if it kept climbing.

Use the fear. Use the fear.

But the fear gripped her too hard, quaking shivers through her body, launching flashes of memory she fought to keep at bay.

Phoenix would come. She'd rescue her. The PK-9 team would show up soon.

If they didn't, Nevaeh was finished.

Branson couldn't remember when he'd ever been so angry. Fury blazed a fiery trail through his veins as he stared at the Fun Land security footage Detective Larson was letting him watch.

What kind of men gunned people down in front of little kids? And roughed up women?

Knowing the answer didn't calm the indignation that rose in his chest when the two thugs grabbed Nevaeh and pressed the cloth over her mouth.

He clenched his hands into fists at his side as the thugs tossed her into the back of their van like she was nothing more than a bag of garbage.

"See anyone you recognize? Anything familiar?" Detective Larson's scratchy voice halted the anger spreading like wildfire in Branson's system. Slowed it anyway.

He forced himself to relax his hands, uncurling the fists. "No."

The van was common enough, the angle of the camera wrong for anyone to make the plate. Probably stolen anyway. And the men were dressed in plain jeans and black sweatshirts, ski masks covering their heads. No chance of recognizing them.

"Thanks for letting me see the footage."

The middle-aged detective turned away from the monitor in the manager's office. "It was worth a shot."

"Did Darren say if he saw what direction the van drove when it hit the street?"

Larson pulled a tablet from the pocket of his blazer and flipped it open but didn't lower his gaze to check it. "North. The suspects had already been gone about five minutes when our boys arrived, according to Tremblay, so they didn't try to pursue."

Made sense. The police would gather as much evidence as they could before making their next move.

But Branson couldn't wait that long. Not while Nevaeh was in danger. "Mind if I go out back and take a look at the scene?"

Larson watched him for a moment.

Branson met his gaze.

The detective must've liked what he saw because he nodded. "Just stay out of the way of the lab techs back there, and don't touch anything."

"Thanks." Branson walked at a quick clip from the office and past the officers clustered near the trampolines.

He pushed through the back door into the small parking lot.

The footage from the camera above the door hadn't shown where the first men had come from, but the large trash bins to the left were a likely guess.

They'd shot Darren right away, his body barely visible on the camera before he fell out of view.

That had left Nevaeh all alone to defend the kids.

And she'd done an incredible job. Made every decision the way Branson would've. Even avoiding use of her firearm when it could've hit the kids or drawn return fire that could jeopardize their safety.

Branson stepped away from the door, not going behind

the trash cans since two lab techs were scouring the ground there already. He followed Nevaeh's movements as he recalled them from the footage, scanning the faded blacktop for a sign of something, anything that could offer a clue as to who the kidnappers were and where they might've taken Nevaeh.

Right about there. He paused where he estimated she'd caught up with Samson and Destiny. Where she'd hunkered down to defend the three kids, no matter what.

He shook his head as the image of her standing there with her K-9, the kids clinging to her, pumped both awe and anger through his veins.

She hadn't shown a moment's hesitation or uncertainty from the time the first shot was fired, and she'd always kept the children's safety, not her own, as her obvious objective. She'd used the tools she had—her dog, her gun, and her martial arts training—expertly.

That should've been enough.

He walked a few more feet. There. Could be where she'd switched to the other side of the kids to face the new attackers from the van.

His gut twisted. She hadn't flinched. She'd instead given them the fight of their lives. Looked like she'd broken the arm of the one guy.

But it'd been four against one at the end. Not exactly a fair fight.

She'd gone limp a couple seconds earlier than he'd have expected if they'd used chloroform on the rag they pressed over her mouth.

He wouldn't be surprised if she'd done that on purpose to get the kidnappers away from the kids. He'd have to ask her when he found her.

Because he would find her. He had to. He clenched his jaw as he moved toward where the black van had pulled up and stopped.

His gaze caught on black streaks. Tire tracks from hard braking. Good.

The lab techs could probably get an impression from those that could lead them to ID the type of tire. Hopefully lead them to the van itself.

But that would take time. Too much time. Nevaeh could be…

He didn't dare finish the thought. He'd find her.

He turned around, scanning the blacktop again.

Sunlight glinted off of something.

He crouched. A pool of liquid. Looked like oil.

Maybe the van had an oil leak, and it pooled in the minutes it had parked there.

He stood and stepped over the puddle. Walking a few yards, he kept his gaze on the ground. No more drops. No trail to follow.

Discouragement flickered on his radar for only a second. Doubt and despair were two things he couldn't afford right now. His days of active duty had taught him to keep moving, keep using his skills and stay on target, no matter what.

Victory was just around the corner if he got there first.

Darren had told the police the van turned left out of the parking lot, traveling north.

That's where he would go, too.

He jogged around the building and reached his blue Silverado within thirty seconds. He escaped the parking lot as quickly as he could, turning left.

The kidnappers already had a significant lead of—he checked his watch—seventy-two minutes. It was a long shot to retrace their possible route. Exactly why the police weren't bothering to waste their manpower better used in gathering evidence.

But Branson had to do something. And he'd seen long shots pay off before. He'd picked up some tracking techniques during his service. Might as well see if they worked in the big city.

He owed it to Nevaeh to try. Owed it to anyone who cared about her.

Wait. Her family. He should've notified them. He'd been

so caught up in trying to get her back that he hadn't thought to let anyone else know. She probably had family in the area.

Her boss would know. And he should tell her what had happened anyway.

Branson grabbed the phone he'd left in the console and pressed it into the holder on the dash. He navigated to the saved number for the Phoenix K-9 Agency.

"Phoenix K-9 Security and Detection Agency." The soft, friendly voice of the woman who'd answered when he'd called before came across the line. "Hi. Cora, right? This is Branson Aaberg."

"Hello, Mr. Aaberg. Is something wrong?"

His voice must be broadcasting the tension that clenched his chest. "Yes. Nevaeh has been kidnapped."

A sharp intake of breath came through the phone's speaker. "I'm going to transfer you to Phoenix." Cora's voice sounded stronger than he'd expected. "I'll tell her what you said. Please hold."

Three seconds lapsed as he scanned the street in front of him and the businesses that lined the sidewalk.

"Aaberg." The deep voice of Phoenix Gray was strong and firm. "Do you have details?"

"It happened seventy-four minutes ago." He rapidly brought her up to date on what he knew, finishing by telling her he was on the road, trying to retrace their possible route.

"I have a recent location on her phone."

He blinked. Phoenix must've already been running a trace while he talked. His pulse sped up. "Where is she?"

"The phone was last on Reed Street, three blocks north of Fun Land."

"I'm almost that far now."

"What street are you on?"

He looked for the street sign as he approached a stoplight. "Jacksonport." He braked for the red light.

"Take a right there."

Already in the correct lane, he flicked on his blinker. No oncoming traffic. He zoomed into the turn.

"Then the next left."

"Got it. Then where?"

"Two streets farther, then a right onto Reed."

"Great. Thanks."

"My team and I are on our way."

"Can you notify her family about what's happened?"

A pause met his question. "It won't be necessary to worry them. Nevaeh can tell them afterward if she wants to."

Now that was confidence. He was starting to really like Nevaeh's boss.

"Keep me posted."

"Will do."

"If you beat me to her, don't wait. We'll be right behind you."

"Yes, ma'am." His lips angled in an almost-smile as she ended the call.

She had more bravado than he did. And something told him she could back it up.

He hoped she could. Because he wouldn't mind the help if it meant finding Nevaeh sooner.

He slowed as he pulled onto Reed Street. Not much traffic.

He kept his gaze moving, darting from the road to the sidewalks.

Something dark caught his eye. Not big enough to be a phone, but...

He pulled over to the curb and hopped out of the truck.

Leaning down, he looked at the object. More than one.

Pieces. Smashed, broken insides of a phone.

Frustration heated his chest as he turned back to his pickup.

But this meant he was on the right track. They'd been here, apparently intending to drop Nevaeh's destroyed phone into the trash receptacle that stood on the sidewalk behind the clothing boutique there.

He glanced up the street. Had they continued from there? Or turned around?

A dark streak on the pavement grabbed his gaze.

His gut clenched.

Could it be what he'd been looking for this whole time?

He barely kept himself from running out into the street in front of a passing car.

As soon as the sedan drove by, he dashed into the closest lane. He crouched by the stain.

Oil. From the same van?

He hoped so.

Sliding back into his pickup, he took off at a much slower pace than his itching muscles wanted him to go. But he couldn't miss the trail. If there was one.

He drove over the streak of oil, his gaze pushing ahead, searching for more.

Another streak slashed the pavement.

"Yes." He pumped a clenched fist in the air.

More oil marks marked a path he followed for the rest of the block.

Until he reached an intersection. No stop sign or light. But which way had they gone?

He slowed, probably annoying the driver of the gray sedan behind him.

Wait. Looked like a trickle of fluid on the street to the right.

He whipped the wheel to turn onto the road. He followed the trail of oil for another two blocks.

Then it stopped.

No. It couldn't stop. Not yet. Not until he found Nevaeh.

Frustration rose from his stomach to his chest as he pulled into a driveway of a parking lot for a bank, then backed out to reverse direction.

He lifted his gaze this time, no longer keeping it locked on the road as he headed for where he'd seen the last oil spill.

A couple stores. A bar. Restaurant.

And an alley.

Or was that a driveway?

He slowed and pulled into the drive he'd mistaken for an alley before.

It was long enough he couldn't see what it led to from the road.

But as he drove a little farther in, a large building met his gaze. A warehouse. Looked old, which explained why it was an anomaly hidden behind more modern-looking buildings that housed newer businesses.

Adrenaline seeped into his veins. This could be it. The perfect place to hide a kidnapping victim. At least for a little while.

He scanned the parking lot that expanded out from the driveway and lined the front of the warehouse. He needed a place to park his Silverado where it wouldn't be spotted.

Four vehicles parked in stalls along the building. Maybe hidden in plain sight was the way to go.

He pulled up between a black sedan and a silver SUV. He dropped out of the pickup, leaving the driver's door to rest against the frame.

If the kidnappers were here, no need to bring them all down on him at once thanks to a door slamming.

He crept behind the other two vehicles, then along the warehouse, aiming for the left side of the building where he hoped to find an entrance.

He crept to the corner of the wall and peered around it.

A black van stood under a carport awning. A van exactly like the one in the security footage.

And two men in black sweatshirts stood talking on a loading dock.

He'd found more than an entrance. He'd found Nevaeh.

TWENTY-SIX

Zip ties off her wrists. Horrible tape off her mouth.

Nevaeh focused on her mental escape checklist. Nothing else. Not the panic that simmered close to the surface anytime she thought of fighting the kidnappers up close. Mainly that biggest guy.

Her breaths shortened as memories knocked on the door she battled to keep closed to them.

She wasn't at that step yet. She'd need to get out of this office first.

Especially if she didn't want to face the thugs head on.

She was lucky they hadn't returned so far. From the snippets she'd heard when the two talkers were near the office, it sounded like they were waiting for someone. And they weren't happy about it.

They'd opted to leave her alone. Something about the *he* they were waiting for not liking it if they messed with her.

It seemed she'd been taken by the hired help of the actual kidnapper. She'd figured that the moment she'd seen these jokers.

It could be a good thing if the person who hired them showed up here. Then she could identify the culprit. Sounded like it was a man. That knowledge alone could narrow their list of suspects for who had it in for D-Chop.

Unless the head honcho here was still hired by someone else, like Jill.

Going for his kids was definitely an escalation from the previous scare tactics.

What would the culprit do now that the plan had failed and they'd gotten her instead?

Might try to leverage her with D-Chop, see if he cared about a lowly security contractor.

She could see the headlines now: *Iconic Rapper's Female Security Guard Kidnapped...A Lover's Tiff?*

She snorted at the perfect imitation of a tabloid's take on this situation.

The inner humor took her mind off the men she'd have to face outside the office. But it wasn't helping her get past the lock on the door.

Who would've thought such an ancient lock still existed? One that needed to be opened with a key from either side. This is when she could really use a hairpin. If she owned one.

Or a pocketknife like Sofia always carried.

Nevaeh made a mental note to get one as soon as she got out of here.

Past the three or more men.

She forced herself to take a breath despite the tightening in her chest. She could do that. She just needed to take them on separately. One at a time.

She'd handled that one guy who grabbed her first in the parking lot. She nodded to herself. She was strong, dangerous. They'd better—

Noise outside the office stalled her pep talk.

She leaned closer to the door.

Voices. Movement.

Maybe the person they'd been waiting for had arrived?

She crouched and inched toward the closest window.

Another noise. A shout?

A pop cracked the air. No mistaking that sound.

Another gunshot exploded.

She peered out the bottom of the window.

Couldn't see anything.

Shots meant conflict. An enemy to the kidnappers.

The PK-9 team? Or a double cross by whoever hired the thugs?

She needed to be ready in case her second guess was the right one.

She backed into the corner behind where the door would swing in when opened.

What if the bigger guy came in first? Her throat started to close. She needed Alvarez here. He could take the man down for her.

She needed someone. Anyone but her. Alone. Against a man like Walter.

His face broke through her defenses, loomed in front of her with that twisted grin. He—

"Nevaeh!" The deep voice shattered the memory. "Nevaeh!"

Was that—

The door crashed in, halting the surge of hope that shot through her body.

The man who must've kicked it in stood in the doorway, filling it with his huge size, a mountain of muscle and power.

Branson.

Nevaeh came out of nowhere, flying toward him. She landed against Branson's chest, hard enough he had to brace himself to keep from stepping backward. But he'd never felt anything so good in his life.

He wrapped his arms around her, forcing himself to be gentle when what he really wanted to do was squeeze her so tight, she could never be taken from him again.

Her body trembled.

"Nevaeh, are you all right? Did they hurt you?"

Her hair tickled his chin as she moved her head against his chest, shaking it in denial.

"They didn't hurt you?" His heart pounded against his ribs as he waited.

"No." Her voice was weaker than normal, but the answer calmed his pulse. For a second. Until he became aware of how she felt pressed against him, fitting him like a glove.

His heart rate sped for a different reason as heat traveled through him all the way down to his toes.

What if he'd lost the chance to hold her like this? What if he'd lost her?

Another question followed on the heels of the first instinctive ones. When had holding her become important, something he wanted?

The answer rushed into his mind just as fast, as unexpectedly—when there was a chance he might never see her again.

Or maybe these feelings for her had been growing every day that he thought about her, saw her, talked to her.

He wanted to talk to her more, get to know all about her. Wanted to hold her like this for much, much longer.

But she pulled away. Not far. Her small hands still lingered on his sides, and she stayed within the loose hold of his arms.

She was even more beautiful up close. Her flawless skin tempted him to lift his hand and run his thumb over her cheek, just to feel if it was as soft as it looked. But he kept his hand where it was, nearly as happy to rest gently on her back.

She finally lifted her lids, tilting her head up so her gaze reached his face.

His breath caught. Signs of stress and fear lingered around her eyes, but the dark brown orbs were filled with relief, maybe gratitude, and something else. Something so soft and wonderful that it made him want to lean down and taste her full lips.

But those lips moved as she spoke. "Thank you." Her eyes seemed to search his.

"You're welcome." He wanted to say much more, something that didn't make it sound like she owed him. Because, if anything, he owed her for risking her life to protect D-Chop's kids. He cleared his throat. "You were amazing."

Her eyebrows lifted.

"I saw the security footage at Fun Land. Thank you for protecting the kids."

She twisted slightly in his arms, glancing toward the open doorway. "I should've asked. Where are the men? The ones who took me?"

"They're incapacitated at the moment." He'd been able to render them all unconscious as he'd worked his way to Nevaeh. Thankfully without lethal techniques.

Her mouth quirked as she scanned him from his chest to his face. "You like a giant Amalia Pérez or something?"

His turn to lift his eyebrows in question.

She chuckled. "That was Sofia when she was with the CIA. Girl has crazy skills you wouldn't believe." As she spoke, she relaxed in his arms in such a comfortable way that his heart pumped faster.

He could get used to this.

A sound echoed. Inside the warehouse.

A dog barking?

"Alvarez!" Nevaeh pulled away completely, leaving his arms feeling empty.

Or maybe that was his heart, bereft without her.

"The PK-9 crew is here." She moved toward the empty doorway, then paused. She looked back with a smile that nearly stopped his heart "You coming?"

Then she did it. She held out her slim, lovely hand, low and angled in a clear invitation.

He covered her hand with his, interlocking their fingers as he followed her out of the office to meet the Phoenix K-9 team. He ignored the warnings in his head that told him he shouldn't hold her hand, shouldn't send the wrong signals when he couldn't date a non-Christian.

Because right now, his heart's will was stronger, telling him to follow her anywhere and never let her go.

TWENTY-SEVEN

Nevaeh watched the women of PK-9 and their dogs in the breakroom at headquarters, smiling at the way Sof teased Cora and Bris about wedding colors and flower arrangements. She stroked Cannenta's short fur as the corgi mix sat on her lap, warming her legs.

"May I get you more coffee, Nevaeh?" Cora smiled from the love seat where she was poised on a cushion, Jana lying on the floor by her feet. Even from this distance, Nevaeh could see the worry that added thin lines to Cora's milky white skin.

"I'm good, thanks."

Poor Cora had been hovering since Nevaeh arrived about five minutes ago. Cora's mothering instincts meant she had to make sure every team member was okay at all times. She'd better have some kids soon so she could make good use of all those mama tendencies. "Is there anything else I can get you?"

Nevaeh chuckled. Cora was probably worried because Nevaeh wasn't as talkative or peppy as usual. "Nah, I'm fine, Cora. Really." And she was. Thanks to a surprisingly calm night of sleep, probably because she knew Phoenix and Dag were patrolling outside her house, Nevaeh felt about ninety percent better today.

Except for the weird feeling she hadn't been able to shake since the first time she'd thought of Branson that morning, about two minutes after she woke up. It was almost like she missed him. The gigantic, muscular bodyguard. The man who'd rescued her singlehandedly.

"I know that smile." Sof's voice drew Nevaeh's attention reluctantly away from the handsome face and the soft blue eyes that had darkened just before they'd lowered to her lips. Like he was going to kiss her.

"What exactly were you and your bodyguard doing before we showed up?" Sof grinned from the armchair near Bris, who sat on the other end of the love seat with Cora wearing a matching grin.

A flush crawled into Nevaeh's cheeks. But thank goodness nobody would see it. No way was she going to share she'd thrown herself at him or that he hadn't seemed to mind a bit. That she'd wanted to stay in his arms forever and then some. That she kind of wished he'd kissed her. "He was making sure I wasn't hurt."

Sof and Bris laughed, Jazz joining in with a chuckle from her seat on the sofa next to Nevaeh, her hand stroking Gaston's furry ear.

The big Newfie had somehow claimed the end cushion before anyone had managed to sit there. He'd turned around at some point to rest his head on Jazz's lap, the rest of his body sprawled to the end of the sofa.

Flash didn't seem to mind the claim on his partner. He looked pretty content lying on the floor between the coffee table and Jazz's feet.

"Just how did he do that?" Sof snickered.

"Really, ladies." Cora's pale cheeks showed every bit of her blush. "I'm sure he was a perfect gentleman."

"Oh, of course he was." Bris sent Nevaeh a grin. "But you can't expect us to resist the chance to rib Nev. After all, this is the first time she's fallen for a guy since I've known her."

"I haven't fallen for him." Nevaeh floundered to find

some argument that could deny the truth her heart had been confirming all morning.

"Oh?" Bris's teasing twinkle sparkled in her eyes. "Then I suppose there's some other explanation for why you two were holding hands when we came to your rescue?"

Nevaeh swallowed. They'd seen? She'd let go of his hand right away when she'd reached them. Apparently not soon enough.

"You forget, Bris." Jazz gave the brunette a glance with a deadpan tone. "He beat us. He came to her rescue first."

"Oh, I see." Bris gave an exaggerated nod. "So we would've gotten all that affection if we'd been first."

"Of course." Sof's serious expression broke with her laughter.

Alvarez popped up from his lying position in front of Nevaeh, giving her a perfect excuse to look at him instead of trying unsuccessfully to convince the girls of something they all knew wasn't true. She'd expected Alvarez to join Raksa and Toby in the open area beyond Phoenix's armchair like he usually did, but he stuck to her like glue today. Her brave boy. She'd missed him, too.

She scratched behind his ear in his favorite itchy spot as he sat beside her knee. They both would need a little recovery time from the events of yesterday.

Phoenix and Dag entered the breakroom, and the usual momentary hush fell over the jokesters.

But eagerness pressed words against Nevaeh's closed lips. She'd been planning an argument all morning to convince Phoenix to let her go on patrol at D-Chop's estate tonight. She'd get to see Branson that way. But springing it on the boss probably wouldn't get the answer she wanted. Phoenix would likely say Nevaeh needed more recovery time.

The boss sat in the armchair, Dag looking just as ready and alert as his partner as he lay on the floor beside her. Phoenix lifted her wrist to check her watch. "We'll have a debrief in two minutes, provided our guest is here."

Nevaeh looked at the other girls, but they watched

Phoenix with confused expressions, too. Well, except Sof, who Nevaeh suspected was never surprised or confused and Cora, who probably knew what the boss was talking about.

Nevaeh landed her gaze on Jazz. But Jazz just shrugged and shook her head.

A buzzer sounded, making Nevaeh start.

Her nerves must not have gotten the message they could chill now. Though she'd probably only heard the buzzer one other time in all the years of team meetings in the breakroom. "Isn't that the front door?"

Cora nodded and glanced at the open screen of her notebook computer that sat on the coffee table. Probably checking the security camera feed. "Mr. Aaberg is here."

Nevaeh's heart dropped into her stomach. Branson? Here?

"Bring him in."

Cora hurried from the breakroom as heat coursed through Nevaeh's veins, and her pulse raced.

Phoenix stood and walked around the love seat toward the open door, Dag keeping pace at her side. "I've invited Aaberg to share intel concerning his client." She paused and angled toward the team. "We're going to find the culprit behind the kidnapping and end the threat to Nevaeh. Aaberg can help us do that faster with the information he has."

"Great idea." Bris nodded.

Jazz nudged Nevaeh's elbow. "Hey." She lowered her voice to a whisper as she leaned close. "You aren't going to swoon, are you?"

Nevaeh shook her head.

But then Branson followed Cora into the room. He stopped by Phoenix, and she said something to him.

Nevaeh couldn't hear that or anything else. Her pulse pounded too loudly in her ears.

He looked her way, and a smile curved his mouth, brightening his blue eyes.

Goodness. She just might swoon after all.

If Branson's heart thumped any harder against his ribs, the whole Phoenix K-9 team might hear it.

"Branson?" Cora's soft voice drew his attention reluctantly away from Nevaeh, probably just in time before his enjoyment in looking at her was too obvious. "You can sit there, if you like." She gestured to the empty cushion on the love seat next to Bristol Jones.

The furniture was oversized, so that would work. Better than one of the armchairs that looked like they were sized for women, not a full-grown man.

"Thanks." He walked over to sit where she indicated, bumping into the too-close coffee table. Talk about being the proverbial bull in a China shop.

Two, then three dogs crowded around him, somehow fitting between the furniture better than he had.

He petted the head of the black Lab, the most exuberant of the bunch. "Toby, right?" He glanced up, and Bristol nodded. "Jana I just met out front." He stroked the golden retriever's ears. "And...," he gave the striking German shepherd a scratch under the chin, "starts with an *r*?"

"Raksa." Sofia gave him a smile.

His gaze immediately drifted across the way to the person he'd most like to see a smile from.

Nevaeh's widened eyes darted away. She wasn't back to being nervous around him, was she? Even after what had happened yesterday?

He nodded at Jazz and returned the beaming, maybe somewhat amused smile she gave him. What would it be like to sit where she was, right next to Nevaeh?

The woman somehow grew more stunning every time he saw her. The red sweater she wore this morning complimented her skin and lips.

A small dog he'd never seen before sat on her lap. He nodded toward the cute mix. "Who's your friend?"

Nevaeh's eyebrows lifted as if she was surprised he spoke

to her. Why that would be surprising, he didn't know. They'd just held hands yesterday.

"Cannenta."

He smiled at the dog who watched him with soft, amber-colored eyes. "Nice to meet you, Cannenta."

"Do you know everyone else here?" Cora's voice carried the smile she wore.

He glanced around the room. "I think so. Except for the Newfoundland there." He grinned at the chocolate-colored, rug-like dog sprawled on the end of the sofa by Jazz.

"That's Gaston. He's very at home here." Sofia's deadpan brought a grin to Branson's face.

"I can see that." He also spotted the hint of a smile that angled Nevaeh's lips. His pulse skipped a beat in response. What could he do to generate a real smile from her?

"We were about to begin our debrief of yesterday's events." Phoenix's serious tone brought him back down to earth. And to the reason she'd invited him here.

Cora went to a large whiteboard on wheels at the far side of the room and pulled it around the sofa, parking it in front of what looked like a snack table. "Oh, may I offer you some coffee, Branson?"

He shook his head. "No, thanks." Never wanted to be dependent on caffeine to wake up in the morning.

The board featured a sketch on the far left side drawn in black marker. Looked like a visual representation of the attack that had resulted in Nevaeh being kidnapped.

He clenched his jaw. The memory of the security footage, what they'd done to her, still boiled his blood.

"Okay. As you see, we have a reconstruction of the incident." Cora glanced at Phoenix, who stood on the other side of the whiteboard with her tan dog.

Funny how the leader of the Phoenix K-9 Agency was so much smaller than he'd expected. When he'd met her at the warehouse yesterday, he'd realized he must've pictured her as an unusually large woman with the size to match her deep voice and commanding persona.

But she was only slightly taller than Nevaeh with a slim figure. Very pretty, actually, though she seemed to hide her looks behind the baseball cap she wore then and this morning.

He'd learned within only a few minutes in her presence that she didn't need size. The confidence he'd admired over the phone was even more palpable in person, defining her entire demeanor and giving her an air that reminded him of Captain Killian, the fiercest Naval officer he'd ever served under.

"We've all seen the security footage, and I can make the copy available to anyone who wants to examine it further." Cora wrote a heading next to the sketch that read, *Suspects*. Then she added another heading of *Motive*.

"Branson," she directed her blue eyes at him, "we're hoping you can help us fill in these lists more accurately. Do you feel D-Chop's wife belongs here?" She pointed the tip of the marker at the *Suspects* list.

"Absolutely. After the fireworks incident, she moved to the top of my list." He glanced at the women, all their attention trained on him. As a man, he couldn't miss how lovely they all were. Each one of them was beautiful enough to fit in with the celebrities he was used to being around, even with about a quarter of the amount of makeup. These women weren't trying to be noticed. And that made them far more attractive in his book.

"Would you mind sharing why that is?"

He nodded at Cora. "Sure. Peter Volrath, D-Chop's assistant, escorted her into the garage the morning of the fireworks. She stayed in there for six minutes and forty seconds alone before she drove her Ferrari out and left. That's enough time for her to have set up the fireworks and remote activation."

"Would she have the knowledge to do that?" Bris's question, so similar to the thought process he and Louis had walked through, made Branson's mouth twitch with a smile.

"She's not mechanical, but she's smart enough to have learned how to do it if someone showed her."

"Her motive?" Cora wrote *Custody* in the *Motives* column.

"That's right." Branson nodded. "But you could also add the settlement. Her lawyer's actively negotiating with D-Chop's lawyer for a bigger financial settlement. It's possible she could sweeten her deal and gain custody if she makes D-Chop look unsafe for the children. She could use custody as a bargaining chip."

"Would she do that?" Cora looked at him with her eyebrows pinched together, as if she were genuinely bothered by the idea.

Branson thought through what he knew about Jill and chose his words carefully. He didn't want to slander anyone. "I believe she cares about her kids. But she's also used to a certain lifestyle and is highly career focused. She always wants to keep climbing the ladder."

"Of popularity?" Bristol turned her head toward him.

"Yes. She lives for media attention, but she also wants the money that comes with notoriety. There isn't much she wouldn't do to get that."

"Even kidnapping her own kids?" Sofia's dark gaze landed on Branson from the armchair where she sat.

"I'm not sure." It was the question he'd turned over in his mind several times that morning. "I don't think she'd want to scare the kids. But if she felt they would be safe, ultimately, and that it would get her what she wants, she might do it."

"She'd do that to her children?"

He shifted his gaze to Cora. "I think she could rationalize it if she convinced herself it was better for them. Maybe as a way to jumpstart their popularity for a future career like hers. Her own mother pulled some drastic stunts and had Jill do things no normal parent would to further her career in the public eye."

"You mean the reality show and all the...other things." Cora's eyes filled with what looked like sadness.

"Exactly. She might think of the kidnapping as a sort of reality show moment for her kids that would put them in the public eye and gain them sympathy. She already has social media fan accounts for each of her children."

"How sweet." Sofia's tone carried obvious sarcasm.

Sadly, such behavior and mentalities were common in the world Branson worked in. But they didn't need to hear about the systemic problems among celebrities.

"It makes sense." Bristol looked toward the whiteboard. "In my years as a cop, I saw people do some crazy things, even parents, for less motivation."

So she used to be a cop. That explained a lot. How many of the others on the team had law enforcement backgrounds? Hadn't Nevaeh mentioned Sofia being with the CIA?

"Have you isolated other suspects?" Phoenix gave him an unreadable stare. Having her stand so close to Cora, on either side of the board, was a study in contrasts.

The willowy and elegant blonde seemed to wear her heart on her sleeve. Phoenix, dressed in functional clothing that looked as tough and matter-of-fact as she seemed to be, didn't give away a thought let alone emotion. Her ready, wide-legged stance was much more practical and prepared than elegant. Really did remind him of Captain Killian. No one had been able to figure him out either. But they'd all respected him.

"I've created a list. There's the staff." He rattled off their names and positions, figuring the team had probably already thought of them.

"I wasn't aware of the chef." Cora finished writing his name, Bartlemay Cox, on the board. "How often does he come to the estate?"

"Every evening before dinner. And I should mention I don't think Marsha would be involved, especially in the kidnapping. She adores D-Chop's kids. I can't see her putting them in any danger."

Cora added a question mark to Marsha's name on the board.

"What about motives for the other staff members?" Sofia glanced at him.

"I don't see a motive for any of my security staff, and, of course, I trust them since I already put them through a thorough check before hiring. Not sure what Cox's motive could be unless he was paid by someone else. But he wasn't on the grounds the day of the fireworks. I think D-Chop had a fling with Jaycee when he first hired her as a maid, but that's cooled. She could hold a grudge. The security footage didn't show her entering the garage the day of the fireworks, but she could've jimmied the window off-camera. It was so smashed by the fireworks, we couldn't tell if it had been forced or broken."

"You said the groundskeeper went into the garage that day?" Cora tapped her marker next to Brian's name on the board.

"Yes. Again, I don't know of a motive, but people can hide those things. I've thought about interviewing him to see if he has a past with D-Chop I don't know about. Something that could make him resent his boss."

"What about Larry LeSalle?" Nevaeh's voice made his heart skip a beat and brought his gaze happily to her gorgeous face. "It was all over the news when D-Chop fired him."

Branson couldn't help the smile that stretched his mouth, just from looking at Nevaeh. "Yeah, LeSalle was pretty steamed. He manages other major celebrities, though, so it didn't break his career. He still lives in Los Angeles, so the logistics would be tricky for him, especially the fireworks incident."

"Unless he's working with Jill or someone else." Nevaeh met his gaze for a moment before glancing away.

"Good point." He kept his attention on her face, glad he did when her eyes lifted again at his remark. "There could be more than one person behind this."

"Let's include Frank Jones on the list." Phoenix looked at Cora, who wrote the bitter father's name on the board. "He's been released from jail since D-Chop dropped the charges, but he has a verified alibi for the time of the kidnapping. However, he could have hired the men for that and perhaps paid the groundskeeper to set up the fireworks. Or the incidents could be unconnected."

Cora nodded, then glanced at Branson. "What about other friends or acquaintances of D-Chop? I could only find the obvious ones the media highlights."

"That's where the list gets very extensive." Branson ran a hand over his hair. "I asked Peter to give me a list of all D-Chop's friends and associates now and in the past."

"Bet he loved putting that together." Nevaeh's mouth shaped in a cute smirk.

Branson grinned. "He wasn't too happy about the idea. And I could see why, once I got the list. It's five pages. And he also pointed out that most of the people on that list love D-Chop. He's a generous guy, always ready to help his friends."

Nevaeh nodded like she knew from personal experience. Probably why she'd told D-Chop she owed him the first day she came on patrol.

"Would you be willing to share that list with us?"

"Of course." He switched his gaze to Cora. "I'll email it to you."

"What about the band members?" Jazz glanced at Branson. "Do any of them have reasons to be unhappy with D-Chop? Or want money from a ransom?"

All eyes turned to Branson again. "I've spoken with Kicker at the hospital. He doesn't seem bitter, especially not against D-Chop. He seems to feel he took one for the team and is glad D-Chop wasn't injured. D-Chop gave him his big break hiring him as his hype man. He's always seemed grateful."

"What about the other band members and the new hype man?" Jazz tucked her red hair behind one ear. "The new guy could've sabotaged Kicker intentionally to get his spot, or if that was random, one of the others could be trying to get at D-Chop."

"Jonesy Baker is Kicker's replacement. He's pretty new to the business. Doesn't have much experience yet, but according to D-Chop, he's the nephew of one of his old pals."

"Another favor." Nevaeh drew Branson's attention as easily as a fire alarm. "Did Baker have reason to expect he'd be next in line?"

"D-Chop said he was going to pick K. I. Deep, but he had just taken a job with ZayDee, another rapper. D-Chop apparently didn't even know Jonesy was a hype man until he happened to be talking to the guy's uncle on the phone after the fire."

"Could have been planned, but not necessarily." Phoenix folded her arms across her dark gray sweater. "It would've been difficult to predict with any certainty who would be injured, if anyone, in the fire. That makes intimidating D-Chop, damaging him financially, or the custody issue the most likely motives."

She leveled her gaze at Branson. "Do you know of anyone in Jacquet's entourage—a staff member, or any suspect we've listed—who drives a black Dodge Ram pickup?"

Odd question. Branson cycled through the vehicles he'd seen among the people associated with Jill or D-Chop. Jill probably had a rule against pickup trucks, given how much she disliked them. She and D-Chop had a huge blowup one time when the rapper wanted to get one to drive to an event. "No, I don't believe so."

"Have you seen a vehicle like that following you or your client?"

He watched Phoenix more intently, looking for something in her expression that would clue him in on the reason for these questions. "No. I always check for tails, whether I'm with D-Chop or not." A lasting symptom of having served overseas. "There haven't been any." He still couldn't interpret anything from her expression or her eyes. "Why do you ask?"

"Since you're assisting us in finding the party or parties behind the threats to your client, you should know the additional trail we've been following." Phoenix lowered her hands to her hips. "The culprit, or the person hired to carry out some of the incidents, could drive a black Dodge Ram."

"How do you know that?"

"Because he was following me." Nevaeh's response nearly knocked the wind out of him.

His gaze instantly swung to her face. "What?"

Nevaeh glanced at her boss before continuing, hesitation in her tone. "Someone in that kind of pickup started following me after the fire at PowerSource."

Jazz nodded. "And I saw the same truck in the lot that night. No one was in it."

Nevaeh looked at her friend. "I could never get the plate number because it's splattered with mud."

"You said 'he.'" Which meant she'd seen the driver, the stalker. The word stuck in his craw even though he hadn't said it out loud. Nevaeh had a stalker. The woman who had already been through so much. The woman he—

"Yeah. I got a look at him—not a very good one—when he..." Nevaeh slid her tongue between her lips and glanced away. "When he looked in my window one night."

"He *what*?" Branson leaned forward, his whole body tensing with his tone.

Every woman in the room looked at him, along with more than one dog. Several of them protection dogs who stared at him a little too intently.

He let out a slow breath and forced himself to lean back. "Sorry. I didn't mean to raise my voice."

Cora smiled. "We understand." Something in her gaze said she understood a little too much. That she realized he cared for Nevaeh.

He wasn't exactly doing a good job hiding that from anyone at the moment. He unclenched his fists and forced his hands to rest on his legs. "Did he...," Branson locked his gaze on Nevaeh's brown eyes, "...hurt you?"

A grunt drew his attention to Sofia and the smirk on her

face. "More like the opposite. She and Alvarez gave him the scare of his life."

"We did charge out after him, and he took off." Nevaeh grinned, infusing Branson's taut muscles with relief. "I couldn't ID him because he wore a ski mask, but it was obviously a man. Big build. In a black sweatshirt and jeans."

"Has he come back?" Branson wasn't sure he wanted to hear the answer. But he had to know. And had to find out who the man was who would dare stalk Nevaeh.

"Nope." Her tone was casual. "I don't think he'll try that angle now that he knows the welcome he'll get."

At least she didn't seem too bothered by the man. That unexpected courage showing itself again.

"Especially with Flash and me there." Jazz nudged Nevaeh with her elbow, earning a smile.

"Oh, yeah. Ain't nobody gonna mess with you two."

"We think that fits one of our theories as to his identity." Cora wrote *Masked Man* in the suspects list on the board. "Given that his vehicle was at the PowerSource Center the night of the fire, and he began tailing Nevaeh soon after, we believe he could have been the one to set the fire and could be tied to all or some of the subsequent threats against your client."

"But why would he follow her?" Branson glanced at Cora. "If he felt threatened by the additional security and the K-9s around D-Chop, why not target Sofia and Jazz, too?"

"That's what we wondered." Jazz's mouth straightened into a serious line. "We think the guy must believe Nevaeh saw him at PowerSource, maybe doing something to the equipment or being somewhere he shouldn't have been. Something that could identify him as the culprit."

Branson swung his gaze back to Nevaeh.

She shrugged. "If I did, I didn't notice anything suspicious about him. I saw your security people that night, and Peter, of course. The band members. Stagehands. But no one who seemed out of place or up to no good. I checked everyone I saw for IDs."

"Could one of the band members or stagehands have monkeyed with the pyrotechnics while you were there?" Bristol leaned forward and looked at Nevaeh.

"They were all near that equipment on stage, but I wasn't watching them very closely since they were cleared to be there."

"Of course." Jazz's tone took on a slight defensive edge as she spoke up for her friend. "We were only supposed to watch for people who weren't allowed back there."

"I don't think anyone would have chanced tampering with the equipment when they could be seen anyway."

Branson nodded at Sofia's good point. "I agree. That would've been foolish, and someone would've remembered seeing it if the culprit had done it in front of witnesses. But I could see the perp being afraid Nevaeh saw something that wasn't obvious to anyone but him."

"If that's true," Sofia pushed her fingers through her thick black hair, "then having his cronies accidentally grab Nevaeh during the kidnapping attempt could've been his chance to get rid of her."

Branson's gut twisted at the idea. And the memory of finding Nevaeh locked in the warehouse. The way she'd thrown herself into his arms. He swallowed back the lump in his throat.

"I think he was maybe going to. I heard the men talking about waiting for someone to get there to find out what to do with me." Nevaeh's gaze landed on Branson. "But you showed up before they could do anything." Her eyes softened, filling with trust, admiration, and another emotion he didn't dare identify.

He stopped breathing. He'd never had a woman look at him like that before. As if he was…a hero.

"It's a viable theory." Phoenix's statement made Nevaeh look away. "But not the only one."

Cora seemed to take that as her cue, and she added a new section at the bottom corner of the board titled *Nevaeh*.

Branson's chest tightened. Given the news she had a stalker, what kind of list was this going to be?

"I traced all of the inmates the record shows were at Whitlow Heights Prison when you were." Cora glanced Nevaeh's direction.

Nevaeh was in prison? Disbelief sucked Branson's oxygen away as he looked at her. That couldn't be possible.

"To boil down my findings to the most pertinent information, six who were released live in the Twin Cities area." Cora rattled off six first and last names, and then wrote them under the new heading in neat handwriting. "Nevaeh, do you think any of these people would have a grudge against you?"

"No. I don't even remember meeting three of them." Nevaeh stared at the board. "And I knew all the inmates in the pods I was assigned to. But it's a big facility."

Of course. Relief soothed the tension coiling Branson's insides. She must have worked there as a correctional officer, which would've given her security experience prior to Phoenix K-9.

"Should I still keep them on the board?" Cora looked at Phoenix.

Her baseball cap bobbed as she gave a short nod. "They could have grudges Nevaeh isn't aware of."

So they were considering that the stalker could be unrelated to D-Chop's situation, too. Good to cover all the possibilities. His respect for the Phoenix K-9 Agency grew even more. They seemed skilled at investigating as well as security. It would be challenging to get the kind of information Cora was saying she'd tracked down.

"What about..." Nevaeh paused, her gaze dropping to her lap.

"The other possibility?" Cora's vague terms perked Branson's senses. Was he the reason she was being vague?

"All of our information still indicates Los Angeles. But we haven't been able to obtain physical confirmation yet."

"I'm putting more pressure on my contact to verify the current location." Phoenix turned to the board, appearing to scan the contents. "In the meantime, we continue to pursue the possible connection to D-Chop. It may be the quickest way to eliminate Nevaeh's problem."

As if a stalker who could be violent was a minor, everyday type of difficulty she could solve without breaking a sweat. Branson hid the smile that wanted to emerge. This Phoenix Gray was great.

She rotated toward the group. "We need more information. Aaberg and Nevaeh, I want you to interview the primary suspects together. In the meantime, we'll gather more intel through our sources."

Phoenix's last sentence was virtually lost on Branson as his gaze hopped to Nevaeh.

Her brown eyes were already on him.

"Aaberg, do you have time to interview Jill Jacquet with Nevaeh today?"

Branson couldn't pull his attention from Nevaeh as he responded. "I have to bring our new security guard up to speed when his flight gets in mid-morning." Travis Taylor had been on the security team when Branson had worked for Modella Hughes. The experienced protection specialist should have no problem covering the estate with Louis. And Branson wasn't about to let anything keep him from spending time with Nevaeh. "Then I'm all yours."

Nevaeh's mouth opened in a brilliant smile.

This was going to be a very good day.

TWENTY-EIGHT

"You know, I wouldn't be talking to you if you hadn't done what you did." Jill Jacquet leaned forward from the sofa to lift her wine glass off the marble coffee table in front of her. The bent-over position let her surgically enhanced assets hang mostly uncovered, barely tucked into a lowcut top that was cropped and tied in a knot above her belly button.

Nevaeh glanced at Branson, sitting in a large striped armchair, to see if he was drooling yet.

The man opened the small notepad he'd brought for the interview and jotted something with a pen, as if D-Chop's soon-to-be ex-wife had said something significant.

Was he trying to avoid looking? That would be unusual for a guy.

"I suppose I should thank you." Jill stared at Nevaeh over the rim of her glass as she leaned back.

"You don't have to."

The woman pursed lips she must've covered with an inch of lipstick. "Don't get me wrong. I'm grateful you protected my kids. And I'm sorry you were kidnapped." She paused like she wanted a response.

Nevaeh gave her a nod.

"But D-Chop is bad news. I knew my kids weren't safe with him. That's why I want custody."

"Has anyone been watching your children, or has anything unusual happened around them when they've been with you?"

Jill shifted her dark gaze to Branson, lifting her sculpted eyebrows with the haughtiness of royalty. "Certainly not. They're perfectly safe with me."

"I understand." Branson wrote something else in his notepad. He was really taking this detective role seriously. "Do you have any idea who might have wanted to kidnap your children?"

"Why should I know something like that?" Offense lifted the pitch of Jill's voice.

Alvarez stood from where he'd been lying by Nevaeh's feet in front of the sofa she occupied facing Jill. Nevaeh stroked his head to calm him.

She could tell Jill had evil intent almost as easily as the K-9 could in this case. But was that evil aimed at D-Chop, her children, or everyone who didn't prioritize Jill Jacquet above all else? The woman acted more like a spoiled brat than an adult with a billion-dollar fortune.

Even so, if they were going to get anything useful out of this interview, they'd have to get on Jill's good side. Nevaeh forced a smile. "I know most people adore you." Out the corner of her eye, she saw Branson throw her a look. But she kept her focus on the privileged woman in front of her. "I mean, why wouldn't they?"

A self-satisfied smile cut into the stretched olive-toned skin that had seen too many plastic surgeries. "Exactly. I don't know anyone who'd want to hurt me or my kids."

"Jealousy is a powerful motivator."

Jill's smile faded, but she held Nevaeh's gaze without irritation.

"You know tons of women are jealous of you. Your beauty. The life you lead. Maybe one of them would want to target you or your kids?"

Jill's lips pressed together. "It's true. Every woman wants to be me."

Not every woman, honey. Nevaeh kept the smile plastered on her face as she forced down the retort she wanted to launch.

Jill sighed dramatically. "And I suppose some of them are jealous because they can't be me. But harming me? I don't know about that."

"We believe ransom was probably the goal in the attempted kidnapping." Branson glanced at Nevaeh before returning his attention to Jill. "Could be someone who simply wants money."

A sultry laugh came from deep in Jill's throat. "Oh, baby. Doesn't everybody?" Her gaze skated over Branson's muscled physique. "Although there are other things in life just as enjoyable."

Nevaeh stifled an eye roll. Was there anything this woman didn't get that she wanted?

Branson met Jill's gaze. "Like motherhood?"

A snicker bubbled up Nevaeh's throat, and she tried to choke it back. Which turned it into a cough instead.

"You okay?" Branson leaned toward her.

But she spotted the twinkle in his blue eyes. He knew exactly what he'd done.

Heat spread through her torso, and not from the coughing. How many men would've knowingly shot down a chance for a fling with Jill Jacquet? He had the looks to catch her eye, and he probably knew it. But he hadn't ogled her once since they'd arrived. And even when she started coming on to him, he'd answered with a spectacular misdirect.

"Yeah." Another little cough escaped. "I'm good."

He gave her a smile, then turned toward Jill again. "I don't want to take up more of your time, but we're trying to ensure your children's future safety with these questions. As their mother, I'm sure that's important to you."

She shifted before setting her wine glass back on the table. "Of course."

"Great. Just a few more questions then." Branson waited until the woman straightened before looking at her again. Man, the guy was too much. Was he on his best behavior because Nevaeh was with him? Most men she knew wouldn't even hide their wandering eyes with their girlfriends right beside them.

"Do you think this kidnapping attempt will jeopardize D-Chop's chances at custody?" Branson threw her the direct question.

"I sure hope so." Jill let out a smug laugh.

"That's not what I asked." His deep voice firmed. "Do you think it will help you get custody?"

Her eyes narrowed. "It could."

"Why did it take you six and a half minutes to leave the garage when you took your Ferrari from D-Chop's estate?"

Jill blinked. "What does that have to do with anything?"

"It has to do with your children's safety. You care about that, right?" Branson held her gaze without blinking. But no challenge or accusation showed in his gaze, at least from what Nevaeh could see from her angle. Good call, since Jill would probably get angry or clam up if he went too far.

"I couldn't find the keys."

"Peter said he gave you the keys when he took you out there."

Jill paused, her gaze flitting to Nevaeh, then something beyond her. "I'm not very mechanical. It took me awhile to remember how to start it."

Nevaeh squelched the urge to snort. Who did Jill think would believe that story?

"So I'm assuming you wouldn't know how to set up fireworks to start remotely?"

Jill's eyebrows dipped only far enough to avoid a wrinkle appearing on her suspiciously smooth forehead. "What are you talking about?"

"Does that mean you don't know how to remotely start fireworks?"

"Why would I?" The confusion in her eyes did look genuine. But she was avoiding a direct answer—a lie if she'd set off the fireworks.

Branson turned his head toward Nevaeh. "That's all I

have. Do you have any other questions?"

"Just one." Nevaeh met Jill's gaze. A defensive glint now shone in the superstar's eyes. "How are the kids today?"

"Fine." Jill raised one shoulder. "They're at school."

"They weren't too scared or rattled to go today?"

Jill lifted her gaze past Nevaeh again. "They're kids. They bounce back."

"You weren't worried about another kidnapping attempt?"

"Why would there be another one?"

Nevaeh forced one more smile. "Thanks for your time."

"Sure." Jill shrugged and didn't get up when Branson and Nevaeh did. "Wendy." Jill reached for her wine glass as her personal assistant stepped forward.

"I'll show you out." The young blonde who had enough natural beauty to be a model without plastic surgery led them to the massive double-door entry of the mansion Jill had inherited from her parents.

As soon as the assistant closed the door behind them, Branson threw Nevaeh a glance. "Well?" He started down the stone steps to the elegant driveway where they'd parked his pickup a short distance away. In case Jill didn't want him seen in front of her house, Branson had said.

"Not sure that accomplished much." Nevaeh kept pace beside him, something she suspected he made easier by shortening his strides. "She hates D-Chop and isn't a very good mother, but we knew that already."

"So she definitely has motive." Branson walked around the truck with her. To keep talking longer? "Did you notice how she avoided directly answering several of the questions?"

Nevaeh nodded. "Like she wanted to avoid a head-on lie." Nevaeh reached for the door handle, but Branson's large hand beat her to it.

She glanced at him, and her pulse ratcheted up. Man, he stood awfully close. But heat instead of the cold rush of fear surged through her body this time.

He pulled open the passenger door, giving her a second to find her voice.

"You don't have to open doors for me." Though she had to admit, only to herself, that she didn't mind it now or when he'd done it when they'd left PK-9 headquarters.

"Okay if I want to?" The sweetness in his question pulled her gaze up to his gentle eyes. To his teasing half-smile.

She couldn't help the grin that curled her lips. "Whatever makes you happy." She glanced down at Alvarez, whose tail wagged in anticipation of a ride. "Al, in."

The rottie mix jumped onto the floor in front of her seat and then clambered into the extended cab's back seat.

"How does he know to go in the back right away?"

Nevaeh stepped up to sit on the passenger seat. "He's used to riding in my Chevy."

"Oh, yeah. I saw you have a Silverado, too. Good taste." Branson smiled as he gently closed the door.

Nevaeh couldn't help watching him as he rounded the front of the truck and reached the driver's side. For such a big man, he sure moved nice. A confident, easygoing stride without the cockiness of the guys she'd grown up with, their swagger trying to earn or maintain their status in the hood.

He gave her a cute little smile as he slid onto the driver's seat. His large body seemed to fill the cab, his bulging bicep crossing halfway over the console between them just from the astounding circumference of his arm.

But the close quarters caused something very different than fear to flutter in her belly.

Branson cleared his throat as he started the engine. "Can I ask you a question?" He pulled into the center of the driveway and headed for the road.

Tension squeezed her chest. That question itself never sounded good. And there was more than one thing he could ask that she wouldn't want to answer. "Shoot."

"Does it make you uncomfortable, riding in the truck with me?"

A flush rushed to her cheeks. Yeah, that would definitely be on the list of things she didn't want to answer.

"I know at first...when we first met, it seemed like I maybe made you...uneasy?" An uptick of his voice made a question of the statement.

She swallowed. "That was before."

"Would you..." He glanced at her, his soft blue eyes touching her gently before bouncing back to the road. "Would you tell me why? Was it something I did?"

Her heartbeat pounded in her ears. The man had saved her life. She owed him some answers. "No. It's me."

"Does it have to do with your PTSD?"

She shot him a glance. But no judgment lurked in his open expression. "Yeah."

"I hope I don't remind you of whatever happened. I hope I'm not..."

Was he going to say *a trigger*? She couldn't let him keep thinking that. Or at least not that it was his fault.

Her mouth turned dry. She took a breath. "You maybe figured from what we said at the PK-9 meeting that I used to be a correctional officer at Whitlow Heights Prison."

He nodded.

"When I was there...working...an inmate caught me by surprise." She drew in a shaky breath. "And he jumped me."

Branson's fingers tightened on the wheel as Nevaeh continued the story he'd asked to hear but almost didn't want to now.

"The inmate attacked me. Pretty much went crazy. I couldn't..." Her voice choked. "I couldn't do anything but hope I'd be rescued."

Branson strangled the wheel as if it were the monster's neck. His imagination filled in details she didn't give. He braced himself to hear more.

But she stayed silent, turning her head away from him

toward the passenger window as they drove through the opulent residential neighborhood.

"I'm sorry, Nevaeh." The words were inadequate. But he had to say them, had to try to express a fraction of the grief and anger knotting inside his chest.

Resolve hardened his gut as he gritted his teeth. He would never let anything like that happen to her again. Not on his watch.

"I'm okay now."

But she wasn't. Not really. She still had PTSD—fears that kept her captive. He'd seen the evidence of that. Especially around him when they'd first met. His throat tightened as he realized the problem. "Am I…like the man who…"

She turned her head toward him, the weight of her dark gaze falling on his face. "No. You're not."

A smidgen of relief loosened the tension in his stomach.

"The inmate was big and muscular. So strong." She glanced down at her hands in her lap, hands that twisted each other.

His gut mimicked the motion. This was stressing her out. Should he change the subject?

"Men who are the same—built the same, I mean—can… make me nervous."

So that was it. He was a similar size and physique as her attacker. Great. No wonder she'd been hesitant, even downright fearful around him before. Especially when he got too close. "I'm so sorry. I had no idea."

"I know." She met his gaze as he looked over. "It's not you. I know you now. You're nothing like him."

Thank the Lord she realized that now. A lump lodged in Branson's throat as her mouth turned up slightly at the corners. He nodded and directed his gaze back to the road.

Raindrops accumulated on the windshield, and he clicked on the wipers.

Another question burned on the tip of his tongue. He had to know. Had to be prepared. "Is he in prison now?"

"He got out seven weeks ago."

His stomach clenched. Not the answer he'd hoped to hear.

"Do you think he'd come after you again?" His voice was tight as he locked his gaze on her.

She glanced at him. A flicker of fear sparked in her eyes.

He had to check the road briefly, but he quickly met her eyes again, trying to convey what he felt with only a look. That he'd protect her if that monster ever tried anything again. That the guy had better not if he valued his life. That no one could hurt her on Branson's watch.

The fear in her brown orbs dimmed as they softened. Message received.

He reluctantly broke eye contact to watch the road and surrounding traffic.

"The judge gave him a lifetime restraining order with the condition he'll go back to prison if he comes near me. He'd have a lot to lose if he tried anything."

That helped. But it wasn't enough to slow the rush of protectiveness that pumped through his veins. "Is he the 'other possibility' you asked Cora about at the Phoenix K-9 meeting this morning?"

"Yeah. Phoenix or Cora—I'm not sure which—tracked him to L.A., where he's supposed to be working on a stock car pit crew."

"Supposed to?"

"Phoenix has been trying to get physical confirmation that he's really there right now. You know, showing up at work, has an alibi." Nevaeh gazed out the windshield. "Phoenix told me before we left that she's going to put more pressure on her contact in L.A. to verify herself that he's there."

"Phoenix has contacts in California?"

Nevaeh threw him a grin. "The boss is more connected than the FBI and CIA put together."

"How'd she manage that?" Branson caught Nevaeh's shrug from the corner of his eye.

"Nobody really knows. At least, none of us on the team

do. I don't think. She's tight with FBI agents, the police, and she even fixed something for Sofia with the CIA."

"Sounds very mysterious."

"That's Phoenix. She pretty much saved my life." Nevaeh's voice tightened as if with emotion as she turned her head toward the passenger window. "Got me back on my feet when she gave me this job. And she gave me Cannenta and Alvarez. So I don't care if she has secrets. Anything she does is good with me."

Appreciation welled in Branson's chest. He didn't have a right to, but he felt like thanking Phoenix Gray himself for how she'd helped Nevaeh. He could tell it had made a big impact.

And he could continue her progress. "I'd like to help, too."

Silence followed his statement, but that didn't stop a plan from forming in his mind.

"Some friends of mine have helped women in your situation recover by equipping them with skills to defend themselves in the future. Just knowing they can protect themselves helps eliminate the fear."

Her lovely curls bobbed as she nodded. "I already do that. Phoenix trains me in jiujitsu so I can beat a bigger opponent."

"Is it working?"

She lifted her eyebrows.

"I mean, can you defeat someone bigger? Someone like me?"

"I hope so."

That's what he'd thought. "You need to know. How about I train with you? Give you someone larger to practice on?"

Her eyes widened before she glanced away. "I don't know."

"It probably sounds…" He stopped himself from saying *scary*. He didn't want her to feel he was judging or demeaning her in any way. "Uncomfortable."

Silence hung between them again. Except for Alvarez

panting behind his head. Maybe he was pushing her too much. "Does being close to me still make you uneasy?"

She looked at him again, something different in the gaze that darted up from his waist to his face. "No."

A smile settled on his mouth as his insides warmed. "Good. Then I'm your chance to see that you can really do it. That you can defend yourself against a man, someone who outweighs you." By a lot, he could've added as he quickly scanned her curvy but small figure. "Or have you already practiced with a man?"

"No. Only Phoenix. Because of..."

Her PTSD. She didn't need to finish for him to know what she meant. If being close to a man terrified her and triggered her PTSD, it made sense she'd avoid that possibility. "I get it. But wouldn't you feel better knowing, not just hoping, you could defend yourself against someone my size?"

She didn't answer as she aimed her gaze out the windshield.

"It won't happen again, Nevaeh. You won't need the skills." He tried to infuse his voice with the promise he made inwardly. The promise to keep her safe, no matter what. "But it could do wonders to *know* you could protect yourself, if you had to."

Her gaze flitted over him again, and he caught a glimmer of fear in her eyes before they darted away.

"I was a Navy SEAL and served two tours. I've seen the effects dangerous situations have on different people. And I've seen a lot of fear."

Images of their faces, men turning to flee, others staying to fight to their deaths, cycled in his memory. "Fear can be our worst enemy. You can't let it fester, or it'll grow until it controls you. You have to beat it."

She jerked her head toward him. "That's not what Phoenix says. She wants me to use my fear as a tool. She says it can help me."

Branson pressed his lips together. It wasn't the first time he'd heard that popular philosophy. People loved to believe fear was natural and even helpful. But the only thing natural about it was that it belonged to the fallen, sinful nature of mankind.

Truth was, it was never helpful. It was a deadly obstacle, a sin to be defeated just like any other. And like other sins, fear became all the more powerful when people mislabeled it as good. But he doubted going all preachy on Nevaeh would convince her to fight her fear.

He clicked on his blinker and slid the pickup onto an entrance ramp to access the freeway. "I've seen people try to use fear, try to tell themselves it's a good thing that helps them survive. But as someone who has weathered his fair share of dicey situations, I can tell you I don't need fear to warn me of danger or to help me survive. The senses and intelligence God gave me do that. Training helps, too."

He glanced at her, catching the pensive look in the eyes that watched him. "Believe me, fear only interferes with beating the enemy. It turns us into irrational, instinctual beasts. You have to beat fear, or it will destroy you, one way or another."

The memory he'd hoped wouldn't surface flashed quickly in his mind.

His buddy Grady, panicking, screaming that they weren't safe. Dashing out from their cover, straight into the line of fire.

The horrible memory drove Branson to say more. "Fear blinds you and controls you. But you can get rid of fear if you learn to handle whatever scares you and come out on top. Fear loses its power if you know how to defeat the thing that scares you."

That might not be enough. When fear was as deep-seated as Nevaeh's, true victory over it could only be achieved through a spiritual battle. But he kept that bit of truth to himself. Maybe he could share it with her another time.

He'd said enough for now. Probably more than enough. He drew in a breath and let out a chuckle. "Sorry. Didn't mean to lecture you."

"No. It's okay." Her voice was different than usual. Thoughtful, maybe?

"So, did I convince you to let me be your guinea pig? You may not find another volunteer so willing to let you beat him up." His effort to lighten the mood earned a gorgeous smile.

"Okay."

"Okay, you'll let me train with you?"

"Yeah."

He held back the urge to pump his fist and instead settled for a big grin. "Awesome."

"On one condition." Her mouth curved in a charming, closed-lip smile.

"Ah. What's that?"

"My grandpa wants to meet you."

"He does?" Branson's pulse shot off at a sprint. She'd told her family about him?

"Yeah. He wants to meet the man who rescued me."

The man who rescued her. The words swelled in Branson's chest. He wanted to keep rescuing and protecting her. For the rest of—

"My sister is moving out of my grandpa's place to an apartment on Saturday. Do you want to come help? We could use some muscles for the heavy lifting." The way her appreciative gaze moved over his bicep made his chest expand even more.

"I'd be honored to help." He met her gaze. "And to meet your family."

She laughed. "You may not say that after you meet them. We can be a crazy bunch."

"Hey, I grew up with seven siblings. I can do crazy."

Her eyes grew larger. "Eight kids? Wow, that's more than my sister has. Let me guess, you're the oldest."

He gave her a sideways grin. "Does it show?"

"A little, yeah." She laughed again.

The delightful sound trickled into his ears and right down to his heart. This was how Nevaeh should always be. Happy and free.

He'd do whatever it took to keep her that way.

TWENTY-NINE

"Looks like we're already back at the pool, Al." Nevaeh smiled at how quickly she was completing each patrol round tonight. It wasn't a race, but she couldn't tell that to her feet. Seemed like she was walking on air—practically bouncing on air tonight.

She glanced at D-Chop's mansion as she unlatched the gate and walked through to the patio with Alvarez. Branson was in there somewhere.

The thought warmed her torso, warding off the chill of the crisp wind.

Considering it was three thirty a.m., he should be sleeping now. But somehow she still felt different just knowing he was there. Safer. That was it—protected and safe.

That's how she'd felt with him in his pickup when they'd driven to and from Jill's place. The close quarters should've scared her. Terrified her. But she'd had to fight the urge to shift closer to him, especially when he'd said he wanted to help her. Well, once she'd gotten past the initial surge of panic at the thought.

His urgent tone as he'd talked about fear and how to beat it had slowly smothered the panic. He cared. It was obvious in every word he'd said and the concern in his eyes when he'd looked at her. He wanted to help her, not harm her.

She'd realized something on that drive. She trusted Branson Aaberg. Trusted him with her life. Trusted him not to hurt her, which was an even bigger step.

Considering Branson was the only man Phoenix had ever invited to a PK-9 meeting at headquarters to consult, Nevaeh obviously wasn't wrong to trust him. Phoenix had agreed to let Branson train with them tomorrow, too.

A tingle of nerves fluttered in her belly as she angled away from the pool and walked toward the alcove where tables and chairs were clustered. Okay, so maybe she wasn't completely chill about the idea yet. Or were these flutters from excitement instead of fear?

Maybe something he'd said in his talk about fear had already helped. Because she'd never felt so far from her PTSD, so far from having an episode, so free from her fear as she did right now.

What would it be like to always feel like this? To live like this? Confident and unafraid.

Would having Branson in her life make this her new normal? He'd proven he could keep her safe and—

Her gaze caught on something white on a dark brown table.

Looked like the maid had missed something.

Nevaeh veered that way. If it wasn't anything gross, she could pick it up and throw it in the trash.

The shadows cast on the table shifted as she moved closer, the angle of her viewpoint changing.

Was that—

A black handle stuck into the air, attached to a blade. A butcher's knife?

Alvarez pulled to keep moving on patrol. "Hang on, Al." The K-9 stopped at the end of the leash.

She stood by the table and stared at the knife. The heavy blade stabbed into the wooden tabletop.

The white object beside it appeared to be a piece of paper. She picked up the folded half page and opened it.

Her mouth dried as her gaze fell on typed text.

You owe me. I'll kill you or your kids if you don't pay up. You pick who dies. I'll send you a bill soon.

Nevaeh knocked on Branson's bedroom door. Not far down the hallway from D-Chop's suite, she tried to avoid being loud enough to wake the rapper, too.

Here was hoping Branson was a light sleeper.

Shuffling sounds came from behind the door.

She lowered her fist and took a step back.

The door swung open.

Whoa.

Branson's tall height meant her gaze hit chest level first. A very broad, very muscular, bare chest. Yeah, Hercules was a better description than she'd thought. From the sculpted display in front of her eyes, she'd say he outclassed Thor, too.

"Nevaeh? Is something wrong?" Branson's voice, deeper and rougher than normal, sent a thrill tumbling through her belly. Or maybe it wasn't his voice.

She dragged her gaze from his chest and climbed the long trek to his face.

His blue eyes blinked, worry pinching his mouth.

She cleared her throat. "Sort of." Her gaze bounced to his chest again before she meant to let it.

"Sorry. Hang on a second." He pulled away, shutting the door.

As if he needed to apologize for that jaw-dropping sight.

The doorknob rattled within seconds, and the door opened to reveal a fully clothed Branson.

Disappointment cooled the heat tumbling through her. Though she couldn't help noticing how the gray T-shirt he'd pulled on skimmed closely across his muscular torso.

The note, girl. The reminder moved her hand to her jacket pocket where she'd stuffed the paper. "I found this on my rounds."

She handed it to him.

His large fingers brushed hers, shooting a shiver up her arm.

She swallowed as he read the note, her gaze moving over his handsome features, the strong brow wrinkled with concentration.

Good grief, she was sounding like a girl in a romance novel.

She mentally shook off the nonsense and straightened.

A small squeak pulled her gaze to the floor. The tiny white cat rubbed against Branson's leg, his massive foot bare beneath loose-fitting pants.

Branson scooped up Princess with one thick arm and held her against his chest. "When did you find this?" His eyes were darkened and his features pinched as he looked up from the note.

But Nevaeh had to fight to keep a smile off her face at the sight of the little puffball in Hercules' arm, nuzzling his chest and climbing up to his neck. The twitch of her mouth told her she was failing to hide her amusement. She tried for a serious tone. "Um, five minutes ago. It was folded and sitting on top of the patio table by the pool."

"Had you been back there earlier tonight?"

"No, that was the first time tonight. Jazz told me on coms she had been there and hadn't seen it. But she also said she didn't walk through the patio furniture in the alcove. I don't know why I did. We usually just go past, because the dogs will tell us if someone's hiding anywhere back there."

Branson nodded. "I'll change and talk to Travis. He may have seen something on the monitors, someone going back there. We could have a security breech on the grounds. Maybe a break in the fence again."

"That couldn't have happened tonight." Nevaeh shook her head. "Nobody would get past Alvarez and Flash, and we didn't see any holes in the fence on patrol."

Princess rubbed her mini head against Branson's chin, nuzzling him while her little paws dangled over his big hand.

A chuckle pushed up Nevaeh's throat and fell out.

Branson lifted his eyebrows, looking at her over the cat as if completely unaware of the incongruous, totally adorable picture he and his furry friend made.

"Okay, you have to tell me how you got that cat."

"Princess?" He looked down at the feline who was only the size of a small kitten. Some of the tension on his face lessened as his lips shaped into a smile.

"Yeah, you can't tell me you decided to get a cat one day and went to a shelter and picked *her* out."

"Why not?"

She paused, not sure how to answer the seemingly serious question. Then she caught the twinkle in his blue eyes.

Her pulse jumped. Man, if he was going to start teasing her like that, she'd be in trouble. She grinned, and his smile broadened.

"You're right. Princess kind of picked me, I guess. Or really, God picked us for each other."

There it was again. One of those God mentions he liked to drop in at odd moments.

"I worked as a personal protection specialist for a certain celebrity who…had a lot of issues."

"Don't they all?"

His mouth angled in another smile. "Good point. But hers were particularly bad. I felt sorry for her. She fired everyone who worked for her in the time I was there, hiring replacements she'd fire soon, too. I knew I wouldn't last forever either. She posed for a photo shoot with kittens once and decided on a whim she had to have one. So her people brought Princess home, though she had a different name back then."

He scratched the fluffy cat under her chin, eliciting a purr that made Alvarez wag his tail as he watched the feline. "Princess and I took a liking to each other right away. My client didn't really do anything with her, but her staff did the feeding and essentials. Until my client had one of her episodes one night."

The amusement in Branson's eyes faded. "She had substance abuse problems and would fly into rages. Princess was the target of that particular rage. In the wrong place at the wrong time, I guess. I intervened, trying to become the target instead."

A rueful tilt lifted his lips as he glanced at the tiny cat that burrowed down farther into the crook of his elbow. "It worked, but she still threw Princess out on the street before I could stop her. It took me an hour to find Princess, but, thank the Lord, I did. And we both got out of there, didn't we, girl?" He lifted Princess closer to his face as his voice softened into something very close to baby talk.

Nevaeh couldn't help the light laugh that escaped. Who would've imagined Hercules would baby talk to a mini feline named Princess?

Warmth ballooned inside her torso, starting in her belly and reaching her chest. Could Branson be for real? If he was any more perfect, he really would be mythical. And he'd be way out of her league. Who could date a perfect man? An infallible hero who was strong but gentle and loving?

"Want to hold her while I change?" He extended the white creature toward her.

"Sure." The cat was suddenly in her arms, a warm ball of fur softer than Nevaeh had imagined.

Branson closed the door, but Princess didn't seem to mind. She made herself at home, burrowing her little face under the collar of Nevaeh's jacket until it tickled. Nevaeh laughed and smoothed her hand over the cat's soft body.

Alvarez bumped into Nevaeh's leg, making it known he'd like to meet Princess, too.

"How would you like to say 'hi' to a doggy?" Nevaeh carefully lowered the cat for Alvarez to sniff, watching both animals carefully for friendly body language.

But her mind drifted to the man behind the door. And the fact that even if he was perfect, she'd very much like to date Branson Aaberg. To be the other special girl in his life besides Princess. To be the other one he protected and loved.

Her racing heart told her she probably wanted that way too much. If he didn't feel something for her, she could be placing herself in danger of a different kind than she was used to confronting.

THIRTY

"Now the standing rear attack." Phoenix's unemotional voice was the distraction Branson desperately needed.

He nodded and stalked up behind Nevaeh. He slipped his arms around her waist, clenching harder than he'd like. But Phoenix had already scolded him for being too gentle three times during this training session at the martial arts studio. She had a point. He wouldn't do Nevaeh any good if he was too easy for her to escape from.

But it was one of the biggest psychological challenges he'd ever faced, trying to stay detached and apathetic about the physical contact. Because he did care. A lot.

The fragrant, fruity scent of her hair, the warmth of her body, the way her eyes had looked at him this morning—soft and trusting—all of it lured him to wrap his arms around her and hold her close for an entirely different reason.

"Go again." Phoenix's even tone jolted him to the realization Nevaeh was reaching back to grip his ankle. "Speed is everything." The woman's baseball cap blocked her eyes from view, at least from Branson's high vantage point, but she was clearly talking to Nevaeh. "If he were an attacker, you'd be dragged or on the ground by now. Again."

Branson released his hold and walked away, using the opportunity to take some deep breaths. He'd trained with a couple other women when he'd sought more martial arts training on his own after the SEALs. He'd never had any problem being close to them and keeping his mind only on the objective. *Discipline, Aaberg. You got this.*

Phoenix gave him a nod, and he marched up to Nevaeh, gripping her waist even tighter this time to drag her.

She instantly dropped forward at the waist, reached behind to hook his ankle, and leaned back to knock him to the floor.

The triumphant grin she tossed him over her shoulder as she held his leg in a breakable pose shot a bolt of heat straight to his heart.

He tapped her calf to signal she should stop the stretch on his knee. "Nice." His mouth smiled around the words that sounded a little breathless. Hopefully, she'd think it was from the exertion.

She let go and extended her hand as if to help him up. If he really gave her his weight to lift, he'd pull her over right into his lap. Not that he'd mind. But he brushed off that enticing image in a hurry and took her hand, hoisting most of his weight himself as he stood.

He released her hand, but it took her a second to let go of his. He glanced at her face, but she was looking at Phoenix. Had he imagined her lingering touch?

You're here to help, not flirt. The self-admonishment came just in time to clear any strange emotion from his face before he found himself the subject of a Phoenix stare.

The woman had the most fascinating lack of expression on her face and even in her eyes. But what was always there was the confidence he'd noticed from the first time they'd talked over the phone.

Something about her silent gaze made him turn his thoughts inward, as if he had to search his conscience. Had she noticed he was enjoying the close contact with Nevaeh? Or that she may have held on to his hand longer than required?

"Did you see anything on the security footage from last

night?" Phoenix's question made him want to let out a relieved breath.

But he released the air a bit at a time instead as he brought his mind to the unexpected topic. "No. Nothing unusual. D-Chop had a girlfriend with him by the pool late. He likes privacy for that, so no one was with him. But Travis was observing on the monitors as needed. I'm checking into D-Chop's guest. He had just picked her up that evening. Some friend of a friend."

"Could've been paid by someone or have a personal connection."

"True." He nodded. "I can look into her."

"Give me her name, and we'll do that."

"Sounds good." He wasn't about to argue with Phoenix Gray. He'd already deduced she had more extensive connections for investigating people than he did. And something about her told him it wouldn't be a good idea to oppose her on anything unless absolutely necessary.

"D-Chop agreed to have the police lab analyze the note, so we could get a lead there." Branson ran his hand over his hair as he glanced at Nevaeh.

She'd seemed nervous when they'd started this training session. She had stiffened under his touch and darted him frightened glances. But after only a few minutes, she'd relaxed, and the trust that he felt all the way in his gut had replaced the fear in her eyes.

"How will the financial motivation affect your interviews?" Phoenix's question reined in Branson's wandering mind. But she was looking at Nevaeh this time.

Nevaeh watched her boss with an open, thoughtful expression. "I think the same suspects are still likely. Though maybe not the father of the boy who killed himself?"

Phoenix stared at Nevaeh for a silent moment. "He could internalize what he's owed as having a monetary value, depending on his personality. He wants it paid. That could be the only way he sees that being accomplished."

"I guess so." Nevaeh pressed her full lips together. "But

the location of the knife and note this time suggests an inside job, doesn't it?" She shifted her gaze up to Branson. "You said Marsha went out there to serve food and drinks?"

"Yes. I still don't think she would be involved in this, though. Peter went out while D-Chop was there and talked to him about something. Probably going over his schedule or giving him his messages."

"What other staff members were still on the grounds after D-Chop returned to the house?" Phoenix aimed her question at Branson.

"Jaycee, the maid, stayed later than usual. She left at one fifteen a.m., shortly after D-Chop and his girlfriend came inside. She didn't go to the patio after D-Chop was there unless she used a different route off camera. The girlfriend went back out by herself an hour and a half later. She lit a cigarette on camera and then stepped out of view. She went inside about ten minutes later."

"You said the alcove isn't covered by the camera, right?"

He nodded to Nevaeh. "Correct. The camera is primarily to cover the entry point to the house. And all of those people stepped out of the camera's view at one time when they were back there."

"I suppose this rules out the chef and the groundskeeper." Nevaeh looked at Phoenix.

"Unless they were hired by someone only for some tasks or hired an accomplice themselves." Phoenix jerked her thumb over her shoulder. "Go again." Her abrupt topic change made Branson straighten as if Captain Killian had called him to attention. "This time, you're on the mat." She shifted her gaze to Branson. "You're in mount."

Nevaeh shot him a wide-eyed glance that did nothing to calm the surge of his pulse. This should be interesting. That mental—no, emotional—battle he was having? It was about to get much more intense.

She'd expected this. Nevaeh reminded herself of that over and over again as she lay with her back on the mat and waited for Branson to lower himself onto her.

And she'd already gotten over her nerves once. She'd thought it would be bad when Branson first touched her and took her in tight holds for the standing attacks. But instead of fear, Nevaeh had felt only attraction. Her only problem had been staying focused on defensive techniques instead of enjoying the contact.

But this was different.

Branson lowered above her, being so careful to touch her as little as possible, bracing his arms on either side of her torso.

The sweetness of his caution washed like a cooling wave over her nerves. This was Branson. He wasn't going to hurt her.

And as his leg made contact with hers and the warmth of him charged the air around them, a much more pleasant reaction filtered through her system.

"Too gentle, Aaberg. Pin her down." Phoenix's command shot a jolt of fear through Nevaeh's heart.

Branson lowered his weight onto her hips and bent his upper body down, so close.

This was practice. Phoenix knew this was what Nevaeh needed. She knew it would trigger Nevaeh, that the trigger had to be there to mimic the real-life scenario.

Nevaeh forced the reminders into her mind. But they weren't loud enough to hear over the rushing sound in her ears. The panic flooded her system.

Walter's face leaned close. The sneer. His breath hot as he pinned her down.

His weight crushed her.

She couldn't move. Couldn't fight. Couldn't save herself as he pummeled her nearly to death.

"Nevaeh."

Strange. He hadn't said her name before.

"Nevaeh."

A different voice. She knew that voice. The sweetness of it.

"Nevaeh, it's me." Air whispered against her ear. "It's Branson."

Her vision cleared as he lifted his head, his face appearing above hers. She knew those features, those soft eyes.

The panic receded, her chest rising and falling rapidly with the quick breaths that would take longer to calm.

He smiled the gentlest of smiles. It was Branson.

She was safe.

THIRTY-ONE

"Can you see okay?" Branson glanced down at Nevaeh, so close her hair brushed against his shoulder.

"Yeah, I think so."

"Would it help if I moved my arm?" He lifted his left arm and draped it behind her on the sofa instead.

She scooted even closer, her leg touching his.

Heat shot from the point of contact through his whole body. *Easy, boy.* He wasn't trying to flirt with her. Only trying to be sure she could see and be seen by the camera of his laptop computer for the interview with their next suspect.

She tilted her head up to look at him, her beautiful face only inches away. And she smiled. "Yeah, that's loads better." The way her gaze caressed his face lit the fire in his chest he'd just tamped down.

A beep from his computer came just in time to save him from doing something stupid. Like kissing the woman.

He pulled his arm from behind her as he leaned forward to tap acceptance for the new party to join their meeting.

Another camera view popped up on the screen. Larry LeSalle. D-Chop's ex-manager attempted a smile that was about as successful as a wet match. "Hello."

"Hello, Mr. LeSalle. I'm Branson Aaberg here with Nevaeh

Williams, another of D-Chop's security specialists. Thanks for agreeing to meet with us today."

"Your email was very persuasive."

Branson hid a smile. "Glad to hear it." He'd suggested in his email to LeSalle that D-Chop wasn't happy with his current manager and might be looking for a replacement soon. All completely true, since D-Chop was pretty much never happy with any of the three managers he'd had since Branson had worked for the rapper.

"Now I know you've said you always had D-Chop's best interests at heart. But would you mind sharing what led him to dismiss you as his manager?"

LeSalle straightened in the chair placed in front of a large blue and white painting in a modern, abstract style. "Let's just say D-Chop didn't always hold that same perspective."

"You mean he didn't trust you were doing what was best for him?" Nevaeh's sweater sleeve brushed against Branson's arm as she leaned in more.

"That's a good point." LeSalle nodded as if he were answering the question. "Trust is important between a manager and his client. Once that's gone, even if through no fault of the manager's, it's hard to rebuild the relationship."

"So you would say D-Chop had no reason to mistrust you?"

LeSalle's gaze drifted down a bit, maybe to where Branson appeared on his screen. "Of course, he didn't have a reason. Not a good one." An edge lined LeSalle's voice. "Certain... influences around D-Chop convinced him I couldn't be trusted. But that was never true. I always did only what was best for his career."

"D-Chop said you were pressuring him to give up his interest in fashion design."

Branson glanced at Nevaeh. How did she know that? Maybe the tabloids.

"I may have suggested it was too far of a departure from his brand and primary revenue. That's sound business advice. Not pressuring or misguiding." The edge returned with the last words. LeSalle definitely wasn't okay with what had happened.

"So based on the way D-Chop wouldn't listen to you and misrepresented you to the press, you probably wouldn't even want to manage him again if he asked you." Branson kept his eyes locked on the screen, homing in on every detail of LeSalle's response to the question.

The man forced a smile that held longer but didn't reach his eyes. "I would be delighted to represent D-Chop."

"Why?" Nevaeh threw out the perfect question—quick and to the point.

Enough to catch LeSalle by surprise, judging from the way his smile faltered. "Even the closest of families have little tiffs now and then. But if we didn't forgive and move on, where would we be?"

"Good point." Though Branson didn't buy this guy having any familial affection for D-Chop. More like a love of D-Chop's profit margin. "Speaking of where you are, I understand you're in Paris right now?"

"Yes."

Branson wasn't about to take the word of the manager's secretary for it. "Can you verify that somehow for us?"

"Why would I do that? You don't suspect me of something, do you?" The man's brown eyebrows lifted. "Did something happen to D-Chop?"

News of the attempted kidnapping of D-Chop's kids had leaked out and was being featured on all the major news sources. How would his ex-manager have missed that? Unless he really was overseas and wasn't staying in touch with events back home. Or he could be faking.

"I wondered why his security personnel were conducting his interviews." LeSalle's eyes narrowed. "I thought it was some kind of clearance procedure D-Chop wanted."

"In a way, that's true."

"Well, look at my social media. I've been posting photos of Paris. Or check my flight itinerary. Isn't that how these things are done?"

"Sure." It was a good sign the man didn't seem reluctant to have his alibi investigated. Though he could be bluffing.

"Now, when do I talk to D-Chop?" The manager's gaze tracked downward again, probably looking at Branson instead of the camera lens.

"You know D-Chop. I can't say for sure."

"I see."

Even if LeSalle was in Paris, that didn't eliminate him as a suspect. He could've hired someone to carry out his threats and the kidnapping. Someone from D-Chop's staff, if it was an inside job as Branson was starting to suspect. "Do you know D-Chop's current staff members?"

LeSalle blinked, silent for a moment. Covering something or genuinely surprised? "Do you mean his personal staff? I don't know if I'm familiar with all of them."

"Which ones do you know?" Nevaeh's question prompted the man to move his gaze to the right, perhaps where she was on his screen.

"Well, the housekeeper. And his assistant, of course. I believe his hired chef changed with his move."

Interesting that LeSalle seemed confident Marsha and Peter were still on staff. As if he'd kept tabs on them or on D-Chop.

"Do you know the groundskeeper?"

A smirk settled on LeSalle's lips as he answered Nevaeh. "I don't believe I ever had the pleasure." Probably considered associating with that level of staff beneath him. Branson doubted he'd admit to knowing the maid then, either. And the current maid was local, a new hire since D-Chop had moved to St. Paul. That didn't mean LeSalle wasn't in contact with the groundskeeper or the maid, though.

"When was the last time you spoke to any of D-Chop's staff members?" Branson tried for casual but steady eye contact. Difficult over an online video call.

"I couldn't say."

Because he didn't remember or didn't want to admit something? "Within the last month?"

"Oh. No. Not after I was last at D-Chop's residence in L.A."

"So you haven't had any contact with them over the phone or online?"

"Of course not." LeSalle frowned. "I'm not chummy with them, if that's what you meant. I only saw them at the house and dealt with Volrath for scheduling purposes." He glanced away from his screen and nodded as if someone was there. "I really have to go now."

"Sure. Thanks for your time."

"Tell D-Chop I'm looking forward to his call."

"Enjoy your trip." Branson watched LeSalle until the man tapped out of the session. He flipped the lid of his notebook computer closed and turned his head toward Nevaeh. "That was interesting."

She didn't move away, even though the call was over.

His heart thumped as she stayed close and looked up at him. He lifted his left arm and draped it on the sofa behind her, only to give her more room, of course.

She melded into his side, soft and relaxed. His pulse sprinted, careening at an erratic tempo that had to be unsafe. But he didn't care. Not when she felt so good, so perfectly fitted to him.

"He seemed like he was hiding something."

The interview. Yes. He forced himself to focus on her statement rather than the powerful urge to move his arm forward to cradle her shoulders. "I agree. But when I knew him in L.A., he always seemed to be hiding something. I think that's partly why D-Chop let him go. Never could tell what LeSalle had up his sleeve. He'd say one thing to placate D-Chop and then turn around and do the opposite."

"So he might not be hiding anything related to the attacks and threats." An adorable frown settled on Nevaeh's full lips. "Did the police get back to you about the note and the knife yet?"

He nodded. "Just this afternoon. No prints on the knife. It's a professional-grade butcher's knife. I checked with Chef

Cox, and he said he's missing his butcher's knife. He said he used it last night for dinner prep but can't be sure he saw it after that."

"Or so he claims." Nevaeh brought her brown eyes up to Branson's face, nearly making him lose his train of thought.

"Exactly."

She looked away, enabling him to focus on the topic again.

"The only prints on the note were yours and mine. The paper was a common type used in home printers, and the ink was from a standard printer, too. Nothing traceable."

"So it could still be anyone."

"Anyone with access. I don't believe our security was breached last night. You and Jazz had your K-9s. Like you said, they wouldn't have let anyone past them, and I don't think an intruder would've risked the dogs. Nothing unusual shows on the security footage either. Other than the pool area having more traffic than usual with D-Chop, his guest, and the staff."

"Too bad that table isn't actually covered by the camera back there."

"Whoever planted the knife and note knew that." Another indication of an inside job. But it was hard to picture any of the staff members Branson knew doing anything to hurt D-Chop. "We should interview the staff next. Starting tomorrow."

Nevaeh's curls brushed Branson's shoulder as she nodded. "Totally."

Her reply brought a smile to Branson's lips. And inched his arm close enough for his fingers to gently touch her shoulder.

The light contact brought her gaze to his. Her mouth curved in a smile.

She apparently didn't mind.

His arm slid more fully onto her shoulders as if of its own volition. His heart pounded into his ribs hard enough she could probably hear it. "Would you like to stay for dinner before your shift tonight?"

Her eyes widened slightly. Then her lips pressed together and shifted to the side with what looked like disappointment. "I'd like that."

He heard a *but* coming.

"But I need to go home to my dogs. Get them fed and bring Alvarez back with me for patrol." The reluctance in her voice kept her response from feeling like a rejection. She didn't seem to want to decline any more than he wanted her to. "Probably should get some sleep, too."

She shifted away slightly but turned her head and body more toward him as if she wanted to see him better. "You remember how you said you could help out with my sister's move on Saturday?"

He moved his fingers to caress the small shoulder still cupped in his hand. "Yes. Looking forward to it." Did she think he wasn't going to show?

"Cool." She glanced away, her tongue sliding over her lips. "How would you like to go to Cora's wedding with me later in the afternoon?"

She brought her attention back to his face, probably just in time to see the surprise he tried to hide. And the pleasure that rolled through him. Was she asking him to be her date for a wedding?

"The girls keep telling me to bring someone. But if you don't—"

"I'd be honored." The grin that split his face from ear to ear likely looked as goofy as it felt. But he didn't care. Nevaeh had just invited him to be her date. "Anything in particular you want me to wear?"

"The wedding's super formal." She skimmed him with her brown eyes. "You got a tux?"

"Yes, ma'am."

"That'll be somethin' to see." The way she let the words roll off her tongue sent a thrill through his veins.

Good thing she was about to leave right now. Because he

seemed to be losing a bit more of his self-control with every minute she lingered. And that wouldn't do either of them any good.

He reluctantly pulled his arm away and stood. Then he turned to her and extended his hand.

"Aren't you the gentlemen?" She smiled before slipping her small fingers into his palm.

He aimed to be. But with the space between them came more clarity to his mind. What was he doing? Flirting with her, holding her on the sofa. Agreeing to go to the wedding.

He hadn't actually declared intentions he shouldn't. Not verbally anyway. But had his actions conveyed more than he could promise?

He pushed the doubts and questions to the background of his conscience as he escorted Nevaeh out of the house and to her pickup outside.

Only as she drove away did he let his thoughts turn toward the two messes he needed to untangle. His increasing attraction to Nevaeh, and the other little thing of someone threatening to murder his client.

Nevaeh had never felt more confident. At least not in the last six years. She moved through the darkness of D-Chop's estate with Alvarez, the lyrics and beat from one of the rapper's earliest recordings timing with her steps in her mind.

She'd break into a dance move, but that wouldn't exactly be professional. She snickered at the thought.

"Excuse me?" Jazz's amused voice sounded in Nevaeh's ear over coms.

"Oops." Nevaeh laughed. "Sorry." Must've left it open. At least she was on the channel she and Jazz used privately when they wanted to chat without the new security guy hearing.

"Somebody's in a good mood. Are you ever going to tell me what happened between you and Branson today?"

Nevaeh grinned as she angled her path to head toward the outbuilding at the rear of the grounds. "What makes you think anything had to happen?"

"Because I haven't seen you this giddy since Gary Benson asked you to prom."

Another laugh tumbled from Nevaeh's lips.

"Scratch that. I've never seen you like this." The smile was obvious in Jazz's voice. "Did Branson ask you out?"

"Kind of."

"What do you mean, 'kind of'? Don't tell me a guy like Branson would do the backhanded invite to avoid rejection? He has to have more guts than that."

"No, he was cool. Straight up asked me to stay for dinner."

Jazz took in a quick breath. "Really?"

"Yeah. I couldn't 'cause I had to take care of the dogs."

"Girl, I could've done that."

"I know but…it's good not to be too available."

Jazz's snort carried across the coms. "Since when do you play those games?"

"I don't. I needed to get sleep, too."

Alvarez paused to smell something in the grass.

"Did you feel uncomfortable with him? With the idea of a date?" Jazz's tone took on a concerned note. "It's a big step with someone who made you so uneasy before."

"That's not it." At least, Nevaeh didn't think it was. Had she been protecting herself? They had already been alone for a while at that point. Had her instincts been guarding her against more solitude with him in the big house?

No. She trusted Branson. The fact he was in the house tonight was the reason she didn't feel a hint of her PTSD. If she sounded an alarm for any reason, he'd come running to her rescue. She knew that deep down in her bones.

She'd even cuddled with him on the sofa. Outside of hugs

with Pops and that jiujitsu training session, she hadn't been that close to a man since…

The attack didn't count. And Walter didn't need to be in her thoughts right now.

Strange how the brief thought of him didn't make her tense or start to see things she didn't want to.

She smiled. Apparently, Branson was where her mind wanted to linger.

"You still there, Nev, or should Flash and I start a search for you?"

Nevaeh rolled her eyes as her feet found the concrete walkway that led to the outbuilding. "I'm still here."

"Then why didn't you have dinner with him?"

Nevaeh wasn't sure herself. She trusted Branson. But something held her back. Maybe it felt better to be the one in control. "I wanted to ask him to the wedding instead."

Jazz's squeal stung Nevaeh's ears, but she laughed anyway.

"Girl, you gonna make me go deaf if you keep that up."

"I'm proud of you, Nev. You two will make such a gorgeous couple."

"Hey, nobody's a couple yet." Though the idea was definitely appealing.

"Sure. You can't hide these things from your BFF." Amusement filled Jazz's voice.

"Hey, you'll be the first to—"

A noise jerked her gaze to the outbuilding.

Alvarez growled, staring at the door as they approached.

Was someone in there?

"Nev? You okay?"

"I just heard something in the outbuilding." She scanned the darkness surrounding the structure as she walked the few remaining feet of the path to the door.

The security light above the single entrance lit the concrete walkway.

"I'll meet you there. What does Al say?"

The dog rumbled as they stopped by the door.

"He doesn't like it either." Nevaeh reached into her jacket pocket and pulled out the keys Branson had given them for the outbuilding. "I'm going to check it out."

"Stay on coms the whole way."

"Yeah."

Nevaeh shoved the key into the slot and turned. The lock moved with the motion like it should.

The door had still been locked. Should mean no one was inside.

But the noise...

She slowly turned the knob, then pushed the door in as she shifted to the side of the open doorway. She pulled her Sig and checked the angle to the left first.

A dark interior stared back at her.

"If you're in there, you'd better throw down your weapon and come out. I'm armed and have a protection K-9."

Silence met her warning.

She shifted to the left and peered into the right side of the building. Using her flashlight would make her a better target, so she kept it pocketed.

Her eyes started to adjust to the dim lighting enough to see a parked tractor, a tiller, and shovels leaning up against the wall.

Alvarez wasn't growling, but his body was tense and ready.

If she remembered correctly, the light switch was to the right of the door.

She took a breath and ducked inside.

Al stuck with her as they darted to the right of the door, and she flicked the switch.

Light illuminated the rectangular building.

She kept her Sig raised as she took it all in.

No one moved among the machines, landscaping equipment, and storage containers.

Shelves lined the entire left wall, holding boxes and big lidded tubs.

"Looks clear so far." Nevaeh gave the report to Jazz as she

started forward. Someone could still be hiding in the remaining shadows.

"Okay."

Alvarez swung his head toward the open door behind and let out a low growl.

Nevaeh's muscles tensed.

"We're coming up to the door now."

Nevaeh chuckled and relaxed her stance. "Yeah. Al just told me."

The dog swished his tail as he recognized his friends silhouetted in the doorway, the security light bright behind the slim redhead and her K-9.

Nevaeh spun back around. She still hadn't fully cleared the space. Someone could be waiting for them in here.

Jazz and Flash stepped inside. "We'll take the left."

"Roger." They kept the coms open even though they were close enough to talk directly. But not having to speak loudly could be an advantage if an unwanted visitor was there.

They stayed silent as they cleared the two sides of the long building. Nevaeh checked every shadow and crevice between the machinery and tools.

No surprises.

"We're clear here." Jazz glanced across the space.

Nevaeh walked toward her. "The other side, too."

Jazz's gaze skimmed the boxes and containers. "Any idea where the noise came from?"

"No. Al didn't like it either." Though they both knew guard dogs tended to react to any unexpected noise first and ask questions later.

"Sure is a lot of stuff in here. I see some of it is labeled with record names I remember from your D-Chop fangirl days."

Nevaeh sniffed. "You talk like those are over."

Jazz laughed. "Won't never be over, right?"

"Duh."

"Maybe you can find some cool collector's items in here

and talk D-Chop into letting you have them." Jazz fingered the corner of a box. "You did save his kids, after all."

"Yeah, 'cause that would be so professional." Nevaeh walked along the row of boxes and containers, taking in the labels. It would be cool to see some old stuff from D-Chop's early rapping days. Maybe he even had keepsakes from earlier in here. From their childhood. Before things got so dark. Before Jordy was—

"Since when is professionalism your priority?" Jazz threw Nevaeh a grin.

"Since I had to start covering up for you. Gotta grow up for this job, girl. None of your goofing off."

Jazz snorted. "Oh, I see how it is."

Nevaeh's gaze stopped on a stack of containers next to the last set of shelves. Papers and file folders were piled precariously on top and scattered on the floor. "Might've found what made the noise." She squatted to look at the papers and folders on the concrete floor.

Jazz stepped closer, and Flash ran his nose over the folders nearest him. "You think they fell?"

"Could've."

"With help?"

Nevaeh glanced up at her tall friend. "Could've just been off-kilter, I guess." Nevaeh reached for the papers to start gathering them into a pile, but she paused. "Better leave these for someone who knows how they should be organized."

"Good idea."

Nevaeh stood. "Well, I guess this was a bust."

Jazz shrugged. "Not for you."

Nevaeh met her friend's eyes, the twinkle there signaling more teasing to come.

"Now you'll get to report everything to Branson. Think you'll wake him up again? Just because that's totally necessary." Jazz's lips twitched at the corners.

Nevaeh narrowed her eyes. "I never should've told you about that."

Jazz's eyes widened with very fake innocence. "You mean about shirtless Hercules? Why would you keep the best thing to ever happen to you from your best friend?"

"Because she's super annoying." Nevaeh punched Jazz's shoulder before turning away with a grin.

Jazz's laugh chased her as Nevaeh and Alvarez headed for the open door. "What's the big hurry?" The teasing tone followed close behind. "He'll still be sleeping by the time you get there."

"You just wait till—" Something white on the doorframe caught Nevaeh's gaze, killing the retort on her lips.

"Is that..." Jazz's unfinished question came from behind Nevaeh's shoulder as they both stopped.

Nevaeh reached for the folded paper taped to the wooden doorframe. It opened easily with a light touch from the tip of her pinky.

Her eyes locked on the typed text.

I haven't forgotten you. I'm watching. You'll be next.

THIRTY-TWO

A blood-curdling scream penetrated the walls, jolting Branson awake and out of bed in one fluid motion.

He snatched his Glock from the nightstand and darted for his bedroom door, yanking it open.

His gaze cleared the empty hallway as he went to D-Chop's suite. He knocked on the closed door. "D-Chop?"

He gave it one second. Any longer could be too long.

Gripping the nob, he turned it. Unlocked, as expected.

He swung the door in and lifted his gun.

The lounge attached to D-Chop's bedroom suite was a mess, throw pillows on the floor by the white sofa, empty wine glasses on the coffee table.

But it was empty.

Branson stepped inside, gaze locked on the open doorway that led to D-Chop's bedroom.

Movement made him level his Glock in that direction.

A young woman stumbled through, her hands pressed over her face, covering her eyes as she whimpered.

Branson had seen the petite woman only briefly last night when she'd come to visit D-Chop. Another fan the rapper had picked up, this time at the Wilton High concert.

Branson's gut clenched at the thought of what could've

caused her hysterics now. He skirted past her as she headed for the sofa.

He ducked into the bedroom, weapon ready.

He scanned for D-Chop.

The rapper stood at the side of the king-sized bed in his boxers.

Relief slowed the adrenaline coursing through Branson.

Until he followed the direction of D-Chop's stunned stare.

A butcher's knife stabbed into a pillow at the head of the bed. Had D-Chop been sleeping there?

"D-Chop?" Branson lowered his gun as he moved toward the rapper, scanning him for any sign of injury. "Are you all right?"

The man stared at the knife, unblinking.

"D-Chop? Branson?" Louis's shout came from the lounge area. He was staying overnight in Darren's bedroom now, much farther down the hall.

"In here!" Branson answered just as Louis reached the bedroom doorway, his Glock drawn.

"Everyone okay?"

"I think so." Branson jerked his head toward the bathroom. "Clear the bathroom, will you?"

Branson stepped closer to D-Chop, who still stared at the knife. "D-Chop? What happened?"

"What happened?" He whirled on Branson, eyes snapping. "You can see what happened, man." His voice pinched with anger and a touch of anguish. "Somebody tried to kill me."

"Did you see who put the knife there?"

"You mean who tried to stab me? No, man, I was sleeping. Right there." D-Chop jabbed a finger at the pillow next to the knife, then marched to the silk robe that lay on the floor. He snatched it up and shoved his arms through the sleeves with closed fists as if he was ready to punch someone.

Branson's jaw clenched at the brazenness of the threat. It

was a threat, not an attack like D-Chop thought. If whoever put the knife there had wanted to stab the rapper, the person clearly could've accomplished that. And the girl in the next room would've screamed for an entirely different reason.

He walked closer to the knife. "Is this where the young lady was lying?"

"Sure. Lucky she was in the bathroom."

The square outline of a white shape distinct from the pillow caught Branson's eye. Paper. The blade of the knife stabbed through it.

He glanced around for something to pull the knife away without obliterating fingerprints. Though he was ninety-nine percent sure there wouldn't be any, given the previous knife incident by the pool.

He grabbed a tiny paper napkin off the console table by the wall and used it to grip the base of the knife handle. He pulled the knife out and lay it on the pillow before he picked up the note.

His gaze took in the words, typed like the previous notes.

I can get to you anywhere. You're not safe until you give me what you owe. You'll get instructions for the drop in 24 hours. No cops.

Branson lifted his gaze, catching Louis's nod as he emerged from the bathroom and holstered his weapon.

"Give me that." D-Chop stared at Branson.

Handing the note to him, Branson watched as the rapper read the message.

D-Chop's jaw twitched. Then he crumpled the paper into a wad and chucked it.

The paper didn't go far, dropping to the floor before it reached the bed.

"We should have the police look at that. As well as the knife, and this whole suite."

"No way." D-Chop shook his head.

"This was too close, D-Chop."

"No cops."

"Because of what the note said?" It wasn't like D-Chop to be intimidated.

"'Cause I ain't gonna have cops crawlin' all over my house!" A rare surge of anger erupted in a shout as he angled toward Branson. His eyes flashed. "My house, my business. You take care of this, man. That's what I pay you for. And if anybody gets this close to me again, you're finished. You hear me?"

Branson grit his teeth as his gut clenched. His dad's life depended on this job. On Branson.

And so did D-Chop's. "I hear you." Branson met the rapper's hard gaze. "This won't happen again. You have my word."

Branson would keep the promise, even if he had to personally attach himself to the rapper twenty-four seven. The stakes were much too high if he failed.

"Everything all right?" Travis stepped halfway into the room. He wouldn't have seen much on the security cameras since D-Chop didn't want coverage in this hallway.

Branson nodded. "We're clear."

"Tried to reach you on your phone. We've got a situation." Travis darted a glance at D-Chop before returning his focus to Branson. "Nevaeh found another note."

This night just kept getting better.

Nevaeh mentally reviewed the threatening words of the note she'd found as she watched Branson read it.

I haven't forgotten you. I'm watching. You'll be next.

Something about the threat seemed more ominous this time. More—

"This one is different." Branson lifted his gaze from the note.

Had he been reading her thoughts? But he could mean anything by that. "Different from what?"

The chandelier above them in the entryway of D-Chop's mansion cast shadows across the planes of Branson's face.

Darker coloring hovered beneath his eyes. He looked tired. Stressed.

Her chest pinched with a strange desire to help him somehow. To make him smile.

"The one on D-Chop's pillow."

"What?" Jazz looked at him with widened green eyes.

Nevaeh and Jazz listened in silence as he told them about a knife and message in D-Chop's bedroom. On the rapper's pillow while he slept. No wonder Branson looked stressed.

He handed Nevaeh the crumpled note to read.

I can get to you anywhere. You're not safe until you give me what you owe. You'll get instructions for the drop in 24 hours. No cops.

"A payoff?" Nevaeh handed the note to Jazz as she glanced up at Branson.

"Looks that way."

"Whoever this is, they're getting bolder by the minute." And more dangerous. Nevaeh pressed her lips together. "Do you know who could've gotten into D-Chop's bedroom?"

"The security system wasn't breached."

"So we're looking at another inside job." Jazz returned the paper to Branson, the set of her mouth grim.

He nodded.

Nevaeh thought back to their first night on duty and Branson's tour of the house. "You said there are no cameras in the hallway there, right?"

"Correct." Because D-Chop wanted his privacy, Branson had said.

"So anyone could've entered the bedroom?"

Branson slid his large hand down his face, pinching his thumb and fingers along his stubbled chin. "Unfortunately. I've cautioned D-Chop to lock his door overnight as an added precaution, but he never does." Frustration tightened Branson's deep voice. "And he had another woman in there tonight. He doesn't really know them and doesn't give me time to run security checks on them."

"You think she could've been in on what happened tonight?" Jazz watched Branson intently.

"It's possible. She could've put the knife there herself and then screamed."

"But what's the motive for her?"

Alvarez shifted at Nevaeh's side when she asked the question. She stroked his head. Poor guy wanted to be out on patrol, not standing still indoors.

"Could've been hired to do it." Jazz glanced down at Flash as the Belgian Malinois kept a close eye on the front door. "But I don't get why they'd leave two notes in one night."

"That's what I'm wondering." Branson scanned the paper Nevaeh had found. "This one sounds different. Not like any of the others before." He landed his gaze on Nevaeh. "I think it's meant for you."

"For me?" Surprise pitched her voice higher.

"Look at it." He handed the note back to her. "No mention of what D-Chop owes the person like the other notes. And the 'you'll be next.'"

Nevaeh's eyes locked on the words as he repeated them.

"It indicates there's someone who's first. D-Chop, I assume. Then you."

Her belly tightened as her breath pinched. Her old companion lurked in the shadows, waiting for an opportunity to sneak up on her again. No. She wouldn't let the fear back in.

She shook her head. "I don't think it has to mean that. It doesn't have to be for me. Maybe the writer wanted the groundskeeper or Peter or...you to find it. Other people use that building, right?" Her plea probably sounded a little desperate.

Branson's blue eyes softened as he watched her.

Did she look that worried?

"Yes. Other people use the building." It was a concession. She could hear it in his voice. He still thought the note was meant for her.

No big deal. She could handle a stalker. An extortionist trying to get money from D-Chop and maybe revenge. Somebody who didn't like her because he thought she could blow the whistle on him. Or her.

I'm watching. You'll be next.

The words staring up at her from the page blurred as her hand trembled.

She stepped closer to Branson.

He didn't have to touch her. Just his look was enough. The fierce protectiveness in his blue eyes.

She didn't have to be afraid. Branson would keep her safe.

THIRTY-THREE

Branson smiled at the housekeeper when she gave him that disconcerted, confused look again across D-Chop's dining room table.

Could Marsha sense the tension that tightened his muscles? Or was she nervous about the interview? Maybe she had something to hide.

The need to suspect the woman he'd always respected galled him even more than the boldness of the latest threat. First the patio by the pool, and now the knife in a pillow by D-Chop's head. Whoever had risked that had to know D-Chop was a sound sleeper, often helped along by alcohol.

It was a brazen attack that not only threatened Branson's client but also put his job more at risk than it had ever been. Which put his dad's life in greater danger, too. How would Branson pay for the cancer treatments if he lost this position?

But even that pressing concern didn't bother him as much as the note in the locked outbuilding. Where Nevaeh had been patrolling alone.

He glanced at the beautiful woman who sat beside him, facing the housekeeper. She wasn't as close as yesterday on the sofa, but still close enough to keep his pulse running more rapidly than normal. Close enough to be very aware she was there and cognizant of the effect she had on him.

An effect that made him worry for her safety even though he knew she did this kind of work for a living. She was a professional who could take care of herself. Except when she couldn't.

He wished she'd taken his suggestion to head home after her shift. She was probably exhausted after the long night.

Even Alvarez had collapsed at Nevaeh's feet under the table where he slumbered with an occasional snore.

And Nevaeh would likely be safer at home, away from the person who'd left the note he still thought was aimed at her. But she'd been firm when she'd said she wanted to stay.

The determination in her eyes had stopped him from arguing. She seemed to want to end the threat against D-Chop as much as Branson did. And Branson wanted to end the danger to her even more. Neither one of them wanted to wait to interview the staff after the note on D-Chop's pillow.

Twenty-four hours. And then instructions for leaving money somewhere? Or another attack to make sure D-Chop felt unsafe?

"Fifteen years." Marsha's answer to a question from Nevaeh that Branson must've missed brought his thoughts back to the interview. Their second this morning.

With the locations of both notes last night, he was even more suspicious these threats and attacks were an inside job. There were no signs of break-in. A key had to have been used to access the outbuilding. And there'd been no lapse in the security system protecting the house. Which meant a member of D-Chop's staff, someone the rapper had thought trustworthy, was responsible. Or possibly hired to do someone's bidding.

Branson and Nevaeh had started their interviews this morning with Brian Cornwall, the groundskeeper. The middle-aged man Branson had already liked still seemed like a down-to-earth guy who loved plants and the outdoors. As well as dogs, apparently. He'd asked to pet Alvarez more than once.

The man also wasn't high on Branson's list of suspects

after last night. He could've planted the note in the outbuilding, but not the knife in D-Chop's pillow. Brian had left at five o'clock in the evening as usual, and the gate guard and cameras hadn't caught him returning.

The suspect pool had shrunk abruptly with the knife in D-Chop's bedroom. Only Marsha, Peter, and Branson's security staff stayed at the house overnight. At one forty-two a.m. when D-Chop's girlfriend screamed, no daytime staff members were at the house. The woman with D-Chop, who Branson had finally learned was a twenty-two-year-old named Kim Jameson, was an unknown. He hadn't had time to check into her yet but Nevaeh had passed along the name to Phoenix. Maybe she could give him a reason to not have to suspect the kind housekeeper who sat in front of him now.

"In those fifteen years, have you ever had a problem with D-Chop?"

Branson heard Nevaeh's question this time and watched Marsha for her answer.

The older woman gazed at Nevaeh carefully, but no hostility or tension showed in her eyes. "I know what you're getting at. Some people haven't been happy working for D-Chop. Though I suspect they only fabricate those stories to get attention from the press when they're dismissed."

She transferred her gaze to Branson, then back to Nevaeh. "I've never been anything but happy working for D-Chop. He's always been kind and fair to me. And I appreciate the trust he places in me, even letting me care for the children."

Marsha's gaze softened as she referred to the kids. More affection for them radiated from her than their mother. "I don't have family of my own, you see." She looked down at her folded hands on the table. "It's been...so lovely to have those children around." Her eyes glistened as she looked up.

Branson glanced at Nevaeh.

Her lifted eyebrows and pressed lips reflected what he was thinking. Marsha wouldn't try to extort money from the father of children she treated as if they were her grandchildren. And she certainly would never terrify them and put them in danger with an attempted kidnapping.

"Thanks, Marsha." Branson smiled. "You've been very helpful. You can go now."

"Oh." Her eyes widened slightly as if surprised they hadn't been rougher. "Thank you."

Relief he hadn't had to be stern or tough filtered through Branson as the woman stood and left the dining room. He wouldn't want to damage his working relationship with her.

"I think she'd like to adopt D-Chop's kids as her own grandbabies." Nevaeh's warm voice easily drew his focus to her heart-stopping smile.

The smile that made him throw caution to the wind and do rash things like ask her to dinner. A warning had flared in his mind the moment the invitation had slipped out yesterday after their interview with LeSalle. He couldn't ask her on a date. She didn't share his faith. Didn't believe in the God he lived for. In the Savior Who was everything to him.

He knew better than to try to build a relationship on such a shaky, mismatched foundation. And he'd never wanted to date just to date or play around. He would never toy with any woman that way. Especially Nevaeh.

A lump slid into his throat as he watched her smile down at Alvarez. She deserved only the best man, fully committed to her for life. No games. No selfishness. Just sold-out love and commitment to her forever in marriage the way God intended. The kind of marriage Branson wanted someday.

Nevaeh's phone vibrated, and she grabbed it from the table, flipping it over to see the screen. "Cora. Oh, here we go." Nevaeh's eyes lit as if she'd received good news.

They could use some about now.

"You were right to wonder about Kim Jameson."

"I was?"

Nevaeh tossed him a smile. "Don't sound so surprised."

"Of course. I should've known I was right." He adopted a pompous tone. "I always am."

She rewarded him with a laugh that danced through his ribs and settled softly in his heart.

"So what exactly was I right about?"

The grin stayed on her face as she looked at her phone. "Cora found Kim Jameson's social media accounts. Pictures of her with D-Chop's chef Bartlemay Cox and—get this—our pal, Larry LeSalle." Nevaeh turned the screen toward Branson.

He peered at the screenshots and scrolled with his finger to see both the photos. "Would you look at that."

"Cora also says Kim competed in a modeling competition where Jill was a celebrity judge. They were pictured together."

He lifted his gaze to look at Nevaeh above the phone. "Looks like our suspect pool just widened again."

"Yep."

Thank the Lord. He didn't want to believe Marsha or Peter, D-Chop's trusted personal assistant, could be so evil. And he knew his security team couldn't be behind any of it. But Kim could've been hired by Jill, Chef Cox, or LeSalle to deliver the message to D-Chop.

"You wanted to see me?" Peter entered the room with an expression as bored as his tone.

"Yes. Thanks for coming, Peter. Have a seat, would you?" Branson gestured with his hand toward the chair on the opposite side of the table.

"I don't have much time." Peter tapped the smart tablet that he laid on the table as he sat. His tone was more distracted than put out as he checked the screen.

"I know you're busy. We'll keep this as short as we can."

"Great." Peter lifted his gaze and used one finger to push his glasses up from where they'd slipped down his nose. "You want to talk about the note you found last night?"

Surprise made Branson pause for a moment. Peter was always so quiet, Branson hadn't expected him to say anything unless asked. But maybe it was his way of hurrying things along. "Yes. What do you know about it?"

Peter's bushy eyebrows dipped beneath the rim of his glasses. "What Marsha told me. D-Chop isn't awake yet." He glanced at the tablet and tapped the screen. An avoidance tactic? Or Peter being Peter? He rarely seemed to look up from the device at any time.

"Did the noise wake you last night?" Seemed unlikely he could've slept through the scream, given that Peter's bedroom was on the other side of D-Chop's.

"What noise?" His blank expression appeared equal parts unknowing and disinterested.

"There was a scream."

"D-Chop screamed?" That raised the man's eyebrows.

"No." Branson held his gaze. "Kim Jameson."

"Ah." Peter checked the smart device.

"You didn't hear a scream?" Nevaeh jumped in with the question. The technique had worked for them so far, switching off whenever one person wasn't getting where they wanted or when the subject wasn't responding well.

Peter's gaze went to her. "When one has a room next to D-Chop, one wears earplugs."

"I see your point." She didn't break eye contact with the man. "Did Marsha tell you about the knife?"

"Oh, yes." He looked at his screen again. The man had the attention span of a six-year-old. Though he did have a lot of responsibilities, so maybe that excused it. "Marsha made sure to tell me we would need a replacement pillow and pillowcase."

"So, Pete." Nevaeh rested her arms on the table as she leaned forward. "You know everything that goes on around here."

That comment got Peter to lift his gaze, though his eyes narrowed slightly behind his glasses. Maybe flattery was not the key to his confidence.

"Who do *you* think left the knife?

"I try not to get involved in D-Chop's personal affairs."

"You're his personal assistant."

"Yes." Peter watched her, his gaze devoid of any apparent

awareness of the contradiction there. But maybe there wasn't one in his mind. Or he could be intentionally stalling.

Branson mimicked Nevaeh's position and leaned forward. "I'm going to be straight with you, Peter."

"I would certainly hope so."

"You, Marsha, and Kim are the only ones who could've done this."

"Other than your security personnel, you mean."

Branson squelched the urge to blink at the ready answer. An accusation it almost seemed like Peter had prepared in advance. Or was he that clever? Branson hadn't thought he was, but come to think of it, the man never spoke enough for Branson to get an accurate estimate of his intelligence or wit.

"And either of you, I suppose." Peter looked down at his tablet as he launched the even more personal insinuation. But the slight twitch at the corner of his mouth gave him away.

He was enjoying this. Or at least relishing his own cleverness.

Peter just moved higher on Branson's list of suspects.

"We're ready for you in five, Chef." A guy in his early twenties with a brown beard long enough to brush his black T-shirt popped around the end of Bartlemay Cox's leather sofa.

The wannabe celebrity chef waved a dismissive hand at the man who seemed to be the director of the TicTube video Bartlemay said they were about to record for his channel.

Most TicTubers Nevaeh had seen used their own limited equipment for their videos. But Bartlemay had a small crew and enough equipment to transform his large apartment into something that looked like a TV news studio.

The chef draped his long, skinny arm along the black sofa cushions as he looked at Nevaeh. He'd been staring at her most of the time since she'd arrived, ignoring Alvarez and Branson almost entirely.

"Nevaeh." Bartie Boy smiled. "Heaven in reverse. It's perfect for you."

Nevaeh barely stifled an eye roll. The guy must want to add *playboy* to his resume along with *celebrity chef*.

"I'm having a party here tonight. To celebrate my contract with 'Wake Up, Minneapolis.'" He lingered on the name of the popular morning talk show, as if that was supposed to impress her. "I'd like you to come as my special guest."

She glanced at Branson just in time to catch his eyes narrowing at Bartie Boy. Branson's jaw muscle twitched, and his fingers dug into the navy blue armchair he sat in, a small table with a lamp separating him from Nevaeh.

Was he jealous? Or just being protective? Either option was fine by her. Warmth heated her belly as she swung her gaze back to Bartie Boy—a name that fit him much better in her mind. She tapped the arm of her chair. "I've had smoother pickups, Bart."

The chef's professionally shaped eyebrows lifted at that. But he grinned. "I like a challenge."

"You got one. Like explaining why your girlfriend stuck a knife into D-Chop's pillow last night."

His smile froze, then dropped as he stared at her.

Somebody had to show him women could think.

"I don't know what you're talking about."

"Kim Jameson." Branson's voice rumbled deeper than usual.

"Who's Kim Jameson?"

Alvarez sat up at Nevaeh's side. He'd kept his attention locked on Bartie Boy since they'd arrived. Something about the man put Al on edge. And his instincts on people were never off. Could Al tell Bartie Boy was lying now?

"I can show you the photos from her social media account." Nevaeh pulled her phone from her jacket pocket.

"You said Kim Jameson?" Bartie Boy's tone turned more cooperative. Funny thing.

"Yes." Branson didn't look amused.

"I do know a Kim. I wasn't sure what her last name was. We met at an event—someone's party, I think." Bartie Boy landed his eyes on Nevaeh. They were blue like Branson's but a darker color—cool and flat. Eyes that made her want to look away instead of move close like every time Branson looked at her. "But she's not my girlfriend. I don't have one at the moment."

Uh-huh. Because he liked to play the field. Didn't have to be a genius to fill in the blanks with this guy.

"Did you know she was going to D-Chop's last night?"

Bartie Boy dropped a fake chuckle, barely looking at Branson. "First you think she's my girlfriend, and then you think she'd tell me when she's having a sleepover at D-Chop's?"

Nevaeh leaned forward. "But you did introduce them."

He smiled at her like her statement didn't rattle him a bit. "Anything you say. Has anyone told you how fabulous your skin is? Flawless. You would shine on camera." He tilted his head, his bleached blond, long-on-top locks falling to graze the shaved side of his head. "How would you like to go on with me? You could be my assistant." He grinned, and his eyes lit with a glimpse of life. Dude was in love with his own idea.

She held his gaze. "I'd like it better if you answered our questions. You agreed to."

Bartie's mouth straightened into a forced sober line. "Of course. Anything for D-Chop. It's been a delight to cook for him and his guests." And to use D-Chop's name and the association to leverage himself higher in status.

"Glad to hear it." Impatience edged Branson's voice—something she'd never heard from him before. He really didn't like this guy.

Neither did Alvarez. The K-9 sat alert, watching the chef.

Both her protective guys smelled something wrong about him. Did that mean he was guilty of something worse than being a player?

"How long have you known Kim Jameson?"

Bartie Boy glared at Branson. Probably thanks to the sharpness of his tone. "Only since the party where we met. Which you apparently have documentation of. Probably a month ago."

"Did you know she was going to D-Chop's house last night?"

"I already answered that." Bartie glanced at Nevaeh.

"No, you didn't." Branson's hard answer snapped the chef's gaze back to him.

"Okay. No. I had no idea. Because I don't talk to the woman. We may have had a thing a couple of times, but not for weeks now."

"Will your phone records back that up?"

Ooh. Good one. Nevaeh fought to hide a smile as she glanced at Branson before checking for Bartie Boy's reaction.

The chef's eyes narrowed. "You don't have that kind of access."

"No, but the police do."

Bartie sneered at Branson. "I know D-Chop. He won't want the police involved in this."

Branson leaned forward, pinning the chef with a stare. "There was a knife in his pillow."

Bartie dropped his arm from the cushions and looked away. "You'll need a search warrant and the police to get anything more from me." He pushed to his feet, glaring down at them from his tall height.

Alvarez let out a low growl.

A spark of fear glinted in Bartie's eyes as he looked at the dog. "I have work to do. And I don't allow animals in my home."

Funny he hadn't mentioned that when he'd let them in and said her dog was cute.

"We'll be in touch." Branson stepped to Nevaeh's side as she got to her feet. His large hand cupped her elbow, sending yummy shivers through her arm.

"Come on, Alvarez." She followed Branson's lead as he guided them from the apartment.

Bartie Boy didn't look back as he rounded the sofa and went to take his position behind the massive counter where dishes and ingredients were prepped.

Branson shut the large door to the apartment behind them and let out a heavy breath.

"Don't take it so hard." Nevaeh gave him a grin. "I'm sure I could get him to invite you to his party tonight, too. If I bat my eyes a little." She blinked three times, widening her eyes.

Branson's mouth smushed like he was trying to squash a grin. But a laugh escaped along with his adorable smile. "You're hilarious." He reached out and touched her arm lightly as if to turn her toward the hallway that would take them to the elevator. Funny how he seemed to be doing that more. Touching her. Nothing inappropriate or dominating. Just sweet little natural touches, like Pops might do.

But she sure never had butterflies take flight in her stomach or bolts of heat shoot through her body when Pops touched her.

And she'd never had any man look at her the way Branson did. He seemed to like the way she looked, given how often she caught his gaze going to her lips or lingering on her features. But it was more than that. Different. It was the look he had sometimes when she talked or joked around.

Like just now as he let her enter the elevator with Alvarez first. He had a light in his eyes and a lingering smile on his lips that made her think he enjoyed her. Liked being with her for who she was.

She could get used to dating a guy who made her feel safe, attractive, and appreciated at the same time.

But they weren't dating. Caution waved a flag at the back of her mind as the elevator traveled down. She'd better not get ahead of herself. She should see how things went with her family first. Then the wedding.

"You're awfully quiet." Branson's voice curled around her

along with the heat from his closeness in the elevator. The compartment seemed so small with his muscular body taking up half the space. But it didn't scare her a bit. She had to resist the urge to lean into him instead. To feel his strong arm around her shoulders like that time on the sofa.

"He didn't bother you, did he?"

"Bartie Boy? Not a chance."

"Bartie Boy?" Branson lifted one eyebrow higher than the other as his mouth curved up at the corners.

"Fits him, don't you think?"

Branson chuckled and shook his head. "Only you."

"What? Like I'm going to sit there and be able to call him 'Bartlemay' with a straight face."

Alvarez stood up and wagged his tail.

"See? Al agrees."

Branson laughed. "Al is right. I really wish you would've called him that to his face."

The elevator doors slid open, and she stepped off with Al, glancing over her shoulder as Branson followed. "Let's go back up, and I will. I just didn't want to mess with your interrogation techniques."

"Right." His smile dimmed as they headed through the small lobby to the glass doors. "I wish it'd been a little more successful."

"I think it was. We got him to admit he knew Kim, and he practically lawyered up the moment you challenged him on his fib about not talking to her for weeks."

Branson pushed open the door and held it for her. "So you think he was lying?"

She stepped through the opening, not bothered in the least when her arm brushed his sweater. "For sure. He's hiding something."

"Exactly what I thought." Branson angled toward her as they paused on the sidewalk outside the apartment building. "I wonder if we should—"

Alvarez growled loudly between them. His body went

rigid, as he stared up the sidewalk where another high-rise was followed by some stores.

"What is it, bud?" Nevaeh stepped closer to him.

Pop-pop-pop.

"Get down!" Arms of steel grabbed her as she identified the sound. Gunshots.

THIRTY-FOUR

Branson held Nevaeh against his chest, wrapping his body around hers as they ducked behind a black sedan parked on the street in front of the apartment building.

More shots punctured the air.

The sound of glass shattering followed the gunfire. Close. The rear window of the car that shielded them.

Alvarez barked, stinging Branson's ears.

"Let me go." Nevaeh lifted her head and pushed back against his hold.

He instantly dropped his arms, though his heart screamed he shouldn't let her go. Not until the danger passed. Maybe never.

"We have to stop the shooter before he kills somebody."

Like Nevaeh. She could've already been hit. A vise squeezed his chest.

She pulled out her Sig.

"No." He put his hand on her wrist. "You can't. You could get hurt. I'll go."

"You could get hurt, too." Her mouth quirked. "It's what we do, right?" How could she make light of a moment like this?

Didn't she know what it would do to him if she got shot?

Injured or worse? The air to his lungs stopped somewhere in his chest as his ribs seemed to crunch inward.

He hadn't known either. Not until this moment—the first time in his life he hadn't rushed out to stop the bad guy. Because there was something more important. Someone.

Oh, man. He didn't just care for her. He loved her.

"I'll take the street. You take the sidewalk?" She already moved toward the front of the car with Alvarez, ducking as she prepared to go around it, to leave their protected spot. She paused and glanced back.

He swallowed. He'd get out in front and entice the shooter to focus on him, not her. He'd keep her safe. He nodded. "On three. One, two…three."

He dashed into the open.

"Thank the Lord you're both all right." Cora's smile and affection were so comforting, Nevaeh didn't mind the overdose of Christianese that came with it.

She sat on the truck bed of Branson's pickup that they'd dropped open.

Alvarez had jumped up beside her and lay with his front legs by her knee, holding his head up as he panted.

The sun had come out, pushing away the clouds that had cloaked everything in an overcast gray before. The warm rays permeated her jacket, chasing away the chill.

Or maybe the cold feeling was leaving now that Branson was safe.

Her gaze found him easily among the cops that questioned him next to the high-rise, probably asking the same questions they'd asked her. He stood head and shoulders above them all, his stance so strong and confident.

But he could've been shot.

The knot in her belly twisted, refusing to relax since the first rounds had sounded. She'd grown up hearing gunshots nearly everyday in her neighborhood. They didn't phase her. But it was different with Branson there.

Her heart cared. Really, really cared.

Jana stepped closer and stretched up to push her muzzle between Nevaeh's knees. The golden retriever's senses were nearly as good as Cannenta's for knowing when comfort was needed.

"Did you tell her?" Phoenix's deep voice drew Nevaeh's gaze to see the boss suddenly standing to her right with Dag at her side. Nevaeh had given up a long time ago trying to figure out how Phoenix could appear and disappear so silently.

"I wasn't sure if this was the best timing." Lines crossed Cora's forehead as she looked at Nevaeh. "Are you doing okay?"

"Tell her." Phoenix seemed a little brisk even for her today. She was usually gentler with Cora.

The blonde looked at the boss before she brought her attention back to Nevaeh. "I dug deeper into Peter and Marsha, and I learned something unexpected."

"Not about Marsha?" Nevaeh stroked Jana's soft head. "I can't see her doing anything to put the kids in danger."

"No. It's Peter."

"The mousey assistant?"

"He has a surprising side to his character." Cora glanced toward the cops as she moved in closer to Nevaeh. "To begin with, Peter Volrath is not his real name. He's Peter Ipsen, and he has an assault record."

Nevaeh stared at Cora. "You're kidding. That guy?"

"Yes." Cora nodded, her mouth in a serious line.

"What'd he do, throw his smart tablet at somebody?" Nevaeh let out a laugh.

"Worse than that, I'm afraid. He attacked a rapper who dismissed him from a small hip-hop group. He used a knife."

"Wait." Nevaeh tried to push through the disbelief slowing her brain. "He attacked someone with a knife? And he was in a hip-hop group?"

"He was the rapper's hype man until he was dismissed."

Nevaeh's mouth fell open. She tried to picture Peter as a hype man. She shook her head at the goofy mental image of the little guy with glasses and mousy demeanor on stage trying to jack up a crowd. No way.

"We'll inform the police of what we discovered."

"What about Bartie Boy up there?" Nevaeh shot a glance at the high-rise. "It can't be coincidental that we were shot at as we left his place. And the guy moved way up my list with our little chat. He's hiding something."

"Quite possibly." Phoenix met Nevaeh's gaze with her steady blue eyes. "But Peter could have overheard where you were going next."

Nevaeh thought back to what they'd said before leaving D-Chop's house. Peter could've heard if he'd lingered outside the dining room out of sight.

"We'll continue to look into Cox, but Peter's record points to him as the most likely suspect for D-Chop's extortionist. Perhaps they have a history we aren't aware of, or he carries generalized resentment for rappers."

Nevaeh nodded. "But it's not enough to arrest him."

"Sadly, no." Cora pressed her lips together.

"If we could tie him to this shooting, we could nail him." Nevaeh glanced toward the cops. "Have they found any evidence?"

"Not that they've told us. I'm going to access the footage from the nearby security cameras and hope we can see the shooter." Good ol' Cora. Her skills always came in handy.

"Dagian tracked the shooter's trail to Baird." Phoenix put her hand on Dag's head as he stood patiently next to her.

Baird was the cross street at the intersection two blocks up.

"He or she appears to have taken a parked vehicle from there."

"That's a lot of cameras to avoid on a stretch that long."

"Exactly." A small smile curved Cora's lips. "I'm praying

he made a mistake, and we can find the evidence we need to arrest him."

She could pray until she was blue in the face, but Nevaeh wouldn't hold her breath for a gift to drop from heaven. She'd put her money on Branson and the PK-9 team to crack this case and end the threat to D-Chop.

She just hoped it was soon. Before anyone got hurt. Especially the tall, strong man who held her heart.

THIRTY-FIVE

"Isn't it a little late for you to be up?"

Branson smiled at his dad's words—exactly what he'd say when Branson passed his study too late at night as a teenager. "Keeping a curfew for me?"

His dad chuckled, but the sound disintegrated into a cough.

"Are you okay?"

Another few coughs, each one cinching Branson's chest. Was the cough a sign of something bad? The cancer?

"Yes, I'm fine. I just know you're usually early to bed and early to rise."

Branson dropped to sit on the side of his bed. "And are you still late to bed and early to rise?"

Princess jumped up next to him and rubbed her soft little head against his hand.

"I suppose I am." His dad's tone of voice signaled he wore the gentle smile Branson could easily picture. "But you didn't call me to talk about the hours I keep, did you?"

Perceptive as always. "No." Branson ran his tongue over his lips. It had seemed like a good idea to warn his dad. Tell him his job—the income that supported the cancer treatment —may be coming to an end.

With the intel on Peter from the Phoenix K-9 team, they

could be about to close in on the culprit behind everything that had been happening. They didn't have any evidence they could arrest him for yet. But hopefully Phoenix or the police would uncover something soon.

The threat to D-Chop would end then. But would the threat to Branson's job be over? Not likely. D-Chop was slow to become angry with anyone. But once a person got on his bad side…there usually wasn't any recovering from that.

"What is it, son?" Another cough followed his dad's question, each scraping sound twisting Branson's gut.

He couldn't tell him the treatments were about to end. This was a battle for his life. Branson couldn't fail to protect him from this disease. There had to be another way.

The investor his friend Cooper had talked to about Branson had to come through. Then he could be his own boss and provide for his family in a security specialty that didn't pull him away from his faith so much. That didn't require him to keep quiet and turn a blind eye to people who lived such sordid lives.

"Are you sure that will be what you're looking for?" Andrew's words echoed in Branson's memory. Strange that his mentor had brought up Branson's childhood dream of becoming a pastor. He'd only wanted to be like his dad as most boys did.

"I would've made a terrible pastor." The statement spun off from his spiraling thoughts.

Silence met the words he instantly regretted. His dad had always been disappointed Branson hadn't followed in his footsteps.

"What makes you say that?"

Because he was letting his faith slide. Wasn't in the Word as much as he should be.

"Have you asked God what He wants you to do?" Andrew's question sounded in Branson's head as loudly as if he were on the other end of the line instead of his dad. "I just couldn't do what you do."

"God calls each of us to the work He created us for. If you had pursued becoming a pastor, you would've been the minister God wanted you to be. Different than I am, I'm sure. But still striving to serve God to the best of your abilities."

Unlike what he was doing now. His dad probably didn't mean that implication, but the words stung anyway.

Branson was protecting people, though. That was something God wanted His people to do. Preserve human life. Take care of others. Branson was serving Him and others in that way.

The rationale sounded desperate even in his own mind. Kind of like the attempt he'd made to excuse the fact he'd fallen for a woman who wasn't a Christian.

He hadn't even been able to face Nevaeh tonight when she'd arrived for patrol. He'd told Travis to greet her and Jazz instead while he hid in his room like a coward.

But how could he face her, talk to her, when he didn't know where to go from here? He loved her, but he shouldn't. He couldn't act on it. Not when she didn't share his faith. He may not be doing great staying close to God, but he wasn't about to disobey God's mandate to not attach himself to a non-believer.

The urge to talk to his dad about Nevaeh pressed against Branson's lips. But how disappointed would his dad be if he knew Branson had let himself fall in love with a non-Christian?

"How are the treatments going?" He pushed out the safer question instead. "I mean really. You sound sicker."

"Well...It does seem like the treatment is worse than the disease some days." A sound like his dad was trying to repress a cough broke across the line. "I'm so grateful you're able to pay for it, though. I want to beat this."

"And you're going to." Branson tightened his jaw. "I'll make sure you can keep going with the treatment as long as you need it." Somehow. Even if D-Chop did fire him and the investor fell through.

"I worry this is putting too much of a burden on you."

Had his dad detected Branson's stress? Branson tried to

force a smile he hoped would lighten his tone. "It's not a burden at all. I want to get you through this."

"It's not up to you, son. Even with this treatment, there are no guarantees I'll pull through."

"You will." Branson couldn't consider any other outcome.

"That's in God's hands."

Branson blew out a breath, trying to loosen the worry clogging his chest. "I guess I'm used to facing attacks I can see. Enemies I can take down."

"Our God is mighty to save, Branson. He is my stronghold, my ever-present help in trouble. I'm not worried."

But hadn't God given Branson his well-paying career exactly for this purpose? To save his dad's life? He couldn't fail his family. "I should let you get some rest."

"Before you go, your mom wants me to ask about the young lady you mentioned the other day. Nevaeh, was it?"

"Oh?" Heat crawled up Branson's neck. His mom didn't miss a trick when it came to her kids' significant others.

"Yes. You know your mom. She's convinced there's something there." The higher pitched tone of his mom's voice sounded in the background. "She wants me to ask if you're going to ask her out."

"Well..." Branson stood and paced along the bed, searching for the best answer. Honesty was always the best course. "I'd like to, but she's not a Christian."

"Oh, that's too bad. Have you talked to her about Jesus?"

"Not much, no." Guilt lodged in Branson's throat.

"It could be that's why God put you in her life, to point the way to Him. You could have an eternal impact on her, son."

The words fell heavy on Branson's conscience. "Thanks, Dad. I'd better get some shut-eye. Give Mom a hug for me, will you?"

"Sure thing. We're praying for you."

"And I'm praying for you. Love you both."

"Love you, too, son. Goodnight."

Branson lowered his phone and caught Princess staring at

him, her tiny paws hanging over the edge of the bed. "I know. He's right. Maybe I'm not in Nevaeh's life for my sake. Maybe I wasn't supposed to care for her like I do. I should focus on leading her to God. Helping her beat her fear and heal, right? Like I've been doing, but more God, less emotion."

Wide blue eyes stared back at him.

"You're ridiculously cute but not much help, you know that?" He scratched the kitty's plush cheek with his finger.

He glanced at the clock on his nightstand. *11:30 p.m.*

Much too late to fit in a good night's rest by four thirty in the morning.

But his instincts rebelled against the idea of going to sleep while Peter was in the house. Branson had posted Louis outside D-Chop's bedroom door overnight and called in Kal Lawrence, another personal protection specialist he'd worked with in L.A., to arrive in the morning. That way, D-Chop would have added security at his bedroom every night with Kal and Travis alternating between guard duty and monitoring security cameras, while Branson and Louis rested up for the daytime shifts.

Nevaeh didn't have extra protection, though. And if Peter was the one behind the threats and incidents targeting D-Chop, then he was also responsible for the note Branson was sure had been meant for her.

And the nighttime visit to her house. When the perp had looked in her window.

The idea heated Branson's blood and curled his hands into fists. He could end the threat to Nevaeh right now.

He didn't need to wait for more evidence Peter was the culprit if he could find it himself.

D-Chop had to know something about the man he'd hired for his most trusted position. If the rapper wanted Branson to handle this, he'd have to tell Branson what he knew.

"I'll be back, Princess." He gave the kitty a final stroke and stalked to the door.

It was time to end this.

No threatening notes. No knives randomly stabbing into furniture and décor. At least so far.

It should be a good night.

But unease curdled in Nevaeh's stomach as she and Alvarez patrolled D-Chop's estate in the crisp night air.

She wasn't supposed to feel like this anymore. At least not when Branson was around. And he was in the house now, probably sleeping.

Maybe that was the problem. She hadn't seen him tonight.

Jazz had been as surprised as Nevaeh when Travis had met them at the front door instead of Branson. Actually, Nevaeh had been worried more than surprised at first.

But Travis had said Branson was there, and he was fine. The guy looked like he hadn't known what to say to her inquisition. Probably a good sign Branson hadn't coached him to say anything. But the sudden change in the routine Branson had established since they'd started patrolling the estate threw her off-balance.

She blew out a breath that steamed the air in front of her face, creating a cloud for her to walk through as she scanned the fence along the perimeter of the front yard.

Who was she kidding? It wouldn't have mattered if she had seen a supervisor before starting a shift at any other gig. It only mattered because it was Branson.

Because she needed to know that everything was okay. Had to know *she* was okay—a state which seemed to be linked to his presence, dependent on seeing his smile and knowing, really knowing, he was close by.

Especially after that morning. The gunshots, the near miss.

Though since when had gunfire bothered her so much?

The question hit its mark in the story she was apparently trying to sell herself. Okay, fine. She mostly needed to see him to know *he* was okay. Because he could have not been okay today. If one of those bullets had hit him.

And that bothered her more than she'd have expected.

Was it because she needed him? Because he was the reason she wasn't afraid anymore? Or was it something more?

Her heart beat out the answer in the silence of the night. An answer that scared her more than a little.

Could she risk loving a man? What if the PTSD came back? What if he ended up not being who she thought he was? She'd been fooled before.

The shadows of the memory pushed at her mind. Tendrils of fear reached for her, waiting to grab her if she looked back.

No. She wouldn't. She'd only look forward. To a future that could include Branson if she didn't let her fears and doubts ruin the possibility.

Branson wasn't like the monster who'd tried to kill her. She knew that. She'd stake her life on it. And she'd even stake her heart on it.

But she did need to find out if he felt the same. She thought he did, especially after the way he'd acted today. Jealous of Bartlemay Cox's flirting and oh-so-protective when the gunfire started. But why hadn't he wanted to see her tonight?

"Come on, Al. Let's cover the house."

It was a good idea Branson had to have them make more frequent passes inside the mansion now. Should deter anyone on the inside who had ideas about attacking D-Chop. They were only hours away from the twenty-four hour deadline, and instructions for the money drop still hadn't shown up.

At least now Nevaeh had a reason to visit the house where Branson was. Probably sleeping, but she could muster up some excuse to wake him. Would wanting to ask if he loved her be a good enough excuse?

She snickered as she picked up the pace toward the well-lit door at the nearest end of the house. Wouldn't hurt to get out of the cold for a bit either. It had to be under forty tonight. She'd have to switch to her winter jacket tomorrow.

She reached the door under the security light and typed in the access code on the keypad.

As it clicked open, she turned the knob and pushed in the door.

Warm air greeted her. Along with raised voices. Shouting.

Alvarez growled.

THIRTY-SIX

Men's voices, raised and angry, sounded somewhere nearby.

Alvarez rumbled again, pressing to the end of his leash.

"Where are they, Al?"

The rottie mix headed through the mudroom and pulled to the right, down the short hallway that led to the bedrooms.

The voices grew louder. More intense.

Was that Branson? She'd never heard him angry or loud before.

And who was the other man? The second voice was kind of familiar, but different enough she couldn't place it.

Alvarez led her around the sharp corner with another growl.

Her gaze jumped ahead to the light from an open doorway. Wasn't that Peter's room?

She drew her Sig and kept the weapon low at her side for now. If Peter was really D-Chop's extortionist, the man who'd stalked her and hired the kidnappers, this could get messy.

You'll be next.

If Peter was the one who'd left that note in the outbuilding and he'd meant it for her like Branson thought, he could say it again to her face.

"With me." She whispered the command to Alvarez as she slowed by the open doorway.

"Then how do you explain this?" Branson's voice bellowed from the room, strong, powerful. Safe.

"I don't know what you're talking about!" If Peter wanted anyone to believe him, he'd better calm down and stop shouting.

Confident that Branson must have things under control, Nevaeh stepped into the doorway.

Alvarez let out a well-timed growl that silenced both men, drawing their stares.

Peter stood near a desk that held a computer and printer off to one side of the huge bedroom.

Branson hovered about six feet away, his stance wide and ready, a sheet of paper in his hand. He hadn't drawn his gun. Should be a good sign.

"Everything okay in here?"

"Nevaeh." The way Branson said her name and the way his eyes lit at the same time, lessening the tension around his mouth, did crazy things to her pulse. He was happy to see her.

She couldn't help the smile that found her lips. "Hey."

"I don't need a crowd in my room." Peter glared at her—the most emotion she'd ever seen on the little man's face. "I'll thank you all to leave now."

"Oh, we're not going anywhere, Peter. But you are." Branson stepped closer to Nevaeh, ratcheting up her heart rate and warming her through just with his proximity. "Louis is with D-Chop in his suite just in case." He said the words in a low, quiet tone, as if sharing a secret. He kept his gaze locked on Peter as he held out the paper toward her. "I found this on Peter's printer tray."

She glanced at the text, exactly the font and size of the other threatening notes.

$25 million. By tomorrow noon. We both know you can afford it. You owe me. Leave the money in a suitcase, locker #15, Jackson & 9th

St. Ramp. If it isn't there by noon, I'm coming for you. You won't survive this time.

Nevaeh lifted her gaze to the little man who glared at Branson, then at her. As if they were to blame for what he was doing. But why was he doing it? Because he had some vendetta against rappers from his bad experience? Seemed a stretch. "Why?"

"I don't even know where that paper came from. Someone must have broken into my room. Like you did." He aimed the remark at Branson, anger shooting from the eyes behind his glasses.

"D-Chop just told me Peter wanted to be his hype man." Branson didn't take his eyes off Peter. "D-Chop said no. More than once."

"So? Is that a crime?"

"No." Branson took a step toward Peter. "But extortion is. Kidnapping is. Arson, damage to private property, endangering children...Shall I go on?"

"You can talk until you're blue in the face. You can't prove anything."

"I think this note will do that for us, Peter. And the fact that it'll be on your computer, along with all the other threatening notes. Knowing you, I'm sure you saved each one, neatly labeled."

Peter clenched his round jaw. But his fingers shook as he adjusted his glasses.

Hard to believe this small, seemingly shy and harmless man could be behind everything. That he would do that to D-Chop, who'd treated him well. Anger for her friend, for the guy who'd helped Jordy and so many others, rose in Nevaeh's chest. "D-Chop gave you a really good job. He didn't have to do that. Why would you think he owes you?"

A harsh laugh popped from Peter's mouth. "You know what he said when he offered me this lackey's job?" Peter's lips curled in a humorless smile. "He said it would give me a chance to watch and learn. From him. From the hype man he hired instead. As if I needed to learn."

Peter whirled to face his desk, planting his hands on the chairback in front of it. He gripped the leather, squeezing until his knuckles turned white. "I was born for rap. He never gave me a chance. Just made a slave out of me."

A slave who already made more money in one year than most of Nevaeh's family members would see in four. She stifled an eye roll at the man's pathetic entitlement complex. Reminded her too much of her sister, but at least Sherinda didn't go so far as violence.

A wailing sound came from outside. Sirens?

"You called the police?" Peter didn't turn around.

"Yes." Branson's voice was calm, but firm. "It's over, Peter."

The man's shoulders sagged, his grip on the chair appearing to be the only thing that held him up. "No. No, it isn't."

His denial, a desperate man's grasp at hope, almost tempted her to pity him. Almost.

But after all he'd done, he deserved to be behind bars. Everyone would be safer with him locked up.

Nevaeh had done it. She'd paid D-Chop back for her family's debt. Mission accomplished.

The satisfaction that should've come with the closure was tainted. Because if the job was over, so would be the reason for seeing Branson. This giant of a man who'd filled every corner of her life with his strength and claimed her heart.

A different kind of fear trembled her pulse. He was her protector. The key to her newfound courage. She couldn't lose him. Ever.

Branson should be thrilled. Or at least deeply satisfied. But as he watched the police officer cuff Peter and escort him from the suite, a sinking sensation filled his torso.

He didn't have to guess why.

Two officers brushed close to him, forcing him to sidestep out of their way. And bump into Nevaeh.

"Sorry." His hand automatically went to her arm in case he'd made her lose her balance.

Her full lips curved into a smile as her gaze drifted from his hand to his face. No trace of fear lurked in her eyes, the frightened response to his closeness. Only warmth shone there now. Warmth, affection. Dare he hope…love?

But that wouldn't solve the problem. The reminder made him drop his hand. He gave her an awkward smile. "Hard to believe it's over, isn't it?"

"Yeah." The smile still hovered on her closed lips as she looked away toward the officers who searched the room.

"I'm glad it is." He dragged his hand across the back of his neck. "The danger to D-Chop. And especially to you." He risked looking at her again. She had to know it mattered to him, at least. "I can't believe Peter would've had the guts to stalk you like that."

She shrugged. As if it didn't matter someone had violated her privacy and threatened her. "I don't think he did it himself. The guy I saw was a lot bulkier and taller. Peter probably hired the dude. Maybe he was one of the kidnappers, too."

"Well, either way, I wouldn't have minded a little time alone with Peter to make sure he never did that to a woman again."

Nevaeh rewarded his protective sentiment with a grin. But just as quickly as the burst of light had arrived, it faded, her mouth transitioning to a frown as she looked away. "I guess you won't need us for patrol anymore now."

Was that disappointment in her voice and causing her frown? The possibility shot hope through his system, a short-lived elation because she was right.

On the other hand, D-Chop probably wouldn't object to having Nevaeh stay on. Especially with their past connection, the apparent friendship they had. He'd probably still think having the K-9s around was cool, too.

"Actually..."

Her gaze shot up to his at the first word.

A smile stretched his mouth as he continued. "I could tell D-Chop I'd like you to stay on. He might go for that." Branson didn't care if his wording revealed his feelings for her. He wanted her to know. Wanted to tell her in the sweetest words he could manage.

But he couldn't.

"It could be that's why God put you in her life, to point the way to Him." His dad's words rang in his ears.

That should be his goal. Not winning her heart for himself but winning her soul for God. Telling her the best news, the truly sweetest words and most glorious truth anyone could ever hear.

He would focus on that goal from now on. Something he couldn't do unless he kept her on for security. He needed to stay in her life to tell her about Jesus.

And if she did come to the Lord. Well...

"I'd like that." Nevaeh looked at him, the hope that welled up inside him reflected in a smaller way in her gaze. "So are we still on for tomorrow?"

"Tomorrow?"

"Moving my sister. The wedding." She adopted a casual tone as she glanced away.

But her words—*the wedding*—tripled the hope seeping through him, making his heart thump against his ribs.

"I wouldn't miss it for the world."

THIRTY-SEVEN

Now that was a sight a girl could get used to. Nevaeh paused in the middle of filling glasses with lemonade and stared out the kitchen window.

Outside on the driveway, her own Hercules hefted a bookcase into the trailer alone, his massive muscles straining against his T-shirt sleeves, the cotton skimming his rippling back.

She couldn't believe that impressive display of strength and fitness used to spook her.

"He's a good man."

Nevaeh jumped and whirled, sloshing the lemonade in the pitcher as her gaze landed on Pops.

"Careful." He eyed the pitcher in her hand. But his eyes redirected over her shoulder so quickly that suspicion rose in her mind. Pops loved his double meanings. Though what he was hinting at this time, Nevaeh had no clue. Unless he didn't approve of her liking Branson.

"You like him, don't you, Pops?"

"I do." He stepped around Cannenta, who lay at Nevaeh's feet, and stopped by the counter to peer out the window.

She turned to look again, too.

Branson and her older brother TJ laughed about something. TJ never even smiled around folks he didn't like.

LeBron sauntered up to the two men and smacked Branson on the back as he said something she couldn't hear.

Branson didn't wince or startle, instead gripping LeBron's shoulder and giving him a hearty shake with a grin. He appeared to answer LeBron back. Knowing her kid brother, LeBron had probably ribbed the older guys about getting back to work.

"He's good for the boys."

Nevaeh smiled at the approval in Pops' voice. "Yeah."

"Good for you, too."

"I'm glad you think so." Nevaeh set the pitcher on the counter and rotated so she could get a better look at her grandpa. "I saw the two of you having a serious conversation out there a little while ago. What'd you talk about?"

"Men talk." Pops gimped from the window to the breakfast table and pulled out a spindly chair next to Alvarez. The poor dog lay panting on the vinyl floor, not enjoying the absence of air conditioning in Pops' house.

"Aw, come on, Pops. It was about me, wasn't it?"

He lowered himself into the chair and let out a breath that sounded too much like a wince for her taste.

"Your leg hurting today?"

"Every day, honey."

She frowned. There should be something they could do about the discomfort. Maybe a physical therapist. She'd have to check to see if his state insurance or Medicare would cover that.

"Don't worry about me, child."

"What makes you think I'm worrying?"

He chuckled. "Since you was a little girl, you always got them lines between your eyebrows and that cute pucker whenever you was worried about something or somebody."

"Okay." She lifted the pitcher and stepped to the table. "Seeing as you don't want me to worry, then you better give me something else to think about." She grabbed the empty glass that sat in front of Pops and filled it with lemonade. "Like what you and Branson talked about."

"We talked about the most important things."

"Like?"

His lips formed the pucker he'd just accused her of having. "He's a real good man. A man of faith."

Nevaeh narrowed her eyes as she lowered the pitcher to the table and sank into the chair kitty-corner to Pops. "Why do I get the idea you're saying that's bad?"

"It's good. Real good. He could do *you* good."

Apprehension clustered in Nevaeh's stomach as she watched her grandpa closely. His expression wasn't giving much away except that he hadn't said all he had to say yet. "But?"

"I know you sweet on him."

She straightened. A smile found her face. Not the wording she'd have used, but she couldn't deny it. Didn't really want to. And it was probably written all over her, anyway, especially when she'd just been mooning over the man as she watched him through the window.

"Yeah, Pops. I'm sweet on him." She covered his hand with her own. "But that's good, right? You said he's a good man. And I know you like that he believes in God like you do."

"Honey, the problem is you need to get right with God before you can be with a man like Branson."

Nevaeh pulled back, surprise hitting her like a slap in the face. She removed her hand, letting it rest on the edge of the table. "What do you mean? Did he say that?"

"He don't have to. I know these things. You could never jive with each other. You'd be tugging two different directions every day of your lives. 'Cause Branson, he a man of God."

Nevaeh pressed her lips together. "So I wouldn't be good enough for him?"

"Now come on, honey, you know that ain't it. You rejected God after you got beat up. I saw it soon as you pushed Him away."

Frustration surged up from Nevaeh's belly. She shoved

back her chair and stood, stalking to the counter just for something to do other than talking back to Pops. She'd been raised never to do that.

"Thing is, you rejected Him, but He never left you."

Pops' voice hit her back as she faced the kitchen window.

Branson set down a box to lift little one-year-old Crieg over his arms and land him on those muscular shoulders. Handon, only two years older and always competitive, pulled on Branson's arm until the big man swept that boy up, too, and held him high against his chest. Branson was even amazing with her nephews and nieces.

Felice had been following him around most of the time since he'd arrived, clearly nursing a crush, and his presence had inspired too-cool-for-work-Dawton to join the men carting furniture and boxes.

"Who you think let you get up this morning? And Who's letting you keep breathing right now?" Pops' voice dragged her back to the preachy lecture she'd really like to avoid. "And Who brought that boy into your life, the one you can't stop watching long enough to listen to your old Pops?"

Nevaeh rolled her eyes before she turned to face him. But the humor she'd expected to see in his dark brown eyes wasn't there. Only the serious stare that meant she'd better listen.

"Thought that might get your attention. You hear what I been saying?"

"Yeah. I hear you, Pops."

"Good, 'cause I got one more question for you. Who do you think helped you survive that man beatin' you at that prison and used it to make you stronger?"

Nevaeh took deep breaths as she folded her arms in front of her, grappling for control. She wouldn't sass her grandpa. But the denial that boiled in her chest pushed up into her throat, fighting for release. "It sure wasn't God. He didn't do nothin' for me there." She'd been completely, utterly alone against the monster. Helpless. Powerless.

"God's God, child. He does what he wants and ain't nobody can stop Him."

Nevaeh glared at the floor, giving the old, faded vinyl the brunt of her glare.

"Nevaeh, look at me."

She clenched her jaw and dragged her gaze to her grandpa's face, to the weathered skin that was becoming as old and worn as the flooring in this place.

"What He wants is for you to be His child. That's what I want for you, too, baby. No matter what it takes." Something glinted in Pops' eyes. Moisture? It couldn't be. Pops never cried. She'd never seen him cry once, not even when Grams had passed.

"God ain't always done things the way I want either. Like when he took your grams before me. But I learned a long time ago, I got to trust Him 'cause there ain't no stopping Him."

So God was the great bully in the sky? That would explain why He had let Walter beat her nearly to death. And that was exactly why she'd leave Him alone just like He was leaving her alone.

"I better get this out to the crew." She put the pitcher on the tray with the glasses and hefted the load, heading for the screen door.

"Nevaeh?"

She closed her eyes and stopped. Then she slowly turned to face him.

"You hear what I said. That boy won't have you if you ain't right with God."

The words stung, even though she didn't believe them. Branson hadn't said anything about her feelings toward God. Hadn't even asked. But she was pretty sure he liked her anyway. He wouldn't have come here otherwise or said he'd go with her to the wedding this afternoon.

"But worst is that fear you can't shake. It's gonna own you forever if you don't take it to Jesus."

Not that again. And Pops was wrong this time anyway.

The fear didn't own her anymore. She was done with it, thanks to Branson.

She hurried outside before she said something she'd regret. Pops loved her and always had her best at heart. She knew that.

But he was finally wrong about something.

"Hey." Branson's deep voice and welcome smile made her pulse trip, followed by her feet.

He reached for her, his warm hands landing on her waist to steady her. "Whoa, there. I'm hoping to drink some of that lemonade, not wear it." The twinkle in his soft blue eyes melted into a different kind of glimmer—one that matched the way his breaths grew shallow and quicker.

Yeah, Pops was wrong this time. Branson liked her a whole lot. Maybe loved her.

Nothing—not fear or how she felt about God—was going to stand in their way.

THIRTY-EIGHT

Cue the most beautiful bride Nevaeh had ever seen.

The classic wedding march belted from the organ as Cora glided gracefully up the aisle, her steps timed to the music perfectly. Her slim arm entwined with her dad's, she was a vision in a classic, long-sleeved gown covered in intricate lace.

Cora had chosen a veil that left her face uncovered, the fabric attached to a glimmering headband that crested her upswept hair, a few blonde tendrils left out and shaped to frame her delicate features.

But more than the getup was the expression on Cora's face. She was always happy and sweet, but—wow. Nevaeh had never seen her look so...blissful. As if she'd been transported to the heaven she liked to talk about. And her gaze and smile were aimed right at her groom. She was breathtaking.

Kent obviously thought so, too. From where Nevaeh stood next to Bris on the steps at the front of the cathedral, she had a good view of the groom's face. He waited for his bride on the top step near the minister. Kent's brother, Rem, and Michael stood on the lower steps beside him in gray tuxes.

Nevaeh couldn't believe it. A huge smile split the handsome man's face.

Sure, Kent had been smiling a lot more these days thanks to the effect Cora apparently had on him.

But the man she'd always teased Cora was a brooding bad boy could pass for a choir boy at this moment. She'd never seen him look so happy. So giddy.

Jazz nudged her with an elbow, and Nevaeh answered her friend's smile with one of her own. Jazz's unspoken sentiment was spot on—these two were perfect for each other. And all kidding aside, she couldn't be happier for them both.

Cora's dad passed her hand to Kent, and they faced each other in front of the minister. Kent held Cora's hands in his, smiling at her like a man who knew how lucky he was to catch such a gorgeous bride.

Cora's dad went to the empty seat in the front row. At least he'd shown up for the big day. She and Sof had predicted he wouldn't make it, given how absent he'd been during Cora's life. Her brother, Bradley, was there, too, sitting next to their dad.

Nevaeh's gaze skirted past him to search the other people in the full pews. She'd tried to spot Branson on her walk up the aisle but hadn't been able to. Surprising, given he'd be head and shoulders above everyone else.

There. He sat about four rows back toward the outer wall, which explained why she hadn't been able to see him past all the people filling the row. But even from this distance, she could see he was watching her. Could feel the warmth of his attention. It drew her to him, tempting her to go down there and sit with him. Especially since he looked drop-dead gorgeous in the navy blue tuxedo that intensified his eyes even from this distance.

Then he smiled. That warm, gentle smile.

And suddenly an image of him at the front of the church, watching and waiting for her to come to him, burst to life in front of her eyes.

Her heart surged in her chest.

Is that what she wanted? Marriage to Branson?

Thanks to him, she'd felt freer and happier these last few days than she had in the last six years. She hadn't even needed to bring Cannenta with her to the wedding. Cora had said she could if she needed Cannenta's support, though the formal wedding and reception venues wouldn't allow the other K-9s to come.

The potentially crowded spaces around men she didn't know would've normally made her nervous. But knowing Branson was going to be at the wedding with her had been all the comfort she needed. And she had a feeling he could be exactly what she needed for the rest of her life.

"That boy won't have you if you ain't right with God." Pops' words rang in her ears, deflating the confidence that had felt so solid a second before.

Was he right? As soon as they'd moved her sister's stuff to the new apartment, Nevaeh had to dash to get to the wedding in time for all the preparations. She hadn't had a moment to talk to Branson about what her grandpa had said. Not that she wanted to. They seemed to be moving along just fine without that complication.

She'd hang on to what they had and trust Branson. He wouldn't string her along, wouldn't play with her feelings like some guys. She was as sure of that as she was that she could trust him to keep her safe. Now, and hopefully for a very long time into the future.

Her gaze sought his again.

He still watched her as she'd hoped. But his mouth formed a straight line, pinched at the corners. And his eyes held an expression she didn't know how to interpret from this distance. One that didn't look good.

His lips abruptly relaxed and slid into a smile. Probably because he'd seen her watching him. But it was too late.

Doubt stirred in her belly. She switched her attention to the bride and groom and tried to listen to their vows.

She'd be able to talk to Branson soon at the reception. But her nerves didn't seem to find that thought comforting.

Maybe because they knew she wouldn't like what he had to say.

It was almost over. Regret lodged in Branson's chest as Cora's father stepped away from the microphone where he'd just told everyone they would soon gather in the lobby to send off the happy couple on their honeymoon to Europe.

It was too soon. Not to send off the couple he barely knew, but much too soon to say goodbye to Nevaeh.

He looked at her, sitting in the chair to his left. She leaned away, talking to Jazz on her other side. Laughing and happy.

She took his breath away. Every time he looked at her in the blue dress that perfectly draped over her curves, emphasizing her femininity with grace and elegance. When she'd walked up the aisle and stood up front during the ceremony, his mind had easily taken leaps it shouldn't have. He'd pictured her in a white dress instead, standing there with him. As his bride.

But he had no right to picture anything of the kind. She wasn't his bride and never could be unless things changed in a big way.

Not likely, given that this may be the last time he'd see her. The painful thought stuck in his throat. He hadn't even had a chance to tell her about Jesus yet. To point her to her Savior.

But he'd run out of excuses and time to be around her. His idea to ask D-Chop to keep her on for security wouldn't work. When Branson had stopped at the house before the wedding to change and make sure the security detail was set to cover the rest of his day off, D-Chop had given him the bad news.

The rapper was moving back to L.A. His wife had finally agreed to a settlement that included a split custody agreement, so he didn't have to keep staying in Minnesota to look good to a judge.

D-Chop wanted Branson to return to California with him. The invitation would've seemed like positive news before. Branson wasn't being fired. That was a good thing.

Except it meant staying in the shallow, immoral, and anti-Christian world he was trying to escape.

And it meant leaving Nevaeh, putting hundreds of miles between them.

But he didn't have any other option. The email he'd seen on his phone twenty minutes ago had made sure of that.

The investor considering Branson's corporate security proposal had declined. Maybe they'd gotten wind of the security troubles with D-Chop. Or maybe they had other reasons not to invest. He'd probably never know.

All that mattered was he didn't have the funds to start his own security business. Not while still supporting his dad through the cancer treatments.

He should just be grateful he had a job left at all after everything that had happened.

But it was going to take him away from the woman he loved. Maybe if he could stay here, he'd devise an excuse to keep seeing her. He could offer his services to the Phoenix K-9 Agency or get some job as a security guard in the Twin Cities.

He was dreaming. None of those options would pay enough to fund his dad's treatments. Not even close.

He had to stay with D-Chop and the lucrative career he was coming to loathe.

He had to leave Nevaeh.

As if she sensed his attention, she turned her head toward him, her gorgeous brown eyes landing on his face.

Her smile faded as she watched him.

Too much of his inner turmoil must be showing.

He tried to force a smile. After all, he was looking at the most beautiful person he'd ever seen in his life. A smile shouldn't be hard.

But it was. Because he couldn't ignore the reality that this was one of the last times he'd have the opportunity to smile at her. Probably the last time he'd ever sit next to her like this. Be close, be part of her world, her life.

"Should we go, guys?" Jazz's voice drifted past Nevaeh to reach Branson's ears.

Go. Exactly what he didn't want to do.

"Want to throw some rice at people?" Nevaeh's full mouth quirked in a half smile.

A chuckle bubbled from his throat. Leave it to Nevaeh to make him laugh, even when his heart was aching. "Absolutely." He stood and extended his hand toward her.

Her eyes widened slightly like she was startled, but she smiled as she slipped her hand in his.

He kept it—her hand—even though he had no right to, as they moved with the crowd of guests out of the reception hall and to the large lobby at the front of the building.

The people clustered, bottlenecking at the double doors they had to take out of the reception hall.

Branson shifted Nevaeh in front of him, releasing her hand to cup her shoulders and keep her shielded from the people bumping into each other. He didn't mind the excuse to hold her close.

The grin she shot him as she tilted her head up and back said she didn't mind either.

A surge of heat pulsed through him. This was what he wanted. To be always near her. Always protecting her—from jostling crowds, from PTSD, from anything that arose. He wanted to make her happy. To keep that grin on her face forever.

But he wouldn't sacrifice his faith, wouldn't be disobedient to God, to be with her.

So when they reached the lobby where the people spread apart, he dropped his hands from her shoulders.

"Over here, guys." Bristol waved them to the front of the two sides that were forming an aisle between them. "You didn't get rice." She glanced past them. "Oh, Sofia. Good."

The petite woman in a navy blue pantsuit hurried toward them with a small plastic bucket in her hands. "Rice for everyone." Sofia grinned as she extended the bucket for them to grab handfuls. "Though I don't think the cleaning crew is going to be thrilled the farewell moved inside."

Branson didn't miss the way her husband's hand went to Sofia's back when she swung the bucket toward him. And the way their daughter beamed up at them with an excited, joyous expression of a child who had a happy, safe home.

Branson shook his head at himself. He'd heard weddings could do this to people—make them imagine marriages and families of their own. Make them want those things so much it hurt. But he'd never experienced the wedding effect before. Not until Nevaeh.

"Are you okay?" The woman of his thoughts stepped close, her arm brushing against the sleeve of his tuxedo jacket, sending a jolt of awareness straight to his heart. "You look like you got bad news."

His chest squeezed, the ache strengthening its grip. He put his arm around her shoulders. He couldn't seem to help himself. He had to hold her, to try to banish the concern in her eyes. "Nothing important." Except the news he was trapped in the career he no longer wanted. And the news that he had to leave with D-Chop in less than forty-eight hours, that he'd probably never see Nevaeh again. That he probably shouldn't.

"Here they come!" Someone's shout at the back of the lobby drew everyone's attention to the makeshift aisle they'd created for the couple to pass through to the door.

Rice started flying above the crowd, and Branson's height enabled him to spot the dark head of Kent, Cora's husband, before they reached the front.

The couple's smiles beamed as they drew close, walking quickly through the shower of rice and well-wishes. They'd changed out of their wedding garb into slightly less formal wear, Cora in a pale blue suit jacket and skirt, and Kent in a blazer and jeans.

"Love you." Cora kissed her hand and moved it outward

toward her Phoenix K-9 co-workers with an especially large smile.

"Love you back!"

"Safe travels!"

"Congratulations!"

The Phoenix K-9 women shouted the wishes in return as they tossed the rice.

Kent put his arm around Cora's waist and hurried her forward, probably afraid she'd stop and chat when he wanted her all to himself.

Branson grinned and tossed his handful of rice over the couple as they reached the doors.

A thick wall of fog crowded up against the glass, swallowing Kent and Cora as soon as they stepped outside. No wonder Cora's dad had announced they were moving the sendoff indoors. The lights at the entrance slightly illuminated the fog there. But at nearly seven thirty, it was probably dark beyond the lights. Should make driving Nevaeh home a challenge.

Driving Nevaeh home. Wishful thinking again.

Nevaeh and Branson had driven separately since she'd had to arrive earlier for the wedding preparations. He didn't get to escort her home. Didn't get to do a lot of things he wanted to.

Including telling her he didn't want to leave. That he didn't have to leave.

But he did have to leave. Very soon.

"You were right, Sofia." Bristol cringed as her shoe crunched the rice on the floor. "There's probably a reason people usually do this outside. We should sweep this up, so the cleaning crew doesn't have to."

"Sure." Sofia nodded. "I'll grab a broom from the maintenance closet by the bathrooms."

"I'll get it." Michael smiled at her. "You enjoy your friends."

She returned the smile that seemed to carry some secret message between husband and wife.

"So sweet." Bristol's teasing tone matched the grin she gave Sofia.

"Isn't he?"

"Sweet? Yeah, I really am." The masculine voice seemed to surprise Bristol, and she turned toward her husband, Remington, with a beaming smile.

Jazz let out a quiet groan as she swung toward Nevaeh. "Save me from all the happy couples."

Branson knew what she meant. Didn't help a bit to see all that marital bliss at the moment.

"I'm going to stuff my face with cake. You want some?"

Nevaeh laughed. "Sure, grab me a slice. I'll be right there."

"You got it." Jazz glanced past Nevaeh to Branson as if she knew something he didn't. Was Nevaeh going to tell him something? Say something important?

He held his breath as she turned toward him and lifted those big brown eyes.

"Care to dance?"

His pulse stalled. What had he hoped she'd say? That she suddenly wanted to know more about Jesus? That she wanted to work for D-Chop and move to L.A.?

"Sorry. You're probably not a dancer." Her mouth dipped into a frown as she looked away.

He'd be anything for her. The words he wanted to voice died on his lips. He did enjoy dancing, and if it meant he could hold her in his arms, he'd dance with her all night long.

But it would only postpone the inevitable. Only prolong the goodbye that must be said. Only make him fall in love that much more with this woman he had to leave.

"I guess I'll go find Jazz." Disappointment was written all over her face as she moved away.

"Nevaeh, wait." Branson caught her hand.

She turned back to face him.

If this was the final evening they had together, maybe

even the last time he'd see her, he couldn't leave her like this. Disappointed and maybe hurt.

"I'd love to dance with you."

Her eyebrows lifted.

"I'm actually a pretty good dancer, believe it or not. Especially ballroom."

A beautiful smile lit her face. "You're kidding."

"Nope. My mom had all us kids learn."

"Is there anything you can't do?"

"Um..." He looked toward the ceiling as if pretending to think. "Play the violin? I tried, but I couldn't get into it. Piano was more my thing."

She laughed. If only he could bottle up that sound and keep it with him wherever he went.

"Okay, let's see those mad dance skills."

He offered his arm, and she placed her hand there.

It seemed like only seconds later when Bristol approached them on the dance floor during a slow dance. "Hey, guys. Rem and I are going to head home. Toby's waiting for his dinner."

Nevaeh pulled back from the cradle of Branson's arms.

He reluctantly let her go as she glanced around the room, probably looking for the clock on the far wall.

"Eight thirty?" She glanced at Branson.

He looked from the clock back to her. "Time flies." *When I'm with you,* he wanted to add. Holding her in his arms for dance after dance, with a few breaks for visiting with her friends, had made an hour feel like five minutes.

"I'd better go, too. Cannenta and Alvarez are probably wondering where I am."

"Sure." Branson gave Nevaeh a smile that likely looked as sad as his sagging heart. He should probably tell her the bad news—that he had to go back to L.A. But he couldn't find the words. Not yet. Maybe when they said goodbye for the night. Which could be goodbye forever. "I'll go tell the valet to bring your pickup."

"You don't have to do that."

He met her gaze. "I want to." It was only a fraction of what he wanted to do for her.

Her beautiful eyes were filled with hesitation—or was it confusion? She opened her mouth like she was going to say something, then closed it.

Hope floated like a bubble in his stomach. Maybe she would say something that would work as an excuse to see her again before he left.

Her lips parted. "Thanks."

The bubble burst. But what had he expected? Their working relationship was over. He was pretty sure she liked him, but he couldn't be sure how much. And he'd have to leave regardless. Even if he could stay somehow, that would only mean the torture of having to tell her he had feelings for her but couldn't act on them unless she shared his faith.

Disappointment seemed to strain her features, too, as she turned away and went to the table where the other Phoenix K-9 women were grouped, some gathering their things.

Branson took in a breath and pulled his gaze from her. He marched off the dance floor and headed for the lobby.

He could do this. He was a soldier. He'd done many things he didn't want to for the sake of the greater cause, for the sake of what he knew to be right.

The stakes were pretty similar now. He needed his job for his dad's lifesaving treatment. And he needed to be obedient to God, no matter what. He had to do the right thing, even when it hurt.

He pushed through the glass exit door and stepped outside. Good grief, the fog was so thick he could barely see two feet in front of him.

The valet podium should be somewhere to the right.

Branson took two steps in that direction.

Something crashed down on the back of his head, careening pain through his skull.

THIRTY-NINE

"Are you okay?" Jazz kept her voice low as she looked up at Nevaeh from her seat at the round table assigned to the PK-9 team.

Nevaeh paused midway in lifting her long red coat off the chairback. She stepped around the chair and sat down instead, sliding the wool coat onto her lap.

Bris and Rem chatted with Sof and Michael on the other side of the table, not paying attention.

Phoenix and Dag still stood by the wide doorway that connected the lobby to the reception hall, apparently on security detail even though Cora had tried to convince Phoenix to relax and enjoy the reception. As it was, the boss had only agreed to attend the reception when Cora had her dad convince the ritzy country club people to bend their no-pet rules for Dag, though he wasn't an assistance dog.

Nevaeh leaned forward toward Jazz, squishing her folded coat on her lap. "I thought he'd ask me out. Or...something." She shrugged.

"You mean he didn't?"

Nevaeh shook her head. "Nothing. But we don't have anything set up to see each other again after this. The patrol gig is done unless he got D-Chop to approve keeping us on. I thought he'd mention that, but he didn't say a word. And he looks so grim tonight. I figure D-Chop must've said no. We could still see each other, though. Outside work."

Jazz's eyebrows dipped. "Did something go wrong when he helped with your sister's move?"

"No. Everything was terrific. My family adored him." A smile stretched Nevaeh's mouth as she remembered her brothers' approving remarks and the things Pops had said. "Even Pops liked him."

Jazz grinned. "Well, if *he* approves, you know you've got a keeper."

Nevaeh chuckled. Of course, Pops had also said a lot of other things. Like his prediction that Branson wouldn't have her because she didn't believe in God the way he did. Was that why Branson wasn't asking her out now?

"So nothing bad happened here either?"

"No." Nevaeh thought through the afternoon and evening. "Like I said, he looked really down a couple of times. Or like he was thinking about something heavy. But then he'd shake it off."

"Maybe that's it." A laugh from the others drew Jazz's gaze away. "Maybe he was just distracted so he forgot about asking you out."

"Could be, I guess." Nevaeh sighed and straightened. "Well, he's probably waiting with my pickup, so I'd better go." She stood.

"Oh, hey, I know." Jazz rose from her chair. "He's probably planning to ask you out now, when you're alone outside. In private, you know? More romantic that way."

Nevaeh laughed. "Yeah, in the fog." She slipped her arms into her coat sleeves.

"Heading out?" Sof glanced across the table from her chair next to Michael.

"Yeah. The dogs probably want to go out by now."

Sof nodded. "Michael ran home between the wedding and reception for our boys. But we'll have to drag Grace away soon to get her to bed."

Nevaeh glanced at the dance floor, instantly finding the

skinny girl with straight hair bobbing her head and dancing wildly to the music with a few other kids. "She's gonna crash when she gets home."

"Don't think she'll make it that far." Michael grinned, and they all laughed.

Nevaeh glanced at Jazz, still without a coat. "You staying?"

"For a little while." Her gaze drifted toward the other tables as she answered.

"Hmm. Some hot guy you got your eye on?"

A sly smile curved Jazz's mouth. "You never know."

Nevaeh gently punched her friend's arm. "You're telling me everything later." She turned her head toward the group. "Have a good night, gang."

"You, too." Bris's farewell was echoed by others.

Nevaeh waved over her shoulder as she left the reception hall, her pace picking up along with her pulse.

Branson was waiting for her. And Jazz could be right. He might've wanted to wait until now to set up their next thing. To ask her out on a date. Or maybe...her step hiccupped. What if he was going to tell her he loved her? Maybe even...

No. This would be way too soon for a marriage proposal. Wouldn't it? And did she want him to propose? She was so comfortable with him now and trusted him completely. But marriage...

Her heart pounded as she approached the glass doors, plastered with so much fog she couldn't see out.

But she could see Branson in her mind. His sweet, gentle smile. Those soft eyes.

She pushed the door open and walked into the chilly, damp fog. Oh, yeah. If he popped the question, she would say—

Hard steel clamped around her neck. Crushing, squeezing. Pulling backward.

Arms. In a choke. A man.

She gasped for breath and started to slide her hands into

position to hang her weight low, stop him from dragging her. Then she'd step back and—

"Hey, baby." The deep, scratchy rumble in her ear froze her blood.

She couldn't move. Couldn't think. Panic flooded her system.

No. It couldn't be.

His large head bent over her shoulder as he squeezed harder.

Her peripheral vision could just make him out.

The face of her nightmares. "You miss me?"

Walter was back.

Burning. Searing. The throbbing pain pierced through the blackness and dragged Branson to consciousness.

He moaned.

Someone was touching him, his wound.

He reached back, opening his eyes. A blurry view of light blue fabric greeted him.

"Lie still." A female voice.

His hand connected with skin behind his head. A smaller hand. It withdrew.

He tried to rotate his head upward, to see the face he suspected was there. Pain shot through the back of his head. He sucked in an involuntary breath, his eyes closing.

"Careful." The same voice. Bristol? "You'll rub the wound. You have a gash on the back of your head."

He forced his eyes open again. He hefted his head slightly as he rotated it this time before gently lowering it again. The effort ricocheted spikes of pain throughout the front of his skull, though he'd probably only managed to lift it a quarter inch. "What happened?" His gaze finally found Bristol's face, her grayish blue eyes filled with a blend of intensity and concern.

"We found you unconscious outside minutes after Nevaeh left."

Nevaeh left? Why hadn't he seen her leave? Or had he? He blinked. His brain felt so foggy.

Fog. He'd stepped outside the reception hall, the lobby. Walked into the fog. To get Nevaeh's pickup.

Something had smashed into his head. "Someone knocked me out."

"Yes."

Adrenaline surged through his veins, and he tried to push to sitting.

Hands landed on his shoulders from behind, pressing him down with surprising strength. "Hang on. You're not ready to go anywhere yet." A masculine voice. Maybe Sofia's husband, Michael?

Branson angled his eyes up, trying to see, but that only elicited more throbbing in his head.

"Were you able to clean the wound?" Cora's voice? But she sounded different, as if on a recording or...

"Yes, I think so." Bristol glanced to the side, drawing his gaze to a smartphone she had lying on the coffee table where she sat.

They'd apparently put Branson on a sofa by the table. A too-short sofa, judging from the way his feet and lower legs stuck out into the air past the end at an awkward angle.

"It's not as deep as I initially thought." Bristol lifted the phone and held it in front of her face. "Had a lot of blood, but that seems to have stopped."

"Praise the Lord." Cora's words drifted over him as his eyelids grew heavy. "Try to have him lie still until the paramedics arrive."

"Right."

"What about Nevaeh? Have you found anything?"

The mention of her name shot Branson's eyes open. "I thought you said she left. Went home." Concern pinched his chest.

"Easy." The male voice again. And the pressure on his shoulders, holding him down.

Bristol lowered the phone to the table and focused on him with an expression that looked too much like pity, or maybe caution, for his taste. As if she was afraid of how he was going to react to what she was about to say. "We don't know where Nevaeh is."

"What?" The word burst from his lungs, and he pushed his fists into the sofa, trying to push up.

Didn't help that the guy kept trying to pull him down from behind.

"Let me up." He barked the order as he pushed through the resistance.

Bristol nodded at the phantom captor behind his head, and the pressure released.

If only he could say the same for the explosive pressure in his head. His skull felt like it was collapsing inward from his forehead back. But he managed to reach a sitting position. He sagged against the cushions behind him as the room reeled. He closed his eyes, which didn't seem much better.

"He'll likely be dizzy and possibly nauseous. But it might pass as his body adjusts to being conscious again." Cora's voice listed his symptoms as if she were experiencing them herself. She'd better be right about this passing. Because he wasn't going to just sit here if his foggy brain had correctly comprehended what Bristol said.

"What do you mean?" He pushed out the words through clenched teeth as he forced his eyes open and picked Bristol's nose as the fixed point to focus on.

"The last we saw her, she was headed outside to meet you and go home. Did she meet you outside?"

He squinted, pushing through the slog of memory. Had he seen her? That's right. He was going to find the valet and have him bring up her pickup. Had he seen the valet? "The fog was so thick. I couldn't see the valet. I walked in the direction I figured he was. And then…"

Branson's hand went to his forehead and pressed—a futile

effort to reduce the burning pain. "I don't remember anything after that."

Bristol's lips pressed together.

A small hand entered Branson's limited view, then a petite body slid onto the table to sit next to Bristol. Sofia. She grabbed the phone as she sat down and looked at the screen. "What's your ETA?"

A deep voice spoke, muffled in the background, before Cora answered. "Kent says fifteen minutes. The fog is starting to clear, which should help, but the traffic has been heavy all the way from the airport."

"Roger." Sofia glanced over her left shoulder. "Did you put in Phoenix's call?"

"Yes. I'm waiting to hear back."

Sofia stood and set the phone down next to Bristol again.

"Hear back from whom?" Branson winced as another jolt of pain seared his skull.

Bristol's attention swung to her left, and Branson managed to turn his head enough to see Phoenix stalk toward them with her dog.

Did she have news? He couldn't tell. Her expression was exactly the same as always. Unreadable.

Frustration surged in his chest, and he opened his mouth, but she spoke first.

"Her pickup is still in the lot. The valet confirmed he never drove it up." Phoenix's cool gaze went to Branson. "Never saw Aaberg either."

Was he supposed to respond to that? He opened his mouth to explain, but she beat him to the punch again.

"Dagian tracked her around the back of the building, where it dead-ends. She was likely put into a vehicle in the employee parking lot."

Put into a vehicle? The statement cinched Branson's ribs, squeezing his breath away.

But the woman continued as if she could care less. "We found this in the lot." She pulled something from her pocket and held it up.

Dizziness swirled as he followed the motion. A red smartphone?

Someone sucked in a breath. "That's Nevaeh's new phone." Jazz stepped into view a few feet from Phoenix.

Of course. He should've recognized it. "Hold on. You think Nevaeh was…taken? Abducted?"

Phoenix's gaze tracked somewhere other than him. "I reached my source in L.A. Johnson hasn't shown up at his job or his girlfriend's apartment where he was living for three weeks."

"Why didn't the FBI agent tell you that sooner?" Frustration pinched Jazz's voice.

He knew how she felt.

"She only learned it yesterday but got tied up on a case."

"Who's Johnson?"

A pause answered his question.

"Someone Nevaeh used to know." Jazz's green eyes landed briefly on Branson. And he didn't like what he saw in them. Fear. Worry. Whoever they were talking about, it wasn't a friend. Could it be—

"I think this is the callback from your source at MPD, Phoenix." Cora's voice from the phone cut through his thoughts. "Hold on."

"Go now." Phoenix's order was directed somewhere to Branson's left.

He turned his head in that direction, surprised when only minimal dizziness greeted the movement.

"Roger." Sofia darted past Phoenix.

"I'll take Grace home."

Sofia gave a little salute to Michael in answer, not breaking her quick stride toward the exit.

"Will someone tell me what's going on? Who took Nevaeh?" Branson let his frustration strengthen his tone. "Peter's still in custody, right?"

"As far as we know, yes." Bristol's answer did little to ease the knot forming in his gut.

"I'm afraid I have bad news." Cora's tight voice cinched the knot even more.

Bristol leaned forward and looked down at the phone. "Did Peter get released?"

"No."

Branson breathed again.

"But he confessed he wasn't making the threats against D-Chop for himself."

"What do you mean?" Jazz stepped toward the coffee table from the opposite side.

"He says he didn't attack the gate guard or start the fire at the PowerSource Center. And the threatening notes and fireworks were not his idea. Peter was forging checks when he was working for D-Chop."

"Let me guess, someone found out and blackmailed him?" Bristol leaned toward the phone.

"Exactly. And the blackmailer who required Peter to threaten D-Chop as payment for his silence is Walter Johnson."

"No." The one word sounded strangled as it escaped Jazz's mouth. She rounded the table, stepping in front of the sofa where Branson sat, and stared down at the phone. "Are you positive?"

"It's what Peter said in his confession. He also claims Johnson was behind the kidnapping. He wanted to scare D-Chop by faking a kidnapping attempt on his children."

"Faking?" Disbelief clenched Branson's insides.

"Yes." Emotion thickened Cora's voice. "According to Peter, Johnson's real target was Nevaeh. He told the men to capture her."

Jazz dropped to the table as if she didn't have the strength to keep standing. "No. This can't be happening."

Bristol reached over the phone between them to put her hand on Jazz's shoulder.

Dread curdled in Branson's stomach. "Walter Johnson. Is that the man who—"

"Tried to kill Nevaeh?" Jazz's head jerked up, her gaze

slamming into Branson's as anger sparked in her eyes. "Yeah. That's the one."

Branson's mind tried to absorb what she'd just said. "Nevaeh told me she was attacked. What do you mean he tried to kill her?"

"The monster tried to beat her to death. And he almost succeeded."

"He wanted to kill her? Why?"

"Because she wouldn't give him her car keys." Bitterness edged Jazz's voice. "He wanted her to help him escape and give him her keys. Idiot didn't believe her when she told him the COs couldn't keep their keys with them in the prison."

"That made him want to kill her?"

Jazz gripped the table edge with her hands on either side of her knees. "She begged him to stop, begged for her life. But he kept going. He would've killed her if it hadn't been for the other inmates."

"The other inmates?"

A *ding* pulled Jazz's gaze to Bristol.

The brunette pulled a phone from her back pocket and looked at the screen. "Rem picked up Toby and is on his way here."

"We're only a few minutes away now." Cora's voice floated up from the phone on the table.

But Branson barely heard her or the other women's voices as they continued talking.

Nevaeh had been taken. By the man of her nightmares. The brute who'd caused all her pain, her fear, her PTSD. A monster who'd tried to kill her with his bare hands.

He would show her no mercy. He'd try to kill her again.

Rage burned through Branson. But not all of it was aimed at Nevaeh's abductor.

Branson had left her unprotected. The woman he'd sworn he would keep safe no matter what.

The woman he loved had been taken on his watch. And now she was in the hands of a killer.

FORTY

Blackness surrounded her. She was shaking.

No. Something was shaking her. Pushing her.

Nevaeh opened her eyes.

To a nightmare.

Walter's face—the bulky features, the scar across his forehead, the sloppy sneer she could never forget—loomed above her.

She must be lying on the ground. A floor, since there was a dark ceiling above made up of exposed boards. The floor was hard and cold beneath her shoulders. Like concrete.

Where had he taken her? A basement somewhere?

Like it mattered.

Walter was here. And she was at his mercy. That might be the last thing to ever matter in her life.

"Bet you thought you'd never see me again, huh—"

She tried to keep her face blank as he called her the degrading name. She'd been used to that at the prison. The taunts and insults from the inmates. She'd barely noticed them after a while.

But Walter hadn't actually called her names or slurs. He'd acted friendly and polite. Almost sweet at times.

Until the day he'd tried to kill her.

"Ain't you gonna talk to me?"

"Ain't you gonna help me?" The words he'd shouted when he first attacked her at the prison ricocheted through her memory.

The feel of his fist crashing into her face. Her bones crunching as he kicked her.

The fierce pain seared her like it was happening now, accelerating the fear pumping through her body.

She pushed the memory away. She couldn't get consumed by it.

But her fear was supposed to help her.

Use it as a tool. Phoenix's voice sounded in Nevaeh's ears.

The fear had primed her nervous system. She was ready for fight or flight.

She moved her fingers and hands slightly, feeling the grit on the cold floor.

He hadn't tied her up. Must've drugged her or knocked her out with a choke hold. The last thing she remembered was being pushed onto the floor of his pickup truck.

"Don't tell me you shy now?"

Her fear would warn her when he was going to go from chatty to violent. She just needed to listen to it. Be ready to react. And not do anything to fuel his anger.

Because she could see it in his eyes. Above the fake smile he was trying for, his dark eyes held the same look she'd never forget. Hatred. A hatred that had flamed in those eyes as he beat the life out of her.

She'd wait. Not make a move until he did. She'd trained for this.

Yes. Like practicing with Branson. She forced herself to see his face above her instead of Walter's. Branson closing in to help her train her ground techniques.

If Walter tried to attack her down here, she had the advantage. Phoenix had trained her for years for this moment. To be safe even on the ground, even in the worst-case scenario.

It didn't matter that Walter was bigger and stronger. She'd been able to escape Branson's holds and submit him during training. She could do it again. For real this time.

"Hey. I'm talking to you. Think you're too good for me now you sent me up for six years?" Walter lowered his massive frame into a squat beside her.

Her pulse raced as panic torqued her insides. *Breathe*. She tried to think. Ran through the response to a side mount attack. She'd practiced with Branson. With Phoenix hundreds of times before that. It was muscle memory. She was ready.

"I never forgot you." Walter's voice turned into a snarl. "Then what happens soon as I get out? You get in my way again." He lurched forward and grabbed her neck with both hands.

He pressed her head into the hard floor as he squeezed.

Terror burned through her.

"Ain't nobody here to save you this time." Walter's growl pushed through his smile as his fingers tightened more.

But Branson would save her. He'd come to her rescue. Like last time.

She just had to hang on until he came. The memory of him kicking in the door at the warehouse, her handsome rescuer, fueled strength into her limbs. She quickly rotated her lower body toward Walter, positioning to—

His grip suddenly released, and a hammer-sized fist slammed into her cheek, smacking her head against the concrete.

Pain seared her bones, her skin, her skull. The same pain she'd tried to forget.

He laughed. That horrible laugh.

"I been lookin' forward to this. I'm gonna finish you slower this time. And you're gonna beg again. Beg *me*." His massive hands gripped her arms, and he lifted her off the floor like she was a doll. He chucked her in the air.

She landed hard, her shoulder and hip slamming against the concrete.

His laugh, higher pitched, more hysterical, followed her from behind. Then his footsteps. Loud. Heavy.

He was so strong, so big, she couldn't—

A blow struck her back, making her lurch. A bone-crushing kick.

He laughed again.

The cackle had grown more hysterical with each kick, every punch.

No. Nevaeh tried to will the terror away. She couldn't have an episode now. Couldn't give in. She'd be helpless.

She had tried to block her head, protect it with her arms.

But he yanked her arm away.

Tossed her onto the ground. Kicked from behind.

Her head, shoulder, ribs. Didn't matter.

He just wanted to hurt her. Kill her.

And she couldn't stop him.

He landed on her with his full body weight. Crushing, pinning her beneath him.

She couldn't tell what was memory and what was real.

But the horrible truth pulsing through her was real. Even Branson couldn't save her this time.

She was powerless against the monster.

He was going to kill her in the worst way she could imagine.

"That's good enough, thanks." Branson resisted the urge to push the EMT's hand away from the back of his head and stood instead. He turned to give a forced smile to the woman.

"You really should see a doctor. You probably need stiches."

Branson snatched his phone off the round table in the reception hall populated by the Phoenix K-9 team and spouses, the couple police officers who'd come in response to the abduction report Bristol had called in, and the two EMTs. "I'll do that as soon as I can. Thanks."

The EMT looked at the guy working with her and sighed. Probably used to difficult patients.

But Branson had a good reason not to care about his own health at the moment.

He tapped D-Chop's phone number for the tenth time in the last thirty minutes and held the device to his ear as he stalked toward the lobby.

The rapper's generic, computerized voicemail message answered. Again.

Branson groaned and lowered the phone. D-Chop had probably turned off his phone or left it somewhere like he usually did when he was busy with a new girlfriend.

Which was why Branson had called Louis. He'd filled Louis in on what had happened to Nevaeh and told him to get D-Chop to call him. But that was ten minutes ago. Still nothing.

Branson pocketed his phone as he marched across the empty lobby and stopped by the glass doors.

Was the fog thinning? Yes. He could see a little farther, more of the concrete walkway outside the door.

Phoenix had cited the fog as the reason for stopping Branson from rushing out earlier to take his pickup and canvas the area for any signs of the mud-splattered Ram the women had ID'd from before. They deduced now the truck had to be Walter's. And he'd been watching Nevaeh all along. Ever since the PowerSource Center fire.

Branson gripped the long push bar on the door. How could he have failed to protect her?

Protecting people was his goal in life, ever since the shooter came to his church when he was a kid. He'd spent years training and working to be the kind of man who would always be able to beat the bad guys and keep them from hurting others. And now his whole career was dedicated to protecting people from brutal criminals like Walter Johnson.

Branson shoved the door open and stepped outside. He could see the nearest pillar of the carport now. If the fog kept thinning, he could have a chance to find something, to see where Johnson may have taken Nevaeh.

Who was he kidding? Despair surged up his throat, threatening to choke him.

As hard as he'd tried, he was obviously nowhere near the hero Andrew Allen was.

Branson couldn't even protect the woman he loved. The woman he'd promised he would keep safe, especially from the monster who had her now.

She'd trusted him. But he couldn't even protect her from one man.

What was the monster doing to her now?

Branson closed his eyes against the terrible possibilities that swirled in his mind. A tremor quaked through his body. Not from the cold, but from the horror of what he'd let happen on his watch.

If anything happened to Nevaeh…

He walked to the pillar and squeezed it between his palms, half-wishing it were his own neck. How could he live with himself if that monster hurt her…if he…killed her?

Branson's breath stuck in his chest.

If he couldn't protect the woman he loved, how could he protect anyone? And what was his life worth if he couldn't protect the people he loved? What was it all for? That was what his life was all about. If he couldn't save people from danger…

"That's in God's hands." His dad's voice came to him as if carried on the fog.

Air returned to Branson's lungs as he remembered the rest of what his dad had said.

"Our God is mighty to save…"

The truth hit him like a punch in the gut, making him drop his hold on the pillar.

When had he become so arrogant that he thought he was stronger than God? He had completely overestimated his own strength and abilities. Training and skills seemed like they would supply all he needed to be able to save the day. Every time. As if he were some kind of superhero.

But prizing physical strength and fighting skills, and even

the intelligence to create secure environments, above all else was a slippery foundation for life. Because he was only human.

Even superheroes were defeated sometimes. And Branson didn't have superhuman powers. But he'd sure acted like he did, thinking he alone could keep Nevaeh and everyone else protected at all times.

Only God was mighty enough to accomplish that. Branson had forgotten that truth somewhere along the way to trying to impress others and be a hero people would look up to, like Andrew.

He'd wanted to be a man who made a difference and saved lives. That wasn't a bad thing.

But he'd determined having superior human strength was far better than pursuing the kind of strength his dad had. It was ironic, because though his dad didn't save physical lives, he was the means God used to save souls. He made the most important kind of impact on people's lives.

The kind of impact Branson could've had on others, even in the celebrity culture. He'd blamed his silence about God and Christianity on the consequences he'd incur if he risked sharing about Christ. But the job hadn't silenced him and made him drift away from God. He'd done that himself. Because he hadn't trusted God to take care of the fallout if he spoke the truth with boldness. He should've been speaking out and standing firm, no matter the risks.

Thanks to his mixed-up priorities, he'd missed having the most important kind of impact in Nevaeh's life. He could've done more to point her to Christ, to help her gain freedom from her fear by telling her about the only way victory over fear was possible—through God's power.

The same power that was accessible to Branson right now.

Hope stirred in his stomach as he walked away from the pillar and stopped beneath a tall lamp that pushed light through the thinning fog.

He could do something to help Nevaeh. He could access the superhuman powers available to him. He could pray.

"Lord, I'm sorry. I've been selfish and arrogant in my aspirations for my career, for my life. I didn't even ask You what You wanted me to do with my life. And I may have missed the chance to tell Nevaeh about You." His voice choked on the words as remorse, worry, and desperation clogged his throat. "Please give me another chance, Lord. Please protect her."

God could keep her safe. Branson knew that. Andrew had always said God had put him in the church at the right time, in just the right position to be able to take down the shooter. It was God, not Andrew, Who had protected the people that day.

And it would be God now, not Branson, Who would protect Nevaeh if that was His plan.

"I know You can do so much more to help Nevaeh than I can, Lord. Only You know all things, control all things, and have power over evil. We need Your help right now, Lord. Nevaeh needs You. Please, protect her from danger. Deliver her."

His phone dinged in his back pocket.

He reached for it as he swiped away the tear track on his cheek. He checked the screen.

D-Chop.

His heart lurched as he smacked the phone to his ear. "D-Chop?"

"Hey. Heard about Nevaeh. You're getting her back, right? I can't believe Buzz would do something so stupid."

"Buzz? You mean Walter Johnson?"

"Yeah, he always been Buzz to us."

Branson gripped the phone tighter. "Have you known him long?"

"Sure. Grew up in the same hood. Ran with the same...kids." He'd probably stopped short to avoid saying *gang* instead. "Got him a job not long ago with a pit crew back in L.A."

"Then maybe you can tell us where he'd go to hide out. If he wanted to keep Nevaeh hidden, where would he go around here? A place he'd know about that he could use."

"I wouldn't know nothin' like that." D-Chop's tone firmed.

Branson had heard that edge often enough to know he was hedging. He never snitched on his pals. Never revealed his own indiscretions either unless they painted him in a helpful light for his career. "D-Chop, Johnson is the one who's after you, too. He blackmailed Peter into writing the notes and planting the knives. But Johnson beat up the gate guard and started the fire at PowerSource."

A pause answered Branson instead of the information he'd hoped for.

"He didn't hurt me with that stuff."

Good grief. How much did it take to make a guy like D-Chop do the right thing, even when that meant looking like a fink?

"He's going to hurt Nevaeh." If he hadn't already. The thought cinched Branson's chest until it hurt. "Maybe kill her. Unless we get there first."

Please, Lord. Get through to D-Chop if he can help us find Nevaeh.

A sigh came across the line. "A'ight. I might know a place."

FORTY-ONE

She only had a few more minutes to live.

Nevaeh sat folded in the fetal position in the corner of her prison, the basement she'd die in. Tremors shook her body.

Walter had left her for now. Called away by some unfriendly male voice above the stairs. Probably someone who'd join in killing her before he'd lift a finger to help.

Cold. She was so cold. Walter must've taken her coat before she came to. The cap-sleeved bridesmaid dress did little to warm her. Her fingers, wrapped around her legs to pull them tight to her chest, felt numb. As numb as her insides, those internal organs her frame wouldn't be able to protect much longer from the monster determined to crush her.

And she couldn't do a thing to stop him. She was helpless. Just like before.

She'd been such a moron. Why did she think anything had changed?

All her training and preparation didn't make a difference. All Phoenix's help and Nevaeh's hard work amounted to nothing. Her skills didn't help her against Walter. He was too strong, too deadly.

Maybe if she could've kept it together, not let the PTSD

take over. But wasn't the fear supposed to help her like Phoenix said?

It had nearly gotten her killed. Would get her killed as soon as Walter came back. She'd freeze again, go into another episode. She'd be useless to defend herself, unable to remember or execute any of the techniques that might help.

She thought she'd beaten this—the crippling fear. It had been gone for a few blissful days. Thanks to Branson.

She'd felt so safe with him. So protected. No more worries about Walter or any man hurting her.

But Branson hadn't come to her rescue this time. He couldn't. He probably didn't even know where she was.

It wasn't his fault. She'd been so stupid to think he'd always be able to protect her. To think he could somehow guarantee she'd never feel powerless again.

Nothing Branson or Nevaeh herself could do—even with Phoenix's help and all the training in the world—could equip her to survive this.

The fear was rendering her defenseless, making her an easy victim, just like Branson had said it would.

Panic rolled through her, trembling every part of her battered body.

She wasn't going to make it through this. Walter would come back at any moment. And it would be over.

But not quickly. It would be painful and slow, like he wanted.

And the fear would paralyze her again. The fear would make sure she didn't survive.

If only someone stronger like Branson were here. Or anyone more powerful and courageous than her—like Phoenix, Jazz, or Sof.

"That fear gonna own you if you let it."

Pops. His words, his voice in her head brought hot tears to her eyes. He was more right than she'd known.

"Keep fighting, honey. God will help you. You just got to ask."

Her breath caught. Another tremor tumbled through her.

She could see Pops' face as he'd said those words, leaning

in the window of her pickup the morning she took the kids to school. He was so confident, so certain.

But she'd asked God for help the last time. Cried out to him to save her life, to stop Walter from murdering her. It hadn't done any good.

"Who do you think helped you survive that man beatin' you at that prison and used it to make you stronger?" Pops' question that day in the kitchen with Branson outside, helping with her sister's move, had grated on her nerves. But was he right?

She swallowed, her throat thick and dry.

Walter had only been stopped that day because the inmates still locked in their pods saw him beating her. They saw it and used the phones in their pods to call outside for help. They'd called the police and told them what was happening.

The police had gotten hold of the other COs to alert them. And they'd been able to come to her rescue.

She stared across the empty, cold basement. Had that been God? Had He been there? Had He answered her prayer?

Was He here now?

"God's God, child. He does what he wants and ain't nobody can stop Him."

If Pops was right, then somebody more powerful was here. Right now.

God.

Even Walter couldn't stop God.

She never saw it until now. But God had rescued her the last time.

He had ended the beating. He'd saved her life. He'd protected her.

Warmth flared in her chest.

Was God more powerful even than her fear?

Pops had told her to take the fear to Jesus or it would own her forever. He'd been right about everything else. He had to be right about that, too.

"God." The word came out weak and raspy. She swallowed and tried again. "You know I need help. I'm not gonna make it unless you help me." She pulled in a shaky breath as tears dropped down her cheeks. "I know you can save me again. I'm sorry I didn't see it before. That I didn't believe you'd rescued me when you got those inmates to call for help. But I need your help now, God. You're my only chance out of this."

A thump above her head made her jerk.

A surge of fear shot her pulse into overdrive. Panic gripped her from the inside out. Her hands shook as she tried to hold her knees.

"Oh, God. Please." A sob escaped. "I'm taking this fear to you, Jesus. Please, help me beat this. I don't want to be controlled by it anymore. It's killing me. Take it away, God. Take it away."

"He does what he wants and ain't nobody can stop Him…What He wants is for you to be His child."

She moistened her lips as her grandpa's words echoed in her head. "Okay, Pops. Okay, God. You want me? You got me. I'm sorry I haven't lived the way You want me to. That I haven't believed in You. That I pushed You away like Pops said. But I know Cora and Bris always talk about how forgiving You are. And that all a person has to do is be sorry and ask for forgiveness."

She tilted her head up, staring at the cobwebs decorating the ceiling, the closest to heaven she could see right now. "I am sorry, God. Sorry I rejected you. Sorry I thought I could do life on my own. I'm a mess. You know that."

A sardonic laugh bubbled up her throat. Here she was, sitting in the fetal position, waiting for somebody to come back and kill her. Yeah. *A mess* was putting it mildly.

"I can't do any of it alone. I need you, God. I want to be your child. Please, forgive me. I want what the girls have. What you did for Bris and Sof. Cora was probably born that way, I don't know. Give me the peace and courage they have, God. Please. Rescue me."

She shut up and waited. Listened. For what, she didn't know. A voice from heaven?

The muffled sound of two male voices upstairs was all she heard.

But the warmth under her ribs fanned into a hot flame and surged outward. Heat flowed through her veins, pumping in strength and life where she'd been preparing to die.

Hope. Rescue. Was this what it felt like?

Something slammed.

A door. At the top of the stairs.

Walter was coming.

But God was more powerful than Walter. More powerful than Nevaeh's fear. God had beaten Walter before. He could do it again.

The truth filled her with a sense of power she couldn't explain.

Even as Walter pounded down the stairs.

Even when he scanned the basement, and his hate-filled eyes found her.

Even when that horrid, gleeful sneer slashed his face.

"Not trying to hide from good ol' Buzz, are ya, baby?" He laughed and stalked toward her.

She lowered her arms and flipped to her back, lifting her foot high, ready to kick at him if he approached. A ridiculous position in the bridesmaid dress, but at least Cora had picked a loose, gathered skirt that allowed for the movement.

"Oh-ho. Look at you." He grinned. "Got some fight back, huh? That'll make it more fun."

He tried to move around her.

She swiveled, pushing one foot off the ground and keeping the other lifted up in a ready position to block him and kick if he came close.

He did.

She kicked, but he threw his massive body over the low kick, slamming her leg down as he crashed onto her.

She instantly grabbed his torso, her arms locking tight around him as far as she could reach.

Muscle memory. The fear was gone. She laughed.

Walter froze beneath her hold.

He should be the scared one now.

She climbed higher, still holding her body tight to his chest.

He tried to reach for her head, tried to punch. But each attempt required him to lift a hand off the floor, his brace to hold himself up.

She trapped his leg with her foot, planted the other between his legs, and bridged into a roll away from the wall.

She took him with her, landing him beneath her on the floor before he knew what was happening.

His hiss as they rolled told her she'd caught his fingers under their weight at a painful angle.

He swore and swung his fists as he tried to sit up.

She flattened her head against his chest to duck under his blows, then shot her arms up to grip his shoulders and brace his arms wide, preventing the punches.

She waited for a pause between his attempts to punch.

Now.

She jerked up and threw an elbow jab into his face.

He yelled, grabbing his nose as she rapidly pushed off his hips and launched backward to her feet.

She shuffled back, then turned and sprinted for the stairs.

"Hey!" His shout couldn't catch her.

Her gaze locked on the light under the door as she ran up the steps. She could make it.

The door swung open. "What's—" A bearded man stood in the bright doorway. With a gun.

He lifted the weapon, aiming it at her face. "Don't think you're supposed to be up here."

FORTY-TWO

"Coms check." Cora looked at Branson before he could close the back doors of the souped-up van she'd driven him in. She pointed to her ear.

He switched on the earpiece she'd given him. "What's my call signal?"

"You'll be F1."

"F?"

"Freelancer." She smiled. "For you, Rem, and Kent. Phoenix is Team Leader. Sofia, Jazz, and Bristol are PT1 and so on. I'm Base."

"Got it." He glanced at the monitors Cora sat behind in the back of the van. Images came up on the screens as the Phoenix K-9 team members activated the body cams Cora had explained they had.

This operation was even more professional and advanced than he'd realized. No wonder Phoenix had insisted they didn't need to wait for SWAT. They were the SWAT team.

But now wasn't the time to gawk. It was time to rescue Nevaeh.

Though he prayed God had already done so. If God hadn't intervened yet, they would be too late. And if God didn't give them greater strength and skill than the enemies they were about to face, they could still be too late.

"Help us, Lord." He whispered the words as he turned away from the van.

"Amen." Bristol's voice came through his earpiece.

Had he said that over coms? He glanced back at Cora.

She gave him a warm smile.

He grinned. "Does that count for a coms check?"

"Best one I ever heard." Sofia's response carried over coms with a chuckle.

"Aaberg." Phoenix's voice behind him nearly made him jump. He'd thought everyone else had already moved out to get in their positions. He had the shorter route since he was attacking the front of the house. At least that's what Cora had said when she'd persuaded him to wait longer in the van while she checked the bandage on the back of his head.

He faced their leader who stood in the light cast by the nearby streetlight. Her wide stance and unflappable demeanor were the kind that instilled unshakable confidence in her troops.

Her dog adopted a similar stance and expression at her side, his erect ears aimed forward along with his gaze, as if he was looking ahead to the house they were about to breech.

Both Phoenix and her K-9 wore black armored vests like the rest of the team. Cora had been apologetic when she'd told him they didn't have one in his size, but he couldn't care less right now.

"Alvarez." Phoenix turned her head toward the other side of the van just as Branson spotted the leash in her left hand.

Nevaeh's rottweiler came toward them, passing the van's bumper to greet Branson with a slight swish of his tail.

A lump formed in Branson's throat as he bent down and put his hands on either side of the dog's face. "Hey, Al." Branson didn't know if he was imagining it or not, but he could've sworn Alvarez's dark eyes held sadness. "We're going to get her back. Don't you worry."

"Alvarez will go with you."

Branson jerked his head up. "What?"

Phoenix didn't blink in the shadow cast by the bill of her gray baseball cap. "He's Nevaeh's partner. He'll be the best weapon you could have in there."

"But I don't know anything about working with a protection dog."

Phoenix thrust the leash toward him. "Alvarez knows how to do his job. You just worry about doing yours and don't get in his way."

Branson swallowed as he took the leather handle.

"Loose leash at all times. If he wants to go somewhere, let him rip."

"Yes, ma'am." The response was instinctive, as if she were his superior officer in the Navy.

"Dagian and I will breach the front with you." She switched to speaking into coms. "Team Leader, we are a go. Report your positions."

She lifted a hand and swung it forward to signal Branson to fall in step behind her.

"PT1 to Team Leader, in position." Sofia was the first to answer. The rest of the team checked in, all of them in position and ready.

Phoenix led the way along the shrubbery that lined the sidewalk, making good use of any concealment along the way to the house.

They'd parked a block away to avoid being detected, but Sofia had gone ahead to scout the abandoned house D-Chop had said Johnson could be using. The rapper had said he and Johnson used to hang out in the old house with their homeboys. And Johnson had holed up in it when he'd been hiding from the police before the last time he'd gotten arrested. According to D-Chop, Johnson claimed it belonged to his uncle, though no one had believed him.

Sofia had reported suspicious activity at the house. A few vehicles parked on the street nearby. Two unidentified men she saw enter, apparently armed.

And a mud-splattered Ram pickup parked alongside the house.

Alvarez quietly kept up with Branson as he followed Phoenix's quick clip toward the house. The dog's panting was the loudest sound he made.

There it was.

In the dim light from a streetlamp, a gray house that looked like it should be condemned stood apart from the closest house, which appeared to be in only slightly better condition. The siding of Johnson's hideout was mostly disintegrating, all traces of paint gone. Visible splotches of something dark—probably mold—spotted the walls instead, an appropriately decaying visage for the house of the violent man who wanted to kill Nevaeh.

But it was the pickup parked in the dirt driveway that arrested his gaze. A black Ram, mud obscuring the license plate. Walter Johnson.

His fingers twitched with the urge to sprint to the house, find the monster and—

"Easy." Phoenix paused next to an overgrown bush at the edge of the yard that probably belonged with the old structure. She didn't even glance Branson's direction. How did she know what he wanted to do?

He tried to harness the adrenaline flowing into his veins. Telling him to rush forward. No good came of pulling a Geronimo. He needed to trust their leader and her team. Needed to trust God.

"Team Leader to Base, in position to breach. Status report."

Branson breathed out a calming breath.

Just as Alvarez growled.

"Team Leader, this is Base." Cora's voice sounded firmer than usual as she responded. "Cameras show no activity outside."

"Roger, Base." Phoenix stared in the direction of the house. "Ready to breach in twenty seconds. Base, start countdown now."

"Twenty…nineteen…" Cora counted the seconds off, her tone steady.

Phoenix didn't move.

Alvarez growled again, his stare locked on the house, his flopped ears lifted high. He tilted his nose up into the air.

Did he smell Nevaeh?

"Easy, boys." Phoenix didn't look at either of them as she held maddeningly still.

"Fifteen…"

"Follow me." Phoenix finally moved, a picture of stealth and tactics as she stayed low and darted quickly from a trash can to the pickup, to a tree, then a bush, her Glock in hand.

Branson followed her lead, keeping Alvarez's leash in one hand as he drew his weapon with the other. Nevaeh had teased him for wearing the Glock to the wedding, concealed beneath the tuxedo jacket he'd since ditched at the country club. He hoped it would help him rescue her now.

As they stepped onto the rotting porch, he anticipated Phoenix would step aside and signal for him to knock in the front door.

But exactly as Cora counted the last second, they reached the door, and Phoenix kicked it below the knob.

The door crashed in. "Dag, on it."

Her K-9 launched himself into the house with snarls that would've turned Branson's blood cold if he'd been on the receiving end.

Phoenix darted in after the dog.

Branson followed on her heals with Alvarez.

Just to the right of the door, Dag swung from a man's arm, hanging on with his teeth as he snarled over the perp's yells. A gun had fallen to the floor at his feet.

Branson snatched up the weapon and stuffed it in his waistband as he glanced toward Phoenix.

She was engaged with another thug in the corner, a muscled guy twice her size. She must not have been able to shoot him before he'd grabbed her. He held onto her from behind, his arms across her shoulders and waist as he glared at Branson.

Branson took a step toward them to help.

"Find Nevaeh." Phoenix delivered the order in a sterner tone than normal, but her eyes held the same indecipherable expression she always wore. No fear. No anger.

He couldn't just leave her behind to get beat up.

But before he could decipher the best approach to help, she twisted and dropped the man down to the ground. She was suddenly on top of his back, choking him out as she stared at Branson. "Go."

She was good. Very good.

Branson nodded and spun away.

Alvarez strained at his leash, barking.

More growls and yells came from the back of the house. Sofia, Jazz, and Kent must've breached the back with their two dogs as planned. Bristol and Rem would wait outside initially to catch any escapees, then enter if none snuck out.

"Find Nevaeh, boy." Branson dropped the leash, hoping the dog understood. Maybe he knew to find her on his own.

Alvarez sprinted through the nearest opening.

Branson ran after the dog, ducking into a narrow hallway with a low ceiling.

Two doorways opened onto the hallway.

Branson forced himself to slow as he reached the first one on the right. He should clear it before potentially stepping into the line of fire.

A man flew out of the doorway with a growl that riveled the dogs', a knife in his hand.

Branson ducked and charged into the guy's torso with his shoulder, slamming him against the wall with a frustrated grunt.

Every second he delayed could mean Nevaeh was being hurt. Or worse.

The thug he was fighting wasn't Johnson. Cora had shown him a photo of the monster.

He prayed the man was really here. Or at least that Nevaeh was.

Help her, Lord. Give her strength.

The guy with the gun had helped Walter turn tables on her again. With the gun aimed at her head, Nevaeh couldn't risk a move.

Walter had come up behind her and flung her to the floor. Her head had banged against the concrete, disorienting her long enough for him to get in two more blows.

Now he was on top of her hips, pinning her arms to the floor with his hands on her wrists.

He looked down at her, his features bigger and more repulsive from gravity's weight as he laughed.

The guy on the stairs joined in with a cackle. "I'm next."

Walter's position was meant to intimidate her. To make her feel helpless.

But she wasn't scared anymore.

This fight wasn't over. Not by a long shot.

Shouts and shuffling upstairs made Walter glance toward the stairs.

In one single motion, she swept her elbows downward and bridged her hips.

Walter plummeted forward as she broke his grip. His chest collapsed on top of her, but she'd moved her head to the side so he wouldn't slam her nose.

She locked her arms around his torso again as he got his arms under himself and lifted. She started to climb, prepping for another roll.

But he dropped his body down on her again, hard.

The full weight of him slammed the back of her head against the concrete. Sparks spattered her vision as pain seared through her skull.

Her hold weakened.

He jerked back and lifted his fist with a grin.

Something pounded down the stairs.

"What the—"

A snarling, glorious ball of movement crashed through

the gunman's legs, jumped off the stairs, and hurled himself into Walter.

The man fell off Nevaeh as Alvarez spun back to him and grabbed on to the nearest hand.

Walter let out an ear-splitting shout as Al bit down hard.

Nevaeh scrambled to her feet while Walter swung at Alvarez with his free hand. But the K-9 took the captured hand with him as he dodged.

"Shoot it!" Walter looked wildly toward the stairs.

The guy with the gun.

Nevaeh's heart dropped as she checked for him.

He was just getting up, still holding his weapon.

She moved toward him but froze when a muscled man thundered down the stairs behind him.

The man's head came into view as he grabbed the gunman from behind, knocking the gun from his hand.

Branson.

Her heart squeezed in her chest. He had come for her.

Grunts jerked her gaze back to Walter just in time to see him kick at Alvarez.

The K-9 couldn't dodge the blows forever.

She hurried back to help her partner and dropped to the floor behind the flailing man. She wrapped her arm around his neck for Sof's favorite chokehold.

Seconds later, Walter was unconscious.

"Alvarez, out."

The K-9 instantly released his bite as Nevaeh pulled away, letting Walter slide to the floor. He wouldn't be out for long.

Strong hands came into view. Branson.

He rolled Walter onto his front and wound a zip tie around his wrists.

"Are you okay?" Branson's deep voice traveled through her, infusing her with excitement, peace, and happiness, all at the same time. His fingers cradled her elbows, and he gently lifted her to stand, guiding her away from Walter.

The man of her nightmares moaned as he came to.

But she barely heard him as her gaze feasted on the sight of the man of her dreams.

He'd rolled up the sleeves of his white dress shirt, revealing the muscular arms that the fitted shirt couldn't hide anyway. His tie and jacket were gone, his slacks wrinkled. Similar wrinkles creased his forehead as he stared at her, blue eyes filled with worry. For her.

"Oh, yeah. I'm having the time of my life." She grinned. "Can't you tell?"

A disbelieving smile crept onto his face. He shook his head. "You are incredible, you know that?"

"Oh, yeah. I get that a lot." Her grin stretched wider. "In fact, I—"

In one quick motion, he closed the gap between them and claimed her lips with his while his strong arms cradled her in heavenly warmth.

A laugh bubbled up even as she savored the incredible thrill of his kiss. She couldn't help it. She was just so crazy happy.

He pulled back, keeping her in his arms as he gave her that adorable look of bemusement, like he couldn't figure her out but loved her anyway.

Loved her.

Nevaeh's heart lurched. Was it true?

"I'm sorry, Nevaeh."

Her dancing pulse slowed. Not the words she'd expected to hear.

"I shouldn't have kissed you." He slid his hands down her arms as he stepped back. "I can't date you because—"

"Wait." She moved closer to him again. "Is this because of how I don't...," she searched her memory for the terms she'd heard Cora use, "share your faith?"

Furrows formed between his eyebrows as he nodded.

"But I do now." She pressed even closer and slid her arms around his waist. "God showed me a lot of things today. And I guess I'm a Christian now."

A whoop and cheer made Nevaeh jump, and she swung her gaze toward the noise.

Bris and Sof clapped and whistled as they and Jazz started down from the halfway point on the staircase where they'd apparently been standing with their K-9s.

"We were going to ask if you're all right, but I guess you're better than all right." Sof's grin beamed.

"And then some." Jazz gave a meaningful glance to Branson, whose arms had encircled Nevaeh again.

His eyes sparkled as he looked down at her, the happiness there matching his huge smile. "So am I now."

"Welcome to the family, girl." Bris moved in to hug Nevaeh, making Branson let go to give them some room.

"I'd hug you, too, but you know." Sof gave her a shoulder punch instead as Nevaeh laughed. Sof didn't need to be a hugger for her to know how much Sof cared about her getting right with God. The glimmer of moisture in the tough woman's eyes said plenty.

Jazz stepped closer and threw her arm around Nevaeh, squeezing hard. "I was so worried. I'm so glad you're okay." Tear tracks wetted Jazz's face as she pulled back. She let go before Nevaeh did and backed away farther with a glance to the side. As if she felt awkward or something.

"Thanks, Jazz. I knew you'd have my back."

She nodded but didn't meet Nevaeh's gaze. Weird.

"Are you—"

Movement in the shadows of a dark corner cut Nevaeh's question short.

Phoenix and Dag came into the dim light. How long had she been there, watching silently?

Knowing Phoenix, she'd probably reached the basement right after Branson. Then kept out of sight for reasons known only to her. "Sofia, stay on Johnson until the police come for him."

"Roger." Sof went to stand by Walter with Raksa.

"Bristol, Jazz, go help Thomson and Jones secure the others. Cora will bring the police up to speed as they arrive."

Phoenix and Dag stepped closer to Nevaeh while the other women walked to the staircase. She met Nevaeh's gaze with her steady blue eyes. "Well done." Phoenix gave a nod that felt like something much closer to an award along with those words.

Pride swelled in Nevaeh's chest as her throat clogged with sudden emotion.

"Let's get you looked at."

"Looked at?" Nevaeh glanced from Phoenix to Branson.

His eyes scanned her face. "You're bleeding."

"I am?" Weird. Though now that he mentioned it, the pain she'd felt before started to return, rapidly pushing to the front of her consciousness. Probably thanks to the adrenaline wearing off.

"And you look like you're about to collapse." Good ol' Jazz hadn't left with Bris after all. Even in defiance of Phoenix's orders. The redhead stepped close to Nevaeh's elbow like she thought Nevaeh was going to go ahead and keel over right then and there.

"Aaberg." Phoenix's one word seemed to be all the encouragement Branson needed.

He bent and, slipping his arms behind her back and knees, swept her up against his chest like she was light as a feather. Which she definitely was not.

A laugh tumbled from her lips.

He looked down at her, his handsome face close enough to kiss. "You shouldn't be laughing. Not after everything you've been through."

She laughed harder, earning a sting of pain from her ribs. "You're right. It hurts."

His mouth shaped into a severe frown. "What did he do to you, Nevaeh?"

She shook her head. "It doesn't matter. The only thing that matters is what God did *for* me. He saved me." She scanned Branson's face, memorizing every feature. "And He sent you to me."

"He is mighty to save." Branson's low murmur rumbled his chest as she laid her cheek against the firm muscles there.

He carried her out of the house and into the night toward the flashing lights of police squads. An ambulance pulled up, reminding her of the bruises and fractures that were painfully making themselves known.

But cradled in Branson's arms and held in the hands of God, she'd never felt more invincible.

EPILOGUE

Six months later

"I can't believe we're hiking." Jazz glanced at Nevaeh as they trudged up the path's steep incline with Flash and Alvarez on leashes. "For fun."

Nevaeh wrinkled her nose at her friend. "You're the one who suggested it."

"Yeah, but you've never said 'yes' before." She shook her head, her red ponytail bobbing with the movement. "You sure have changed since you started dating Branson."

Nevaeh grinned. "Afraid I'll get in as great shape as you?"

"Not possible." Jazz shot her a teasing smirk. "But I can see having a boyfriend who's into fitness is rubbing off on you. Has he gotten you to join him for five a.m. workouts yet?"

"Uh, no." Nevaeh lifted her water bottle and thumbed the cap loose. "Love ain't made me crazy."

"If you say so."

Nevaeh gave Jazz's arm a playful shove before bringing the bottle to her mouth for a drink. It was good to see Jazz smile and joke around again. Seemed like she'd been getting more serious lately.

She often had a weird expression on her face when she looked at Nevaeh or Branson. One Nevaeh couldn't interpret, which was stranger still. She could always tell what Jazz was thinking. At least up until now.

Maybe Nevaeh couldn't read her because they hadn't been hanging out as much since she spent most of her free time with Branson. Weekends and evenings were the only chances they had to see each other between Branson's studying for seminary and his temp job.

Or maybe the awkwardness with Jazz had something to do with Nevaeh becoming a Christian. It was the first thing they couldn't really share, that Jazz couldn't understand.

That's why she'd immediately agreed when Jazz asked if she wanted to go for a hike this Saturday. Branson had said he needed to spend today prepping for some big test, so she had the time free to reconnect.

And to enjoy the fresh spring air. She inhaled deeply as they walked. The air was still on the crisp side this early in April, but some grass and plants were starting to grow anyway. Signs of warmth ahead after the long winter.

Alvarez paused to smell some spot on the short, muddied grass by a connecting path, then lifted his head and barked.

Nevaeh jumped inwardly. "What is that all about?"

"Hey, there." Bris and Toby appeared from behind bushes on the narrower path that joined the main one Jazz and Nevaeh were following.

"Bris?"

Toby wriggled his way toward them, his whole body wagging with his tail to convey his excitement at finding friends on the trail.

"Hey, bud." Nevaeh chuckled as she petted the Lab's head. "What are you guys doing here?"

"We hike here all the time. Did you know there's a beautiful waterfall ahead?"

"Is there?" Nevaeh glanced at Jazz. She hadn't mentioned that was their destination. "Cool."

"Mind if we join you?"

"Of course not." Jazz's response was quick and eager. Maybe she didn't need this hike to be only the two of them.

Once the dogs greeted each other, they all continued up the path, Bris and Toby falling behind since there wasn't room for three across with the dogs.

"So how's it feel to be the girlfriend of a future pastor?"

Nevaeh glanced over her shoulder to catch Bris's teasing smile. Nevaeh grinned back. "What, can't you picture me as a pastor's wife?"

"I admit it's something I never imagined before."

Nevaeh snickered. "Neither did I." She'd had the same thought when Branson had first told her he wanted to quit security work and go to seminary to become a pastor. She'd also felt a small degree of panic. Could she be a pastor's wife if they got married some day?

But when Branson had shared his story of wanting to be a pastor when he was young, of the shooter at his church, his mentor, and now the clear call God had given him to serve as a pastor, she couldn't do anything but support him.

Since there was a seminary in the Cities he wanted to attend, he was able to stay close, renting an apartment only fifteen minutes away from her house. And every day spent with Branson in her life convinced Nevaeh that God's call for her was connected to Branson and doing whatever she could to serve God alongside him.

Movement by a tree trunk caught her eye.

A golden retriever emerged from a path that veered off the main one a few feet ahead.

Wait… "Jana?"

Cora followed Jana onto the main path, connected to the golden by a leash.

Nevaeh and the others stopped. "What are you doing here?"

Cora smiled. "Hiking, of course."

"But you don't hike." Nevaeh would've bet Cora didn't even own hiking boots, but she sported a pair now. That looked suspiciously new.

"Kent is always telling me I should try new things."

Nevaeh narrowed her eyes. Something was going on. "Am I about to get pranked?"

Cora's gaze was as innocent as always. "I don't prank people."

She couldn't argue with that. Cora didn't prank anyone. But Jazz, Bris, and Sofia were a different story.

She scanned the two other suspects, but they were busy letting their dogs smell vegetation along the path.

"Mind if I walk with you?" Cora's sweet smile looked far too angelic to be up to no good.

Even Jana gave Nevaeh the same expression with a swishing tail.

"Love to have you girls."

"Thank you." Cora fell in step beside Nevaeh as they continued on while Jazz joined Bris behind them. "I've been wanting to ask you how Branson is doing."

"Branson?"

"I mean with his father's passing. It was so sad."

"Oh. Yeah, it was. Though it was so cool to see how his church and community supported him through the crowdfunding campaign when Branson couldn't pay for the cancer treatments anymore."

Branson had shared with Nevaeh when he decided to leave his job with D-Chop that it was a leap of faith. He explained how he'd believed he was his dad's only hope, that he had to save his dad's life by paying for the treatments or they wouldn't happen. He'd carried that so far that he'd ignored God's prompting to leave celebrity security and become a pastor, even though he knew his career had been hurting his relationship with the Lord.

But God had proven again that He was in control and didn't need any help providing for His children. Andrew Allen had the idea to set up a crowdfunding campaign, and between the community and church support, Branson's dad had received more than enough funds to continue his treatments.

Still, despite the experimental treatments, Branson's dad had passed away three months later. "You know, I've never seen people grieve like Branson's family." Nevaeh glanced at Cora as they continued up the path that seemed to get steeper with every step. "I mean, they're sad, but they're happy, too. Because they know he's in a better place, and they know God's in control of it all."

Cora nodded. "That makes all the difference."

"I'm thankful I got to meet him before he passed."

"Yes, that was—"

"Well, hey." A friendly voice cut Cora's reply short. "Fancy meeting you here."

"Sof?"

The raven-haired superspy seemed to pop out of nowhere, but she must've been standing behind the pine tree along the path.

Raksa panted at her side, probably in on the joke, too.

Nevaeh planted her feet and leveled a stare at her teammates. "Okay, what is going on?"

"Well, hello to you, too." Sof grinned.

Nevaeh landed her eyes on Sof. "You can't tell me you all just happened to be here."

"Of course not. You said you're not a fan of surprises, so we're making this as obvious as we possibly can. Something is going to happen at the waterfall ahead."

"And the person who set this up wanted all of us here to share the moment." Cora smiled.

"The person who..." Nevaeh pieced together Cora's words, trying to see what they added up to. *The moment?*

Her pulse skipped, then danced.

She didn't have a birthday coming up soon. And she hadn't won any awards or done anything special.

She could think of only one other possibility for a setup that might involve a beautiful vista and the PK-9 team being there to share the moment.

A smile split her face as she hurried up the slope that leveled off in a small clearing.

Phoenix and Dag stood in the shade of a large tree.

Disappointment sank to her stomach. "Hey, Boss. Good to see you. Though I hope this wasn't all buildup for you to tell me bad news about Walter or something."

"No." Phoenix's tone and expression were even and steady, just like always. Totally unhelpful under the circumstances, but she'd be the last one to ever give anything away. "He began his thirty-year sentence yesterday. I witnessed his arrival at the prison myself."

"That's a relief." Nevaeh still had a hard time believing Walter had risked everything to try to get even with D-Chop and her. D-Chop had only been guilty of getting away when he and Walter had broken into a pawn shop as teens. Walter believed his arrest then and the many after were the only reasons he hadn't achieved the fame and riches D-Chop had. In his twisted mind, D-Chop owed him because he ran off and let Walter take the fall alone.

But Nevaeh didn't have to think about Walter anymore. And thanks to Phoenix's verification, she could be confident he really was behind bars, and the danger was over. "Thanks, Boss." The simple word didn't say nearly enough for everything Phoenix had done for her and continued to do.

Nevaeh had learned through all this that Phoenix wasn't always right. She'd been wrong about fear. It wasn't helpful. And it wasn't a tool to be used. It was a danger—a sin, Nevaeh understood now—that wanted to control her.

She hadn't always been fearless since that night when God took her fear away completely as she faced Walter. The PTSD still showed up sometimes, and grim memories occasionally visited her as nightmares. But she knew how to fight the fear now. She knew how to beat it—through unshakable trust in God's power. And she tasted small victories over her fear every day.

But even though Phoenix wasn't quite as perfect as Nevaeh had thought, she always had the best at heart for the PK-9 family. And she stopped at nothing to help them.

"Someone's waiting for you around that bend." Phoenix

directed her gaze to the bushes and trees where a path left the clearing.

"Really?" Nevaeh's feet moved before waiting for an answer, her heart pumping into overdrive.

Alvarez trotted alongside her with his ears perked like he was excited, too.

As she rounded the bushes, a man stood before her.

But not the one she'd expected. "Pops?"

He extended his free hand as the other leaned on his cane. "Bet you're surprised to see me up here."

She blinked at him. Surprised didn't even touch it.

"You got a clever young man there." Pops leaned in, and she took the hand he offered. "There's a road up the other side. He drove me right up here."

He had to be Branson.

"Is he here?"

"Come with me, honey." Pops' bony hand gripped hers, and they walked slowly on the narrow path until another clearing opened up before them. This one was much larger than the first. It sloped up on either side to frame a rock wall with a waterfall cascading down.

The view was stunning. But nowhere near as gorgeous as the tall, muscular man who stood only six feet away, wearing the sweetest smile she'd ever seen.

Her heart dropped to her stomach and then bounced right back up to bang into her ribs.

Pops gently tugged on her hand, and she walked with him to Branson. Pops slipped her hand into Branson's larger one, giving their joined hands a squeeze before he let go.

"I'll take this fella with me over here." Pops reached for Alvarez's leash.

Nevaeh handed over the leash with a smile she then directed up at Branson as Pops moved away. "I knew something strange was going on."

"Strange?" His mouth twitched. "Is that what you're calling me now?"

Her heart melted at his teasing. Amazing how quickly

he'd picked up on her sense of humor. He managed to make her laugh at least once a day and usually more.

"I'll call you worse than that if you don't tell me what you're up to."

"As clever as you are, I'm guessing you already know." He lifted his free hand and opened his fingers to reveal a square velvet box.

Her breath caught.

He lowered his massive frame to kneel on one knee and looked up into her face. "Nevaeh Williams, I love you more than I can say."

A smile stretched across her face at the start of what could only be a proposal. And the three little words she would never tire of hearing.

"You are God's greatest gift to me. From the moment we met, I couldn't shake the feeling we'd been made for each other. And it turns out, God did make us for each other." His blue eyes sparkled as he looked up at her. "You make me want to be a better man and a better Christian. And I want nothing more than to love you and take care of you for the rest of my days. Will you do me the honor of becoming my wife?"

The answer she wanted to give fought to get out. But she couldn't resist the chance to tease him a little. "Are you sure you want to risk having me for a pastor's wife?"

He grinned. Didn't even have the decency to look nervous that she hadn't answered him yet. "I can't think of anyone more perfect for the job."

"Oh, so it's a job application, is it? Kind of like you saying you had to prep for a test today?"

"You clearly have no idea what it's like to ask your grandfather for permission to marry you."

She snorted. "Did you pass the test?"

He winked, kicking up a bunch of butterflies in her stomach. "With flying colors. How am I doing with you?"

"Get up, and I'll show you."

His eyebrows lifted, but he held his position. "I'd like to, ma'am, but I'm waiting for the answer to a very important question."

"Yes."

"Yes, what?"

She laughed. "Yes, I love you, and yes, I'll marry you. Now will you get up and kiss me already?"

He let out a whoop as he stood and swept her off her feet, literally, lifting her above him into the air.

Then he lowered her down against his chest and planted a kiss on her lips that left no doubt she'd said *yes* to the right man.

The sound of clapping ended the kiss earlier than she would've liked, but she smiled at Pops and her PK-9 family as they watched and cheered.

Nevaeh didn't move toward them yet, though. With so much joy filling her heart that there was no room for fear, she wasn't about to leave the arms of the hero God had given her anytime soon.

Turn the Page for a Special Sneak Peek of

GUARDIANS UNLEASHED, BOOK 4

LETHAL DANGER

COMING 2024

EXCERPT OF LETHAL DANGER

"Sir?" Hawthorne braced his knee against the beams, ignoring the discomfort of the metal digging into his bone as he let go with one hand to reach for the unmoving passenger.

He pressed his fingers to the guy's clammy neck, feeling for a pulse.

Soft beats thumped against his fingers.

Thank the Lord.

Hawthorne leaned forward to get a better look at the guy's head where it had slammed against the spoke.

Blood oozed onto the steel from an apparent wound. Not good. Was it still actively bleeding?

Hawthorne mentally cycled through the First Aid course he'd received in basic training.

He should apply pressure, but with a clean cloth. Given how sweaty his clothes were by this point, a torn scrap from either his shirt or pants wouldn't suffice. Maybe he should wait for the rescue squad to try it.

Hawthorne glanced down below. Wow. Way below. Glad he hadn't looked down earlier. And he was especially glad heights didn't bother him.

Wait a second…

Something moved, but not on the ground. On the Ferris wheel.

A person in a black shirt climbed up the spokes and beams exactly as he had done. Was that the redhead?

Sure enough, a dark red ponytail swung to the side as she shifted her body toward a spoke.

A strange feeling stirred in his chest as he watched her. She moved quickly—faster than he had climbed, actually. Her movements were fluid and strong. No hesitation or caution. Only athleticism and skill, apparently, since she didn't miss a hold in her almost rhythmic climb.

She disappeared under the cluster of connecting beams at the center. But only for a moment.

Then her head appeared above the horizontal spokes where he waited with the injured man.

She sprang onto the beams and crawled toward him nearly as fast as the monkeys he used to watch at the zoo when he'd volunteered there. Coiled rope hung from her shoulder and angled across her shirt.

"How is he?" She didn't even sound out of breath as she came up beside Hawthorne, close to the passenger's head.

Hawthorne turned back toward the injured man, whom he probably should've been watching instead of the remarkable woman who'd just free-climbed halfway up a 156-foot Ferris wheel without breaking a sweat.

He reached to check the man's pulse again. "His pulse is steady. But a little weaker. Maybe slower."

The redhead moved closer and pushed up to sitting, balancing on the middle of the crossbeams' *x* with her feet braced on the two beams where they angled away. She aimed big eyes at him. "The rescue squad is on the way. ETA ten minutes. But one of the onsite nurses is waiting below. If we can get him down, she can start treating him."

The woman was fascinating. With only a few feet between them, there was no missing she was even more beautiful than he'd first thought. And she wasn't slathered in makeup like so many women her age who wanted to be attractive.

Her smooth, creamy skin was sun kissed to perfection, and the sun glinted off her shiny red hair. Her full lips didn't need more than the gloss he guessed she wore. But her eyes were her most stunning feature. A brilliant emerald green that made him rethink his statement that he'd never seen a green as intense as the color he'd seen in the fields of Ireland.

The woman had beauty, brains, courage, and toted a gun and a knife he was sure she knew how to use. It couldn't get any better than that.

"I'll get on his left side here. You can go on his right, and I'll pass the rope under him to you." Her statement brought him out of his observations to see she was hefting the coiled rope off her shoulder and over her head.

Occupational hazard to get lost in observations and imagination. But he couldn't help it this time. He'd been searching for weeks for the right idea for his next series. And now, she was staring him in the face.

"What's your name?"

"Excuse me?" She shot him a glance with raised eyebrows as she unwound one end of the rope.

"Sorry." He scrambled for an excuse for the oddly timed question that would also get her to answer it. "I just want to know what name to yell if I'm about to fall."

His joke earned a charming laugh that sounded like she was hitting notes in a musical scale.

She handed him the loose rope end. "Jazz Lamont."

Jazz. Even her name was perfect. Though she'd probably never agree to let him use that in print, too. But either way, he'd just met the heroine of his next bestselling thriller novels.

She never invites visitors. But visitors sometimes invite themselves.

When a winter storm brings more than snow, May Denver is forced to flee from her home and fight for her life. Can she trust an unwanted neighbor and risk her greatest fear in order to survive?

GRAB THIS ROMANTIC SUSPENSE STORY FOR FREE WHEN YOU SIGN UP FOR JERUSHA'S NEWSLETTER
www.FearWarriorSuspense.com

Shop the *Guardians Unleashed Series*
at
JerushaStore.com

ABOUT JERUSHA

Jerusha Agen imagines danger around every corner, but knows God is there, too. So naturally, she writes romantic suspense infused with the hope of salvation in Jesus Christ.

Jerusha loves to hang out with her big furry dogs and little furry cats, often while reading or watching movies.

Find more of Jerusha's thrilling, fear-fighting stories at www.JerushaAgen.com.

facebook.com/JerushaAgenAuthor
instagram.com/jerushaagen

It's up to a K-9 handler and her canine partner to stop a bomber before it's too late.

www.RisingDanger.com

Made in United States
North Haven, CT
14 August 2023